THE WHITE HUNTER

BOOKS BY GILBERT MORRIS

Through a Glass Darkly

THE HOUSE OF WINSLOW

1. The Honorable Imposter
2. The Captive Bride
3. The Indentured Heart
4. The Gentle Rebel
5. The Saintly Buccaneer
6. The Holy Warrior
7. The Reluctant Bridegroom
8. The Last Confederate
9. The Dixie Widow
10. The Wounded Yankee
11. The Union Belle
12. The Final Adversary
13. The Crossed Sabres
14. The Valiant Gunman
15. The Gallant Outlaw
16. The Jeweled Spur
17. The Yukon Queen
18. The Rough Rider
19. The Iron Lady
20. The Silver Star
21. The Shadow Portrait
22. The White Hunter
23. The Flying Cavalier
24. The Glorious Prodigal
25. The Amazon Quest
26. The Golden Angel
27. The Heavenly Fugitive
28. The Fiery Ring
29. The Pilgrim Song
30. The Beloved Enemy

THE LIBERTY BELL

1. Sound the Trumpet
2. Song in a Strange Land
3. Tread Upon the Lion
4. Arrow of the Almighty
5. Wind From the Wilderness
6. The Right Hand of God
7. Command the Sun

CHENEY DUVALL, M.D.[1]

1. The Stars for a Light
2. Shadow of the Mountains
3. A City Not Forsaken
4. Toward the Sunrising
5. Secret Place of Thunder
6. In the Twilight, in the Evening
7. Island of the Innocent
8. Driven With the Wind

CHENEY AND SHILOH: THE INHERITANCE[1]

1. Where Two Seas Met

THE SPIRIT OF APPALACHIA[2]

1. Over the Misty Mountains
2. Beyond the Quiet Hills
3. Among the King's Soldiers
4. Beneath the Mockingbird's Wings
5. Around the River's Bend

LIONS OF JUDAH

1. Heart of a Lion
2. No Woman So Fair

[1]with Lynn Morris   [2]with Aaron McCarver

03B

The White Hunter

Gilbert Morris

BETHANY HOUSE PUBLISHERS
MINNEAPOLIS, MINNESOTA 55438

Published by Bethany House Publishers
A Ministry of Bethany Fellowship International
11400 Hampshire Avenue South
Bloomington, Minnesota 55438
www.bethanyhouse.com

Printed in the United States of America by
Bethany Press International, Bloomington, Minnesota 55438

Library of Congress Cataloging-in-Publication Data

Morris, Gilbert.
    The white hunter / by Gilbert Morris.
       p.   cm. — (The house of Winslow ; bk. 22)
    ISBN 1-55661-909-X
    1. Titanic (Steamship)—Fiction. 2. Winslow family (Fictitious characters)—Fiction. 3. Americans—Africa—Fiction. 4. Hunting guides—Fiction. 5. Africa—Fiction. I. Title.
    PS3563.O8742 W47   1999
    813'.54—dc21   00502455
                                          CIP

To Mildred Fitzgerald—
my very special friend.
You have brightened my life
with your lovely spirit.

GILBERT MORRIS spent ten years as a pastor before becoming Professor of English at Ouachita Baptist University in Arkansas and earning a Ph.D. at the University of Arkansas. During the summers of 1984 and 1985, he did postgraduate work at the University of London. A prolific writer, he has had over 25 scholarly articles and 200 poems published in various periodicals, and over the past years has had more than 70 novels published. His family includes three grown children, and he and his wife live in Alabama.

CONTENTS

PART FOUR
MASAILAND

HOUSE OF WINSLOW

★ ★ ★ ★

THE HOUSE OF WINSLOW

★ ★ ★ ★

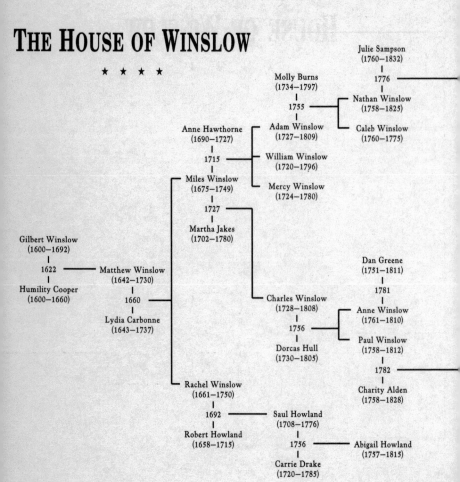

Julie Sampson
(1760—1832)
|
1776 ————

Molly Burns
(1734—1797)
|
1755 ———— Nathan Winslow
(1758—1825)

Adam Winslow
(1727—1809)

Caleb Winslow
(1760—1775)

Anne Hawthorne
(1690—1727)
|
1715
|
Miles Winslow
(1675—1749)

William Winslow
(1720—1796)

Mercy Winslow
(1724—1780)

1727
|
Martha Jakes
(1702—1780)

Gilbert Winslow
(1600—1692)
|
1622 ———— Matthew Winslow
(1642—1730)
|
Humility Cooper   1660
(1600—1660) |
Lydia Carbonne
(1643—1737)

Dan Greene
(1751—1811)
|
1781
|
Anne Winslow
(1761—1810)

Charles Winslow
(1728—1808)
|
1756
|
Dorcas Hull
(1730—1805)

Paul Winslow
(1758—1812)
|
1782
|
Charity Alden
(1758—1828)

Rachel Winslow
(1661—1750)
|
1692 ———— Saul Howland
(1708—1776)
|
Robert Howland   1756 ———— Abigail Howland
(1658—1715) | (1757—1815)
Carrie Drake
(1720—1785)

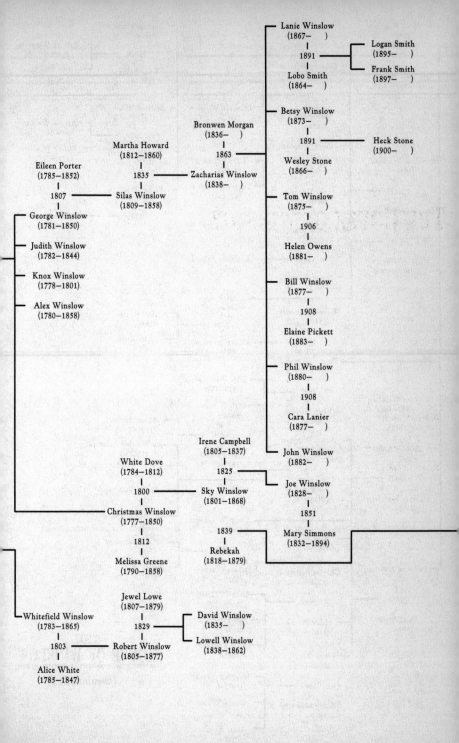

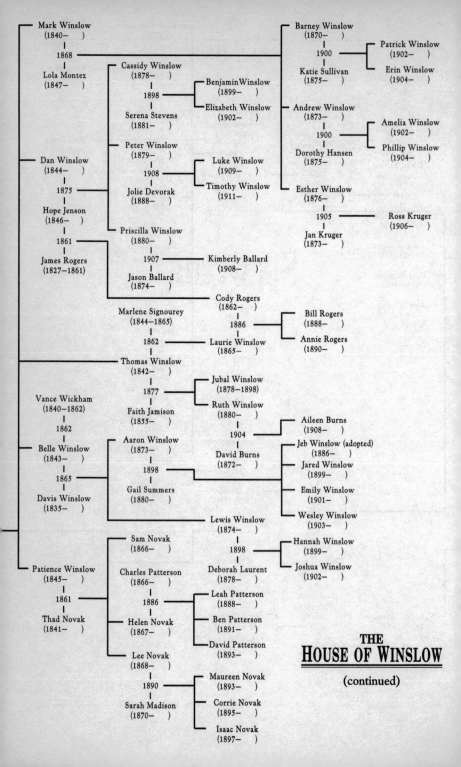

THE
HOUSE OF WINSLOW
(continued)

PART ONE

SEEDTIME

★ ★ ★ ★

CHAPTER ONE

KISSING COUSINS

★ ★ ★ ★

"Oh *dear*! I can't wear this old rag to meet Jeb!"

Annie Rogers stared at her image in the mirror, her face cloudy with discontent. Ordinarily she was a sweet-tempered girl, but now her brow was furrowed and she gnawed at her lower lip. With a quick motion of disgust, she reached up and ran her hands through her bright red hair, a habit she was trying to break. Dropping her hands, she whirled and fixed her dark blue eyes on the mirror again as if she could transform the offending garment into something much more glamorous. "It's too little for one thing— and, besides, I never did like it."

The garment in question was a simple blue affair, with white lace around the neck and the sleeves. Annie had bought it only six months earlier but had made the mistake of getting a perfect fit. Now at the age of fifteen she had experienced a sudden spurt of growth, and the beginnings of a womanly figure strained the dress at the seams. Annie should have been pleased, for she had matured so much later than most of her other friends that she had sunk into despair. Once she had cried out plaintively to her mother, "I'll never have any figure *at all*, Mama! I won't be anything but an old garden rake!"

She had refused to listen to her mother, who pointed out that some young women matured later than others and that she had nothing to worry about. The explanation had done nothing to soothe Annie's feelings. Now, as she stared grimly at herself, she found no satisfaction in the thought that at last she was passing from girlhood to young womanhood. "What good does it do to have a figure," she muttered rebelliously, "if I don't have a nice dress to wear?"

Moving over to the window, she stared outside and watched as her father labored over the automobile he had purchased only two months ago. It ran erratically and apparently had a will of its own. As Annie watched him struggle to fix the car under the blazing June sun, her lips twisted bitterly. "Now I don't have anything to wear, and we won't have any way to pick up Jeb except in a wagon! Won't that show him what *hicks* we really are?"

She returned to the mirror and studied her face, finding it unsatisfactory. She took no pleasure in the smooth contours of her cheeks or the fine bone structure that hinted of a beauty only half born. Instead, she fixed her gaze on the bluish birthmark shaped like a butterfly on the left side of her neck. It was no more than an inch wide and low enough to be hidden by a high collar, but Annie hated it so utterly that she tried to hide it whenever possible. It was inevitable that she would be teased about it by other children as she was growing up. She thought suddenly of an advertisement she had seen that offered a salve guaranteed to obliterate any skin blemish. She glanced at the calendar on the wall and glared at the picture of a beautiful woman holding a small jar of *Dr. Sadler's Facial Cream*. The caption boasted, "I had a birthmark on my nose, but *Dr. Sadler's Facial Cream* made it vanish like magic!" The year 1905 was printed in large gothic letters, and the days were checked off with a pencil. "I ordered it two weeks ago, and it's *still* not here!" She rubbed at the small mark as she had done many times and wondered, *Why did God have to put that thing on my neck? Why couldn't He have put it on my foot?*

A sudden knock at the door caused Annie to wheel around. "Come in, Mama," she said quickly. As soon as her mother stepped inside the room, she spoke up petulantly, "Mama, I can't wear this dress. Just *look* at it!"

At the age of forty, Laurie Rogers still retained most of her early beauty. She had the same smooth skin, clear blue eyes, and shiny brown hair that Annie often envied. Moving over to her daughter, Laurie put her arm around Annie and smiled. "Now, it's only a dress, and I'm pleased to see that you've outgrown it. You're growing up into a young woman very fast, Annie."

Annie gave her mother a disgusted look. "I'm not going! I refuse to be seen in this old thing!"

Such behavior was so unusual for Annie that Laurie was taken aback for a moment. All her life she had looked forward to having a daughter, and this young girl had been nothing but a pleasure. Never once had she caused the kinds of trouble that many other girls had given their parents. Laurie had said on various occasions to her husband, "Cody, we ought to thank God every day that we have a good girl like Annie instead of what we might have had." Now she squeezed Annie, suggesting, "Why don't you wear your pink dress if you don't like this one."

"It's even *worse*," Annie moaned. "Mama, can't we stop off somewhere and buy me a new dress?"

A smile turned up the corners of Laurie Rogers' mouth. "It's too late, Annie. By the time we get to the station, we'll be lucky if we meet the train on time."

"Oh, I wish he weren't coming!"

"Why, don't talk like that! You know you've been looking forward to your cousin's visit."

"I was, but I thought I'd have something decent to wear. What will he think of me wearing an old dress like this that doesn't even fit me? He's from the city, Mama. He's used to seeing girls dress up nice."

"Now, Annie, I'm sure that Jeb won't be judgmental about your clothes. From what his father and mother tell me, he's a well-behaved young man."

"He won't like me," Annie sighed.

Laurie stared with astonishment at the young woman, then shook her head decisively. "What in the world makes you say a thing like that? Of course he'll like you!"

"No, he won't. He's from the East, and his father's a college professor. And you know what his parents say—that he's so smart. He'll think we're nothing but a bunch of cowboys out here. I just know he will!"

The object of their conversation was a young man of nineteen named Jeb Winslow. He was the adopted son of Aaron and Gail Winslow. After Aaron had come back from the Spanish-American War, he had married Gail, who was Jeb's older sister, and settled down from his wild ways into the world of teaching at a college in Virginia. Before Aaron and Gail had adopted Jeb, Laurie and Cody had met them at several family reunions and had taken a real liking to them.

When Annie had received an invitation to visit relatives in Montana, it had been she who had said, "Daddy, let's invite Jeb to go. That way both of us can get a vacation." And so when Laurie had written to invite Jeb to join Annie on her trip to Montana, the response had been enthusiastic. Gail Winslow had written, *It'll be just the thing for Jeb. He hasn't gotten to travel any at all. His head's always in a book. Of course we'd be glad for him to join Annie on a visit to our Winslow relatives in Montana!*

Now Laurie said rather strictly, "Stop this foolishness, Annie! It's going to be all right. Come on, don't dally—your dad's waiting for us."

Grabbing a sunbonnet, Annie hastily tied it under her chin as she followed her mother downstairs. As the two stepped out on the porch her father as she had suspected, had given up on the car and was now sitting in the two-seated surrey. Annie was thankful it wasn't a farm wagon, and as she climbed up in the backseat her father leaped to the ground to help her.

"Well," he grinned, "you all set to meet your kissing cousin?"

Cody Rogers was a trim man of forty-three, contoured and shaped by a life in the saddle. A lifetime of ranching under the sun and winds of Wyoming had tanned him deeply, and when he smiled, his teeth flashed white against his bronze skin. He held her hand for a minute and squeezed it, then winked broadly. "I'll have to keep a watch on you two. I've heard about this kissing cousin business."

"Oh, Daddy, don't be silly!" Annie protested and tried to snatch her hand away.

He held it tightly, though, and leaned forward to whisper, "I guess one little kiss between cousins wouldn't be too bad." He suddenly pulled her toward him and kissed her cheek. "You smell good," he said. "You been in your mama's perfume again?"

"No, it's the perfume you gave me for Christmas!"

"Makes you smell better than the heifers." Cody laughed as he helped Laurie into the wagon, then leaped in beside her. "I'm gonna blow that infernal automobile up!" he said with a baleful look at the machine that sat beside the corral. "They're not worth fooling with! Give me a horse every time. Now, get up, Babe! Get up, Maude!" The team lurched forward, throwing Annie and Laurie back against their seat. Cody laughed, saying, "Hang on, women! We're gonna have to break some records to get to that train on time!"

★　★　★　★

The trip from Virginia to Wyoming had been a long one, but young Jeb Winslow had enjoyed every second of it. It might not have been so pleasant for him except that his great-uncle, Mark Winslow, vice president of the Union Pacific, had seen to it that he had a Pullman to enjoy instead of trying to sleep sitting up in a seat. For the first two days, Jeb was almost unable to rest, but finally the clicking of the wheels on the track had lulled him to sleep. During the day, however, he had missed nothing. Hour after hour he sat beside the window and stared out at the country flashing by. It had been a time of revelation for him, for the large expansive plains had filled his eyes as nothing ever had. Up until this point, his life had been rather constricted, partly by the fact that his family traveled little, for as a professor, his father, Aaron, made few trips. Jeb had grown up on the crowded streets of New York under rough circumstances, and becoming the son of Aaron Winslow had been the joy of his life. He had lacked a father's love and had found that quality abundantly in the big man who spent as much time with him as possible.

"Well, now, you about ready for the Wild West, Jeb?"

Startled, Jeb looked up and saw Mr. Brown, the conductor, grinning down at him. Frank Brown had been friendly from the moment Jeb had climbed aboard, showing him the ropes of travel on a train, including how to order the meals and get into his bed at night. Jeb had taken advantage by asking him numerous questions, a habit he could not seem to break.

"I guess so. How long before we get in?"

"Only thirty minutes. You got some relatives to meet you, you say?" Brown was a burly man with a pair of warm brown eyes and a shock of white hair. He was garrulous almost to a fault, and when he was not occupied with his duties as a conductor, he was talking to one of the crew—or better still—one of the passengers. He had developed a liking for young Jeb Winslow, and the two had become good friends on the long trip. Now he planted himself firmly across from Jeb, pulled one foot up, and removed his shoe. "My dogs are killing me," he groaned. "I done too much walking when I was in the army."

Jeb asked, "Did you go over to fight in the war, Mr. Brown?"

"Sure did. I didn't tell you about that?" Brown blinked with surprise and shook his head. "Well, now, I was there. A lot of good fellows that went over with me didn't come back."

"They were killed in battle?"

"Well, some of them were, of course," Brown nodded. He slipped his shoe back on, and his eyes grew thoughtful as his mind ran over old memories. He gazed out the window at the barren landscape of reddish rocks, sagebrush, and distant mountains. "Most of 'em died of malaria and fever more than got killed by a bullet," he said.

"Did you go up the San Juan Hill?"

"Yes, I went up a hill. It wasn't San Juan, though. It was Kettle Hill."

"That's what my dad said. He was there."

"You don't tell me!" Brown exclaimed. "What was his name?"

"Aaron. Aaron Winslow."

"Why, I seem to recollect him. Was he a big tall fellow, broad shouldered, dark hair?"

"That's him!" Jeb said eagerly. "He and his brother, Lewis, were both there."

"Well, I don't remember much about him. As a matter of fact, I was pretty sick myself, and I got clipped going up that blasted hill trying to follow Teddy Roosevelt."

Jeb had heard many stories of the Battle of San Juan Hill, and he always liked to hear others, so with a little urging he was able to get Mr. Brown going. He listened avidly, his eyes fixed on the man's face.

At last Brown said shortly, "It wasn't a fun time. More fun looking back at it than it was when we were there, I reckon." Suddenly a mischievous light came into his eyes. "Be careful now with the wild Indians out here."

"Are there really Indians in Wyoming?"

"Why, of course there are, boy. What do you think?"

"I don't know. I thought they were all on reservations now."

"Don't you believe it! Still plenty out there. Don't let one of 'em take your scalp. Also, these cowboys are pretty rough. Fellows like Wild Bill Hickok. Why, they'd just as soon shoot a fellow as spit."

Frank Brown loved to spin stories and he loved to tease young people—or anyone else for that matter. So for the next half hour he sat there filling Jeb's head with tales of wild desperadoes and wilder Indians. Finally he asked, lifting his eyebrows, "You can ride, can't you, Jeb?"

"You mean a horse?"

Brown laughed abruptly. "Of course I mean a horse. There's lots of Wyoming, and there's nothing to do but ride. Automobiles may be here someday, but they ain't here yet—not much anyways."

"I've never ridden a horse."

"I guess you were busy playing ball, maybe baseball."

"N-no."

"What! You didn't play baseball? A tall fellow like you! Why, I'm surprised to hear it!"

Jeb Winslow was embarrassed. He was, at the age of nineteen, rather tall at six feet, but he was very thin and had never been particularly good at sports. Perhaps the truth of the matter was that he didn't much care for them. All his life he had loved to read, but only when he had gone to Virginia with his sister and his adopted father did he have a chance to do so. Aaron and his mother, Belle Winslow, had seen that he had all the books he wanted, and for the past months he had soaked himself in them. Now he said rather hesitantly, "I guess maybe I should have played ball, but I was busy reading books."

"Well, that's good, too." Brown looked up and said, "We're coming in to Waymore. That's your stop. Better get your stuff together, Jeb."

Jeb already had his belongings packed firmly in his suitcase, and now he sat there staring avidly out the window, wondering what it would be like to meet his relatives. He was aware, of course, that they were not really his relatives, but somehow he longed to put himself into the Winslow family. He had promised himself more than once, *If I can't be a Winslow by blood, I can be one in other ways.* He had heard so much about Cody and Laurie, who were real westerners and pioneers. Cody had been a cowboy and still was, for that matter, although he now owned a ranch along with his wife, Laurie. The couple had actually toured as performers with Buffalo Bill's Wild West Show—Cody as a trick-rope artist and Laurie as a trick-shot artist. He knew little about them, except the stories he had picked up from the family, and now he looked forward to meeting them, along with their daughter, Annie, and her brother, Bill.

"Waymore—Waymore! All out for Waymore!"

The wheels began to grind harshly, and Jeb stared out the window anxiously. There was nothing much in the way of a town that he could see—merely a few buildings, not more than a dozen, scattered on the Wyoming plain. As the train ground to a stop, however, he saw a family standing there and knew at once that these were the Winslows. Scrambling to his feet, he moved down the aisle, bumping into a farmer, who gave him an irritated look and said, "Stop shoving, bud!"

"Sorry," Jeb murmured. He moved more slowly then, and when he stepped down, the conductor shook his hand.

"Take care of yourself now. Don't let any of those wild Indians get you."

"I won't, Mr. Brown."

Turning toward the couple and the young girl that stood there, Jeb suddenly was struck with an acute shyness. He had led a hard life on the streets, getting into trouble, and now his attempt to make himself appear something more than a street tough proved very difficult. He knew his grammar was bad, and although his sister and Aaron worked on it a great deal with him, he still felt awkward when he talked. In truth, he was a shy young man who was being forced into a new life, and his shyness was sometimes taken for aloofness.

"Well, now, I'll bet my saddle your name is Winslow."

"Yes, sir." Jeb looked up into the bronze face of the man who, smiling broadly, approached and took his hand. "I'm Jeb Winslow."

"Well, I'm Cody Rogers and this is my wife, Laurie, and my daughter, Annie. Mighty glad to see you, Jeb."

Jeb took the hand of the woman who approached with a warm smile.

"We are happy to have you, Jeb. Did you have a good trip?" Laurie asked.

"Yes, ma'am."

"Well, Annie, don't be bashful. Say hello to your cousin," Cody winked.

"Hello, I'm Annie."

"Hello." Jeb could not think of another single thing to say. He had known nothing about this young woman except her name was Annie and that she was fifteen. She was a very attractive young woman with bright red hair and large blue eyes. He met her eyes for a moment and noted that they were almond shaped and shaded with thick, dark lashes. Her nose turned up slightly in an appealing manner. His sharp eyes picked out the birthmark on the left side of her neck, and he understood at once why she kept it turned away. *Why ... she's ashamed of that birthmark*, he thought. He was very quick at understanding people, a skill he had developed on the steets of New York. Somehow the fact that she had a flaw made him feel more comfortable, although he could not tell why.

As for Annie, she was somewhat surprised at the appearance of her "kissing cousin," as her father had called him. She had not known exactly what to expect, but Jeb Winslow did not fit her idea of a city boy. He was pale enough, to be sure, but also tall and very thin. He wore a pair of dark blue slacks with a white shirt and a string tie. He had brown hair that was slightly curly, and his face was so lean that he looked almost hungry. His nose had obviously been broken, and his large ears made Annie think, *It's a good thing they lie flat against his head or he'd look like a bat*. He was, in fact, rather plain, but then he smiled at her, a crooked smile, and his eyes crinkled up.

"I'm glad to know you, Annie. I hope I won't be any trouble to you, or to you, Mr. and Mrs. Rogers."

"Nonsense," Laurie said. "Now, come along. We're going to have to hurry to get back before dark."

Jeb had half expected an automobile, for he knew the Rogers were moderately successful ranchers. When they got to the wagon Cody shook his head, saying, "Couldn't get the car started, Jeb. Here, you want to drive us home?"

"Oh no!" Jeb said with alarm. "I don't know how to drive."

"Why, that's funny," Annie said with surprise. "I thought everybody could drive a team."

"Annie, be quiet. Jeb comes from the city," her father said as he lifted Jeb's trunk into the back of the wagon.

"They have teams in the city, don't they? How do you get around there, Jeb?" Annie asked.

"Why, I mostly walk, now that I don't live in New York anymore."

"How did you get around in New York?" Annie probed. She sat down beside him and was studying him carefully. "You had to go some way."

"Why, I mostly walked then, too, to be truthful," Jeb said. He felt intimidated by Annie Rogers' penetrating questions. In truth, he felt completely out of place in the West and had determined to say little until he found his way around. As the wagon moved out of town, he found himself growing more and more withdrawn until finally he said nothing at all except to mumble an answer to a direct question.

Annie also grew silent as the journey progressed, and when they had reached the house and gotten inside, she whispered to her mother, "Mama, he's just plain stuck-up."

"I don't think so," Laurie said, taking off her bonnet and hanging it on a peg. She kept her voice down so Jeb, who was being shown around the first floor of the house by Cody, could not hear. "I think he's just a little bit out of place. He's never been in the West before. Think how awkward you'd feel if you were thrown into a big city."

Annie did not answer, but she had a reservation about her cousin that she did not speak to her mother.

At that moment Cody popped his head around the frame of the kitchen door and said, "Hey, Annie, why don't you show Jeb to his room? You two can get better acquainted."

"All right, Daddy."

Turning sharply, Annie moved toward the stairs. Jeb followed her silently, and when they had reached the top, she motioned toward a door. "That'll be your room while you're here." She moved forward, opened the door, and Jeb stepped in.

"It looks like someone lives here," Jeb said as he took in the room.

"Well, it's my brother Bill's room, but he's not here and won't be for quite a while."

"Where is he?" Jeb asked. The room was large and airy with a set of double windows on the north wall. The furnishings were simple enough: an iron bed with what appeared to be a feather mattress, two chairs, and an oak desk. There were pictures on the wall, some of them of Annie, he saw, that brightened up the room. He turned to ask, "Is he gone away to school?"

"No, he's on a trip around the world on a ship. The *Marybelle*."

"Really!" Jeb murmured, filled with envy. "Is he a sailor?" His curiosity was taken at once and he moved to stand before Annie. "That would be exciting."

"He just wanted to do something adventurous," Annie shrugged. "So he pestered Mama and Daddy for a year until they finally let him go. Daddy knew the chief officer of the ship, Captain Evans. He promised to look out for Bill."

"Where is it going? The ship, I mean."

"Oh, it sailed first to South America, and then it's going on to Africa." Her eyes began to glow, and she said, "I'd love to see Africa. I'm going there someday."

"What would you do in Africa?" Jeb asked cautiously.

"I'd be a missionary," she answered matter-of-factly. "I might work with my cousins who are there, Barney and Andrew Winslow, and my aunt Ruth and her husband, Doctor David Burns."

"Hey, I know him."

"You *do*?"

"Sure. My sister worked with him in New York. He's a good friend of mine." Jeb continued, "I've read a lot about Africa. It sounds like such an exciting place."

"I would love to hear all about it! I'll tell you what. You tell me all about Africa, and I'll help you learn a little bit about the West. Can you ride a horse?"

"No. Never been on one."

"I'll teach you," Annie said quickly. "Now, let's talk about Africa. . . ."

★　★　★　★

The next morning at breakfast Annie immediately began telling her parents that Jeb knew a lot about Africa.

Laurie listened as Jeb explained about Doctor Burns, who had been a special friend of his and was now serving there.

"Well, the Winslows are well represented in Africa—for missionary work, that is. I'm especially proud of my younger sister, Ruth. I know she got a good husband in David Burns."

As Laurie spoke of Winslow families in Africa, the others ate with gusto. Breakfast was a huge meal, consisting of buckwheat pancakes, sausage, scrambled eggs, fresh buttermilk biscuits, tall glasses of cold milk, and hot coffee. Soon some of the conversation drifted around to the matters of the Rogers' household.

Cody shoved a biscuit in his mouth and chewed it, then shook his head with disgust. "Laurie, I got to go in and argue with that fellow about our insurance policy. We may have to change companies."

Laurie looked over at Cody, asking, "What's wrong with it?"

"I don't know. Who can understand those things with all that little print? It's impossible to read! I'm going to make him tell me exactly what you get in case I go up the flue."

"Daddy, don't talk like that!" Annie said.

"Well, maybe I need to put it a little better," Cody smiled apologetically. "But I've got to go talk to him, anyhow." He washed the biscuit down with a huge draft of black coffee and shook his head. "I wonder who started all this insurance business anyway."

"I think it was a man named William Gibbons."

The three Rogerses all turned to look at Jeb with astonishment. "How did you know *that*?" Cody demanded.

"Oh, I read about it somewhere. I just remembered it."

"A man called Gibbons?" Annie asked. "Where was he from?"

"London," Jeb said. He thought hard for a moment and said, "He had his life insurance for thirty-eight pounds at a premium of eight percent per annum."

Silence hung over the room for a moment and Jeb's face flushed. He felt he had been showing off. "I saw it in some book, I'm sure. Don't know why it came to mind."

"When did all this take place, Jeb?" Cody asked.

"In 1583."

Laurie suddenly laughed aloud. "Well, I can see it's going to be handy having you around, Jeb, if you know things like that. I can never remember who's the secretary of state or anything like that."

"For some reason, I remember. I read a lot," Jeb said his cheeks flushing.

As everyone continued to eat, Annie stared at Jeb and asked him more about his avid interest in reading. Jeb, however, felt humiliated and said as little as he could. After breakfast was over, Annie announced, "Mama, I'm going to go give Jeb a riding lesson. Daddy, will you help her with the dishes?"

"No, I won't. You help with the dishes, and I'll go out and saddle up horses for both of you."

The next portion of the day was a torture for Jeb Winslow. The horse that Cody Rogers saddled for him was a tall, rangy animal with what Jeb considered an evil look in his eye, and as it happened, it seemed he could do nothing right.

"No, you can't get on from that side. You have to mount from the other side," Annie said. She swung into the saddle easily, as she had been doing almost every day of her life since she was a young child.

Jeb had difficulty putting his foot in the stirrup, and when he did try to swing his leg over, the horse sidestepped quickly and he lost his hold on the horn. His foot was hung in the stirrup, and he called out with alarm as the tall sorrel dragged him through the dust of the corral. Instantly Annie was out of her saddle and catching the reins of the sorrel.

"Here, let me help you get your foot out of there."

Jeb lay flat on his back, feeling like an idiot. When his foot was finally free, he stood up and his face was flaming. "I can't do this," he whispered.

"Why, sure you can," Annie insisted. "It's just something new to you."

Jeb swallowed hard. He knew he had to try, and while Annie held the horse still, he struggled and pulled himself on.

"You've got long legs and your stirrups are too short. Let me lengthen them."

Jeb sat atop the horse holding the reins so tightly his knuckles hurt. Finally the stirrup length suited Annie, and she swung back into the saddle, smiling. "Now, we'll take it easy."

That proved to be impossible, for Jeb's horse took a notion to run. He suddenly lunged forward, and although Jeb hauled back on the lines, the horse had the bit firmly clenched in his teeth. "Hang on, Jeb! Don't fall!" Annie yelled. She kicked her own horse in the flank, and the two raced out of the yard.

Cody looked up to see them and laughed, saying, "Well, he's learning to ride right fast."

But the riding lesson did not continue very long. When Annie finally grabbed the reins on Jeb's horse and slowed him down, she said, "He's got the bit in his teeth. You have to hold him tight or he'll run away, Jeb."

"I've had about enough of this," Jeb protested.

With surprise, Annie looked at Jeb. "Well, you've got to learn to ride."

"I know it, but I feel so . . . so stupid."

Annie had never seen a young man who could not ride. All of her friends could. Everyone she knew could, but she tried her best to keep this knowledge from showing in her eyes. "We'll just go at a slow walk. It'll be okay."

Jeb hung on grimly and actually even managed to control the horse a little. But when they finally rode back into the corral, he got off awkwardly and walked away without even saying a word to Annie.

Cody ambled out of the barn where he had been working and

stood beside Annie. "I take it he didn't like riding too much."

"He's afraid of horses, Daddy. I can't believe it."

"Well," Cody said gently, putting his hand on her shoulder, "most of us are afraid of something. Some are afraid of snakes, some don't like being in high places, and some people are scared to get stuck in small quarters. With Jeb maybe it's horses, but don't put him down for that, honey."

Looking up at her father, Annie was silent for a moment. "He sure is different, Daddy."

Cody Rogers put his arm around his daughter and hugged her. "We're all different, Annie. God made us that way. You have to take Jeb as you find him, just like people have to take you right where you are. And me—you've got to take me just like I am. You can't trade me in on a new dad."

Annie laughed and reached up to kiss him, but all that day she wondered at how different she and Jeb were. *Well . . . he's East and I'm West—* She finally shrugged. *I guess he finds me as odd as I'm finding him.*

CHAPTER TWO

THE AWAKENING

★　★　★　★

Somehow it seemed to Jeb Winslow that the hard blue sky of Wyoming was very different from that of New York. As a matter of fact, he had seldom looked up at the sky in the city. In the slums of the lower East Side, the dirty, gray buildings shut out the sun. True enough, when he had moved to Virginia, he had learned to admire the green valleys and the high rolling hills of the Shenandoah, but there the sky had seemed softer and milder than the one he looked up at now, craning his neck and blinking his eyes against the brilliant sunlight.

"Is Montana much different from Wyoming, Annie?" Jeb asked. As he spoke he turned to look at his companion. The two of them had left Annie's home and had been traveling on the spur lines that were much rougher than the main corridors of steel that led from the East in St. Louis all the way to San Francisco. As he spoke, he was aware of the *clickety clack* of the rails and the swaying of the cars and commented further, "The tracks are a lot rougher than they were when I was coming to where you live."

Closing the Bible she had been reading and holding her finger for a marker, Annie glanced out the window. She was wearing a calf-length light blue chambray dress with short sleeves and a sweetheart neckline, with small brass buttons running down the front, and her hair caught the reflection of the sunlight that streamed through the car. "I think it's a lot higher," she said finally, "with more mountains." As she gazed at the barren landscape, she added with a shrug of her shoulders, "Desert's desert wherever you find it, I guess, Jeb. It probably looks pretty barren to you after New York."

"I don't think much about New York anymore."

"Why? Didn't you like it there?"

"No."

Annie's attention was caught by the single, bleak monosyllable. She studied Jeb's face, noting, not for the first time, how lean it was and wondered what he would look like when he filled out into manhood. He had said very little about his early childhood, but she had learned from her mother, who had in turn learned it from some of the Winslows in New York, that Jeb had been practically a gang member for a time. She learned also that his father had been a drunken brute who had victimized his family. It was no wonder Jeb never spoke of him. He had, however, mentioned his mother warmly, but he spoke more often of his time in Virginia with his sister and his adopted father, Aaron Winslow.

"What's it like in Virginia?" Annie asked suddenly, more to get him talking than for any other reason.

Since they had left Wyoming the previous day, he had spoken only in brief, dismal sentences. She knew he was still feeling sorely humiliated over his abject failure with the horse. She liked Jeb but found him difficult to get to know. It had been a disappointment to Annie, for she had hoped that as cousins, even distant ones, they might be more like family.

"It's great," Jeb nodded, and his eyes shown with an unusual animation. "Aaron is the best dad anybody could want. Sis couldn't have done better than marrying him."

"And he's a professor there?"

"Yes. And *his* father is president of the same college. I expect Dad also will be someday."

"And you like books just as much as he does."

"I always have, but I'd never before had much of a chance to read. Now, though, I've got the whole library there at the college, and Dad buys me any books that I want."

"I wish I were as smart as you."

Jeb suddenly gave Annie an odd look, lifting one eyebrow, and an expression of regret swept across his face. "I wish I could ride like you can, Annie."

"You could, with a little practice."

"No, I couldn't."

Annie hesitated, then said, "I know you're a little bit . . . awkward around horses."

"Why don't you say what you mean? I'm *afraid* of them. That's what I am."

"Well, Daddy says everybody's afraid of something. I'd be afraid to go down the streets of New York with all that traffic. It would frighten me, I think."

"Really?"

"Why, sure," Annie nodded eagerly, hoping to put him at ease. "Daddy says people are afraid of snakes, or high places, or all kinds of things. He told me that he knew a man who was so afraid of a hospital that he died rather than let himself be taken there."

Jeb listened as Annie chattered on, talking about people who had different kinds of fears, and it gave him some encouragement. He finally dropped his eyes and said, "I feel like such a—well, such a *flop*, Annie."

"It's just a new way of life. The West isn't like the East. You know, I've been thinking," she continued. She let her hand pass over the cover of the Bible that she held. "When I go to Africa, it'll be a lot more different from America than Wyoming is from New York."

"I guess that's true. Are you really going to go, Annie?"

"I think so. Ever since I became a Christian I felt that God was drawing me to do something."

Jeb shifted uneasily on the red plush seat. He looked down the car that was only half-filled. The air was foggy with smoke that crept in through the open windows, and the cinders that had been drawn in had soiled everything in the car, including the faces of the passengers. Even as he looked around, the mournful, piercing blast of the whistle broke the silence, and he looked out across the terrain to see what was coming but saw nothing. He sat quietly for a while, thinking of what Annie had said. He liked to think things over before commenting on them. Finally he said, "It must be nice to know what you're going to do with your life."

"Well, I don't know. It seems kind of like a dream, Jeb. It's going to take a lot of planning and hard work to get to Africa. Nobody really wants to go there. It's too dangerous."

Jeb examined Annie's complexion. She had, he noted, a few freckles across her nose, and the clean lines of her face were pleasing and gave her an air of innocence. "I wish I knew what I was going to do," he said finally. He tried to summon up a grin. "One thing I *won't* do is be a cowboy, that's for sure. Or anything that calls for riding horses."

Annie suddenly laughed aloud. "Well, maybe you'll be a professor like your dad."

"You know, I might be at that. I like it as well as anything else."

"Like what?"

"Oh, books and study and reading and classes. Sometimes Dad lets me go to class with him. I sit in the back and just listen, and I think it's exciting."

Annie gave him a dubious look. "Not me. I don't care much for school. I never did too well at it. I'm not smart like you are."

"Oh, I'm not smart!"

"Sure you are! Didn't take my folks long to find out about that, or me either. If you lived closer, you'd have to do all my homework for me and help me with my math."

"I wouldn't mind doing that."

"Well, maybe we can do it by mail. Are you going to write me when you go back home?"

"Sure. I like to write letters."

"I like to get them," Annie said, smiling at him. "But I don't get very many. It would make all the girls jealous, you know, getting letters from a college student in Virginia."

"I'm not that yet."

"Well, you soon will be. I could pretend that you were my beau, and you could send me a picture or maybe write me a mushy letter."

"A mushy letter? I couldn't do that!"

"Well, I could write it for you," Annie grinned, "and then you could copy it in your handwriting."

Both of them laughed, then Jeb said, "You know, I almost turned and went back to Virginia when I first got here. I was so disgusted with myself."

"I'm glad you didn't, Jeb. We're going to have fun in Montana. I can't wait for you to meet cousin Zach. You know, he was a gunman when he was younger."

"That's what Dad said, but I didn't know whether to believe him or not."

"Well, he was a gunman and a gold miner, and he fought in the Civil War. He got a finger shot off. This one right here." She held up her right hand and pointed with her forefinger. "Shot off right at the knuckle."

"I wonder if he still carries a gun?"

"Not anymore. I don't think his wife would let him. Her name is Bronwen."

"Bronwen! What kind of a name is that?"

"It's Irish. Well, I guess it's Welsh, really. But you know she was engaged to a missionary—before she met Zacharias Winslow, that is—until he died. So she came over to America to be a missionary to the Indians. Oh, it was a real romantic story! Zach wasn't even a Christian then. But anyway, they fell in love and got married, and I've always wanted to go see their place in Montana."

"Do they have a big family?"

"They've got two married daughters. The oldest, Lanie, is married to a man named Lobo Smith. He was an outlaw in the Oklahoma Territory."

Jeb gave her a disbelieving look. "Oh, I don't believe that! You're putting me on!"

"No, really! He was, and later on he became a U.S. marshal for Isaac Parker, the hanging judge in Fort Smith, Arkansas. And Zach and Bronwen have another married daughter called Betsy. She's married to a lawyer named Wesley Stone."

"The Winslows have no children at home, then?"

"They've got four boys at home, Tom, Bill, Phil, and John."

"Must be nice to have a big family like that."

"I think it is. Anyhow, there are lots of us Winslows. Have you ever been to a family reunion?"

"Not yet."

"You will. I'll bet your dad will take you. When all the Winslows come from all over the country it makes a big crowd."

"I'd like that," Jeb said. He sat quietly for a while, and soon Annie began reading her Bible again. He was somewhat puzzled at how much time she spent reading it. He himself had read it at his sister Gail's insistence, and Aaron, his father, was a firm Christian, too. But he did not find the pleasure in it that Annie did. *I'll have to look into that more*, he thought. Then his mind went on creating pictures of what Montana would be like, and soon he was looking out again at the landscape that flashed by as the train clicked over the rails and swayed from side to side.

★ ★ ★ ★

"Come on, Jeb. This is our stop."

"It doesn't look like much of a town, does it?"

"Nope, but that's it. I think the ranch is about five miles from here, according to what Uncle Zach said in his last letter."

"I hope somebody's here to meet us. It looks sort of barren."

The two stepped off of the coach and made sure their luggage was set on the planks of the station platform. One quick look convinced both of them they were not being met, for they saw no one that looked at all like someone who had come to meet visitors.

The train began to huff, expelling a huge gust of steam as it chugged out of the station. The two were left standing on the platform feeling forlorn. Looking around, Annie saw that the station was a small building no more than twelve feet square, and not a soul appeared to be in it. Moving over, she tried the doors but found them locked. She turned and said with some asperity, "Not much of a station. They lock it up even when the train comes in."

"I guess that's the town over there, but maybe we'd better wait here." Jeb waved toward the collection of weatherbeaten gray buildings that composed the small town of Clarence. There was little stirring, except for a herd of cattle being forced into a corral, and two men on horseback who were pulling up adjacent to the station.

"Maybe we could ask those men if they know where the Winslow ranch is."

"I guess so," Jeb said doubtfully. One look convinced him that the two were not the sort he would choose for company. They were both wearing worn jeans and cotton shirts, one red and the other blue. The one in blue had stopped long enough to look over at the pair.

"Well, looky here. We got some dudes come from the East, Pokey."

"Come on, Will. Let's get out of here," the man called Pokey said.

"What's the hurry? If we get back to the ranch, we'll just have to go to work." The man called Will was a tall, lanky fellow with dirty blond hair that was exposed as he shoved his black Stetson back on his shoulders, where it was held by a leather lanyard. He slipped one leg over the saddle and sunlight flashed on the silver spurs. "There's no rush. Maybe we can educate these young'uns about what it's like to be in the Wild West."

Pokey did not move, but Will strolled toward the two young

people on the train platform. As soon as he got close, Jeb, who was more experienced with such things from his time on the streets of New York, saw at once that the man had been drinking. Immediately he tensed up and wished there were some way to avoid the confrontation.

"Well, hello, Sylvester," the tall puncher said. His eyes were red from an excess of alcohol, and he stopped directly in front of the two, peering down at Annie and winking at her. "Is this your husband, ma'am?"

Annie's face flushed with embarrassment. She also recognized immediately that the cowboy was drunk and refused to answer the question. Taking Jeb's arm, she pulled at him, whispering, "Come on. Let's go into town."

"Why, you don't have to do that, missy!" Drunk as he was, the cowboy was fast. He reached out quickly and grabbed Annie's arm, saying, "You and Sylvester here better put on some better manners. Little bit different out here in the West."

"Let me go, please," she implored.

"Well, I'll tell you what. Let's me and you take a little walk, missy. I'll show you the town. Sylvester, you wait here with Pokey over there. We won't be gone long."

Although Jeb was almost as tall as the lanky cowboy, he could see the strength of the man and knew he would stand no chance in any sort of physical contest. His throat grew tight, and he chokingly said, "Please let her go."

"Please? Well, you have got some manners, ain't you, Sylvester? Well, like I said. You just wait here. What's your name, honey?"

Annie was trying to pull her arm away from the grasp of the man, but his fingers were like steel, and he merely laughed at her attempts. She had never been accosted like this and had no idea of what to do. She wished desperately that someone would come to her rescue, but nobody appeared.

"My name's Will Baxter. I'll just call you sweetie if you won't tell me your name. Come on, I'll show you the town."

As Annie was pulled along forcibly, she cast a look of despair at Jeb, then closed her lips. She knew that pleading would do no good with this drunken man, so she determined simply to accompany him. Once they were in the town surely someone would help her. There must be a marshal or a sheriff—!

Jeb swallowed hard, and then, despite his fear, he moved

quickly and grabbed the puncher's arm. "Turn her loose, mister," he said hoarsely.

Will Baxter turned and grinned rashly. He looked down at the thin young man's hands holding on to him and laughed loudly. "Look at this, Pokey. The tadpole's done riz up. Plum fierce, ain't he?"

"Come on, Will, it ain't worth the trouble."

"You go on back to the ranch. I'm going to have me some fun. I'll bet you ain't never been inside a real western saloon, have you, sweetie?" Without warning he suddenly jerked his arm loose from Jeb's grip and with a vicious swing backhanded Jeb across the face. The force of the blow drove Jeb backward. He tripped on his own feet and sprawled full length on the rough boards of the platform. He lay there with his head spinning, then slowly got to his feet. He could feel his face burning, and there was a cut on the inside of his mouth. He tasted the warm, salty tang of blood, then without thinking he threw himself forward. He knew it was hopeless, for no sooner had he gotten within reach of the tall puncher than a blow caught him on his forehead. The world seemed to turn into a kaleidoscope of brilliant, flashing colors as stars of red and green and purple hues flashed and danced before his eyes. Before he knew it, he felt the boards pressing against him again.

Annie stared at Jeb, and then a temper that rarely showed itself rose in her. "You big bully!" she cried and swung her free hand so quickly that it caught the puncher across the mouth.

Anger flashed into the eyes of the cowboy, and he muttered, "You ain't learned many manners, have you? I got a notion to give you a paddlin'!"

"That's enough, Baxter!"

Annie suddenly twisted her head around, for she had not heard anyone approach, but she saw that a buggy had pulled up and a man had stepped out of it. He approached within a few feet of Will Baxter and now stood almost leisurely, it seemed, examining the drunken cowboy.

"This ain't none of your put in!"

"Guess I'll have to make it mine."

The man who spoke was very tall and well proportioned. He had a wedge-shaped face out of which gleamed very light blue eyes, the lightest Annie had ever seen in a man. He was extremely tanned from the sun, and beneath a pearl gray Stetson that shaded his eyes showed tufts of brown hair, almost auburn. There was a strength in his face that Annie trusted at once, and glancing up quickly, she saw that the man called Baxter had given the newcomer his full attention.

"I'm telling you, stay out of this! It ain't none of your mix!" Will threatened.

At the same time he dropped his grip on Annie's arm. She moved backward and went to stand beside Jeb, who was struggling to his feet. The two of them watched as the two tall men faced each other.

"Will, you been asking for a beating for some time now. I been putting it off, but it seems to me that the time has come."

What happened then caught both Annie and Jeb off guard. The ruffian who had knocked Jeb to the ground without warning threw himself forward. Drunk as he was, he was fast as a striking snake. His right arm came up in a sweeping blow, and the newcomer took the blow on his neck. It staggered him, but he merely laughed and said, "That was your best shot, was it, Will? Well, it ain't enough, son."

Suddenly the Stetson of the newcomer went flying, for he had brushed it off. He stepped forward and drove a powerful blow that struck Baxter high on the chest. It made a hollow thumping sound as the other rider named Pokey hollered, "Stay out of this, Winslow!"

Winslow, Annie thought. *This must be either John or Phil.* She had read about both young men in the letters that Bronwen Winslow had written to her mother, and now she watched as the fight continued. It did not last long. While both men took a battering around the face, it was Winslow who drove the other back with blows that made a meaty sound as they pummeled Baxter's face and body. Finally Baxter's face grew flushed, and when a fist from Winslow caught him in the mouth, he was driven backward. He lay there looking bewildered as Winslow stood over him. "Why don't you get up? I'll give you the best we've got in the house, Baxter."

"I had enough," Will mumbled, rubbing his jaw as he crawled to his feet.

Winslow turned toward the other rider, who was watching, and said, "Pokey, how about you? You care for a waltz?"

"Not me, Winslow."

The tall man turned to the two young people, dismissing the

two cowpokes. "Sorry I'm a little bit late. You must be my kinfolk. I'm John Winslow."

Annie said breathlessly, "I'm Annie Rogers, and this is my cousin, Jeb Winslow." Her hand was immediately swallowed by the big hand of Winslow, and she looked up to see a smile with flashing white teeth. "Sorry about the welcoming committee. We don't usually let Baxter run loose. I guess I ought to have him throwed in jail, but he's not worth feeding. How are you, Jeb?"

Jeb could not speak for a moment, then he nodded. "Fine."

"Looks like you got a little bit of the worst of it."

"It's okay," Jeb said quickly. The cut inside his mouth was hurting, but he shook his head. "I'm just glad you came along."

"Well, come on and get in the buggy. Ma will probably give me a whipping with a broom for gettin' here late and subjectin' you to the worst of the county." He led them to the buggy and helped Annie in, then gathered and loaded their luggage before he leaped in himself and picked up the lines. Jeb settled in the back and held on as the twin grays started forward at a word from John Winslow.

Annie's heart was beating fast. In the short time since they'd arrived in Clarence, she'd already had an adventure such as she had never had in her entire life. She kept stealing glances at John Winslow and thought, in spite of herself, *He's like some hero in a book. What would I have done if he hadn't come along?* As the buggy pulled out of town, all she knew was that John Winslow was the most striking man she'd ever seen. When he turned to face her, his light blue eyes smiling, she could barely answer for the tightness of her throat. She would not have described it as falling in love, but those who knew young people might have identified it as the beginning of some sort of attraction that could lead to infatuation. She was scarcely conscious of the words he spoke, for she was admiring his strong profile, the strength of his neck, and his capable brown hands. *I've never seen anyone like him in my whole life*, Annie thought fervently.

"It's only about five miles to the ranch. I would have brought the car, but we had a flat tire, and I didn't have time to fix it." John Winslow turned back over his shoulder and winked at Jeb. "Quite a welcome you got. Gettin' into a fistfight with a skunk like Baxter."

"Is he really a bad man?"

"No. He's not bad. He just smells bad," John laughed. "I been meaning to have a few words with him. He tried to steal my girl at the last dance and I let him get by with it." He turned then to Annie and gave her a warm look. "Ma's been talking about your coming for a long time. I hope you stay for a long visit."

"I hope so, too," Annie whispered.

"Well, you'll have lots of company."

"Company?" Annie was startled. "What kind of company?"

"Why, a pretty girl like you—every long-legged, no-account, trifling cowboy in the county will be filtering over our way." He laughed at his own words and then winked at her. He also reached out and put his hand on her shoulder and squeezed it. "Don't let them scare you now. They'll find every excuse in the world to drop by the house." He chuckled and shook his head. "Horse gone lame . . . brought by some butter from their mother to give to my ma. Oh, they'll find excuses a plenty. And then at the dances you'll have to fight them off with a stick."

Annie, who had never experienced a man's attention in her life, found his words soothing. "I . . . I don't think that'll happen," she faltered.

John Winslow turned to look at his relative. "Well, you're a mighty pretty girl, and there's not many in the whole county. Lots of homely cowboys like me, though."

The buggy moved on and John continued to entertain his two passengers with intriguing stories. Once he looked over his shoulder and said, "I'll make a real cowhand out of you, Jeb."

"I don't think so, Mr. Winslow."

"Just John. I'm not old enough to be your grandpa yet. I'm only twenty-three. How old are you, Jeb?"

"Nineteen." Jeb couldn't help but think that he seemed far younger than four years to John.

"How about you, Annie?"

"I'm fifteen."

"Well, all of us Winslows have to hang together." Once again his hand fell lightly on Annie's shoulder, and he added it, saying warmly, "I'm mighty glad you've come. You'll put some much needed color in our lives. We need young folks around. My brothers Tom and Bill are gone to buy some cattle."

By the time they had come within sight of the ranch buildings, Annie was completely charmed by John Winslow. He paid her an attention that no young man ever had. Always, when he asked a question, he listened to her answer carefully. His smile was quick and friendly, and he paid her many compliments. True, he did the same for Jeb, who sat in the backseat of the buggy, but Annie felt that he was being completely honest. There was nothing flirty about his ways, and several times he said how glad he was they had come for a visit.

Finally John announced, "Well, there's the ranch, and there's Ma and Pa out front waiting for you, and Phil, too. I'm surprised he took time out from his painting."

"He's a painter?" Jeb said.

"Not a house painter. A picture painter. Yep, he's the arty one. Me, I'm just a roughneck."

The buggy pulled up in front of a long two-story house built of wood and painted white. It had two gables in the front, and a long verandah ran along the front. The three who had come down the steps stood there waiting and waving at them. When John pulled the wagon up to a stop, they all came and greeted them warmly. A tall man, obviously John's brother, stepped forward and helped Annie down. He cocked one eyebrow and said, "Well, Annie Rogers, I'm your cousin Phil. The good-looking one. John there, he's the ugly one."

"Will you stop your foolishness, Phil!" The woman who advanced to give Annie a hug had brilliant auburn hair. Middle age lay lightly upon her, and her sparkling green eyes seemed to laugh as she stepped back and exclaimed, "Look at you, Annie Rogers! I'm thrilled you could come, my dear. We've been so looking forward to your arrival."

"That's right. She ain't talked about nothin' else." A big man with strong, powerful shoulders, whose brown hair was streaked with gray, came forward at once. As he put his hand out, Annie noticed that the right forefinger indeed had been neatly removed, probably by a Confederate sharpshooter. "I'm glad to see you. Kindly introduce us to our other relative."

"This is Jeb Winslow," Annie said.

Jeb felt out of place, more or less, as Zach Winslow clapped him on the shoulder and pumped his hand with an iron grip.

"I'm glad to see you. I met your father once. Fine man! Well, wife, are you going to keep 'em standing out here all day in the blistering sun?"

"Well, devil fly off!" Bronwen Winslow responded, her green eyes sparkling. "You're the one that's babbling like an old hen!" She reached over and took Annie's hand and said, "Come in the house, sweetheart. These men have no manners whatsoever."

"Watch out for her, Jeb," Zach winked. "She's a tartar. Come on now. Supper's already on the table. Did you make the train on time, John?"

"Nope. I didn't," he said, casting a look at Jeb.

"He came just in time though, Mr. Winslow," Jeb said. "There was a cowboy there that was—well, he was insulting Annie."

"Who was that?" Zach asked, straightening up with his eyes glittering.

At that moment Jeb could believe that Zach Winslow had been a gunman.

"Oh, it was that trifling Will Baxter," John replied, shrugging his shoulders carelessly.

"Did you shoot him?"

"No, I didn't have my gun along."

"He gave him a thrashing, though, Mr. Winslow," Jeb said. "You should have seen it."

"I wish I could," Zach said. "Break any of his bones, son?"

"Don't think so. May have loosened a few teeth."

"I should have been there," Zach said. "I would have put the scoundrel in the hospital for a long time."

"I'm sure you would, Pa." John smiled and winked at Phil. "But the younger generation's got a more gentle spirit."

"Gentle, my foot!" Zach Winslow bellowed. He had, indeed, been a rough one in his youth, a soldier, a gold miner, and gunman of sorts. He had been considerably tamed by the firm but soft influence of Bronwen, yet the old fire would still rise up in him from time to time. Now, however, he looked with satisfaction at his two tall sons and said, "Well, come on in. Your mother's a poor cook but she does the best she can."

Jeb found out soon that Zacharias Winslow's words about Bronwen being a poor cook were said entirely in jest, for the supper that was set before them was outstanding. Huge platters of thick, juicy steaks were passed around, along with large bowls of mashed potatoes, corn casserole, green beans, homemade bread with sweet butter thickly spread on each slice, apple pie, large glasses of milk, and hot mugs of coffee.

All during the meal Jeb sat quietly. Annie, he saw, could not take her eyes off of John Winslow, and he thought with envy, *She's fallen for him. I don't blame her much. I sure wasn't any help defending her.*

Finally Bronwen prodded, "You men go on in the parlor and I'll do the dishes."

"I'll help you, Bronwen," put in Annie.

"Good for you! We'll let the men do all their worthless talking, then we'll go in and straighten them out."

Jeb found himself dwarfed by the three big men. They were all over six feet—John and Phil at least six two, their father a couple of inches shorter—but he felt weak and pale and washed out next to these bronzed westerners. He sat there listening, answering only when one of them remembered he was there and asked him questions. They were all friendly and wanted to know about his family, especially Aaron, and Jeb did his best to paint a good picture of his adopted father.

Finally Bronwen and Annie came in, and Bronwen said, "See here, we got this new piano, and I'm just learning to play the thing. Do you know how, Annie?"

"No, I don't." She turned suddenly and said, "But you do, don't you, Jeb?"

Jeb flushed. "A little," he admitted.

"Well, come on, Jeb," Zach persuaded. "Let's have a tune."

Reluctantly Jeb got up and went to the piano. He had been playing for a long time, mostly hymns in his church in Virginia, but he had a natural gift for music. "What would you like to hear?"

"Anything, as long as it's good," John said, smiling.

Jeb put his fingers on the keys and began playing. The others fell silent, for the playing was not like the usual amateurish performances they were accustomed to. Jeb, as always, lost himself in the music and soon forgot his audience. He loved music, especially piano, and he began to play the popular songs of the day, like "Wait Till the Sun Shines, Nellie," and "Take Me Out to the Ball Game," but then moved into playing all the favorite hymns he loved to play in the church. He added to them some improvisations that he was so good at until finally his gifted playing filled the room and, indeed, the whole house with deep and profound melody.

Finally Jeb shrugged his shoulders and blinked his eyes somewhat in shock. He looked up and saw everyone staring at him. "I didn't mean to—" He broke off, for they all started applauding. Bronwen came over, stood behind him, threw her arms around him, and squeezed him hard. "I never heard such playing in all my days," she said.

"Why, you could get a job in a music hall," John grinned and winked at Jeb.

"Music hall, indeed!" Bronwen sniffed. "The very idea!"

Phil came over and leaned on the piano. "I wish I could paint as good as you can play the piano," he murmured.

Jeb felt better at that moment than he had since he had left Virginia. He looked over at Annie, who smiled at him and nodded, then said, "Well, it's good I can do something. I sure can't ride a horse."

"Lots of galoots can ride horses," Zach snorted, "but none I know can play like that."

They insisted on more songs, and soon they were all standing around the piano and singing. It was a pleasant hour, and eventually Annie found herself sitting beside John. He suddenly noticed her and, looking down into her eyes, said, "Well, cousin, I'm glad you're here. I told you you'd put some life in the place, and Jeb can put in some music."

At that moment Phil came over and reached down and put his hand under her chin. He tilted her head up, looked into her eyes, and stared into her face. "Oh no! Look out, Annie!" John warned with a broad grin.

"What's wrong?" Annie said with anxiety.

"I know that look," John Winslow went on. "He's going to paint your picture."

"I wouldn't mind, Annie," Phil said. "You've got lovely bone structure."

"Bone structure!" Bronwen snorted. "What a thing to say, talking about . . . a young woman's bones!"

"How about it, Annie? I need a model. Will you pose for me?"

Annie felt their approval and said, "Yes, I will. I've never had my picture painted."

Soon after that Bronwen said, "Now, these young people have had a long and hard day of travel. It's time to go to bed. Come along, Annie. I'll show you your room. John, you take Jeb up to his."

Soon Annie was lying in a soft bed with fresh coverlets about her. The window was open, and she could hear the wind whispering softly outside. A crescent moon grinned in at her, and a bit of wispy cloud drifted across its face for just a moment. Annie lay there thinking about her adventures. *I'm glad Jeb can play like that. He needs to do something well.* But her mind was on John Winslow. Even as she closed her eyes in sleep, she was thinking of how he had come to her rescue and how he had put his hand on her shoulder in the wagon coming home and smiled down at her.

"I've never met anyone so wonderful," she whispered just before drifting off to sleep.

CHAPTER THREE

THE PORTRAIT

★　★　★　★

Time seemed to flow differently for Annie Rogers and Jeb Winslow as the days of their visit in Montana passed. For Annie they seemed to fly by quickly, while time seemed to be frozen for Jeb—he thought the visit would never end. Every day Annie was up at dawn and in the saddle, riding with John Winslow. She was accustomed to such long hours, having grown up on a ranch herself, and John found her company enjoyable. More than once he said, "Annie, you ought to pay more attention to these young fellows who come foggin' in here. You don't want to spend all your days with an old, worn-out bachelor like me."

The last time he had said this, Annie had looked up from the roan mare she was riding into the face of the tall rider beside her. The sun had mellowed his skin to a golden tan, smooth and even, and only the white at the V shirt opening revealed his true coloration. She could not help thinking that she had never seen anyone so young and vigorous as John Winslow. "I like being with you, John," she said breathlessly.

"Well, I guess you just like old folks then."

"You're not old. You're only twenty-three."

"*Only* twenty-three," John chuckled softly. "Seems mighty old to me. Seems like I've been stuck on this ranch for a millennium at least."

"Don't you like the ranch?"

"Oh sure," Winslow said carelessly, "but there's a big world out there, Annie. I want to see some of it. All I see now is a bunch of heifers. Someday I'm going to leave here and get on a ship and sail until it gets out of sight of land and just goes on and on and on until it makes port someplace where they never heard of a saddle or a cow."

The two were riding alongside a river that twisted sinuously across the plain. From time to time it was punctuated by willow trees along the banks. Finally they drew up under one of these to water their horses. Annie had thought deeply about what John said. "I want to do that, too," she said as she watched the river flow along.

"I guess everybody wants to spread their wings a little before they get old. You take Pa. He got to fight in a war, and he went to hunt for gold up north. Ma, she came from Wales. But I've never done anything but nurse these cows."

The two stood there enjoying the cool breeze, and finally they mounted again. "I guess we'd better get back. It's about time for Phil to paint some more on that picture of yours. You going to give it to me when he's finished with it?"

"Do you want it, John?"

Winslow turned to give her a surprised look. "Well . . . sure I'd like to have a picture of a pretty girl, but your folks would like to have it."

"You can have it if you want it," she said demurely.

"You're generous, Annie," he said, "but you hang on to that picture. Your future husband will want a picture to see what you looked like when you were just the age you are now."

Annie did not answer but determined at that moment that she would give the picture to John when it was finished.

When they arrived back at the ranch, John slipped to the ground and took the lines of her horse. "I'll unsaddle. You get on in and let Phil get something done on that picture." He hesitated and his face grew sober. "You know, I think Ma and Pa are in for a shock."

"How's that, John?"

"Well, I've talked about leaving, and so has Phil. I think he's planning on going to England or Spain or somewhere and learn more about how to paint. He doesn't say much about it, but that's all he thinks about. I know him pretty well."

"Your folks would be lonely here, wouldn't they?"

"I guess they would." Winslow ran the lines of the horse

through his strong hands and shook his head. "Life's like that. We get something we like, and then it's snatched away from us."

Annie looked up quickly. "What do you mean by that, John?"

"Why, nothing special." John seemed surprised by her question, but then laughed slightly. "Guess I'm getting philosophical. Run on in, Annie. Let the great artist get started."

At that moment Jeb was standing at the window looking outside at the pair. Behind him, seated on a chair beside the kitchen table, Bronwen Winslow was peeling potatoes. She studied the young man carefully, for she had become quite fond of him during their short time together. She always had a heart for boys, and this one seemed to be in need of approval. He had come to open his heart to her in a way that would have surprised some who knew Jeb, but then she was an easy woman to talk to. She had the gift of silence and a face that invited confidences, and now she knew that something was troubling Jeb Winslow.

"Is that John and Annie come back?"

"Yes, ma'am." Jeb turned, took a seat, picked up a knife, and began to peel a potato. He worked meticulously, shaving the potato almost to a transparent peeling.

"You peel potatoes better than my boys did. When they got through, there wasn't anything left. More potato on the peelings than there was in the middle!"

"I guess I do things pretty meticulously," he shrugged.

"That's the scholar in you. Of course, Phil's careful with his painting if with nothing else. John, now, he flies right at things. Funny how two boys can be so different. Phil so artistic and John so physical."

"I wish I could ride as well as they can."

"Well, if you want it bad enough, you'll find it. I'm not sure it's worth your while, though."

Looking up, Jeb studied Bronwen's face. She was one of the most beautiful women he had ever seen. She had a youthful expression, and her reddish hair and green eyes always struck him as being most attractive. "I guess most people would say I'm a sissy staying in here with you peeling potatoes. Annie's the one that rides and gets outside."

"A difference in people, that's all, and it's not bad. Now, tell me some more about the books you read and what you want to do." Bronwen sat there peeling potatoes, her mind fixed on the spirit of this young man. There was a fragile quality about him that drew her to him. Not that he sought sympathy, but he was vulnerable in a way she was not accustomed to. Her husband, Zach, was a strong, aggressive man, and his sons took after him. Jeb was somehow more—breakable, was the only way she could put it. Physically, of course, he was not as strong as if he had grown up on a ranch. He was growing so fast that he was lean as a rail. *One day*, she thought, *he'll fill out and be stronger. But there's a gentleness in him that most young men lack, and he's afraid of it. He's afraid he won't be manly.* "What do you want to be when you grow up?"

"I don't know. Some kind of a teacher, I guess. That doesn't sound very exciting, does it?"

"It's a fine thing to be a teacher," Bronwen nodded vigorously. "You stay right at it. Just be the best at whatever it is that comes your way."

The two sat there talking for some time, and finally Jeb said, "Annie likes John."

"Yes, she does."

Surprised at Bronwen's quick answer, Jeb looked up, a startled look in his eyes. "But that's not right, is it?"

"Oh, I don't think there's any harm in it," Bronwen shrugged. "She's fifteen years old, and John's a kind and fine-looking man."

"But it's not right for a girl to look at a man that much older."

"She's just waking up, Jeb. I remember when I was younger than Annie. I think I was only fourteen when I saw a young man at a fair. He was throwing the bar—that's a weight that the young men threw in a contest of strength. I'd never seen anyone like him. His name was Kevin," she added dreamily. "I'll never forget him."

"Were you in love with him?"

"Oh, I thought I was, and he was twenty-four years old." She laughed softly at the memory, then reached over and patted Jeb's hand. "Young girls do that. Young boys, too, I suspect, when they see an older woman they admire."

Jeb looked up and flushed, for she had touched a secret spring in him. He had had a similar infatuation just a few years ago.

"You like Annie very much, don't you, Jeb?"

The flush on Jeb's face deepened. "I guess so," he said lamely, "but she would never care for me."

"Of course she likes you. Anybody can see that."

"Well, I'm her cousin, of sorts, but not really. Yet I'm not the kind of fellow a girl would really like. You know what I mean."

Instantly Bronwen's quick mind lay hold on Jeb's problem. *He's smitten with Annie and she's looking at another fellow. He can't see how it will ever work out. He'll probably get over it and Annie will, too, but right now it's tragic and there's no way to help anyone.*

"Well, you'll have to play some more for us tonight," she said, changing the subject.

Jeb did play that night, and it was his one time of triumph. When he finished and he took his seat, Zach began talking about how their visit was drawing to a close.

"Oh, the days have just flown by! I've never seen time fly so fast," Annie said. "Isn't that right, Jeb?"

"No. They've been slow for me, but I like that."

"Funny how time can be slow for one person and fast for another," John said. He was sitting back in a chair, the front legs tilted. He was wearing a light blue shirt that picked up the color in his eyes, and his hair, shaggy and needing a cut, fell over his forehead. He brushed it back and said mildly, "It seems like time should be the same for everyone."

Suddenly Jeb spoke up. "You know, there's a fellow from Germany who's come up with a new theory."

"A new theory?" Zach said. "What sort of theory? These scientist fellows bother me."

"Well, his name's Einstein, and it's called the 'Theory of Relativity.' " Jeb had read a story about the famous professor, Albert Einstein, and it had intrigued him. "He says in his theory that nothing can go faster than light."

"How fast does light go?" Bronwen asked.

"A hundred and eighty thousand miles a second."

Zach grinned. "You know the blamedest things, Jeb. But that's pretty fast. If you had a horse that'd go that fast, he could win any race in the world." Laughter went around the room and Zach ducked his head. "Well, what's the theory, boy?"

"I don't really understand it all. As a matter of fact, I don't think more than half a dozen people do. But basically it says that all time-related things are relative. For example, if you're going to a dentist and you're sitting in the chair and he's grinding on your tooth, why, every second seems like an hour. But if you're having a good time, like catching a fish or something, why, every hour seems like a second."

John Winslow let his chair down and slapped his thigh, grinning merrily. "Why, I could have told him that! Maybe I could be a professor."

"Professor of what?" Zach snorted. "You did good to learn how to read and write."

The bantering went on for some time, and finally Phil said, "Now, I've got a surprise." He looked over and smiled gently at Annie. "I finished the painting today. Are you ready for the unveiling?" Cries of assent went up as he rose to his feet. "You wait right here and I'll get it. No, you wait, too, Annie."

Annie sat there waiting, her back stiffened. Phil had not allowed her to see the painting while it was in progress, and she had no idea what it would look like. Finally he came back holding the back of the painting, which was about eighteen inches wide and twenty inches long. He held it up tantalizingly, saying, "Here it is! Ta da!" Turning the picture around, he held it so all could see it.

Annie caught her breath, for she had not dreamed of something so striking. She had had a tintype made once, but there was something about Phil's painting that was different. He had painted her outside, against the background of the snow-capped mountains. Her lips were slightly parted, and she was looking off in the distance. He had caught the small smile that sometimes came to her with a pleasant thought. She was wearing a green blouse and her hair was drawn back, the red of it catching the brilliant sunset that was beginning to light up the west. Somehow Phil had captured the air of innocence and emerging young womanhood, not just in her attractive figure, but in the eyes and the cheeks and the set of the lips.

"Why, it's you to the life!" Zach said with surprise.

"It's a lovely thing," Bronwen whispered.

"I was never that . . . that pretty," Annie protested.

"You're prettier than that," Jeb said before he thought. And then when Annie looked at him with astonishment, he flushed and dropped his head.

"Do you like it, Annie?" Phil asked, smiling at the young woman.

Annie could not answer. She was studying the painting as if it were someone she had never seen. In all truth, it showed the young womanhood that had come to be hers, but it had caught her off guard. And now seeing herself portrayed, she looked at John and asked, "Do you like it, John?"

"Do I like it!" John exclaimed. "Why, I guess I do. It's the best thing that Phil's ever done. You should have seen the smear he made of me." He came over and stood beside Annie, put his arm on her shoulder, and squeezed her in a friendly gesture. "You'd better hang on to that one. It'll be worth a fortune when my brother gets to be a famous painter."

The painting was widely discussed, and as Annie left to go to bed that night, she stopped to whisper to John, "You can have it if you want it, John. I promised it to you."

Winslow stopped and turned to face the young woman. He had become very fond of her but had no idea of what was going on in her mind. He was a thoughtless young man in many ways, his mind on a future that was uncertain. To him she was no more than a child, and he said gently, "I'd love to have it, but it wouldn't be fair, Annie. You take it home with you. Your parents need to see it."

Disappointed, Annie nodded. "All right, John, but it's yours if you ever want it."

"I'll remember that, but you'll find a fellow that deserves it more than I do."

★   ★   ★   ★

The painting was placed in the drawing room, and every day Annie stopped to look at it, marveling at the skill that had gone into it. "You're a great painter, Phil," she said more than once.

"Not me. I'm just a dabbler. One of these days I'm going to learn how to paint. You'll see."

The days seemed to go by even more quickly, and finally it was time to return east. Annie cried in her pillow for hours the night before her departure. She said little at breakfast and afterward went outside to the porch. Footsteps sounded behind her, and she turned to see that John had come after her. He talked to her pleasantly for a time, then noticed she was silent. "What's the matter, Annie?" he asked gently.

"I hate to go home."

"Well, that sounds good to me." When he saw her look of surprise, he smiled and added, "It means you like us. Maybe you could come back quickly."

"Would you want me to come again, John?"

"Would I want you to? Why, you can believe it! We've had

some good times. I never knew a better rider, Annie, for a woman, that is." He laughed at her then, and his eyes reflected the blueness of the sky. "It's been good. You and Jeb have been good company for all of us."

"I hate to leave you, John."

For a moment John Winslow had a perception that had not come to him before. Quizzically he studied the young woman, and as his thoughts solidified, he cleared his throat. "Well, I'll be moving on, you know."

"Where are you going?"

"Off to college—Yale University. It's Dad's idea. He wants to make a lawyer or something out of me. I don't think he will, though. But anyway, I'll be going in a month or two."

Annie felt she had lost something. "Will you be coming back?"

"I don't know," John said laconically. "But I'll write you and you can write me back."

"Will you really?"

"Surest thing you know. After all, we're cousins, aren't we?" A thought came to him and he leaned down and kissed her cheek. "A kiss for my beautiful kissing cousin."

Annie turned pale and could not say a single word. John didn't notice how silent she was, and finally he left, saying, "Reckon you and Jeb have got packing to do. I'll hitch up the team."

Annie swallowed hard, nodded, then went to her room. After she had gathered her things, she went down and got into the surrey, taking her seat beside John, while Jeb got in the back with Bronwen and Zach. She could not find a word to say, and soon John noted her silence.

"You're not sick are you, Annie?"

"No."

"You haven't said ten words." Studying her face, John said gently, "You sorry to be leaving us?"

"Yes!"

"We'll all miss you. Maybe I'll drop by and see you in Wyoming. Repay your visit."

Annie shot a quick glance at John Winslow, but her throat was tight and she could not answer him.

The train was on time, the baggage was soon loaded, and finally she and Jeb got aboard. Annie's last sight of the Winslows brought a sadness to her. She kept her gaze fixed on John Winslow and cried out, "Don't forget, John! You promised to write!"

"I will, and you answer me!"

The train moved out of the station and the two took their seats. As the train picked up speed, Jeb quietly murmured, "You're going to write to John?"

"Yes. And he promised to write back."

Jeb did not say anything for some time. After a prolonged silence, Annie shrugged her shoulders. She looked over at Jeb, and suddenly a pang of conscience hit her. "Why, we haven't done anything together. I've been out riding all the time. I'm sorry, Jeb."

"It's all right."

"No, it's not," Annie said. She reached over suddenly and took his hand, something she had never done before. "When you go home, will you write to me?"

"If you want me to."

Annie Rogers squeezed his hand. She studied his lean face and noted again that there was something plaintive and almost unfinished about him. She remembered what Bronwen had said to her on one occasion. *Be very gentle with Jeb.* Now she knew what Bronwen meant, and she said suddenly, "I don't care whether you can ride a horse or not."

"You don't?"

"No."

Jeb took a deep breath. "I felt like such a failure. I don't know what to write to you about."

"Write about the books you are reading. Maybe you can educate me a little bit." Annie laughed, squeezed his hand, and then released it. "After all, we're cousins, aren't we?" She had a thought. "Daddy said we're kissing cousins." She leaned over and kissed his cheek and laughed as he flushed. "Look, you're blushing!"

Jeb shook his head but did not answer. He could not look at her for a while, and then he finally did meet her eyes as he whispered, "I'll write, and you write me back, Annie. . . ."

CHAPTER FOUR

"GOD WILL MAKE A WAY"

★ ★ ★ ★

A bitterly cold wind that had already frozen most of the western plains during the last months of 1910 swept around the framed building that constituted Doctor Will Johnson's office as well as his home. A keening wind clawed at the shutters like a fierce animal trying to get inside the house. Annie shivered and longed for the warmth of spring that lay many months away. Thanksgiving was upon them, but years of experience had taught her that with a harsh winter like this, snow and ice and bitter winds could freeze the plains well into the new year.

She quickly slipped into the kelly green dress that had been restyled from a wool coat that had belonged to her mother. It was not the latest fashion, but it had the advantage of being the warmest garment she owned. Quickly she tightened the drawstring in the skirt, slipped into the tunic, buttoned it, and then fastened the wide belt. The fur around the neck tickled her chin but added warmth, as did the matching muff that lay beside her hat on the table.

Very few things were more difficult for Annie than to undergo a physical examination, but since her illness two years previously, shortly after her eighteenth birthday, her mother had insisted on frequent trips to Doctor Johnson's office. Now she quickly moved across the room and opened the door. Stepping into the next room, she found Doctor Johnson sitting behind his desk, basking in the warmth of a potbellied stove that glowed cherry red. A pair of canaries in a bamboo cage chirruped feebly from time to time, seemingly numbed from a cold night in their miniature prison. The doctor sat tilted back in a sturdy oak chair blackened with age, his fingers locked behind his iron gray hair, his eyes staring up at the ceiling. As she entered, he lowered himself, leaned forward, placed his still-folded hands on the desk before him, and nodded. "Sit down, Annie."

Dr. Willard Johnson was in his middle sixties, and years of outdoor travels to patients scattered all over the plains of Wyoming had creased his skin and tanned it almost as deeply as a cowpuncher's. He had silky muttonchop whiskers, of which he was inordinately proud, that he fluffed up with the tips of his fingers from time to time. Now, however, he seemed very serious. As Annie sat down, he studied her for a moment, taking in the young woman's large blue, almond-shaped eyes and thick, dark lashes. His eyes rested momentarily on the small birthmark on her slender neck. *Wish she wasn't so ashamed of that mark*, he thought. *She's let it prey on her mind and give her a bad self-image all her life.* Even now, Johnson noted, she had turned up the collar of her dress with the intention of covering it.

Noting that her cheeks had filled out slightly, he was more interested in her physical condition than in any form of attractiveness. He remembered suddenly how beautiful, strong, and healthy she had been before she had been prostrated immediately after her graduation from high school. Back then she had been tanned and strong, able to stay in the saddle as long as any man on the plains. The sickness had been strange—and extremely frustrating for the physican. At first it had seemed to be the influenza that was sweeping the country, but later on it had turned into something else. Doctor Johnson was a man who hated to be defeated, and his inability to put his finger on the exact nature of her illness frustrated and angered him. It had been a debilitating sickness, and for over a year Annie had scarcely left her room, her mother caring for her constantly. During the second year she had improved somewhat, but she had lost her healthy complexion and now seemed pale and weak.

"Well, what's the verdict, Doctor?" Annie asked quietly. She had been in this office so many times that it was very familiar to her, but now, as always, there was a catch in her throat as she waited for his word. She knew she was not as fit as she had been before she had been struck down, but still, there was hope in her eyes as she waited for his reply.

"It could be worse, Annie," he replied. He fluffed at his muttonchop whiskers and nodded, allowing himself a small smile. "You haven't had one of those attacks in two months now—and that's good."

"Have you figured out what they are, Doctor Johnson?"

"The closest thing I can come to putting a name on it is asthma. It's not that, exactly—but something very like it."

Annie nodded, and the thought of the attacks that came frequently after she had first gotten ill was indeed a bad memory. It was as if the air was being cut off, almost as if a huge hand closed about her throat and she felt herself close to death and unable to breathe. "That's good news, isn't it?" she said brightly.

Doctor Johnson did not answer for a moment, then he shrugged. "Yes, it is. Have you been taking the tonic I've given you?"

"Yes. It tastes so bad that it must be of some value. Why does something good for you have to taste so bad?"

Johnson smiled, his eyes twinkling. "It won't hurt you. It does a young woman well to suffer a few inconveniences." He studied her carefully and then went on. "I believe you've got a little more color in your cheeks. Are you getting much exercise? But no, then, I guess it's too cold. It looks as though the whole country's going to freeze up this winter. Hate to think what it'll be like when December and January hit."

Annie sat listening as Doctor Johnson spoke quietly, and finally he asked, "Are you still busy with all your mission work?"

"Oh, of course, Doctor." The two belonged to the same church, and Johnson, being one of the deacons, was highly appreciative of Annie's activities. It had become her passion to support missionaries around the world. Before her illness she had been a whirlwind of activity—encouraging people to give money, writing letters to various missionaries, including her relatives in Africa, and getting barrels full of cast-off clothes ready to go all around the earth. Her heart went out to those in the foreign countries of the world who had no way of hearing the Gospel unless a missionary would bring the Word of God to them.

"Well, I'm not doing as much as I would like, but I can still write letters," she smiled. "And by the way, I'm taking up a collection for a village in Africa."

"Why am I not surprised about that? How much do you want?"

"All you can spare. It's in the continent's interior. My relative, Barney Winslow, wants to go in with supplies and help them with medical needs and food as he preaches. They've had a severe famine there and people are starving."

Doctor Johnson smiled as he dug into his pocket. He came out with several crumpled bills, looked at them, then wadded them up, reached out, and took Annie's hand. He pressed the cash into it, closed her fist, and said, "There. Now, I want you to go see that worthless brother-in-law of mine and tell him I said to give you a hundred dollars. He can spare it."

"I'll do it, Doctor." Annie rose, smiled back at him, and after receiving familiar instructions from the physican, left the room.

As the door closed, Doctor Johnson went back and sat down. Leaning back in his chair again, he again locked his fingers behind his head and stared up at the ceiling. He was silent for a while, and then he muttered, "That's a fine girl, but she'll never make it to Africa. She's too weak for that. Why, the climate would kill her in two months!"

★　★　★　★

"Here, Mom, let me help you set the table."

Bill Rogers had been sitting in a wooden kitchen chair at the oak table reading the newspaper. He rose now and began to gather dishes, cups, saucers, and glasses out of the large walnut step-back cupboard. He moved awkwardly, as many men do with such tasks, adorning the table first with a white linen tablecloth that had embroidery around the edges, then adding white linen napkins folded into neat squares, silverware with gold etchings, cut glass water goblets, and finally the fine, white china with delicate red roses around the rims.

Laurie Rogers, who had been cooking, stuck her head through the door and wiped her hands on a dish towel. She was wearing a light blue dress covered with a white apron. "I can use all the help I can get," she smiled. For a time she stood there framed in the doorway, her eyes following her son. *He looks so much like Cody*, she thought.

Bill had returned from his voyage to the South Seas with his wanderlust thoroughly extinguished. He had said fervently on his return, "I don't care if I never see anything but this ranch again!"

Laurie snapped out of her thoughts and smiled at Bill. "Now, you hurry up and finish. The roast is done. Annie and your father ought to be here any moment."

Indeed, by the time that Bill had set the table, Laurie came in carrying the roast on a platter, the door slammed. As his sister entered, Bill nodded. "You're just in time for supper, Annie."

"Good." Annie pulled the green cloth cap off, tossed it on a chair, followed by her muff, then came to the table rubbing her hands briskly. "It's freezing out there! That fire feels good." She stepped to the fireplace and stood holding her hands out for a few moments, then came over and gave her mother a kiss. She did the same for Bill and smiled up at him. "You set the table better than I do. You can have it as a regular job."

"No, thanks. I'll stick to herding cows."

Cody then came in, and after kissing his wife, he joined the others in sitting down for supper. He asked the blessing, then looked at the food that was on the table and shook his head. "Well, we're not going to starve to death if we dig into this, are we?" The large roast was done to perfection and was surrounded by small onions and delicately seasoned carrots. Next to the roast was a large bowl of mashed potatoes, a small bowl of gravy, a plate of freshly baked biscuits with butter, and a small bowl of jam. Glasses were filled with water, and cups of hot, black coffee sent steam up into the air. For dessert an apple pie fresh out of the oven filled the room with its tantalizing aroma.

As they ate, Bill kept his family entertained with small talk. He had an eye for unusual facts and events, and soon he announced, "Well, I see the world's coming to an end pretty soon."

Annie stared at him blankly. "What are you talking about, Bill?" she demanded.

"Why, it can't go on much longer." Bill leaned over and picked up the newspaper he had tossed on the floor beside his chair. "Says right here that they started putting curls in women's hair over in England."

"Oh, that's nonsense!" Laurie sniffed. "You made it up!"

"I did not! It's right here!" Bill lifted the paper. "Found out a way to give women curly hair. Permanent waves, they call it."

Cody shook his head. "That's the silliest thing I ever heard of! If God wants a woman to have curly hair, He certainly knows how to give it."

"But that's not good enough for the ladies over in England," Bill grinned. He winked at Annie and said, "What do you say we take Mom down and curl her hair? They use a hot iron to do it, I understand. I believe we could figure something out."

"You crazy thing!" Annie giggled, amused as always at Bill's sly wit. "That'll never catch on."

"No. I guess not," Bill said.

Annie ate little, though, and seemed to have something on her mind. Her parents noticed it, but neither said anything for a while. Bill continued to speak about the events in the paper.

"This new president, Taft—he'll never be the man Theodore Roosevelt was."

"Well, he's twice the man physically. He looks like a whale," Annie said.

"Yep, he's big all right," Bill nodded. "But I don't think he's got Teddy's spunk. I'll miss Roosevelt." He severed a biscuit, smothered the bottom half with rich, yellow butter, then put the top on for a lid. Biting into it, he chewed thoughtfully and said, "You know, that comet is something, isn't it? We'll have to go out tonight and look at it again." He meant Halley's Comet, which was moving across the skies with people all over the country following its progress. A puzzled expression touched his eyes. "How did they know it would come in 1910? I don't see how those astronomer fellows figure that out."

"You know what," Annie said. "It's real strange. Mark Twain was born in 1835, and that's the last time the comet appeared— and he just died. Something strange about that, isn't it? He came in with the comet and he went out with the comet."

Laurie sat thoughtfully considering her daughter and finally nodded. "Yes. That is rather unusual." She hesitated, then asked, "What did Doctor Johnson say, Annie?"

"Oh, he says I'm better," Annie said cheerfully. She knew her parents and her brother were concerned about her and tried to put as good a face on Johnson's remarks as possible. "He said I had more color in my cheeks, and I could take more exercise now. Things are looking very good."

"Well, that's great, sis," Bill said. "Come spring I'll have you out bulldogging steers again, just like before you got sick." He said this cheerfully enough but actually was far more concerned. He had been convinced that Annie would die during her sickness. He himself had never had a sick day in his life. When Annie had become so ill, he did not have the slightest idea how to deal with it. All he knew was that she had practically turned into a ghost for a year, keeping to her room, and each day he had expected one of his parents to come down and say, "She's gone, Bill." Now, however, he said heartily, "Here, buck into some more of this pot roast. It'll put some meat on your bones."

"Oh, by the way—these letters came for you Annie. The mail was late today." Laurie had risen and gone over to the table against the dining room wall, picking up a small packet of letters. "I see there's one from Jeb."

"Jeb Winslow?" Bill said, reaching out for a slice of apple pie. He put it on his plate, cut off a piece with his fork, and shoved it into his mouth. Chewing thoughtfully, he said, "He writes pretty often. What all does he say to you, sis?"

"Mostly he writes about his studies. He's in college now, you know. He's going to be a famous scholar, I think, one of these days."

"From what I hear, he isn't much for riding horses."

"No, he wasn't very good at that. But he's faithful to write, and he writes interesting letters, too."

"Do you ever hear from that cowboy out in Montana, our relative John Winslow? You used to get mail from him quite a bit."

Quickly Laurie's gaze went toward her daughter's face, and as she expected, she saw a slight break in Annie's expression. Laurie well knew that the visit Annie had made to the Winslows in Montana had in no way been forgotten. *She's still got a crush on him*, Laurie thought, *and that's not good. It's one thing for a girl of fifteen to have an infatuation, but Annie's twenty now and should have gotten over it.* She remembered then how Annie had written thick letters, page after page, to John Winslow when she had first come back. He had answered her for a time, but his letters had grown more and more rare until finally they had stopped altogether.

"No, I haven't heard from John in over a year," Annie responded quietly.

"Is he still in college, I wonder? He went to Yale, didn't he?"

"He dropped out of college." Annie looked over at Bill and smiled faintly. "He became a sailor for a while just like you. I get a letter from his sister, Gail Winslow, from time to time, and she says he doesn't write her very often, either. That's too bad; she's so fond of him."

"Well, he can have ships. They're dirty, smelly, uncomfortable things," Bill shrugged.

Cody finished off his pie, picked up his coffee cup, went and filled it from the stove, and said, "I'm going to read the rest of the paper, unless you want me to do the dishes, sweetheart."

"No. Annie and I will do them."

Cody went into the parlor and sat down on his favorite chair covered with black horsehide and propped his feet up on the hassock. Bill joined him. Electricity had not come out to the ranch yet, so Cody turned up the hurricane lamp, which threw a warm, brilliant light over the paper. He read carefully for a while until finally Laurie and Annie came in; then, as usual, he pointed out the interesting parts of the news.

That evening was much like all other evenings for the Rogerses. They seldom went out, and sometimes had family members from nearby ranches in for a meal, but basically they lived very quiet lives.

"Something's troubling you, isn't it, Annie," Laurie finally said quietly.

Cody looked up, for he had had the same thought. "What is it, dear?"

A faint flush came into Annie's cheeks, and her hand went to her throat. It was a moment she had been dreading, but now she took a deep breath and knew she had to speak. "I . . . have something to tell you all." She hesitated for an instant, then said, "The Lord has been speaking to me more strongly lately, and I've made a decision. I've got to go to New York."

"New York!" Cody exclaimed, lowering his paper and sitting straight up. "Why in the world would you want to go to New York?"

"Because," Annie said, "that's where most of the headquarters are for the large missionary groups. I've written to nearly all of them, but none of their responses has been favorable."

"What would you do in New York that you couldn't do here?" Laurie asked. A touch of fear came to her, for she had been expecting something like this. She knew this daughter of hers very well, and now she said, "It wouldn't be easy living in a big city like that, Annie."

"I know it, Mother, but ever since I started improving, God has put it on my heart to go."

Bill shook his head. "You can't do it, Annie," he expostulated.

"It's crazy. What if you had one of your attacks there? Who would take care of you?"

"God will have to take care of me," Annie said, and she smiled as she spoke. "That's the way it is with missionaries in faraway places. He'll have to take care of me in New York just as He'll have to take care of me in Africa."

At her mention of going to Africa, he began speaking earnestly, insisting that it was not a good idea. He gave all of his reasons and finally ended by saying, "You just can't do it, Annie. You just can't!"

"I've got to do it, Bill. It's not my decision. I know God is leading me."

"But how will you do it? It takes money to get over there. And because of your past health, you yourself say the missionary groups won't accept you."

Annie Rogers sat very quietly, and then she said, "God will make a way." Her eyes went to her parents, for she knew that the most difficult part, perhaps, of what she was going to do would be her parents missing her. "I wouldn't leave you, Mama, Daddy, if I didn't have to—or you, Bill. But I have to obey God."

The discussion went on for over an hour, but there was no break in Annie's composure. Her father and mother pleaded with her to wait, but Annie said, "I'll leave right after Christmas."

Bill argued until he grew almost impatient with her, but she knew it was because he loved her. Finally she rose and said, "I think I'll go to bed now. I know you think this is not possible, but I've got to do it." She went over, kissed her mother, hugged her father, then went to Bill and said fondly, "I know you're thinking only of my good, Bill, but you'll see! God will make a way."

As soon as Annie left, Bill shook his head and turned to his parents. "She'll die if she goes to that place."

Laurie Rogers sat silently. Her lips had grown tight, and she struggled with her deep love for her daughter. She had cared for her constantly during the years of her sickness, but now she knew that that part of Annie's life was over. After looking to her husband for assurance, she said quietly, "She's going, Bill, and there's no way to stop her—and God will *have* to make a way."

CHAPTER FIVE

AN OLD FRIEND

★ ★ ★ ★

The first day of 1911 introduced itself to New York with a relatively mild face, but the sun was sullen behind gray skeins of tattered clouds. The last day of the past year had been deceptively mild, but old hands like Pete Frazier knew that the weather was not to be trusted. Frazier, a small man of thirty, peered out from under his black derby at the skies outside Grand Central Station, gave his bushy black mustache a sweep with the back of his hand, and shook his head. Tugging at the lapels of his worn, gray overcoat, Frazier glanced down the line of carriages waiting for business and spoke to his horse as cheerfully as he could manage. "Don't worry, Nellie. We'll get us a fare. Got to make enough to buy you some warm mash when we get home."

Resolution swept over Frazier's lean, pale face. He leaped out of the cab and forged his way rapidly toward the entrance that loomed just ahead. Angry clouds, he noted, were gathering above him. The temperature was dropping like lead and already transformed particles of moisture had changed to crystal flakes that stung his eyes. Dodging through the crowd that hurried to get in out of the coming storm, Frazier moved quickly, sidestepping from left to right and jostling those who were not moving fast enough to suit him. Ignoring the angry stares and muttered curses that followed these tactics, he stepped inside, then made his way to the multiple tracks where the incoming trains would be arriving.

The tracks stretched out endlessly, trains lined up one after another. The engines were spewing boiling clouds of steam and smoke high into the air, and the sound of hissing jets of steam was almost deafening. Frazier's sharp, gray eyes moved restlessly until he spotted a Union Pacific engine huffing to a stop. It gave one last gasp, almost like an animal expelling breath from its steel throat, and then fell silent.

Quickly Frazier moved along, stopping in front of one of the Pullman cars. He was an enterprising man, his wits having been sharpened on New York's streets on the lower East Side, and now he studied the faces of those that got off. Times were hard and fares were hard to come by, but drawing on his years of experience, Frazier quickly spotted his target.

He moved toward a young woman who was wearing a plush dark blue coat trimmed at the collar, hem, and sleeves with beaver fur. Her face was half hidden by the soft hat she wore made of the same material but with a light yellow bow adorning the top. She wore black leather shoes covered with gray spats and was pulling on a pair of woolen gloves as the conductor helped her down. A good judge of character, Frazier thought, *Just in from the farm, it looks like, and don't know much. She ain't rich, but she ain't poor. About twenty, I reckon. If she don't know the big city, I can give her a long ride to wherever she's going, and she ought to be good for a little extra, too.* Stepping forward, he tipped his black derby and said, "Good afternoon, miss. Would you be needing transportation to your hotel?"

Startled by the speech of the small man who seemed to pop up before her like magic, Annie Rogers hesitated for a moment. Her cheeks were already tingling from the cold, and she was weary and stiff after her long train ride. She had slept little and was apprehensive about her odyssey from the plains of Wyoming to the teeming city of New York. Annie studied the man's face and saw that he looked rather lean and hungry. She could also see that he had a good smile, and certainly his manners were polite.

"Yes, I would," she said quickly.

"Well, let me just get your bags, miss. My name's Pete Frazier. Which suitcases would be yours, now? You'll have to point them out to me."

He moved efficiently while Annie identified her three suitcases as they were placed out on the platform by a smiling black porter. Digging into her reticule, she pulled out a small coin purse fished out a dollar. "Thank you, Jefferson. You've been nice to look after me all the way here."

Jefferson's white teeth flashed against his ebony skin. "Yes, ma'am, Miss Annie. Now you be real careful. Watch yourself in this big city, and God bless you, ma'am."

"God bless you, too, Jefferson."

Pete Frazier had taken all this in, especially the generous tip, and figured he'd landed an easy target. "I'll just get these suitcases and we'll step outside, miss. Come this way." He shouldered his way through the crowd, saying, "Gangway—step aside there for a lady—what's the matter with you, Mack? Move it!" When he had bulldozed to the doors and the two stepped outside, he nodded, turning to his right. "This way, miss. Be careful. The street's getting a little bit icy."

Annie followed the cab driver quickly. Looking up, she saw that the skies were gray and gloomy and that snowflakes were beginning to form, some of them almost as large as quarters. She waited until Frazier had put her baggage in the surrey, which had two seats, front and back. It was covered, for which she was grateful, and she accepted his help as he handed her up.

Quickly he scurried around, plopped down beside her, then turned to say, "Where'll it be, miss?"

The question nonplussed Annie. She had assumed that she would have time to think about getting a place to stay, but now that she was here, she had not an idea in the world where to stay. For a moment she wished she had written one of her distant relatives asking them to meet her. God had put it on her heart, however, to make her own way. "If you can't make your way in New York, how will you make your way across the ocean into the depths of Africa?" she had asked herself sternly. She had steadfastly refused any help, accepted minimum financial aid from her parents, and was convinced that God had told her that *He* would make a way. She was determined not to depend on the hands of man. The Scripture that came to her so often was, "He that putteth his trust in man shall fall into a snare, but whoso trusteth in the Lord shall be safe." So she sat still now, praying quietly for guidance, and finally she smiled. It was a pleasant smile that charmed Pete Frazier completely.

"I don't know, Mr. Frazier. I've come from Wyoming, and I don't have an idea about where I'll be staying."

"Do you tell me that!" He wiped his mustache with both hands with a fierce gesture, then fluffed it up and said, "I never heard of such a thing. A young woman like you all by yourself in a big city? It's not a thing that I'd recommend."

"God will take care of me. He always has and He always will."

Frazier studied the young woman's face and liked the quiet confidence he saw. From under her cap bright red hair crept out in small curls, and her large blue eyes seemed innocent and at the same time intelligent with some discernment. A few flakes of snow had stuck to the dark, thick lashes, and as she studied him, he suddenly decided to be honest with her as far as the fare was concerned.

"Well, now," he said. "There's lots of boardinghouses, but some of them cost a fortune."

"I don't have a fortune, Mr. Frazier."

Frazier smiled and shook his head. "Just plain Pete will do, I reckon, ma'am. Well, I've got a friend who runs a boardinghouse on the East Side. Mrs. Alice Simmons. Her husband was killed in the war."

"The Spanish-American War?"

"Right. That's the one. Good friend of mine, he was."

"Were you in the war, Pete?"

"No. No such luck." Pete shook his head regretfully. "I had to stay here and take care of the family. If I had been a young buck, you can believe I'da been there. Anyway, Mrs. Alice Simmons is a fine lady. Runs a respectable house. Clean it is." He looked up at the sky thoughtfully and brushed his mustache again. "I might marry her someday."

"I thought you had a family."

"I lost my dear wife two years ago. It's hard to raise children by myself, so I been thinking I might give Alice a break and provide her a good husband. What do you think?"

"I think we'd better go see Mrs. Alice Simmons."

"Right you are, and put in a good word for me when she gives you a room."

Annie leaned back and filled her eyes with all the new sights of New York as Frazier drove her along, expertly moving the surrey among carriages, wagons, trucks, and automobiles. Her quick eyes studied the deteriorated section of town they drove through. "This looks terrible," she said quietly. "Are all these buildings full of people?"

"Right you are, miss," Frazier said. "Most of the folks in this neighborhood come from across the water. They don't have any money, so they have to live cheap. All these buildings used to be fancy places, but now they've all been cut up into little apartments. And behind them, where their yards were, they built other buildings, so the people in the back don't have no yard or nothing. Sometimes just an air shaft between buildings. But the place I'm taking you to is much nicer than this."

Annie sat quietly listening to the running commentary that Frazier offered, and finally he pulled up in front of a two-story red-brick building. "Here we are, miss. Let me get your suitcase."

"But hadn't we better talk to Mrs. Simmons first?"

"Oh no. My word's good for her, and I know she's got a nice room. Right in the front up there, you see? As a matter of fact," he grinned, "she's been after me to find someone to rent it. So I'm glad I found you."

"I think the Lord must have sent you. You must be an angel of some kind."

Frazier stopped. He had been bending over, reaching to get one of the suitcases, when he turned and raised his eyebrows quizzically. His gray eyes flashed and he shook his head. "I've been called lots of things . . . but never an angel. Come along now."

The snow was coming down harder now, laying a soft, velvety, pristine covering on the street. It already gave the area a fairylike appearance, for the tops of the buildings were covered with snow. The falling flakes created beautiful forms, even of such things as the lamppost, making it look almost magical. Mounting the steps, Frazier put one of the suitcases down and knocked loudly on the door. It opened almost at once, and a tall, black-haired woman of some thirty years opened the door. She had light blue eyes and was wearing a white apron over a brown dress. "Hello, Pete."

"Hello, Alice. I've got your new roomer for that nice room right in the front upstairs. I didn't get your name, miss."

"I'm Annie Rogers, Mrs. Simmons."

"Well, come in. Pete, don't let her freeze out there!" Mrs. Simmons scolded.

When she stepped back, Frazier came in and said, "Shall I take the suitcases right up?"

"Oh, I'm sure Mrs. Simmons will want to talk to me. Just leave them here, Pete. I'll take them up myself."

"Let him take them up. He does little enough," Alice Simmons said. "I've not got a man handy here," she stated. "Not that men are ever very handy. Take them up, Pete. Do what I tell you."

"You see? She's already talking to me like we was married. You're going to have to be sweeter than that if you want to catch me," Frazier grinned, picking up the suitcases. "It takes honey to catch flies."

"I'm not needing any flies," Alice retorted. She turned to Annie, saying, "Come on into the kitchen. I've got some hot coffee on. I could make tea if you'd like."

"That would be nice."

The two women moved back through the long corridor that led to the kitchen in the back. The door on the left opened into a large parlor, and as they passed, Mrs. Simmons said, "You can use this anytime you like. And over there's the dining room. I've got eight boarders now. We'll be having supper in about an hour. You'll have time to freshen up."

Annie was wondering at the ease with which all this had happened, and when she sat down at the kitchen table across from Alice Simmons, she ventured, "I suppose we ought to talk about your rates."

"Ten dollars a week, all meals included."

"That sounds fair enough." Reaching into her reticule, Annie pulled out her purse, extracted some bills, and handed them over. "Here's my first month's rent, Mrs. Simmons."

"Alice will do. Thanks, deary."

At that moment Frazier came in and, with the freedom of an old friend, moved over to the wood-burning stove and opened the lid in the warmer on top. "Ahh, I see you made me another apple pie." Ignoring Alice's protests, he removed it, cut himself a thick wedge, and held it with his hand. "No sense spoiling a dish," he said.

He sat down and Alice poured him a mug of scalding black coffee, and the two talked for a while. Finally he rose up and said regretfully, "Well, I've got to go find me a fare."

"Oh, how much do I owe you, Pete?" Annie asked.

Pete Frazier struggled with temptation, for he knew that whatever he said, the young woman would pay it without question. He also was aware of Alice Simmons' eyes sternly fixed on him, for she knew his habits. Swallowing hard, he said, "Only a dollar."

"Oh no, that's not nearly enough!" Annie said quickly. She pulled a five dollar bill out and smiled. "That's not just for the ride. That's for helping with the luggage, and being there with a friendly smile to meet me, and for bringing me to this place. I wish it were a hundred."

"Well, if you insist, miss," Frazier grinned. He tucked the bill into his inside pocket and winked at Alice. "I'll see you tonight. We're going to that concert, right?"

"I'll be ready."

"Right. I haven't found anybody to keep my kids yet, but I'll find somebody."

"Could I do that, Pete? I'd love to," Annie offered.

Pete Frazier exchanged glances with Alice Simmons. Both of them had seen something in the young woman that they liked, and now he said, "They're a bit of a handful."

"I'm used to children. I'll try to hold my own if it would be of any help to you."

"You sure you're not too tired, dear?" Alice said. "You've come a long way."

"No. I don't mind a bit."

"All right then," Alice said. "This poor benighted man needs a little culture, and I intend to see that he gets it."

"After you marry me, you can culturize me all you want to," Frazier grinned. "I'll see you after supper. How about seven?"

"Fine. Come along, dear. I'll take you up to your room. You've got time to rest for an hour."

Annie followed Alice up the stairs, turned to her left, and stepped inside the door that the landlady held open. When she moved inside, she was delighted. It was large, about twelve by fourteen, and attractive, with its blue and green wallpaper on the walls and worn but well-kept dark green carpet on the floor. There was a large oak four-poster bed covered with a colorful quilt, a small bedside table situated to the left of the bed, and to the right a large armoire of honey-colored oak. The two large floor-length windows at the front of the room were framed with blue, green, and white curtains, and a small pine desk and lamp had been placed to one side, with a dark red easy chair to the other.

"The bath is right next door. Plenty of linens. Let me know if you need anything. Now, you lie down and take a rest."

"Thank you, Alice."

As soon as the door closed, Annie went over to the window and looked out. The snow was coming down now so thick that you could hardly see twenty feet away. On the streets below, horses were transformed into frosty phantoms pulling fairy coaches cloaked with white. She had always loved snow, and now as she stood there, she said quietly, "Thank you, Lord, for going before me and preparing my way." It was a way she had of praying about small things all through the day, and she had found out that waiting at night to catch up was not the best way to keep in touch with God. So now she made it a habit as often as she could to send little prayers up to Him. It was something she had learned from her mother that had stood her in good stead.

The room was cold, but there was a small hot water radiator, and she turned it on according to Alice's instructions. Laying her hand on it, she felt it begin to warm as the hot water forced its way through it. She knew it would not keep the room warm, but it would cut off most of the fierce bite of the cold. She was too filled with excitement to sleep, so she put her clothes away in the armoire and arranged her writing materials and books on the small desk beside the window. She washed her face in cold water, which awakened her even more, and finally walked around the room with a sense of well-being. She went back to the window, pulled up a chair, and watched the procession of carriages, buggies, cabs, cars, and trams as they made their way along the street through the blanket of snow. She thought about how she actually was on her way. "It's a long journey to Africa, Lord," she said quietly. "But I've made my first step. The next step will be up to you."

A faint scratching outside her door drew her head around, and she quickly walked across the worn carpet, opened the door, and looked down to see a large, golden-eyed cat with thick, long, silver-gray fur staring up at her.

Stooping over, Annie picked up the cat, shut the door, and walked over to the chair and sat down. "Where did you come from?" she whispered. She stroked the silky fur, and the cat arched its back in response to the caress. "You're so warm. If I had a fur coat like that, I wouldn't mind this winter at all." She sat there stroking the cat for some time, and finally the animal curled up in her lap and went soundly to sleep. She was still sitting there thirty minutes later when a knock came and the door opened.

Alice glanced at the young woman holding the cat and said, "Oh, you'll have to put him out. He's the world's biggest pest."

"I don't mind. What's his name?"

"His name is Rosie. Named after Teddy Roosevelt. My husband thought the sun rose and set on that man. Now that Rosie's found someone who will pamper him, he'll probably take up residence in here."

"That's all right. We'll get along, won't we, Rosie?"

"Come along. Supper's on the table."

Annie followed Alice down to the dining room, where she met her fellow boarders. One of them, a sharp-faced man named Buford Carmody, peppered her with questions throughout the meal, which proved to be good, indeed.

The others mostly listened, and it appeared that Carmody was the most talkative of the boarders. Quickly he got out of Annie that she was new in New York and that she was determined to be a missionary in Africa.

A big man named Howard Potter, with black hair and mild brown eyes, sat across from Carmody and laughed aloud. "That's just what you need, Buford, a preacher! Maybe Reverend Rogers can do something for you."

"Why, I'm not a reverend," Annie protested quickly.

"I thought you had to be a reverend to be a missionary," Buford demanded.

"Not really. At least I hope not," Annie sighed as she unfolded the white napkin and placed it on her lap.

"You'll have to come to our church, dear," Alice said. "It's not very far from here. Our pastor, Reverend Aubry Sikes, is very mission minded. He's always having missionaries come to speak at the church—some of them from Asia and Africa."

"I'd like to very much! I'm hoping to go to Africa myself."

"You don't have to go to Africa to preach to the heathen," Alice Simmons said primly. "Not all the godless pagans are in Africa. Some of them are right here in New York."

Howard Potter laughed again and winked at Buford Carmody. "I think we're being preached at. Do you feel that, Buford?"

Annie sat quietly for a while and ate the delicious food. Alice had served large cuts of juicy pork, mashed potatoes, corn casserole, green beans, thick slices of fresh bread, and hot apple pie. As Annie ate, she was grateful that she had found a Christian woman whom she felt sure would be her friend. Once again she gave thanks that she had found the exact place God had for her, and then she applied herself to answering the questions that Buford Carmody again determined to toss toward her. She answered as gracefully as she could and finally said, "I'll be going to church with Mrs. Simmons Sunday morning. Maybe you'd like to go, too."

Carmody blinked at the young woman's directness. "Well, I reckon I might at that."

"Well, I'll be!" Potter jeered, leaning back in his chair. "I can't believe it!"

"I'd like to have you go, too, Mr. Potter. I'd feel much better with two escorts such as you and Mr. Carmody. How about it?"

The others waited and Howard Potter suddenly broke out into a loud laugh. "I'll be blowed if I won't do it! Might even make a convert out of the two of us."

"I hope so. Everyone needs Jesus," Annie said. A quietness fell over the table, and both men dropped their eyes. Annie smiled and said no more, but she had learned then that she didn't have to get to Africa to begin her work for Jesus.

★　★　★　★

The Reverend Roger Casement was a small man, almost diminutive. His lack of size, however, did not trouble him. He had learned as a child, then as a young boy growing up, that one's value could never be measured by size. When he was sometimes ridiculed for his smallness, he would turn his piercing blue eyes on the speaker and say, "So you think a six-foot man is more important than a five-foot man? Then you must also think that a gorilla that weighs 500 pounds is more important than a 150 pound man such as yourself?"

Usually such sharp observations would quiet his detractors, but he was by nature noncombative and actually very humble. He did not care whether he was five feet or six feet tall. His biggest concern all his life had been to serve God faithfully. He had worked as a young man and as a pastor in upper New York State. He had been a missionary to South America, where he had almost died of a tropical disease. Indeed, he had left many friends buried there—missionaries who had given their lives. When he had grown too frail to endure the hardship and privations of the missionary life, he had been appointed the head of the mission board of his denomination. In this capacity, which he enjoyed greatly, there was one unpleasant side of his work that he disliked intensely. It was the duty of informing applicants for the mission field that the mission board could not support them. This was al-

ways something that gave Casement trouble, and especially so
when the candidates were as appealing as the young woman who
now sat across from him. His eyes fell down to the letter that lay
before him, and he thought, *I've never hated to say no to a candidate
so much in my whole life, but there's no help for it....*

"Well, Miss Rogers," he said heavily and forced himself to
smile. "I'm afraid I don't have very good news for you."

Annie looked up and studied the lean face of Reverend Casement. "You can't send me as a missionary?" she asked quietly.

"Well . . . not at the present time." Casement spoke with some
hesitation and for one wild moment almost broke his rule. And
despite the medical history that made her a poor choice, he had
to fight down the impulse to approve her. Leaning forward, he
clasped his hands together and shook his head. "You see, Miss
Rogers, we only have so much money. Not nearly enough as you
might well guess. When we make our decisions, we have to use
two things. Divine guidance and human wisdom. In your case my
inclination is that you would make a fine missionary. Just what
we're looking for—in the spiritual sense. I have letters here from
your pastor in Wyoming, fine recommendations from other min-
isters and missionaries that you have supported over the years,
and despite your youth, you meet every qualification in that
area."

"What is the trouble, Reverend Casement? Why can't you send
me?"

Shifting uneasily in his chair, Reverend Casement replied,
"Well, there are two factors. For one thing, you are single. We do
send a few single women, but almost inevitably they are somewhat older than you and have led a much more active life. As far
as possible, we like for couples to go." His eyes grew thoughtful
and he shook his head. "If I hadn't had my dear wife with me
when I went on my first mission tour, I doubt I would have sur-
vived. You know the Scripture, 'Two are better than one, for if one
falls, who shall pick him up?' I can testify to the truth of that.
When you're all alone, away from friends and family, there's nothing but strange faces day after day, month after month. All that
you have loved is gone. I can't tell you how much it's worth to
have a companion there! Although we are not adamant, on the
whole, we feel it would be better if you were married."

"But that's not the real reason, is it, Reverend?" Annie asked.

"Well, no, it's not the *primary* reason. Your health is a matter of concern. I have a letter here from your physician, and while he said you are doing much better, your past health record has not been good."

Annie could not answer this, for she knew well that this was true. "I was very strong as a young woman until the sickness came two years ago. But I've been slowly getting better."

"Have you had any more of these attacks?"

Annie might have avoided the question, but she was honest to the bone. "Yes. I did have one about three months ago. It didn't last long, though, and it wasn't very severe."

"What was it like?"

"I can't tell you very much, Reverend Casement. It's like suddenly the air is cut off and I can't breathe. When I first grew ill this would last for days sometimes. I would have to lie there struggling for breath, but I grew better," she said defensively. "And this last attack only lasted for half a day."

"I admire your determination to follow the will of the Lord, and I have no doubt about your call, but I think you need time. And we need time here at the mission board to pray for you and for your life." Casement once again had an impulse to throw up all restraints and send this young woman. There was a godly air about her, a spiritual aura that he had learned to recognize in people. *She loves God with all of her heart. He can surely take care of her,* was his thought. But he was responsible for many people, and he knew how hard it was to get a sick missionary home again. So now he said regretfully, "Why don't we wait a year? Who knows," he smiled, "you might find a husband in that time. A good stout fellow to stand beside you. And your health could improve even more. We'll keep in touch."

"All right, Reverend Casement."

Casement was surprised. Most applicants would argue in a situation like this, but there was a gentle and meek spirit in this young woman that joined to a steely determination, which he saw in her dark blue eyes. "I wish I could do more," he said.

"Perhaps I could help you some here with your work with the missions. I don't know anything about the work, but I could help with mail and things like that."

Casement's eyes grew warm. "That is *most* generous of you, Miss Rogers—very generous indeed! We are always in need of help here, and I would appreciate anything you could do."

After Annie had left, Casement called his secretary in, a man named Simms. "Simms, that young woman's going to be coming in to help with the paperwork."

Simms, a tall, thin man of forty, studied the face of Casement. "You disapproved her application?"

"Yes, and I'm not sure I did the right thing. But we don't have to worry about this one. She'll go to Africa if she has to crawl on her hands and knees."

Simms grinned. "That would be difficult all the way across the ocean."

"You know what I mean. She's a good one. I think God's got great things in store for her."

★ ★ ★ ★

From the first day that Annie moved into her room, Rosie had taken up residence with her. Every night faint scratching at the door would alert Annie, who would go and open it a crack, whereupon Rosie would come strolling in with his large golden eyes gleaming. During the bleak month of January, having the huge furry cat to sleep with was a blessing for Annie, since he radiated heat like a small furnace. He also liked to get under the cover and curl up down at the foot of the bed, so that he served as a foot warmer for Annie.

Another habit Rosie had developed was rather peculiar. Many days Annie would spend the afternoons in her room studying books on Africa that she had checked out of the library, as well as reading her Bible and praying for an appointment. Annie had learned to treasure these hours alone, but so had Rosie. He learned quickly that after a time Annie would lie down flat on the bed with the light streaming in from the window and read a book. This gave Rosie an opportunity to assume his favorite position. He would leap up on the bed, shove with his blunt head at the book, and crawl up on Annie's chest, his face as close to hers as he could get. He would begin purring, and Annie delighted in the miniature rumble that transferred itself to her body. From time to time Rosie's eyes would half close with the pleasure he evidently felt, then he would reach out gently with his claws sheathed and touch her on the lips. Annie never knew why he did this, but she found it comforting somehow.

It was a month and a half after Reverend Casement had given Annie her first rejection that she was lying flat on her back with

Rosie stretched out full length on her chest. Annie was sleepy. Her head was propped up with a pillow, and she had been reading the book of Lamentations on her way through the Old Testament. The weather outside was inclement, and she had spent all morning going from one mission headquarters to another, as she did one day every week. She now had a collection of rejections from every mission board she could locate. All of them repeated, in effect, what Reverend Roger Casement had already told her. *You're single and too sick.* It was never phrased exactly like this, but every interview ended in another rejection.

Annie had determined never to let herself grow despondent but to rejoice in the Lord. She read over and over again the Scripture, "In everything give thanks." She copied the verse several times and pasted the copies over her mirror, over her bed, and over her desk, and every day in everything she did give thanks. It baffled her, because she did not see how she could give thanks for this. Reverend Aubry Sikes, the pastor of her new church, had spoken with her once in one of their meetings together. "Annie," he had said, "it doesn't say to give thanks *for* everything. For example, I can't imagine anyone wanting to give thanks *for* a toothache. It says *in* everything give thanks. In other words, when you have a toothache, even then you can give thanks. Be thankful that you have a tooth to hurt," he had said, smiling at her gently. "Be thankful that you have health, that you have friends, that you have a church, that you're in the kingdom of God. *In* everything give thanks."

His insightful wisdom had helped Annie tremendously. She appreciated his ministry, and she appreciated the time she spent with Reverend Casement and his small staff at the mission board. As she lay there with Rosie pressing heavily upon her chest, she reached out and stroked his heavy fur, and he responded by stretching out one paw and touching her lips. "You love me, don't you, Rosie?" she smiled. "Well, I love you, too. I'm going to take you to Africa with me when I go, if I can. But you'll probably get eaten by a lion or something."

For a long time she lay there musing, thinking about the many failures she had had, and then almost dozed off until she was interrupted by a gentle knock on the door. "Come in," she said.

The door opened and Alice Simmons announced, "You have a visitor."

"A visitor? Who is it?"

"I don't know. It's a young man."

"Oh. I'll be right down."

Annie sighed as she straightened, picking Rosie up. He dangled as she held him by the middle and gently tossed him on the bed. "There, you can sleep on the bed instead of on me. I'll be back, I suppose, and you can crush me again." She stopped by the mirror, gave her hair a few strokes with the brush, then left her room. Descending the stairs she wondered who it could be, thinking it might be someone from the church or from the mission board asking her to do some extra work. But when she turned into the drawing room she stood stock-still, for there stood Jeb Winslow!

"Jeb!" she exclaimed and rushed forward, holding out her hands. "What are you doing here?"

Jeb Winslow, at the age of twenty-four, was almost as lean as he had been when Annie had seen him five years ago, but now he was six feet three and towered over her. His brown hair was longer, and his face had filled out slightly. His crooked smile came, and he said in a surprisingly deep voice, "Annie, my, it's good to see you!" His large hands enfolded hers until they were lost, and for a moment they stood looking at each other. They had written letters many times over the years, but this was their first reunion.

"Why, Jeb, I'm so glad to see you. How did you know I was here?"

"Your mother gave me your address."

"But what are you doing in New York?"

"Going to school." Jeb was still holding her hands, and very much aware of it. He had thought about this young woman countless times since their parting. They had exchanged pictures two years earlier, but now as he looked at Annie, he saw that the picture had done her little justice. Her eyes were as dark as he remembered, a blue so dark that they almost seemed black at times, and she had grown up into a most attractive young woman. She was wearing a simple green dress, trimmed with lace at the throat and wrist, that clearly outlined her womanly figure.

"Well, what am I thinking? Sit down, Jeb. We've got so much to talk about."

"Have you eaten?" Jeb asked suddenly.

When she shook her head, he said, "Let's go out and get something to eat if you know a place."

"Oh, I know a fine place. Let me get my coat."

Thirty minutes later the two were seated in a cozy restaurant after a brisk walk through the slush that was the aftermath of the snows of January. When the proprietor came over to their table, Annie said, "Devoe, this is my friend Jeb Winslow. He's from Virginia, but he's moving here now. I told him you were the best chef in New York."

Devoe Crutchfield was a rounded man of fifty with warm brown eyes and half a head of very black hair. The front half was bald and glistened under the electric light. "You bet," he said. "What'll you have today? The lamb is good."

The two agreed on their choices, and then as Crutchfield placed steaming cups of tea in front of them, they drank it, all the time interrupting each other in their eagerness to hear everything that had happened since their trip out west.

Finally Jeb leaned back and shook his head. "You've grown up, Annie. What were you, fifteen the last time we met? Now you're twenty. A young woman."

"You've grown, too, Jeb, and so tall! And when did you start wearing glasses?"

"Oh, about two years ago. I'm blind as a bat for close work, although I can see far enough in the distance. It's so pesky. I do so much reading that I just wear them all the time." He pulled the glasses off, leaned forward, and grinned. "It makes you sort of a fuzzy, blurry Annie, not sharp and clear."

"Keep them off, then. I don't want you looking at me too closely. Now, tell me everything about school and what you're studying."

Diffidently, Jeb gave a brief sketch of his college years. "The first two years of college you don't study much of anything special, just general courses. But I know what I'm going to study. I've gotten in with one of the professors, and he's been a great help to me. He's an anthropologist."

"What's *that*?"

"The study of man."

"Which men?"

"Just man. Races. North America, South America, Australia, Africa, the East. You study all about them." Jeb leaned forward and his warm, blue eyes seemed brilliant. He was excited and used his hands, almost knocking over the tray when Devoe Crutchfield brought it and set their food before them. Then he could barely eat for talking. Finally he leaned back and said, "I've instantly become a regular talking machine, Annie. I don't talk this much with anyone."

"No, you were always quiet, Jeb." Annie studied Jeb carefully. His eyes were well sunk in his head and widely spaced, over-shadowed by light brown eyebrows. She had forgotten that his nose had been broken, and it still showed evidence. He had told her once it had been broken in a fight, but she had not asked anything more than that.

Finally Jeb urged, "Now, what's all this about your going to Africa?"

It was Annie's turn to share all she had done over the last few years. Jeb leaned back, sipping coffee from time to time and picking at his dessert. He had known her heart was in Africa ever since she was a young girl, and now he saw a steadiness and a determination that made him murmur, "You're going to Africa. I can see that."

With a half laugh Annie shrugged her shoulders. "I don't know. Nobody wants to send me." She explained her failure to get an appointment with any of the mission boards and ended by saying, "But I'll get there some way or other."

"I think about our visit to Montana a lot. I've never forgotten it."

"Neither have I, Jeb."

"Do you ever hear from them?"

"Oh yes. I got a letter from Phil last week. He's somewhere in New York now, a famous artist, very successful. He married a woman from a wealthy family."

Jeb laughed. "That's one way to get ahead, but I'm glad to hear it. Maybe we can go look at some of his paintings if they're in a gallery around here."

"Oh, I'd like that! I'd like to see Phil again. It's been a long time."

"Do you ever hear from John?"

Instantly something changed in Annie's face. "Not anymore," she said briefly.

It was as if a door had been shut, and Jeb, remembering the infatuation she had had for John, studied her carefully. She had been cheerful, and now it seemed that was replaced by something he could not identify. Her eyes grew hooded and her lips tightened.

"No, I don't expect to hear from him anymore. Even his family doesn't hear much."

After the meal the two walked slowly home, and Jeb said as he left, "We'll have to see more of each other, Annie."

"Yes, we will." She sighed and said, "I get lonesome sometimes. I miss my family."

★ ★ ★ ★

During the next few weeks, they did meet several times and found that they enjoyed each other's company a great deal. A month passed, and Annie grew restless. "Am I never going to get a missionary assignment? I might as well go back to Wyoming," she moaned to Rosie as he lay on her chest pawing at her lips one afternoon.

It was the day after this that God spoke to Annie in a very real way. She had been going to a business school, taking a course in shorthand, and she had become fairly proficient with these new typewriters. It had been in the back of her mind that if she could get a job, she could save enough money in a few years to send herself to Africa. As she lay on her bed, she was thinking, *I've got to do something, Lord. I can't stay in this room forever.* A stillness came upon her room, and she felt the rumble of Rosie's purring as she closed her eyes and stroked his rough fur. She was not exactly praying, but the questions that had been troubling her for some time about what to do with her life seemed to occupy her thoughts more today. Quite unexpectedly she began to feel God's presence in the room and in her spirit in a very special way. This had happened to her more than once, and she had learned that when thoughts came into her mind, sometimes they were from God. Other times, of course, they were not, but she had learned to wait and try to discern between her thoughts and what God was putting in her heart.

Finally something came to her very gently at first, but as she thought on it, a certainty came into her heart, and she knew God was speaking to her. In her spirit came an impression that might have been phrased, *You are going to serve me in Africa. You have been faithful to wait, and I will now do something in your life. You will go to Africa, but I will take you in a way that you will find strange. When I open the door, you will know it. Be certain that you walk through it.*

And then it was over. She continued to stroke Rosie's fur, but she knew that God had spoken, and she whispered aloud, "Thank you, Lord. You open the door, and I'll go through it!"

CHAPTER SIX

A STRANGE EMPLOYER

★　★　★　★

April came, bringing spring showers and an end to the cold winds and ice storms that had frozen New York during the winter. Annie was glad to put aside her winter clothes and be able to walk in the park without wading through snow or slush. The days passed slowly and she filled her time with work at the mission board without pay, where she had learned more about foreign missions than most people know. She also helped the pastor of the local church, throwing herself into any task that required her assistance. She grew stronger, she could tell, and was fervently grateful that none of the breathless asthma attacks had stricken her again. Now as spring came and she began to get out more into the sunlight, color began to bloom in her cheeks, and she looked forward to moving on with God's plan—but what was God's plan? This seemed to be a difficulty she could not solve. Night after night she would kneel beside her bed and plead with God to reveal His will. All that came to her during those days was a repeat of the word she had gotten weeks before. *I will take you to Africa, but it will be by a way you will not expect. Do not trust in man, but trust in me.*

One problem she faced was that her money was running out, and she had determined not to be a burden on her parents. Although Laurie and Cody both sent her cash, her small bank account was not growing. It was still in the back of her mind that somehow she would raise enough money to finance the trip to

Africa herself, and she had become familiar enough with the accounts while working for the mission board to know that it would take several thousand dollars, which she did not have.

On the last day of April, she went to the typing instructor from whom she had been taking lessons for the past two months. Mrs. Lakely was a thin middle-aged woman whose fingers flew over the keys like magic, so it seemed to Annie. She had a sharp tongue and was a critic who dealt out more criticism than praise, but still she had been polite enough. Entering the building, Annie found Mrs. Lakely in her office going over papers and said, "I'm sorry to trouble you, Mrs. Lakely, but I need to ask you something."

"What is it, Miss Rogers?" The voice was sharp and terse, but this was common enough for the teacher. "Oh, by the way. Your last speed test—it was very good."

"Thank you, Mrs. Lakely," Annie replied. She was not asked to sit down, so she continued quickly, "Mrs. Lakely, I'm running a little short of money. I wonder if you know anyone who needs secretarial help. I've been studying shorthand as well as typing. I'm not an expert yet, but I'm improving."

Mrs. Lakely leaned back in her chair and stared at Annie. She tapped her teeth with her forefinger, then said, "It's strange that just now you should come to me with this."

"Why is it strange, Mrs. Lakely?"

"Because about two hours ago I received a request for secretarial help. I have several ladies I'd thought of recommending. Since you're the first, perhaps you'd like to go for an interview?"

"Oh yes!" Annie said eagerly. "I'll work very hard."

Mrs. Lakely had spoken with Annie about her personal life only once—or, rather, Annie had spoken to her, inviting her to church. In the conversation Annie had revealed her intent to go to Africa as a missionary. Now Mrs. Lakely sat up straight and grasped the arms of her chair, saying, "You may not like this. I'm not personally acquainted with the prospective employer, but I know something about her."

"Oh, it's a lady?"

"Well, it's a young woman. Relatively young, that is. Her name is Miss Jeanine Quintana."

"She sounds Spanish."

"She had a Spanish father and an English mother. You've never read about her in the papers?"

"No, ma'am. What does she do?"

An unexpected smile broke the rather frigid features of Mrs. Lakely. "Mostly she gets into trouble," she chuckled almost harshly. "So far she's stayed out of jail, but it wouldn't surprise me greatly to see her land there someday."

Annie could only stare at her instructor with astonishment. "Stay out of jail? Why, I wouldn't want to work for a criminal."

"Oh, she's not a criminal, Miss Rogers. I wouldn't send you to anyone like that. The fact is, she's a very wealthy woman. Her parents were killed in an Atlantic crossing about five years ago. Since then Miss Quintana has gone her own way." Leaning forward, her dark eyes intent, Mrs. Lakely expressed her disapproval strongly. "She's got enough money to be in Mrs. Astor's group, but she's a little bit strong for the taste of the Four Hundred. I don't think they exactly mesh very well."

"What sort of employment does she have in mind? Does she run a business?"

"She has several businesses, so I understand, but I'm not sure she's active in any of them. However, Doctor Taylor, who runs the school, said that she called, and he asked me to recommend someone. I'm not sure what the work would be. He said she needed a companion—secretary. Whatever that is. There would be travel involved."

Annie was highly uncertain of what answer she could return to Mrs. Lakely.

Seeing this, the older woman nodded and said, "Why don't you think it over? As I say, I don't believe you two would get along—any more than she got along with the Astors. She's a very worldly woman and you obviously are not. She's spoiled by her wealth and she's very attractive. I expect she's as hard to get along with as most wealthy people are."

"Thank you, Mrs. Lakely. When would you need to have an answer?"

"I think the matter was urgent. You'll have to let me know by tomorrow."

"I'll be in first thing in the morning to give you my answer one way or another—and thank you, Mrs. Lakely."

"You're welcome."

Annie left the building with her mind confused and headed for home at once. She said very little at supper that night and went to bed early, which puzzled Mrs. Simmons, but the landlady asked no questions, and when one of the boarders remarked that

Annie might be sick, Mrs. Simmons retorted with, "Mind your own business!"

Annie could not fall asleep, so she read the Scriptures, looking for an answer there, but found none. She prayed until her eyes grew gritty, and finally she reached out and embraced Rosie. "I don't know what to do, Rosie." She hugged the feline hard and Rosie reached out one paw, claws sheathed, and put it on her lips.

Annie laughed. "You want me to hush. All right. I will." She got flat on her back, and Rosie got on her chest and stared down into her face. The large, golden eyes of the cat seemed to be studying her intently and Annie stared back silently. Finally she went to sleep, and when she awoke the next morning to Rosie's clawing at the door to get out, Annie suddenly sat up, knowing what she had to do. "I don't know if it's from you, God, but I believe this might be that door you talked about. I'll go see Miss Jeanine Quintana, and if you don't want me to work for her, I ask you, Lord, to slam the door right in my face. Come on, Rosie—out you go."

★ ★ ★ ★

"Fifth Avenue? Well, that's getting down where the rich people live." Pete Frazier handed Annie up into his carriage and moved around to hop up beside her.

"This is the address, Pete."

Frazier looked at the address, then spoke to the horse, which stepped forward at once. "Lots of new mansions in this part of the city, Miss Annie," he said. As they moved along Fifth Avenue, he remarked, "This was just a dirt road not too awful long ago—back when my grandpa lived here. It got started when a Dutch family decided to build a mansion. They called it Brevoort. Then they started building hotels, and then churches, and all the rich folks took a liking to it. They all wanted the name Fifth Avenue on their address."

As they passed by, he named some of the families. "That's where the Vanderbilts live. They spent 15 million dollars on four mansions along here. See that one? That's Madam Restell's place." He gave her a strange look. "And a bad place it is. She takes care of girls that have gotten into trouble."

"Oh, you mean an abortionist?"

"That's what they say. No proof of it, of course. She keeps the police paid off pretty well, I guess."

Twenty minutes later Frazier pulled up in front of an imposing mansion built of dark red-brick and marble. It rose high and was set back farther from the street than most residences. "This is the address. Do you want me to wait?" he asked as he helped her down.

"I think you'd better. I won't be long."

"Right here I'll be."

Walking up the three steps to the entrance of the house, Annie reached up and grasped the huge, shining brass knocker and rapped it sharply three times. She had to wait for a while, but finally the door swung open softly. A sharp-faced woman dressed in black stared at Annie, then demanded acidly, "Yes, what is it?"

"My name is Miss Rogers. I've come to see Miss Quintana."

"What about?"

"About a position. The business school sent me here."

For a moment Annie stood there and saw the dislike in the older woman's eyes. "Come in," she said sharply and stepped back while Annie stepped through the door. Closing it, she said, "Wait here."

Annie stood in the enormous foyer, almost shocked by the ornate and imposing room. The foyer was large, about twelve by twelve, with light streaming in from the leaded-glass panels on either side of the front door with its embossed door pins, hinges, and doorknobs. The floor was covered with a cool gray marble with rugs and runners of deep reds and greens placed down the long hallway. The floor-length windows by the door were covered with a filmy white material flowing down onto the floor. The walls had a deep red satiny wall treatment on the top portion with mahogany wainscoating on the bottom half, and a large fireplace graced one wall, with a large mantel on which sat silver tins of all sizes. A dark wood hall tree with massive branches decorated the wall to the right of the front door, and a towering hall mirror on a marble-topped base graced the wall to the left. Sculptures, family portraits, and etchings were staring out on hanging shelves tucked backed in niches, and three straight-backed chairs and a large cushioned settee were positioned beside a Louis XV occasional table.

"Come this way." Annie's reverie was broken as the tall woman suddenly appeared at the foot of the stairs. She did not wait but turned, and Annie followed her up the winding staircase. When they reached the next floor, the woman angled to her left and went to a massive door. She opened it, saying, "Miss Quintana wants to see you at once. Go in."

"Thank you," Annie murmured. She stepped inside and once again was struck forcibly by the room itself. She took one quick look at the woman who was in the bed, sitting up and reading some sort of paper. The room itself was at least as imposing as the foyer. It certainly reflected great wealth.

"Come over here!"

The woman's voice was pleasant enough, but demanding. Annie moved across the room uncomfortably, for she had expected the woman to be dressed and behind a desk. Instead of that, a small tea table straddled the woman's body, and she poured herself a cup of tea and then looked at Annie over it.

"You came about the job, I suppose."

"Yes, Miss Quintana. My name's Annie Rogers."

"What experience have you had?"

As Annie haltingly answered the woman's probing questions, she studied her prospective employer. She could not be certain about her height, but she seemed very tall. She had hair as black as anything in nature and strange violet-colored eyes. Her skin was olive and her face was squarish with high cheekbones. The lavender gown she wore was very low-cut and obviously made of pure silk. It shimmered in the light from the lamps beside the bed. Her face was determined and her upper lip was thin, though the lower one was full and sensuous.

After listening to Annie, Jeanine Quintana laughed. "So you're going to be a missionary. Well, that might be interesting. Sit down. Would you care for some tea?"

"Why, yes, if it's not too much trouble."

"It won't be any trouble for me, but you'll have to help yourself. There it is over there on that table."

Annie moved over and poured herself a cup of tea, added a little cream, then came back and sat down again.

"How old did you say you were?"

"I'm twenty."

"And you have no business experience?"

"No, ma'am."

Miss Quintana waited for an explanation. Seeing that none was coming, she tsk-tsked and sipped her tea. "Well, at least you don't try to make up things to impress me. I like that. Can you take shorthand?"

"I've had a course. I'm not as fast as I will be later on, but my instructor said I'm doing very well."

"And you've had a course in typewriting?"

"Yes, ma'am."

"Why do you want to work?"

"To save money to go to Africa."

"How much does that cost?"

"Several thousand dollars to stay for four years as I'd like to do."

Once again the bold violet eyes swept over the young woman. Jeanine Quintana seemed older even than her twenty-seven years. There was a worldly knowledge in her eyes that had been put there by experience. Ordinarily she would have sent the young woman off without an adieu, but something about Annie Rogers interested her.

"I can't imagine hiring you."

"Why not, Miss Quintana?"

"Because you are a preacher of some sort, and I am not a godly woman. The first time I drank a cocktail it would probably shock you to death."

"No, ma'am, it would not."

The reply that was rapped out rather sharply amused Jeanine Quintana. "Oh, it wouldn't? You approve of drinking, then?"

"No, ma'am, I do not. But I assume you wouldn't be hiring me to correct your morals."

This reply brought a smile and then a slight laugh from the woman in bed. "You have an edge about you for all that innocent appearance. Though you look like a nun, you're a rather worldly girl. Never been married?"

"No."

"Have you been with a man?"

This blunt question shook Annie. But she lifted her head, and though her cheeks had a rosy tinge, she said, "No."

"Ah, that touched you, I see. Well, you'll hear worse than that out of me if I hire you. What's that mark on your neck?"

"Just . . . just a birthmark."

"You're sensitive about it. Why don't you have it taken off?"

"I never thought about it, Miss Quintana."

"I see. Well, I need someone at once, and it will involve some travel. Do you have anyone who would object?"

"Object, Miss Quintana?"

"Yes—object to travel. Or that you would travel with *me*, to put it more bluntly. My reputation is somewhat tainted, I fear. I don't want a father coming after me with a shotgun because I've corrupted his daughter."

"My father and mother live in Wyoming along with my brother. They trust my judgment and they trust me, Miss Quintana."

Once again the reply and the manner seemed to please Jeanine Quintana. "All right. When can you start?"

The abruptness of the question again startled Annie. "You mean I'm hired?"

"Yes . . . yes, you're hired! When can you start?"

For a moment Annie considered asking about salary, but her mind was working busily. Somehow she had the oddest impression that this was the door God had promised to open, and the thought flashed into her mind, *What could be further from going to Africa as a missionary than going to work for this worldly woman?* Still the impression came more strongly than ever that this was what God wanted her to do. For one brief instant she forgot about her prospective employer and sought God. She looked down at the carpet and prayed, *Oh, God, stop me if this isn't right.*

Across from the young woman Jeanine Quintana studied her. She knew the young woman was praying, and this both irritated her and intrigued her. She had not been to a church for years, not since she was a child. She had put God firmly out of her life and was quite content with how well she had managed. Now the sight of the young woman dressed in very inexpensive clothing sitting beside her bed, obviously praying for direction, stabbed at her in a most peculiar way. *What am I thinking?* she thought. *This could be the biggest mistake I ever made. Well, if she takes the job, I'll make it rough on her quick so that neither of us will have any long-term regrets.*

Finally Annie raised her head and smiled. "Yes. I can start today. Right now if you'd like."

"Good! About pay, I'll pay you half again as much as I'm paying Miss Debrough."

She named a figure that sounded extremely high to Annie, who readily agreed, saying, "That's very generous, Miss Quintana."

"Do you speak French?"

"Why . . . no, ma'am."

"Too bad. We'll probably be in France very shortly. And we'll be going to England next week, so we'll have to get you some clothes. I can't be seen with you dressed like that."

Moving the tea table and throwing the coverlet back, she got to her feet. Annie saw that Jeanine was extremely tall indeed and had a breathtaking figure, full-bodied but slender at the same time.

Now she looked down at her new employee. Reaching out, she touched the collar of Annie's dress and said, "Yes, we'll have to get you some new clothes. Help me get dressed now because you'll have to be maid, secretary, companion, and whatever else I need. At the salary I'm paying I deserve it, don't you think?"

Annie smiled and said, "I'm not sure that any of us get what we deserve."

This enigmatic answer unnerved the older woman. "I don't know what that means," she said finally. Then she laughed briefly. "Come along. I'm going to give you a hard time this week. If you're going to quit, I want it to be on this side of the Atlantic—not when we get to England!"

PART TWO

TITANIC

★ ★ ★ ★

CHAPTER SEVEN

ANNIE MEETS A SAILOR

★ ★ ★ ★

As Annie sat in front of her dressing table brushing her hair, she glanced around and could not help but compare the opulence of her surroundings with those she had grown up in. Just a week earlier she had stepped off the steamship *The Royal Queen* onto English soil. Since that time life had been a whirl for her. The room she studied now was large with two tall windows looking down on the busy streets of London. In between the two windows was a cherrywood tea table that was flanked by red and ivory upholstered easy chairs. The walls were covered in ivory and gilt damask with gilt-framed mirrors all around the room, and the windows were framed with white curtains that reached down to the floor. The ceiling was high and painted a bright white with gilt accents, and the floor was a highly polished wood that was covered with a large area rug with black, reds, blues, and white patterns running through it. In the middle of the room was a large mahogany canopy bed covered with a heavy ivory fabric tied back with red velvet ties on the posts, and a large feather mattress covered in matching fabric. A bedside table with a crystal lamp was on one side of the bed and a large chest of drawers was on the other. A breakfront bookcase with a scrolling pediment had been placed next to a Queen Anne mahogany inlaid desk, and a blanket box took its place at the end of the bed.

With a start she glanced up at the gilt clock over the mantelpiece, replaced the brush on the table, then rose reluctantly. "I'm going to be late," she muttered. "And I don't want Jeanine dressing me down again." Nevertheless she paused for one moment, long enough to pick up a letter she had received from Jeb Winslow. Holding it, she remembered how surprised she was that it had gotten to England only a few days after she had arrived. She smiled slightly as she studied the neat but bold handwriting.

> Dear Annie:
> I already find myself missing you more than I would have thought possible. I knew I would be lonely after you left, but it has been even worse than I anticipated. I go back to all the restaurants where we enjoyed spending so much time together—remember Luigi's? The time that we stayed so late the owner had to ask us to leave? It embarrassed me, but you merely laughed at such a thing. Anyway, I went back to Luigi's and sat for a long time thinking of our days together, but it wasn't the same without you.
> I have been busy with my studies and feel that I will be finished with what I can learn here in two years or, perhaps, even less. What I will do then for a job I have no idea. The world is not beating a path to the door of youthful scholars, so I put it behind me and will worry about it later.
> I also have been faithful to the church, although it seems lonely in the pew there without you. Everyone here asks about you. When will you be back? I could not tell them much, but you made a mark on this church for sure.

Annie continued to read the long letter and finally came to a brief passage that troubled her somewhat.

> I am not much of a fellow with words, Annie, but I think you know how much I care for you. I wish I could have said more about this while you were here, but I'm too much of a coward, I suppose. I think I'm as afraid of young women as I was of horses the time we were in the West together. In any case, it's easy for me to say on paper how much I admire you. So until we meet again—and I hope it will be soon—I remain your faithful friend.
> Jeb Winslow.

Putting the letter down, Annie quickly crossed the room and began to dress. As she pulled her outfit together and slipped into the dress she had chosen, she thought, *I hope Jeb isn't serious about*

*me. We have been good friends for a long time, but I can't think about any
man now. I'm headed for Africa, and Jeb doesn't have the call to go there.*

The dress was one Jeanine had selected for her. Annie had
brought along only very plain clothes from the States, and on the
second day after their arrival, the two had gone on a whirlwind
shopping trip. Jeanine had waved aside Annie's protests that she
had no money to spend for clothes, because she was saving it to
go to Africa. "Don't worry about that. This is a bonus. You can't
go around looking like a scarecrow, Annie," Jeanine had laughed.

The floor-length dress was made of a forest green jacquard
with a round neck and a moss green silk overlay covering the
upper part of the three-quarter-length sleeves down to a deep *V*
under the bustline, where it was held in place by a large, ornate
pin. The skirt of the dress peeked out from under the overlay in
front, and the overlay had a small train that trailed behind her
when she walked. It was worth more than Annie would ever have
paid for a dress, but she saw that it fit her well. She put on the
simple gold chain with a cross around her neck, and her single
other ornament was a pearl ring that had been given to her by her
father when she had graduated from high school.

"Well, that's about as well as I can do, I suppose," Annie murmured. She turned and started for the door, reflecting on her new
job serving as a companion to Jeanine. She already knew it was
not going to be easy. The woman's ways were so different! She
had an immoral spirit that she took no pains to hide, and Annie
was constantly embarrassed by Jeanine's remarks and activities in
public. She had almost refused to accompany her across the
ocean, but still she felt somehow that God was in it, although she
could not see how. With a lift of her chin, she moved outside the
door and down the hall to Jeanine's room. She knocked softly, and
when a voice said, "Come in," she stepped inside and was immediately assailed by Jeanine.

"Where have you been? I've been waiting for you! We're going
to be late! Annie, you're getting to be a sluggard! Come and help
me get dressed now!"

"I'm sorry, Jeanine," Annie said evenly. "I didn't realize the
time." Moving forward, she began to select Jeanine's clothes, but
nothing she selected seemed to suit her.

"Not that dress! I wouldn't wear that to a dogfight! And this
one is simply hideous. The light blue one, Annie—and hurry up!"

As quickly as she could, Annie helped Jeanine get dressed.

From time to time the older woman would take a sip from a glass, and the strong smell of alcohol filled the room. More than once Annie had been tempted to protest, but she well knew what sort of reaction that would bring. Jeanine would hear nothing about her personal behavior—not from Annie, nor from anyone else.

Jeanine was watching Annie rather closely, and a malicious light glinted in her eyes. Picking up a glass, she poured it full of amber liquid, then offered, "Here, Annie, have a sip of this."

"No, thank you, Jeanine."

"Oh, come on! Don't be such a Puritan!"

"I'd really rather not. We've been through this before."

"I know we have, and I'm not asking you to get roaring drunk," Jeanine shrugged. "Just a little drink. After all, it's only wine."

Annie knelt down and began to adjust the hem of Jeanine's dress. She knew this was part of the dark side of Jeanine Quintana. It was not only that she herself participated in such things, but Jeanine would not rest until others joined her. Annie knew that Jeanine had taken it as a particular challenge to get her to drink, and it was a constant battle between them. Rising to her feet, she looked straight into Jeanine's eyes and said quietly, "You know I'm not going to drink that, Jeanine. I'd think you'd be tired of trying to tempt me."

"So you're just too holy to take even a little drink."

"It's something I don't want to do, that's all."

Jeanine drained the glass herself and a flush came into her cheeks. "I don't know why I ever brought you on this trip. What do I need with a preacher?" Malevolence laced her tone, and suddenly her lips drew tight for a moment. "What if I told you that you either drink this or you're fired?"

"Then, Jeanine, I'd have to go pack my clothes."

The simplicity of Annie's reply seemed to stiffen Jeanine's back. She fixed her gaze on the young woman, taking in the steadiness of the large dark blue eyes that were somehow firm and mild at the same time. There was no sign of defiance, and yet there was a calm steadiness in this young woman that piqued Jeanine's temper. "All right, suit yourself!" she snapped finally with a shrug. "Come along. It's time to go."

The two left the hotel and got into a carriage. Jeanine gave the driver instructions in a short, clipped voice, then sat back. The two women felt the surge as the horses moved forward at the driver's command. Jeanine said nothing for some time, nor did Annie try to begin a conversation. Finally, as usually happened, Jeanine's good humor returned, and she asked, "Are you excited about this ball?"

"They're always interesting. So different from anything in America."

"Well, this will be the finest one we've been to. There'll probably be lots of young men there."

"That will be nice," Annie sighed, knowing she was about to be taunted a little more.

"You never say anything about yourself," Jeanine complained. "Have you ever had a sweetheart?"

"Not really."

"Well, that's a phenomenon! Do you ever expect to get married?"

Annie hesitated. "Someday, if the Lord puts me with the man He has planned for me."

"Planned for you? You think God has nothing to do but go around matchmaking?" Jeanine leaned forward. The shadows were darkening in London now and the light was fading. She studied the younger woman, then asked mockingly, "Have you put your order in yet on the kind of man you want?"

Annie turned and met Jeanine's gaze and smiled slightly. "Yes, I have." Her answer took Jeanine aback, for she had not expected an affirmative. "I told the Lord I'd like to have a man who loves Him more than he loves anything on earth."

"You mean—more than he loves *you*?"

"Yes. More than that."

Jeanine Quintana leaned back and stroked her chin. Her bold eyes examined the girl across from her and she shook her head. "I wouldn't want any man that loved anything or anybody more than me. Even God."

"I know that, Jeanine."

The quiet tone of Annie Rogers' voice somehow irritated Jeanine, and she snapped, "I don't know how we're ever going to get along! We're a million miles apart."

"I hope I'll do the best I can for you, but if ever you want me to leave, all you have to do is say the word."

"Oh no, you're not going to get out that easy! It took long

enough to break you in, and now you're not walking off from your responsibility."

Actually, the responsibility had been quite overwhelming. Jeanine had many business interests. She had left them in the hands of a manager back in the States, but she created a steady flow of letters that at times took hours to produce. Annie was not the fastest shorthand expert in the world, and she had felt the lash of Jeanine's tongue when she had stumbled and had to ask her to dictate at a slower pace. Then, of course, typing them up was difficult for her, too. The sheer bulk of the letters had shocked her, and she had gotten to know much about the Miss Quintana's business affairs. She did not know exactly how wealthy Jeanine was, but now she was becoming aware of the extent of her fortune. Annie had never once complained about the long hours, and she knew it would be difficult to replace her.

Within a short time the carriage pulled up in front of a large ornate building built of gray stone. When the door opened, a footman was there to help them out, Jeanine first, followed by Annie. The two women moved up the steps to the doors, which were opened by another servant. As they stepped inside, the faint sound of music came to Annie's ears. She followed Jeanine, and the two women left their wraps in a cloakroom and then entered the massive ballroom, which was grander than anything Annie had ever seen. "I can't believe how *big* this is, Jeanine," she whispered.

"I've been in bigger," Jeanine shrugged. "Well, let's go have refreshments until someone asks us to dance."

As they walked to the refreshment table, Annie gazed at the enormous room with its bright colors, huge windows, and beautiful marble floors. She had never seen such a grand place. She noticed that there was a raised platform at the far end where a six-piece ensemble played softly.

The refreshments were profuse, but Jeanine had merely taken her first sip out of a glass when she was greeted by a slender young man with a pale face and a wide smile. He had blond hair and light blue eyes and greeted her with, "Miss Quintana, I believe."

"Yes," Jeanine said calmly. "I don't believe we've met."

"No, but you have met my aunt, Mrs. Smythe." The young man nodded across the room, and a large, ornately dressed woman with diamonds sparkling from her sausage-like fingers waved and smiled, then called Jeanine's name.

"Take care of my nephew now, Jeanine."

"Oh, that's Hannah Smythe. Yes, I met her last time I was in England."

"My name is Clive Winters."

"I'm glad to know you, Mr. Winters. This is my companion, Miss Rogers."

Winters bowed from the waist in the Continental fashion and acknowledged the greeting, "I'm pleased to meet you, Miss Rogers. Both of you ladies are welcome. You just arrived in London shortly, my aunt tells me."

"Yes. About a week ago."

As the two spoke, Annie kept quiet. She had found one of the punch bowls full of lemonade and helped herself to a glass. Soon she saw Winters leading Jeanine out onto the dance floor where they began to waltz. It was a graceful dance, and the floor was filled with couples who swept around, the dresses of the women adding flashes of color. Many of the men she saw were wearing military uniforms, some of them naval.

For some time Annie stood beside the refreshment table watching the waltzes. Jeanine, she saw, soon had other partners as new dances began. No one approached Annie, and after a while she felt conspicuous. Moving along the edge of the wall, she looked for a place to sit down. She saw three chairs, but a gentleman was sitting in one of them. She hesitated, and looking up, he caught her eye.

Rising to his feet, he said, "May I offer you a seat, miss?"

"Why, thank you. I am getting rather tired."

The speaker was a short man with a very round pale face and a pair of twinkling blue eyes. He looked to be in his thirties, and he introduced himself by saying, "My name is Churchill. I don't believe we've met."

"No, sir. My name is Annie Rogers."

"From America, I take it?"

"Yes, sir."

"You're very welcome here, Miss Rogers. My mother was born in America. Are you here on a visit?"

"I'm the companion of Miss Quintana."

"Oh! Is she here?"

"Yes. That's her in the light blue dress, dancing with the blond young man."

Churchill's eyes swept the floor and he grunted. "I see. Well, that's one of my young men dancing with her. I hope she doesn't run off with him."

Startled, Annie turned to face the Englishman. "Run off with him? Why would you say a thing like that, sir?"

Churchill laughed deep in his throat. He had a hoarse voice that seemed to emerge and bubble over his chest and up through his throat, and she realized that if he wanted to, he could shake the rafters.

"Just a remark. I don't know the lady, of course. She's an American, too, I assume?"

"Yes, sir. She owns several businesses there."

Churchill's sharp eyes went back to the dance floor. He watched as Winters and Jeanine came by, and he studied the pair carefully. Turning back, he shook his head ruefully. "Well, she's the kind of woman that could make a man *want* to run away with her."

Annie was at a loss as to how to take Churchill's words. She did not want to believe that just by a casual glance a man could tell that Jeanine Quintana was a danger to men, but somehow Churchill seemed to have pinpointed her. Casually, she inquired, "Would it be a bad thing if the two of them became interested in each other?"

"Very bad," Churchill responded, then smiled. "You mustn't mind me, Miss Rogers. You see, I'm trying to convince young Winters there to join the navy. I think he could have a tremendous career, but I doubt if Miss Quintana would be a good naval wife."

"Well, why not, sir?"

"Because she's obviously too rich, too beautiful, and too spoiled."

Somewhat astonished at the boldness of Churchill's reply, Annie went on, "How can you tell all that? You've never met her."

"I can tell she's rich by the clothing and the diamonds she's wearing. And I can tell she's spoiled because she's rich. All rich people are spoiled, my dear Miss Rogers. I can tell she wants her own way, also. You see, she's trying to lead Clive out on the dance floor. No, I'm afraid she won't do. You'll have to warn her off, although he's quite a good catch. It's Lord Winters, you know."

"He's a lord?"

"Oh yes. Not one of the wealthy ones, of course, but still, he can call himself Lord Winters, and his wife would be Lady Winters. Yet I apologize for speaking so abruptly. It's a bad habit of mine."

Annie found the Englishman quite captivating. He talked freely with her and seemed to have no inhibitions. He smiled cherubically from time to time and seemed to have been everywhere and done everything. Finally he looked up and said, "There. Now they're finished with that dance. I think I'll dance with Miss Quintana myself, if you will introduce me."

"Certainly," Annie said but with some alarm. She did not know what Jeanine would say to such a straightforward man as Churchill. The couple approached, and Clive Winters said, "Oh, Mr. Churchill. Good to see you, sir."

"Ah, Winters. Good to see you."

"May I introduce Miss Jeanine Quintana."

"I'm happy to know you, Miss Quintana," Churchill said, bowing from the hips. When Jeanine put out her hand, he kissed it.

"I see you've met my companion, Miss Rogers."

"Yes. I forced my attentions upon her. I do that with every attractive young woman I meet—or so my wife says."

"Your wife's not with you, Sir Winston?" queried the young man.

"No. She's confined. So I'm dancing with all the pretty young ladies tonight. May I have this next dance, Miss Quintana?"

"Certainly, Mr. Churchill." Jeanine cocked her head to one side and said, "What is your position, may I ask?"

"Why, he's the new Lord of the Admiralty, Miss Quintana," Clive Winters said quickly.

"And I'm trying my best to get this young man into the naval uniform before he throws his life away on something useless. Come along. I'll tell you all about his bad habits while we dance."

Jeanine Quintana liked Churchill. It was obvious from her smile, and she allowed herself to be led back onto the dance floor. It soon became obvious that Churchill was not as good a dancer as Winters.

"Well, Miss Rogers, you're going to have to help me," said Winters.

"Help you? How can I do that, Mr. Winters?"

"Why, it's obvious that your employer is going to be besieged by men. I want you to put in a good word for me."

Annie smiled first, then laughed aloud. "That would hardly

serve your purpose, Mr. Winters. Miss Quintana does not take my advice on anything."

"Oh, come now!" he protested. "I'm sure that isn't so. She must have confidence in you if she hired you as her companion."

"I'm afraid not."

"Well, come, let's dance and you can tell me about it."

"I would rather not, if you don't mind, sir."

Somewhat surprised at the refusal, Winters replied, "Well, of course. I'll tell you what. We'll get some more refreshments, and I'll show you some of the pictures in the gallery. You haven't seen them, have you?"

"No, sir, I haven't."

"Good. I'll show you the pictures, and you can tell me the way to Miss Quintana's heart."

Not at all content with this bargain, she still found Winters an attractive young man and followed him into the gallery of the mansion. She was fascinated by the large collection of paintings. He seemed to be familiar with all of them, and the artists who had painted them, and had many anecdotes to tell concerning their creations. When they went back to the ballroom, they were met by Churchill and Jeanine.

"So you've taken this young woman off, have you, Winters? Shame on you!" Churchill growled. He looked somewhat like a bulldog, but there was a friendly light in his eyes.

"Not at all, sir." Winters spoke cheerfully, then stepped closer to Jeanine, saying, "I believe the next dance is ours."

"I think I promised it to some other gentleman. What was his name?"

"Admiral Croft. You don't want to offend an admiral if you're going into the navy, Winters."

The foursome stood there speaking for some time, and it was Churchill who mentioned that the largest ship in the world was about to be launched, although it would be another year before it was ready to sail.

"That will be quite a sight. I'm going to see it myself," Clive Winters remarked.

"Where is it?" Jeanine asked.

"In Belfast. Tremendous ship! The biggest in the world."

"I wouldn't mind seeing that myself."

"Well, let me invite you to our party," Churchill said. "My wife will be glad to meet you and your companion."

"And I'll be glad to accompany you also, sir," Winters added quickly.

"Oh, you would? Can't wait for an invitation, eh?"

"You might never give it, Sir Winston," he answered cheerfully. "I can afford to be a little bit demanding now because you want something out of me. Once you get me into a uniform, I'll be under your absolute command."

"All right, then. Have it your own way. It will be next Thursday. That's the thirty-first, isn't it? Last day of May?"

"Yes, sir, it is."

"I'll have a carriage for you. We'll travel together at the expense of the navy."

"What's the name of the ship?" Jeanine asked.

"The *Titanic*," Churchill nodded firmly. "Biggest in the world. Quite a sight to see."

"It is going to be interesting," Winters agreed. "It's a ship that can't be sunk, you know."

Annie shook her head slightly, but Churchill caught the motion. "Why, Miss Rogers, I don't believe you are in agreement with Clive about this."

"I am no expert on ships, Sir Winston, but any ship can be sunk, can't it?"

"Not this one," Winters answered. "She's got watertight bulkheads all along the side. If one of them gets punctured, or two, or three, or four, you get water in those, but it doesn't get into the rest of the ship."

Annie somehow felt uncomfortable. "I grew up on a ranch in America. There's a saying there: 'Never was a horse couldn't be rode, never was a cowboy couldn't be throwed.' "

Churchill burst out into laughter. "By george," he beamed, "I like that! Let that be a lesson to you, Winters. Never was a horse couldn't be rode. . . !"

Winters nodded and then shrugged. "Never was a cowboy couldn't be throwed." Nevertheless, there was a streak of stubbornness in the young man, and he said, "But this is one ship that *can't* be sunk. I've talked to the builders about it, sir. You ought to look into this for your warships in the future. Those watertight tanks, they're the thing."

The evening lasted until very late, and when the two women left, Churchill turned to Winters and warned, "Watch out, my boy. There's a lee shore ahead."

"A lee shore? You mean a dangerous one, Sir Winston?"

"Yes. I'm surprised you don't see it. But you're a young man."

"You mean Miss Quintana. She's a beautiful woman."

"And so are shores sometimes beautiful, but they contain hidden rocks. No, my boy. Find yourself a plain English wife. You must have a home, and there can only be one commander in a home, and with that young woman, she would be it!"

"You may be right, sir," Clive Winters replied, but there was a denial in the warmth of his blue eyes, and he grinned as Churchill chided him for being charmed so easily. "Don't worry about me, sir. The *Titanic* is unsinkable and no woman is unwinnable."

★ ★ ★ ★

As the party approached the docks in Belfast, Annie was more interested in her employer and her attitude toward Clive Winters than she was in the largest ship in the world they had come to see. In the few days since they had met at the ball, Clive Winters had pursued Jeanine Quintana in a most determined fashion. Flowers were delivered every day with cards and letters, and somehow he had persuaded her to go out with him every night.

Winters and the two women had been separated from Sir Winston, who would be standing at the bow of the ship when it was launched. Now Winters was positioning them into a vantage point so they could get a glimpse of the ship. He held Jeanine's arm in a familiar fashion, Annie noticed, and as he spoke there was an excitement in his voice.

"There's no ship like this one. It's eight hundred and eighty-two feet long, ninety-two and a half feet in the beam. It has a gross tonnage of forty-six thousand tons."

Jeanine was very much aware of Clive's grip on her arm. It gave her a puzzled, secure feeling. She had been entertained at first by the young Englishman's determination and had gone out with him for her own amusement. She had soon discovered, however, that there was a real strength beneath the noble manner of the young man. She was always drawn to men of strength, and the fact that he had a title made him even more attractive. Now as they stood pressing against each other in the crowd, she remembered how he had taken her in his arms and kissed her when he had left her last night. It had not been the first time she had been kissed, for she knew men very well, but somehow this had been different. She had been shaken, and although she had not shown it, she found herself drawn to him more than she could ever remember being drawn to a man.

Clive put his arm around Jeanine's waist and said enthusiastically, "Look at that gantry."

"What's a gantry?" Jeanine asked.

"All those beams and hoists overhead that put all the steel into place. It's the biggest gantry in the world. And look at the way the ship's going to slide down. It took twenty-two tons of tallow and soap to lubricate it just for the ship to slide down it!"

"Tallow and soap?" Jeanine asked with surprise.

"Well, there's an enormous amount of weight on those beams. Look, they're going to start now!"

Even as Winters spoke, the ship seemed to move slightly. There was something magnificent about the enormous size of it. It seemed to Jeanine as she watched that it would never float. It was as if a mountain were moving. Winters informed them that the momentum was checked by three anchors connected by seven-inch steel hawsers to eye plates riveted into the hull. With a sigh the massive ship eased itself into the water, the whole process taking only sixty-two seconds.

"Well, that's done," Jeanine announced brightly. "Now I'll be ready to take a cruise on her."

Winters laughed and shook his head. "Not for a time you won't. It will take at least ten or twelve months to get her fitted out."

"Then I can wait," Jeanine said. She suddenly took Winters' arm and directed, "Come now. We're going to explore Belfast. You're going to show me all the sights." Turning to Annie, she asked, "Would you like to come along, Annie?"

"No, thank you. I believe I'll do a little exploring of my own."

"Well, don't wait up for us. We'll be late."

"Very well," Annie smiled. "Have a good time."

An uneasy feeling ran through Annie Rogers as she watched the two stroll away. Jeanine was smiling at Clive and clinging to his arm possessively, and a premonition came sweeping through Annie's mind. She thought of what Churchill had said about Jeanine not making a good wife for a naval officer, but she also saw that there was a stricken look in Clive Winters' bright blue eyes. He was captivated by the beauty of this woman, and Annie was afraid that nothing good would come of it.

She explored Belfast that afternoon, then went out and dined alone at one of the restaurants on the wharf, enjoying fresh lobster for the first time. She made her way back to the hotel room and settled into it, but part of her was thinking about her employer—and Clive Winters. The hours rolled on, and finally she went to bed a little past midnight. She could not sleep and she found herself praying for Jeanine, but she had difficulty with the faith to believe. Fitfully she drifted off to sleep and had strange dreams. They were interrupted by the sound of a door opening and closing. Rising up to rest on her elbow, she looked at the clock and saw that it was just past six o'clock, and she knew that Jeanine and Clive had spent the night somewhere else. A heaviness came to her then, and she lay back and once again tried to pray for Jeanine. *She's headed for a terrible fate. She doesn't know God and neither does Clive, apparently. He's going to be badly hurt over this.*

For a long time she lay there, then finally she rose and dressed. When she went out into the drawing room that separated the two bedrooms, she found Jeanine's door closed, as she had expected. She went down to breakfast, but as she closed the door of the drawing room, a fatal sense of almost despair seemed to settle on her. God had given her a great love for Jeanine Quintana, although it had not been returned. As she moved along toward the elevator, she prayed, "God, help them both, for they're going to need it!"

CHAPTER EIGHT

MEETING MARY WEATHERFORD

★ ★ ★ ★

Sitting on the bench beneath the towering pillar of Admiral Lord Nelson, Annie looked up and studied the statue on top. She could not make out the features clearly, but she had heard so much about Nelson during her ten months in England that she felt a certain admiration for the man. White clouds drifted by, forming a background for the upright figure against the blue sky, and for a time she allowed herself to think of the life of the greatest naval hero of England or, perhaps, of all time. She had read of his victories, but she had also read of his tragic personal life and a sadness came to her. "For a man to have such honor in life from kings," she murmured, "and to have no more wisdom nor judgment about his personal life is sad."

She had come early, as she did frequently these days, sitting outside the British Museum. She had been fascinated by the British Museum and had explored every floor of it time and time again. The vast collection of ancient artifacts from around the world fascinated her, especially the section filled with Egyptian treasures. The mummies somehow seemed to draw her. They looked almost like dolls, brown and wrinkled, and she thought, *These were once filled with warm blood and they were alive. They loved someone and were loved. They hated. They had to find God or else lose it all. They were just like me, and now this is all that's left.*

She had managed to get Jeanine to come with her to the museum for one visit. But Jeanine had merely laughed and said,

"Who wants to look at dead things, Annie? I'm going to spend my time with live people while I have the chance."

Now as Annie lowered her eyes from the towering spire that formed the Nelson monument, she studied the huge carved lions that even now were decorated with children who climbed over their backs. She thought of Jeanine and her affair with Clive Winters. The young nobleman was infatuated with her. Annie had never seen anything like it. Winters came from a noble family that was horrified, she had understood, at their son's mad pursuit of a wealthy and worldly American woman. But Winters ignored the sound advice of everyone, including the Lord of the Admiralty, Sir Winston Churchill. Annie had encountered Churchill twice at social events, and both times he had growled, looking more like a bulldog all the time, saying, "That young fellow Winters is a fool! Your employer may have many fine qualities, but she's not the one for him."

"I don't think she'll marry him," Annie had said.

"I hope not. These affairs often rage with some vehemence for a while and then pass away, leaving the sufferer weak."

As she sat on the bench, Annie shook her head and took out her writing pad and pencil. She began a letter to Jeb, dating it March 20, 1912, noting again with almost a shock that she had spent nearly a year in England.

> My dearest Jeb,
>
> I am sitting in Trafalgar Square as I write this letter, under the statue of Lord Nelson. I come here very often to visit the museum, but lately to watch the people. However, my heart is somewhat confused today. God is not the author of confusion, so I must have created it myself. As I have told you before, I felt that God was in my becoming a companion for Jeanine. It seemed very clear to me that His will was for me to do this, but after many weary months of trying to see some reason in it, I fail to find any.

She looked up to see a young man who had come to sit beside her. He was wearing a pearl gray suit with a very flamboyant red tie and a derby perched on the back of his head.

He grinned and said, "Hello, miss. Doing your homework?"

"Just writing a letter." Annie had had this happen before. She was often approached by such scoundrel young men, and she recognized another looking for an easy conquest.

"You see those lions over there?"

"Yes. I see them."

"You know the story about them, don't you?" The young man's eyes twinkled. "Every time a virgin passes by, they roar." He winked roguishly and said, "They ain't roared in a long time now, babe. How about you and me stepping over to the pub and having a bite?"

"No, thank you. But I have something for you."

"Something for me! What's that?"

Quickly Annie reached down into the leather case she carried her writing notebooks in and withdrew a tract. "Here. It's this. You'll notice the title of it is *How to Become a Child of God*."

Startled, the young man's mouth fell open. He took the tract automatically and stared at it, then scowled. "What are you? Some kind of a preacher?"

"Just a believer in Jesus. Why don't you let me go through it with you? You need Jesus in your life just like we all do."

"None of that! None of that!" The young man rose hastily and glared at her. "Why don't you join the Salvation Army and beat a big drum like the rest of them crazies?" He threw the tract toward Annie, but the wind caught it and sent it on its way.

As the young man whirled on his heels and started marching away, disgust in every line of his figure, Annie called out, "Don't forget! Jesus loves you!" She did not hear his reply, if he made any, but smiled and went back to her letter. She had found out the quickest way to quench unwelcome advances was to begin witnessing and to hand out a tract. To her surprise, three times the young men had not been rebuffed but had shown a sincere interest in the Gospel. Two of them had actually prayed with her and made a confession of their faith in Jesus. She had invited them to the Metropolitan Tabernacle, the local church she attended in London, and they had come and followed the Lord in baptism. Since then she had become good friends with both of them.

"Well, I won't see that one in the Tabernacle," she murmured and then went back to her letter.

And so I spend my days writing letters for Jeanine and wandering the streets of London. She spends her days drinking and going to parties with Clive Winters. I have not spoken of this to anyone but you, for it would be wrong to expose the faults of another. But I am asking you to pray for both of them, Jeb. They are engaged in an immoral affair, and it can come to no good. It grieves my heart, for they are both talented people full of life and ability, and yet they can see nothing but the pleasures of the moment.

Annie continued to write for over an hour until she had filled several pages and then finally closed her letter with a wish that Jeb would continue to write. She folded it up, put the writing materials in the leather bag, then rose and walked past the lions. She looked up at the massive face of one and thought of what the young man had said. "So, you roar when a virgin passes, do you? Well, so much for that myth." She laughed aloud and made her way past the lions, bracing against the stout March wind.

★ ★ ★ ★

A contrary puff of wind caught the triangular mainsail of the small boat, causing Clive Winters to call out, "Duck, Jeanine!" As the boom swept across the cockpit, he reached forward and shoved her head down and laughed. "You have to be a better sailor than that, sweetheart."

White spray, salty and tangy, blew against Jeanine's face. She licked her lips and savored the cold wind and the speed of the boat as it skimmed over the surface of the gray waters. "Faster! Faster!" she cried.

Clive Winters laughed. "If we put up more sail, it'll tear the sticks out of her. Come over and sit by me." He had taken his seat at the tiller, and Jeanine obediently went and sat beside him. She put her arms around his chest, and he embraced her with his free arm. She lifted her face and he kissed her wet, salty lips. There was a possessiveness in her that he had never ceased to delight in, and now as he held her close, he forgot the sea and the wind and the white clouds above and said what he had thought often but had never said before, "I want you to marry me, Jeanine."

The words caught Jeanine off guard. She felt more affection for this man than any she had ever known. But as she looked into his blue eyes, her lips drew tightly together and she removed her arms. Pulling her legs up, she hugged them in a strange embrace. She did not answer but kept her eyes out on the horizon as level and straight as a knife edge. The small whitecaps dotted and splashed against the depths of the sea as she kept her silence.

"You're not surprised, are you?" Clive asked. He had been taken aback by her reaction, and now he reached out and tried to turn her toward him, but she resisted. "What's the matter, Jean-ine?"

"I could never marry you, Clive—or anyone else for that matter."

"What are you talking about? You must marry."

"Why must I?"

"Because it's what women do. You're not a plaster saint, Jeanine. You need a man."

"I have a man, Clive." Jeanine turned and there was a strange expression in her violet eyes. Her back was straight now, and she studied the clean sweep of Clive Winters' features. He was not really a handsome man, but there was a goodness in his face, perhaps what had drawn her to him in the first place. She had known many men who were not good, but she knew that in Clive Winters resided honor and dignity, even nobility, something she had almost ceased to believe in. He was an enigma to her in a way, and long before this, she had decided that she would enjoy his love and affection, but that it could never come to more than that.

"I could never marry anyone," she repeated quietly.

Clive shook his head. The wind blew his fair blond hair into his eyes, and he brushed it away impatiently. All the months he had known her, he had expected that his affections would change. He had expected that it would be a thing of the moment, but now he could not imagine life without her. As he studied her classic features, he realized he knew very little about her, except that she was beautiful and wealthy and that she had stirred a passion in him that no other woman had ever found. "You're talking nonsense, Jeanine," he said, his voice quiet and raised only above the keening cry of the winds that whistled through the cordage and the sails and the slapping of the water against the sides of the small boat. "I love you and I want you to be my wife."

Jeanine shook her head firmly. "You don't know me," she said finally. "I'd make you absolutely miserable."

"That's not true."

"It *is* true. We've had an affair, but we have nothing in common, Clive."

"I don't believe that. Why, we spend hours talking. I'd rather be with you than anyone I know. I never get tired of your company."

"Then enjoy it. Let's take what we have. What do the poets say? *Carpe diem*."

Clive shook his head adamantly. " 'Gather ye rosebuds while ye may.' I don't think that tips our case. I want to grow old with you. I've been in love with you for months, Jeanine."

"And what does your family say about that?"

Clive blinked, for it had been a difficult time for him. He felt Jeanine's gaze steadily upon him and shifted uncomfortably. The boat rose and fell, and he moved the rudder to meet the waves and cast a careful eye on the sails, then finally he turned to her and shrugged. "Well, as you know, they're not enamored of the idea."

"I don't blame them," Jeanine continued quickly. "You're an Englishman, Clive. You have obligations here and your life is here, but I'm American and I'll be leaving here."

"You could stay. You could become a citizen."

"No. My life is in America—and besides, you're the only son. You'll want children, boys to bear your name. I'll never have children."

Clive was struck with that statement. It was something that had never occurred to him. He had never met a woman who did not want children, a family, or a husband, and he set himself to convince her. But it all came to no avail. No matter what he said, she would shake her head, and finally he argued, "You'll want children someday. You don't want to grow old alone."

Jeanine suddenly pulled herself away from him. She moved over to the seat that was built into the side of the boat and braced herself against the rise and fall of the small vessel. The wind blew her hair, for she had loosed it, and now she put her hands up to hold it still and free from her eyes. "I don't want children and you do, and moreover, Clive, I couldn't promise to be true and faithful to you."

"Jeanine!"

"It's true. I've had men before you, and I'll probably have others. Besides that, you're religious and I'm not."

Clive stared at her. "What is that supposed to mean? I've been having an affair with you for months. That's how much my religion means to me."

Jeanine suddenly smiled. "And your conscience has been cutting you to pieces, hasn't it, Clive? You think I didn't know? You think I didn't see how at times you were absolutely miserable because the way we've been living together has gone against your convictions? And remember the time I did go to church with you?

I watched your face, and I saw something there that told me that you know in your heart you're still convinced that sin is sin. Well, I don't believe that."

"But if we married, that would make it all right."

"Marrying you wouldn't change what's inside of me, Clive."

"Don't you love me at all, Jeanine?"

Jeanine Quintana turned her eyes directly on those of Clive Winters. Her voice was clear and there was a hardness in her. "Clive, I feel an affection for you that I've never felt for any man. I like you a great deal." She hesitated for one moment, holding his glance. "But I'll never love anyone—except myself. That's the way I am, Clive, and I won't change. I'm selfish to the bone."

A gust of wind threw the sail around again, and for the moment Clive was busy maneuvering the small boat. When he got control of it, he saw that Jeanine was tying her hair back.

"Let's go back. I've had enough sailing for one day," she said quietly.

"All right."

"And Clive—let's not see each other anymore."

Winters shook his head. "I won't agree to that. There's always a chance you can change."

"There's no chance for us, Clive. You've got a life here, and I'm interfering with it. I hope you'll always remember it, but it has to be over. There's nothing in the future for the two of us."

"I'm going to keep on seeing you, Jeanine."

"You'll get hurt, Clive."

"I'll take that chance." Winters again threw the tiller over and set the sails, and the two said nothing as the boat glided across the water at a greater speed. Both of them knew that things would never be the same again.

★ ★ ★ ★

One of Annie's chief delights and pleasures came from an elderly ex-missionary named Mary Weatherford. She had encountered Mary at a Salvation Army station and was delighted to discover that the woman had served the Masai people in Africa. The two had become very close friends, and Annie went three times a week to take lessons in the *Maa* language. Mary had told her, "That's what Masai means. 'People who speak Maa.'"

Mary Weatherford was a small woman of seventy but looked

at least ten years younger. She had silvery hair, bright brown eyes, and a complexion that had been tanned so deeply by the African sun that it still remained, even though she had been in England for more than ten years. Now as Annie sat before her, she was pronouncing a phrase very carefully. *Oldoinyo le Engai.*

"Now you say it, Annie."

Annie struggled with the words, but there was a tonal quality in the older woman's voice that she could not get. "What does it mean, Mary?"

"It means the mountain of God. Engai is God to the Masai."

"You mean the Christian God?"

"They don't make much difference between gods. Engai is the god that they know."

"I can't believe I found you here, Mary," Annie smiled warmly. "It means so much to me to hear of the people there, and it's made me more anxious than ever to go and share the Gospel with them."

Mary Weatherford smiled fondly at the young woman. "It won't be like you think it is. It never is. It wasn't for me."

"What do you mean, Mary?"

"Well, I mean that you probably picture yourself talking to people about Jesus all day long. But most of the time you'll spend simply learning how to stay alive, how to survive the climate, how to kill the bugs that will eat you alive." Mary smiled. "You'll probably spend as much time fighting snakes as you do preaching the Gospel."

"I don't care. I'm so glad to have a teacher, and that I'll be able to speak their language when I go."

"But you may not go to the Masai people. You might go to another part of Africa."

"I don't think so, Mary. I think God has put you in my path for this very reason, so that I can begin to learn the language and be a part of their lives."

Mary leaned forward and stroked Annie's arm. "You're just like I was, dearie. I couldn't wait to get there, and I would be there still if my health had held out. Even after I lost John, I stayed by myself. I became more Masai than I was English, but bless your heart. You'll be going. I feel that God is in it, and that He's going to anoint you for powerful service."

"Tell me some more words. I'll make a list of them."

"All right. The word for good-bye is *Aia.*"

"Aia." Annie wrote the word down.

"The word for big is *Mkubwa*. It's spelled with an 'M,' but it's pronounced *Kub-wa*."

"Mkubwa. What about the word for lion?"

"*Simba.*"

For over an hour the two women studied, and then soberly, Mary said, "They call Africa the white man's graveyard. The white woman's, too. Many of the missionaries that went over with me are still there. They died for their faith, some of them after a very short time. I'll be praying that you'll have a long, fruitful ministry among the Masai people, Annie. It's a little bit like I would be going back myself." Mary looked at her fondly and shook her head. "It would be better if you were married, Annie. It's hard for a woman to get along without a man in Africa."

Annie flushed slightly. "I'm not thinking about that."

"Come now, all young women think about that! Don't you, just a little bit, have a man that is in your mind and in your heart and is even there now?"

The sudden thought of John Winslow leaped into Annie Rogers' mind. Something of this showed in her face and she dropped her eyes, saying, "Well, I have thought of one man, but nothing came of it."

"Well, God says, 'No good thing will I withhold from him who walketh uprightly.' So I guess you can change *thing* to *man*." Mary laughed and said, "I'll pray with you, dearie, that God will send a strong man to be by your side."

Annie smiled and the lesson continued. Finally she left the Salvation Army station and made her way home. She was surprised to find Jeanine there and spoke to her pleasantly. "I've just had another lesson in the Masai language."

"What do you do all the time that you're not working for me?" she asked. Annie could tell Jeanine seemed restless. There seemed to be an irritability about her and a dissatisfaction.

"Oh, I go to the library. I go to the British Museum—and three times a week I go to visit the poor and help with the Salvation Army work. I'm going today, as a matter of fact."

Jeanine Quintana suddenly gave her shoulders an impatient shake. "I'll go with you," she announced impetuously.

A sudden premonition of disaster came to Annie. She could not imagine what the poor people would think of this wealthy, ostentatious woman, and she said, "I don't think you would like it, Jeanine. It's very rough."

"I want to see what you're doing."

Annie argued for some time, but she had long ago learned that whatever Jeanine decided for herself would be done one way or another. "All right," she finally surrendered, "but please wear very plain clothes. You'll put people off if you wear expensive clothes."

Jeanine laughed. "I'll have to go out and buy some."

"No. Just something less—well, less *ornate* than what you're wearing now."

Jeanine suddenly seemed to find the whole idea amusing. She searched through her wardrobe with Annie's help and finally found a plain outfit—a lightweight serge dress in a muted gray. It had lace ruffles and a choker collar but was not overly frilled. "Do you think this is subdued enough?"

"That'll do fine, Jeanine. Come along, if you're ready."

The two women took a carriage at Jeanine's insistence, and Annie directed the driver to the lower East Side of London in the Soho district. It was a dingy neighborhood, the streets lined with grimy tenements. The air had grown still, as if a storm was coming, and overhead the sky was gray with black clouds scudding along.

As they descended from the carriage, both women picked up large baskets that Annie had prepared. She led the way to a tenement that sat almost on the street and was greeted by cries of children, dirty urchins who ran up and swarmed around her.

"Miss Annie! Miss Annie! Did you bring us sweets?"

"Indeed I did, Cecilia, and another lady has come. Jeanine, maybe you'd like to give the children some sweets."

It was a new experience, that trip, for Jeanine Quintana. She lived in a world far removed from poverty, so the filthy streets and the dirty hands and faces of the children were a shock to her. Then as Annie led her up the crooked stairways to the third floor, her nose was assailed by the smell of cabbage, sweat, human waste, and decay. She braced herself against it, and when they went inside one of the doors, admitted by a small girl no more than four and as dirty as those below, Jeanine's eyes swept the room and she saw what poverty was truly like. The room was small with only one tiny window covered with dirty and torn curtains. The floors were bare wood, caked with dirt and mud, and the walls were a dark gray, with the paint peeling off in large pieces, revealing a much lighter color. An old broken-down and dirty sofa was in the middle of the room, and a small table with four mismatched chairs stood over to one side where the stove was. The chairs were missing back supports, had rags wrapped around the legs that were broken, and the seats were chipped and cracked. Only one small oil lamp placed on the table brought light to the dingy room, and a simple makeshift bed stood in the far corner.

Annie went to the bed over beside the wall and said cheerfully, "Well, Alice, how do I find you today?"

"Not too well, Miss Annie."

The speaker was a frail, thin, almost emaciated woman. The rags that she used for covers were filthy, and her hair was stiff with dirt.

"Well, I've come to do a little cleaning, and we'll start with you," Annie said.

Feeling completely out of place, Jeanine watched as Annie removed Alice's soiled clothing and cleaned her, and finally washed her hair. She continued to watch as Annie dressed the poor woman with a new nightgown and then stood back.

"Now, we're going to do a little cleaning here, and we brought some fruit and some fresh meat. I'll cook you a bit of it, or perhaps you'd like to do that, Miss Quintana."

"Oh . . . yes. I'll do my best." Jeanine went over to the small stove and found only a few pieces of coal. She managed to start a fire, and although she was no cook, she did try.

The two stayed for over two hours, and when they finally went outside, Jeanine took a deep breath as they got back into the carriage. "How do you stand it, Annie?" she moaned. "I couldn't do it at all. I'll pay for the food, but I could never wash anybody like that."

Annie turned to her and spoke quietly. "I couldn't do it either if I didn't have Jesus in my heart. He loves that woman and those children, and I love them, too, through Him."

"I couldn't do it," Jeanine shook her head, her lips drawn tightly together.

"You could if Jesus were in your heart."

Jeanine looked straight at Annie and her voice was hard as granite. "He never will be," she said. "Never!"

★　★　★　★

It was two days after the expedition to the slums of London that Jeanine said abruptly as Annie entered her room, "We're going home, Annie. I've got to get away from this."

Instantly Annie knew that Jeanine's sudden change of mind had something to do with Clive Winters. "When will we leave?" she asked quietly.

"As soon as we can get passage—next week, it looks to be."

"Is something wrong, Jeanine?"

Jeanine rose and paced the floor. There was an agitation in her eyes and in her manner and a nervousness that Annie had not seen in all their time together. "I don't know what's the matter with me. I'm just unhappy, that's all. And don't preach to me! I won't have it!"

"I wasn't going to."

"You weren't going to say anything, perhaps, but you're always thinking it, aren't you?"

"I suppose I am, but, Jeanine, what you are doing is running. You ran away from America, and now you're running away from England. You're running away from Clive Winters."

"Don't say that!"

"You can't run away from God, Jeanine. No matter where you go, He's still there."

"I told you not to preach at me! Now, we're leaving next week."

"All right," Annie said, surrendering. It was not the time to talk to Jeanine about her soul, although she could not really imagine when it would be the right time. "What ship will we be taking?"

"The *Titanic*. You make the arrangements. Book us first class."

"That's the big ship we saw launched."

"Yes. It's in all the papers. She's going to make her maiden voyage. We'll be comfortable. It's a marvelous ship, they say." She went over to the window and stared outside for a time silently, and then she turned, adding, "And we'll be safe. It's the unsinkable ship. You remember what Clive told us."

"I wouldn't put my faith in that. Any ship can sink."

"Not this one. That's the one thing we don't have to worry about. The *Titanic* is unsinkable."

CHAPTER NINE

AN UNEXPECTED PASSENGER

★ ★ ★ ★

"Well, she's certainly big enough." Jeanine Quintana stood on the dock looking up at the massive ship that rose before her and Annie. The mere size of it stunned one's eyes at first, and she shook her head, saying, "That's the biggest ship I've ever seen in my life." She was wearing a lightweight green linen suit with a draped-over bodice and a knee-length tunic. Her skirt was narrow from the knee to the ankle and was trimmed with dark blue lace. She wore a wide-brimmed straw hat ornamented with dark green feathers, and her black hair glistened in the fresh April sunlight.

Annie was less expensively adorned, as usual. She wore a simple light peach dress with a high neck and a bodice draped across the body to form a V-shape. Her hobble skirt was very tight, and she had on a light blue bolero jacket with short sleeves that ended at the elbow with turn-back cuffs. As she looked up at the ship, she murmured, "I've been reading up on shipbuilding a little bit, Jeanine. From what I understand, the Cunard Lines have been building the fastest ships ever since about 1900. The *Lusitania* and the *Mauretania* went into service in 1907. They built the reputation for speed and punctuality." She smiled, saying, "They called them the *Lucy* and the *Mary*. They weren't only bigger than the White Star ships, but they also were very fast."

"How fast will this one go?"

"Somewhere around twenty-two or twenty-three knots, I understand. There'll be three of them, the *Olympic*, the *Titanic*, and the *Gigantic*. It's necessary to have three ships," she said. "They have to have regular service between a British port and New York and back again. So White Star decided to build them. The *Olympic* has already been launched, but it takes all three of them before the schedule will run smoothly."

A smile touched Jeanine's lips. "You know more things than anybody I ever knew, Annie. Come on. Let's get on board."

The two women made their way to the gangplank, where they were directed to the first-class section by the steward as soon as they reached the deck. The steward was impressed, apparently, with Jeanine's appearance and attitude, for he stopped long enough to say, "Perhaps, Miss Quintana, you'd like to look at the first-class lounge."

"Yes. Let's see it," Jeanine agreed. She followed and Annie came quickly behind her as the steward led the way into a lounge that caused Annie to take her breath. It was built in Edwardian, Louis XV style. The ceilings were high, and upholstered chairs were placed around elegantly carved tables. Around all the walls, which were made of walnut, intricate carvings shone forth in the gleaming wood.

"All right. I suppose this will have to do," Jeanine said, winking at Annie.

The steward, offended, gave her a shocked look. "Madam, you would not find a finer room than this in the finest hotels in Europe!"

"I was just teasing. It's very impressive. Come along, let's see what our rooms look like."

But the steward was determined to impress the two women, so he gave them a quick tour. He showed them the dining salon, the reception room, the restaurant, the lounge, the reading and writing room, the smoking room, and then finally the Verandah Cafe in the Palm Court. He even insisted on showing them the accommodations for those interested in sports, which included a swimming bath, electric baths, a squash racquet court, and a gymnasium. There was also a barbershop, a darkroom for photographers, and a clothes pressing room.

Finally Jeanine said, "Enough! Take us to our staterooms, if you please!"

The steward finally surrendered and took them into their stateroom. It was done in the Jacobean decor with a thick Persian carpet covering the floor. The furniture was all made of the finest mahogany, and overhead beams imitated the early English period. Everything was shiny and new, and there were two bedrooms, one off of each side of the sitting room. Jeanine walked around the room and, to mollify the steward said, "This is really very nice, and your service is excellent."

"My pleasure, madam. I'll bring your trunks as soon as they are put aboard."

"Thank you, steward." Jeanine gave him a lavish tip, then when he left, she turned around and smiled. "What do you think of it, Annie?"

"It's very grand, isn't it?"

"Yes, it is. I'll have to admit they've spared no expense. Come on. Let's go take another tour around the deck."

The two explored the ship with interest, and finally they came to stand in the bow.

"I believe we're starting to move," Annie remarked.

"Yes. I can feel the engines."

The two women felt a tinge of excitement as the massive *Titanic* began to ease away from the pier. Slowly and powerfully the massive vessel swung clear and moved through the harbor, breaking the gray water with its sharp bow.

Suddenly, however, Annie cried, "Look at that ship! That one there!" She pointed at a steamer with the title *New York* on its bow. The vessel had snapped her moorings and swung toward the port side of the *Titanic*. Tugboats frantically attempted to get a line on the wayward American vessel. Fortunately Captain Smith of the *Titanic* was able to avoid disaster. He cut his engines, then used the wash from his port engine to halt the swing of the other ship. Even so, the *New York* was dragged relentlessly sideways through the channel, nearly colliding with yet another vessel before the tugboats could stop her rush and put her to safe mooring.

"That could have been a disaster!" Jeanine gasped.

Annie watched as the tugboats pushed the *New York* back into a safer position and moored her to the wharf. "I know," she said quietly. "If things were just a little different, she would have crashed right into us."

Jeanine looked keenly at her companion. "You're not worried about the ship sinking, are you?"

"Not worried, Jeanine, but it could happen. You saw how close we came to an accident, and we're hardly out of the harbor."

Jeanine ran her hand through her black hair, fluffed it up, and laughed shortly. "You don't understand the nature of this ship," she said. "I've been doing a little studying myself, and it's true what we've heard. There are airtight compartments. If that ship over there had crushed one of them, it would have filled with water, but the others would have kept us afloat."

Annie did not argue, but she was uneasy with Jeanine's overly confident attitude. She had been reading much in the paper about the claims of the White Star Lines that the *Titanic* was unsinkable. She knew it was a time when in nearly every area of human endeavor, whether architecture or medicine or science, the Western world had become convinced that man had his destiny in his own hands. All he had to do was apply science, and all problems would be solved. She had no faith at all in this new thought that was sweeping Europe and America in particular. She knew enough of history to understand that man was constantly trying to go places he was never meant to go and to do things he was never meant to do. Sometimes men reached too far and got too arrogant, only to be brought low. She said none of this to Jeanine, however, and the two were leaning on the rail when a voice behind them said, "Well, what a surprise!"

Both women turned and were equally surprised to see Clive Winters standing in front of them. His blue eyes were bright with excitement, and the wind whipped his fine blond hair as he stood observing them.

"Clive, what in the world are you doing here?" Jeanine exclaimed.

"Oh, I just thought it was time for me to take a trip to America. Quite a coincidence, isn't it?"

Jeanine and Annie, as well, knew that the meeting was not at all coincidental. Jeanine shook her head. "Clive, you shouldn't have followed me."

Trying to assume an innocent expression, Clive shrugged his trim shoulders. He was wearing a light gray Norfolk jacket with matching pants, a straw hat with a pleated silk band, a neck band shirt made to be worn with a detachable collar, and brown leather shoes that gleamed in the sunlight. "I hate to be misjudged. I've just taken a sudden interest in seeing your country, Jeanine. So I thought this might be a good time."

Jeanine's lips tightened. She was a woman of firm principles, at least insofar as getting her own way and making her own decisions. She liked Clive a lot and had flirted with the idea of marrying him. But her will was so strong that she believed she could never give it up to any man, no matter how attractive or powerful he was. Having made this firm commitment in her own mind and having told Clive that it was over, it displeased her to find him there. "You shouldn't have followed me, Clive," she repeated flatly. "Nothing can come of it."

Once again Clive made a gesture of innocence with his hands outspread. "Just an ocean voyage. Nothing wrong with that. The ship's big enough that you can run away from me if you want to."

Annie watched the two and understood very well what was going on. Clive, against his own best interest, was following Jeanine, hoping to persuade her to marry him. Annie knew it would be a disastrous match for him and probably for Jeanine as well. Annie had long ago decided that if Jeanine ever married in her current spiritual and emotional state, she would make a man perfectly miserable. She excused herself, saying, "I'll let you two sort this out."

As Annie left, she spent some time exploring the ship, and later in the day the *Titanic* dropped anchor off Cherbourg, France, to embark additional passengers. Annie was fascinated as the *Titanic* left harbor, for instead of plowing straight through, it seemed to change directions quite often. She stopped one of the officers, a short young man with cherubic cheeks and striking eyes. "Why are we changing directions so often, Lieutenant?"

"Oh, it's Captain Smith's idea. I think he's trying to get the feel of the new ship. Ordinarily a ship goes through a great many sea trials, but the White Star was anxious to get the *Titanic* into motion as quickly as possible. So he's just trying her out, much like you would try out a new automobile."

"Will we go straight to New York?"

"Oh no. We'll stop at Queenstown. That's in Ireland."

"Thank you." Annie continued her walk until it was time for dinner. When Jeanine didn't appear, she took her meal in the stateroom. After reading a while, she assumed that Jeanine and Clive were together, so she went to bed. She slept that night with the motion of the ship rocking her to sleep.

★　★　★　★

The next day they reached Queenstown at noon. Annie, once again, was alone. Jeanine had said little at breakfast. Annie could see clearly that there was something on her mind. Annie had learned to read the flamboyant woman's moods well, and it was obvious to her that something was troubling Jeanine. "I hope she and Clive don't marry," she murmured, but there was nothing she could do about that.

As the ship was docked, Annie stood beside the gangplank, watching the passengers who were boarding for the first time. Most of them seemed to be poor immigrants carrying a dream to begin a new life in America. One young woman caught her eye. She could be no more than twenty-two, Annie guessed, but she held in each arm a struggling baby, both faces red from crying. Annie approached the young woman, noting that she had red hair almost like her own.

"Let me help you with one of your babies," Annie offered.

The young woman, who had a fair complexion but wore a worried frown, said, "Oh, would you mind, ma'am? I can't keep up with them and all of my luggage."

"What's your name, dear?"

"Kathleen O'Fallon," the girl said shyly.

"I'm Annie Rogers. And who are these two?"

"This is Michael and this is Mary."

"Well, let me have Michael."

The young woman awkwardly surrendered the baby, and Annie cuddled him in her arms. She touched his cheek and cooed at him, and the yowling stopped immediately. To her amazement a broad, toothless grin suddenly broke out, and a gurgle signified the baby's pleasure. "Why, you little darling!" she said. "If you're not a charmer."

"He's a handful, Miss Rogers."

"Oh, just Annie will do fine. Look, I'll get us some help and we'll find your stateroom."

"Oh, I don't have a stateroom, miss. I'm down in steerage."

"Steerage, then." Annie reached out and plucked the sleeve of one of the stewards and smiled at him brightly. "We need a little help here. Would you mind helping us get this young lady settled?"

"Why, yes, ma'am. I'll be glad to." The steward, a tall, gangly man, had a good smile and at once located Kathleen O'Fallon's luggage. "Let's see your ticket, miss," he said. He took one look at it and instructed, "Right this way. Follow me."

Carrying Michael O'Fallon in her arms and looking at his fat cheeks every once in a while, Annie followed and was in turn followed by the young woman. The steward led them on a labyrinthine path until they reached the lower part of the deck. Immediately, Annie saw that the third-class passengers were thrust into quarters that were a stark contrast to the comfort and luxury available in the first and even the second class. Even here, though, she saw that the quarters were not the traditional "cattle boat" concept of days gone by when passengers simply traveled in one large open space. They passed through a third-class dining saloon and then a lounge, and finally the steward said, "Here's your room, miss." He opened a door, and stepping inside, they found it would take as many as ten passengers. It was clean, of course, being new, and several women were already there.

"Oh, I can't thank you enough," Kathleen said as she sat down on a bunk.

"Well, why don't we see about getting these two taken care of. I'll help all I can. Is your husband coming?"

A look of pain washed across the face of the young Irish woman. "No, ma'am, he's not. He died a month ago." Her lower lip quivered, and the girl bit it to hide her agitation and grief. She could not, however, and tears welled up in her eyes. "It was his dream to take us to America. He was so proud of Michael and Mary, and he said his children would have a better place and a better chance there than in the old country. But then the cholera came and took him off."

The tragedy in the young girl's eyes touched Annie's heart deeply. She sat down beside her, holding Michael in her left arm, and put her other arm around the girl's shoulder. "I'm sorry," she said quietly. "It must be very hard."

"It is, mum! Very hard indeed! We'd . . . we'd only been married a little over four years, and then I lost him."

Annie felt the shoulders shaking beneath her arm and prayed quickly for guidance. "I'm so sorry, Kathleen," she said. "But I'm surprised that you're leaving your home and your friends. Do you have other family?"

"Very little, and it was Michael's dream for us to go to America. I have to do it, Miss Annie. I have to!"

Annie Rogers sat there almost stunned. She had enjoyed a relatively easy life, and now as she considered the courage of this young woman, leaving her native land with two children and probably little money, she prayed, *Oh, God, please help me to be a friend and a helper to this young woman in her time of need.*

"You know, Kathleen, the Bible says, 'A friend loveth at all times and a brother—or sister—is born for adversity.' Did you know that?"

"No, mum. I don't know the Bible. What does it mean?"

"Well, a sister is born for adversity. That means if I'm having difficulty and you can help me, then God will bring you into my life to be a sister and to help me in my need. So I think God is putting me into your life to be a help to you. Would you let me be that sister and friend to you, Kathleen?"

The loving tones of Annie Rogers and the warmth of her arm around Kathleen O'Fallon's shoulders seemed to break the dam. Her shoulders shook and tears ran down her face freely. "Oh, mum," she said, "I need a friend—indeed I do! I don't have anywhere to go, and it's hard taking care of the two little ones. I do need a friend."

"Well, I'll be that friend, Kathleen. But you know, I sing a song sometimes. I don't know if you've ever heard it. It's called 'There's Not a Friend Like the Lowly Jesus.' "

"No, mum, I don't know it."

Annie sang the song quietly. "There's not a friend like the lowly Jesus. No not one. No not one." The tears flowed freely, and finally Kathleen found a handkerchief and wiped her eyes. "I believe God must have sent you to me, Miss Annie."

"Well, it will be a treat for me. I'm going to Africa as a missionary. There'll be children there, and I don't know much about children. I can practice up on Michael here." She bounced the baby on her lap and poked his cheek with her finger and blinked her eyes at him. To her delight he chortled with glee and reached out and grabbed her finger and held to it tightly. "My, what a grip he has! You're going to be a good strong man and take care of your mother, aren't you, Michael?"

Annie stayed with Kathleen and the children for over two hours. She saw her safely settled, and then, each carrying one of the children, they made a tour of the third-class section. She encouraged Kathleen and promised to come back soon. Before she left she gave Michael a hug, saying, "You're a sweetheart, you are." Then she kissed the infant, Mary, on the cheek, and whispered, "You're going to grow up and be a beautiful lady just like your mother." Then she turned and kissed Kathleen O'Fallon's cheek. "You've got a friend now. Two friends, really—me and Jesus."

Kathleen O'Fallon shook her head. "I don't know Jesus, but I know you."

The simple words brought a pang to Annie's heart. *I don't have to go to Africa to be a missionary*, she thought. *Here is a young woman who needs the Lord Jesus, and I'm going to give my whole heart to bringing her to know Him.*

★ ★ ★ ★

Annie resisted Jeanine's urgings for a time, saying, "I don't see why I have to dress up or even why I have to go. I'd just as soon go down to Kathleen and eat with her and the children."

Jeanine was putting on the final touches of her toilette. As she carefully tucked her hair into place, she glanced over and said impatiently, "What's the use of paying for first class on this expensive boat if you don't get any good out of it? Now, put on that dress we bought before we left London!"

Annie shrugged, but she had learned better than to argue with Jeanine Quintana. The woman was the strongest human being she had ever met—at least the stubbornest. She went back to her own room and put on the dress that was much too ornate for her taste. The dress was made of pearl gray silk with a black lace and bead kimono over the high lace neckline and long, slim sleeves. The silk skirt was narrow and showed out from under the kimono, which was caught up at one side with a large pin just above the right knee. Moving back into the sitting room she found Jeanine, who, Annie had to admit, looked splendid. "That *is* a beautiful dress, Jeanine."

"It should be. It cost enough." The floor-length dress was a bright yellow crepe with a low rounded neckline and short sleeves. On top of this was a drape-over dress of white lace and pearls that formed a V-front at the bodice and ended just above the knee in the front and trailed behind her in a long train.

As the two women turned to leave the stateroom, Annie shook her head. "I've already noticed that some women change clothes three or four times a day."

"Yes, they do. That's what people go on a ship like this for, to eat and drink and dress up. Come along now. We're going to the Ritz. They say it's the most luxurious part of the whole ship."

When they reached the restaurant, which was situated on the bridge deck, Annie thought it was beautiful. Jeanine was impressed, but she would not admit it. The two had to wait for a moment while the maître d' seated another group, so they studied the room. It was done in Louis XVII style with French walnut paneling and furniture, and the deep pile Axminster carpet seemed so rich to Annie, she thought she would sink in to her ankles. The elegant paneling was beautifully carved, and the gilded details brought a grace to the room such as Annie had never seen. As they took their seats she saw that the plates repeated the Louis XVII decor. The china plate she touched with one forefinger seemed fragile and yet strong at the same time. Tables were scattered throughout the room, some seating two, and some seating four or more.

The waiter who appeared was a pale-faced man of thirty with a pencil-thin mustache and a pair of sober brown eyes. He spoke with a slight French accent, and a mole dominated the right side of his face. "Here you are, ladies."

The women took the menus and studied them carefully.

First Course—Hors d'oeuvre

Oeufs de Caille en Aspic et Caviar

White Bordeaux or White Burgundy

Second Course—Potage

Potage Saint-Bermain

Madeira or Sherry

Third Course—Poisson

Homard Thermidor

Dry Rhine or Moselle

Fourth Course—Entrée

Tournedos aux Morilles

Red Bordeaux

Fifth Course—Punch or Sorbet

Punch Rose

Sixth Course—Rôti

Cailles aux Cerises

Red Burgundy

Seventh Course—Légume

Asperges Printanieres, Sauce Hollandaise

Eighth Course—Engremets

Macédoine de Fruits

Oranges en Surprise

Sweet Dessert Wines (Muscatel, Tokay, Madeira)

Ninth Course—Les Desserts

Assorted Fresh Fruits and Cheeses

Sweet Dessert Wines, Champagne, or Sparkling Wine

After Dinner

Coffee, Cigars

Port or Cordials

"Well, we are not going to starve—I can see that," Jeanine mused. She was accustomed to fine restaurants and began to explain some of the items to Annie. "This first one, *Oeufs de Caille en Aspic et Caviar*, is only quail eggs in aspic with caviar."

Suddenly Annie glanced up and said, "There's Clive."

"Yes. I asked him to join us."

Clive came over, bowed, and greeted the two women. "I'm starved," he said.

"Well, sit down, Clive," Jeanine said. As he sat down, she grinned impishly. "That's a nice suit. You look very fine indeed. If you drop dead, we won't have to do anything to you except put a lily in your hand."

Clive looked startled for a moment and then laughed. "You

say the awfulest things, Jeanine. I'll have you understand this suit was designed by a Frenchman." It was a white linen, double-breasted sack suit, and, in truth, Clive did look rather good in it.

Looking over the menu, he groaned, "If I eat all this, they'll have to carry me to my room."

He knew practically everybody and began pointing out many of the prominent figures of society who were on the maiden voyage. "That's John Jacob Astor and his new wife," he commented. "And that tall man there. That's Major Archie Butt. He's the advisor to President Taft."

"Is J. P. Morgan on board the ship?" Jeanine inquired.

"No. I understand he was planning to come, but he took ill and canceled out."

"Who is that distinguished looking man with the white beard there?" Annie asked.

"That's the captain, Edward J. Smith. Fine chap. I understand he's about ready to retire, but he's so popular with passengers, they persuaded him to make one more voyage to break the *Titanic* in."

As the meal went on, Annie took in all the enormously wealthy people sitting around the tables. She herself was not impressed by money, and her thoughts were on Kathleen down below. She would much rather have been there, but her employer would not think of it, so she made the best of the elaborate meal.

As soon as she had finished eating, Annie excused herself. "I'd like to go check on Kathleen, if you don't mind, Jeanine."

"Go ahead. I knew you'd run away as soon as you could."

As soon as Annie left, Clive asked, "Who is Kathleen?"

"A young Irishwoman. A widow with two children. Of course Annie's gotten herself totally enmeshed with her. I don't expect I'll get much good out of her on the voyage. She'll be down there caring for those children."

"Would you like a turn on deck?"

"All right."

The two made their way out of the Ritz, and when they were on deck, they began walking slowly. The moon was out, and the glimmering reflection across the waters made a gigantic wedge shape wider than the apex of the moon—the broader part on the ship itself.

"The Vikings called that 'the whales' way,' " Clive murmured.

"Did they? It's very beautiful."

"Not as beautiful as you."

"None of that, Clive."

"Why not, Jeanine?" He stopped abruptly and said, "Come. Let's talk."

He led her to the rail, where they stood leaning over. Far beneath, it seemed, the waters curled and glistened around the sides of the gigantic vessel. The deck itself appeared to be motionless, and the sea seemed to be rushing by. A bell rang, signaling the time, but neither of them knew what it meant. Overhead the stars punctuated the sky with diamond-sharp points of light.

Jeanine said nothing and finally Clive confessed. "I did follow you, of course, Jeanine, and you knew that."

"Yes. But it's hopeless, Clive."

"Don't you care for me even a little?"

"I care for you a great deal, Clive. That must have been clear. Even as rotten as I am, I don't have an affair with a man unless I care for him."

"But isn't it more than that?"

"Not for me. I read books about love and don't understand them. In many of the romances a man and a woman meet, and it's like electricity suddenly connects them. They take one look and suddenly they know they're in love and will be for the next fifty years. I don't believe that, Clive."

"Don't you? I do."

Turning to face him, Jeanine studied his clear-cut features. His lips were firm and his cheekbones high. He had the typical English nose, and there was strength in his face. "You really do believe that, don't you, Clive? That things are going to turn out all right?"

"Yes, I do," he said simply.

Jeanine studied him silently. "I'm glad you do, Clive, and I hope you always will. But as for me, life's not that simple. I don't know what love is."

"It's when you want the good things to happen to someone else instead of to yourself."

"Oh, that's just charity. I have some of that, I hope. Not much. I'm a terribly selfish person. I always have been."

"Jeanine, there's something inside of you. A sweetness, and a goodness, and a charity that you never let out. I don't know how you got this way, but you've built a huge wall around yourself. You're demanding, and you immediately challenge anyone who tries to get you to do something."

Jeanine laughed shortly. "Well, you've made me out to be a pretty domineering sort of woman, and that's right. I am, and I suppose I'll always be that way."

"I don't think so. I think I could make you love me, Jeanine. It might take a while, but I think I see more in you than most men do. Maybe more than any man's ever seen."

"There's nothing in me, Clive, except selfishness, and there never will be."

"I don't believe that."

"Neither does Annie, but she's wrong. You're both wrong."

They stood there together as if they were alone in the world. Overhead the stars glittered and moved, doing their old dance. Deep in the bowels of the ship the turbines hummed and the propellers spun, sending them through the dark waters. It was a moment that Jeanine knew she would not quickly forget. She was uneasy and did not want to prolong it. "Clive," she said almost gently. Then she reached up and touched his cheek. "I don't love. I don't even believe God loves people. How could He?"

"Jeanine, what a thing to say!"

"Well, look at babies dying in fires. Look at the millions of orphans who have horrible lives. Look at all the terrible things. If God were love, and if He were strong, how could He let these horrible things happen?"

He started to protest, but she put her hand over his lips. "No, don't try to talk to me. I've had probably the best preacher in the world. I wouldn't say this to Annie, but she's a good woman. She's a walking Bible, I think sometimes, and she's had more influence on me than she knows. But it's not enough, Clive."

Clive moved forward and took her in his arms. She did not resist as his lips touched hers. As the two stood there and held the kiss, a tempest howled through him, and he knew that this woman was the only one he would ever love.

As for Jeanine, she felt something stir in her spirit, but she could not tell what it was. Whenever it seemed to rise, she quenched it immediately, and now she turned and said wearily, "It's over, Clive. Let's not see each other again. It hurts too much. For you, I mean."

Clive stepped back and released her. He looked at her, and the pain that he felt was reflected in his fine eyes. "I love you more than life, Jeanine," he said. Then he turned and walked away, leaving her alone on the deck. Somehow, when he was gone and she turned back to face the water, there was an emptiness in Jeanine. It had always been there, perhaps, but now she felt it more than ever. "Clive, you're the finest man I've ever known," she said. "But I can't love you. I can't love anyone. Even God." She spoke this aloud, and the deep pain that she kept hidden from the world tinged her words. She bowed her head there, leaned over the rail, and for the first time in years, tears came to her eyes. Her shoulders shook, and she cried out finally, "Why can't I love anyone? Why?"

Overhead the moon was silent looking down on her. The stars far away glittered, but they brought no comfort to Jeanine Quintana.

CHAPTER TEN

"You Can't Run From God"

★ ★ ★ ★

Captain Edward J. Smith straightened his back with a sigh, burdened by the fatigue and pressure of being in charge of the *Titanic*. It brought furrows between his eyes, and he brushed the neatly trimmed white mustache that almost concealed his lips. Smith was the most popular captain on the White Star Line, although no one was quite sure why. He was not, many argued, the most efficient and capable officer, insofar as operating the gargantuan ships. Those who did not admire him were prone to say, "He's merely the most political captain alive and the best host at a dinner table."

Certainly this was part of Smith's role, as was true of all captains of the White Star Line. The captains were to be visible to the passengers—especially the more affluent ones. They were somewhat like the heads of state who constantly went through ceremonials while the prime minister did the grubby business of running the country. Captain Smith's officers, including First Officer Murdoch, were all capable men, and now as the *Titanic* forged rapidly through the gray waters of the Atlantic, Smith ran over in his mind the multitudinous duties that were the lot of any captain. He focused on the date of April the twelfth for a moment and rapidly made calculations concerning the arrival of the ship in New York. He recalled his conversation with Bruce Ismay, managing director of the White Star Line, which he could not seem to shake off. Ismay had insisted that the *Titanic* reach New York at the earliest possible moment. "We've got to show the world that we can compete with the Cunard Line," Ismay had said, his eyelids narrowing and his lips drawn into a firm line under his curling mustache. He was a demanding man, this Ismay, and although he had not directly threatened Captain Smith, still there was, in his tone and in his attitude, an implied warning. "We've got to make all possible speed—or we may have to find a more aggressive captain."

Smith peered out over the choppy waters and through the soles of his feet sensed the throbbings of the giant turbines far down in the bowels of the ship. He had confidence in these powerful engines and in the ship itself, but there was more to navigating the Atlantic than simply throwing the throttle wide open.

Even as Smith thought of this, First Officer Murdoch came to stand beside him, waiting respectfully. When Smith turned, Murdoch said, "Sir, another ice warning."

"Where is it located, Murdoch?" Smith listened as Murdoch gave the location of the ice, but said nothing. He stood there silently for a moment, then finally nodded and left, saying, "You have the bridge, Murdoch."

First Officer Murdoch had expected the captain to change course, to swing farther away from where the bergs were reported. He had also half expected, and even hoped, that the captain would order the speed of the ship reduced. Murdoch was not aware of the struggle between the White Star Line and the Cunard Line. It was a fierce, competitive battle, and Murdoch, being a practical man, concerned himself with the business of running this giant ocean liner. That was enough for him. He had confidence in Captain Smith and filed the matter of the sighting of ice in his mind, then gave his attention to the business at hand.

The *Titanic* was like a beehive in some ways. Down below in the very lowest part of the ship, men, stripped half-naked with sweat running down and making paths through the coal that coated their faces, shoveled fuel into the gaping mouths of the furnaces. It took a man of tremendous strength and endurance to stand a watch at this station, and there was no letup. With the ship running at top speed, there was a constant cracking of the officers' voices. "Pour it on, men! No slacking here! Let's have it!"

Elsewhere on the ship, a huge staff was busy caring for the needs of the 2,223 souls. Most of the work was devoted to the travelers who expected excellent service. In actuality, there were as many staff as there were passengers in the first- and second-class sections of the ship. The majority were involved in preparing or serving food. The huge quantities of raw material were staggering, with separate refrigerators for each type of perishable, including meat, fish, fruit, vegetables, eggs, and dairy products, that lined the corridors. In addition there was separate cold storage for vintage wines and spirits. The books listed cereals: 10,000 pounds. And sugar: 5 tons. Fresh asparagus: 800 bundles. Oysters: 1,221 quarts. The *Titanic*'s supplies were full, pressed down, and overflowing.

For all its size and bulk, the *Titanic* was a tiny microcosm, a small dot, on the enormous expanse of the Atlantic. Yet it was also a cosmos with all the order and pomp and circumstance of an earthly kingdom, even such as ancient Rome itself. It was a little world with its own royalty, Captain Smith being the king. The nobility included the extremely wealthy who had never known want in their lives. There were the poor, the peasants, packed into steerage with little more than the clothes on their backs. The workers were ranked from those who scrubbed the decks to the officers who executed the complicated maneuvers necessary to move this small world through the waters. Overhead the stars did their great dance at night and the sun ran his race each day, coming as a bridegroom out of his chamber. Time moved on, and around the world revolutions came, and plague laid its grim hands on nations. People died and babies were born, but the *Titanic* surged through the cold waters secure in itself, every heart full of confidence and hope, looking forward to the next day and the day that followed that and to the time that would roll on without perturbation. There were no comets to warn of disaster such as came when Caesar died, but only the cold glitter of the stars overhead that had witnessed the tragedies and the triumphs of earth since the beginning. That, and the hard blue-gray sky punctuated by the yellow sun that stared down impassively on the ship as it plowed steadfastly forward toward its destiny.

★ ★ ★ ★

Jeanine could not forget what Clive had said earlier that day at the table. She moved about her stateroom, glancing over from time to time at Annie, who was taking a letter down on her pad. Jeanine finally snapped, "Oh, I can't think tonight! We'll take care of these letters tomorrow. We can't mail them until we get to New York anyway."

Annie folded her pad and asked quietly, "What did you think of what Clive said?"

Jeanine had been standing at the porthole staring out into the dark night. Some of the darkness seemed to seep into her. Annie was unusually sober, and this disturbed her. Whirling quickly, she said, "What do you mean?"

"I mean about his intention to serve God from now on in a better way."

Annie's question seemed to trouble Jeanine. She did not answer for a moment but moved over, poured herself a drink, and took a sip. She toyed with the glass nervously, then shrugged her shoulders, saying with some trace of irritation, "That's fine for him! I wish him the best."

"I think he means it. He's one of the finest men I've ever known."

"In spite of the fact that he's been carrying on an adulterous affair with a fallen woman?"

Annie held Jeanine's gaze for a moment, then shook her head. "Don't talk like that."

"It's true enough! Why shouldn't I say it? You Puritans all think if you say things it makes them worse."

"I think it's good to know who you've been and what you've done, but I don't think it's good to shut the door to a change that can come. And I think Clive has changed."

Annie's simple words brought a pang to Jeanine Quintana, for they were true. She was an intelligent, perceptive woman, and she had seen the change that had come to Clive. There had always been a gentleness in him, but in the latter part of their affair, she had seen something more than that. She had liked Clive more than she had ever liked any other man, yet being firmly committed to living her own life, she had walked away. She knew, however, that she did not walk away whole, for there was something in her heart for Clive Winters that had never been there for another man.

She stalked up and down the cabin and finally flung her arms out in a strange gesture. "What do you want out of me, Annie? You want me to say that I'm glad that he's going to live a good Christian life now? All right. I'm glad." She stood there daring Annie to speak.

When she did not respond, Jeanine walked over and slumped down in a chair. The spoonback armchair was outlined in a dark, highly polished mahogany, had scrolled feet, and was upholstered in light green and ivory damask. She ran her hand over the richness of its fiber without thinking, then she looked up and said abruptly, "You know what he said? He said he loved me more than life."

"Did he, now?"

"Yes, he did, and what's more, he meant it. Other men have said things like that. I've never put any stock in them, but I know somehow that Clive meant it."

"That troubles you, doesn't it? The fact that a man could love you in that way."

"I don't want love like that. I don't believe in it."

"Do you believe he meant it?"

With more agitation than Annie had ever seen, Jeanine paced around the room. Annie saw that her hands were unsteady, and she knew that something was going on inside of Jeanine Quintana that was new, that was different, that was almost startling.

"I don't know. I don't really believe in love like that. He may think he loves me more than life, but if it came down to it, it couldn't be true."

"Jeanine, there was a very famous man years ago who said, 'Inside every person there's a God-shaped blank, and that person will never know peace until God fills it with himself.'"

The words seemed to strike Jeanine like a blow. Her face turned pale, for she had long known that there was an emptiness inside of her. She had tried to fill it up with pleasure, with those things that money can buy, with a frenzy of activity, but she well knew that something was missing deep inside her. She was so moved, she could not speak. Without another word she turned and left the sitting room, entered her cabin, and shut the door.

Annie sat there praying for Jeanine. "Lord, she doesn't know who she is. She's confused. She's unhappy and miserable. Her money hasn't done anything for her except to rob her of that which is valuable, and that's you, Lord Jesus. Now I pray that even now you would convict her heart. Bring her somehow, whatever it takes, to the throne of grace."

Jeanine stopped inside her cabin. Her mind was racing, and a disturbance swept through her like a storm. She moved over to the liquor cabinet, poured a fragile glass full of champagne, drank it down, then set the glass on the marble top.

And at that moment something happened. The glass did a tiny dance. Jeanine stared at it. She felt the vibration through her feet, but she watched as the little glass, almost weightless, bounced across the dark green marble.

This had never happened before, and it frightened Jeanine. She suddenly thought about how fragile the *Titanic* truly was. For all its bulk and size, and for all the steel that had gone into her, she was just a ship. And under the ship, she instantly became aware, were thousands of feet, or perhaps even miles, of dark, cold water. The thought of what lay beneath the hull of the *Titanic* swept through her. She had always been afraid of the dark and hated the cold, and beneath her was the coldest, darkest spot on the face of the earth.

She watched the glass, and finally it stopped trembling. To quiet her fear, she picked up the bottle, poured the glass full, and held it up. She repeated a toast she had heard one of the passengers say: "God himself couldn't sink this ship."

She started to drink the champagne but then stopped. The thought of the cold, dark waters and the depths with unknown creatures below frightened her. She put the glass down, went over to the bed, and sat down on it. She bowed her head and saw that her hands were trembling, so she clenched them tightly together. She had been afraid of little in her life, and now fear gripped her heart with cold fingers. And to her shock, she began to weep.

CHAPTER ELEVEN

Kiss of Death

★　★　★　★

Sunday morning, April 14, 1912, began calmly enough on board the *Titanic*. Captain Smith led the church service for those who were interested in such things. It began at eight o'clock, and for the most part, the passengers in first class were sleeping peacefully as the mighty ship plowed through the gray waters, headed for America. John Jacob Astor, the richest man on board, was rarely seen, except for brief appearances in the restaurants. He did not appear at the service that morning, but Benjamin Guggenheim was there.

Annie, who had offered an invitation to Jeanine and was surprised when the young woman accepted, sat beside her employer and Guggenheim. He was alone, but everyone knew that his young French mistress, a "Madame" Aubert, was no secret. Guggenheim's face was calm, Annie noted, and she wondered, *What must it be like to have all the money that one could possibly use? Mr. Guggenheim could buy any piece of land, or any house, or any carriage anywhere in the world. I wonder if that has gotten old for him? What is really going on inside his heart?* It was a question she could not answer, for Guggenheim's face was placid, and he seemed to be half-asleep during Captain Smith's reading of the Scripture and prayers. Indeed, there was an air of somnambulism over most of the congregation as Smith read from the fortieth chapter of Isaiah, one of Annie's favorite passages.

"Have ye not known? Have ye not heard? Hath it not been told you from the beginning? Have you not understood from the foundations of the earth? It is he that sitteth upon the circle of the earth, and the inhabitants thereof are as grasshoppers; that stretcheth out the heavens as a curtain, and spreadeth them out as a tent to dwell in: that bringeth the princes to nothing. . . ."

Annie shot a quick glance again at Guggenheim and thought of that last verse, "that bringeth the princes to nothing." *I wonder if he has ever really heard the Gospel? Annie thought. Doesn't he know that even kings and princes must stand before God? Has he ever thought about that?*

The reading of the chapter went on, until finally the last three verses came, and Annie moved her lips with those of Captain Smith as he read in a sober tone. "He giveth power to the faint: and to them that have no might he increaseth strength. Even the youths shall faint and be weary, and the young men shall utterly fall: But they that wait upon the Lord shall renew their strength; they shall mount up with wings as eagles: they shall run, and not be weary; and they shall walk, and not faint."

Captain Smith closed the Bible and read a prayer, then dismissed the service.

"Captain Smith isn't much of a preacher, is he?" Jeanine said as the two women left the dining room that had been used as a chapel. "I trust he's a better captain than he is a preacher."

Annie did not answer, although she agreed with Jeanine. She hated to speak against anyone trying to do the will of God and finally remarked only, "I think it was nice of him to hold the service. He's not a preacher, of course, but that Scripture he read has always been one of my favorites."

"I couldn't make much out of it."

"It says that God is all-powerful and that we are helpless and weak. I've always liked that last verse: 'But they that wait upon the Lord shall renew their strength.' I've had to lean on that verse a lot, and I know that it will become even more real when I get to Africa."

The two were walking along the promenade deck. The sun had broken out in the east and shattered itself in beams of light along the choppy waves. The sea was neither blue nor green nor gray, but a murky combination of all. Overhead the sky was a dead slate color, and the clouds that scudded along were tattered and looked like dirty swabs of cotton strung out along the horizon. It was not a cheerful, sunny morning as they had known before, and it depressed Jeanine.

"I'll be glad when we get to New York," she said abruptly, turning and leaning against the rail. "Every time I go to Europe, I'm always glad to get home again."

"I'll be glad to get home, too," Annie said. She looked down at the choppy waters that swirled around the steel sides far below and remarked, "Look how far below it is! It looks like it would kill one just to jump from this height, even into water."

Jeanine looked down and suddenly a shiver ran over her. "I've been having bad dreams, Annie."

"What sort of bad dreams?"

"About the ocean." She shifted uneasily and her violet eyes became half-hooded as she stared down at the water. "I keep thinking about how far it is to the bottom, how awful and dark and cold it is. What it must be like for sailors to fall into that water and drown."

"I don't think much about the depth of it. You can drown as well in six feet of water as you can in a mile, I guess."

"I suppose, but still, it's not what I like to think about." She turned suddenly and said, "You've been a nuisance to me, Annie."

The sudden words spoken almost vehemently shocked Annie. "Why . . . what do you mean, Jeanine?"

"I mean it's impossible to be around you without thinking about God and about . . . hell." It seemed an effort for her to speak the last word, and she said, "I don't know if we can go on together."

Annie knew then that God was dealing with Jeanine. She also knew that she must be very careful, so she said quietly, "I don't think it would help to get rid of me—although that's your choice. The only help for any of us is to allow God to come into that empty place that we all have inside of us. And it isn't hard, Jeanine. What's hard is living a life without meaning. I don't want to be personal, and I've really tried to keep from preaching, but just look at your life. It's one round of parties, of men, of pleasure, and I know for a moment that seems good. But there are bound to be times when it seems awfully futile and empty."

"That's all I have."

"It doesn't have to be," Annie said, and her eyes glowed, for she felt a new surge of love for this woman who had treated her so badly. "When you give yourself to God, suddenly there's more meaning to life than you ever thought. Your life *counts*. God is the same yesterday, today, and forever. And when we become part of His will, we are eternal creatures, not just like flies that I read about that are born in the morning and live their life out and die at night."

Annie's words seemed to strike Jeanine. She closed her lips tightly and shook her head. "I don't want to talk about it," she said as she turned and walked away.

Her back was straight as she disappeared down the passageway beyond, and Annie knew that Jeanine had come to that fork in the road that all human beings come to, when they must once and for all eternity choose between God and the world. She hurried to her cabin, went into her room, fell on her knees, and began to pray for Jeanine.

★　★　★　★

"And where is your home, my dear?"

Annie turned and smiled at the elderly woman who sat next to her. She had come down for lunch with Jeanine and Clive, and they found themselves seated at one of the tables that held half a dozen travelers. She had met Mr. and Mrs. Isidor Straus and knew only that they were extremely wealthy. "I was brought up in the West, Mrs. Straus," she said.

"Oh, indeed!" Interest flickered in the other woman's eyes, and she studied Annie carefully. "That must have been rather exciting. Did you ever see any Indians?"

"Oh my, yes! I grew up on a ranch, and several Indians worked for my father." Annie found Mrs. Straus fascinated by this, and her husband, Isidor, listened in also. He was a heavy man in his middle sixties, and both were dressed as if for a royal coronation. Mrs. Straus was wearing a floor-length, dark blue silk tunic gown with a kimono bodice of white lace and matching long sleeves. She had on a pair of lace gloves and a large wide-brimmed hat with flowers and feathers around the crown.

Her husband was equally well dressed. His three-piece suit was dark brown, single-breasted, and was worn open. His matching vest covered a white shirt with a high wing collar, and around his neck was a knotted black tie. His pants were straight-cut and had turn-up cuffs at the ankles.

Across the table sat Benjamin Guggenheim, the wealthiest

man on board except for John Jacob Astor himself. Guggenheim had been speaking with Clive about the game of cricket, but now he turned and listened to Annie. When she finished, he shook his head. "You must be an admirer of Teddy Roosevelt. He's the consummate cowboy."

"Yes, indeed. I think he's the finest president we've ever had."

"Well, he's certainly no Abe Lincoln," Jeanine asserted. She looked up as the waiter began to bring the food, which consisted of lamb, roasted squab, asparagus salad, and pâté de foie gras. Of course waiters were on hand to serve wines of all sorts.

As they began to eat, Guggenheim asked, "What did you mean by that remark, that Roosevelt is no Lincoln?"

Sipping the champagne from the curved goblet in front of her, Jeanine replied, "Why, I simply mean that Lincoln came from the earth, born in a log cabin. It's become almost a requirement in America. A man has to be born in a log cabin."

Clive grinned suddenly. "I read somewhere that one of your presidents was born in a log cabin that he built with his own hands."

A laugh went around the table and Isidor Straus roared heartily. He was a genial man and much attached to his wife. They were, Annie noticed quickly, a loving couple indeed. Mrs. Straus seemed to be constantly reaching out to touch her husband, and at her touch he would always turn to her with warmth in his fine, brown eyes.

"Is your remark derogatory, Miss Quintana? Are you opposed to having wealthy men from good families serve as president?"

Jeanine smiled quickly. "Not at all. I don't believe having money disqualifies a man for public office."

"I'm happy that you think that way," Guggenheim nodded. "It's getting so bad that when a wealthy man wants to run for president, he has to take lessons."

"What sort of lessons?" Clive asked curiously.

"Oh, how to act small! I have a friend who ran for governor of Connecticut. He had never been on a farm in his life, but he had to learn how to go around and shake hands with farmers and talk about pigs and plowing and picking cotton. Things of that nature." He laughed suddenly. "He made quite a spectacle of himself, I'm afraid. It didn't take them long to find him out. A man's what he is, and if he has wealth and position, well, he needs to make the most of it."

The talk took a curious turn. It concerned wealth and the abundance or the lack of it. Annie had never been around really wealthy people and she listened carefully.

The Strauses said little enough. Mrs. Straus remarked once, "It's only God's will, I think, that my husband and I have a surplus. I could as easily have been born in a slum in New York."

"No, my dear, you were fated," Guggenheim said. He added adamantly, "Never put yourself down because you have wealth. It's not a sin to be wealthy." He looked over at Annie, saying, "The Bible's full of wealthy men such as Solomon. He was the wealthiest man of his day, was he not?"

"Yes, sir, he was."

"Well, there you are."

Annie felt constrained to add, "But at the end of his life when he added up what it had meant, he said of his money that it was merely vanity." She saw this displeased Guggenheim.

Clive said quickly, "Good for you, Annie. I suppose that'll settle the issue."

Guggenheim was combative, and finally he turned to address Clive, who had entered the argument on Annie's side. "Are you a Christian then, Winters?"

Clive Winters suddenly grew silent. All the eyes of those at the table fell on him, especially Annie's. Finally he nodded and said, "Yes, sir, I am—I mean to say, I was."

Jeanine turned to look at him as if his words had touched a nerve. She said nothing, but there was a look in her eyes that Annie did not miss. Clive looked up then and said, "I've been a follower of Jesus Christ since I was seventeen years old. I've gotten away from my first love for God, but I purpose to turn my life over to Him completely."

"Oh, I'm so glad!" Annie said impulsively.

There was a silence at the table, and then the ship's orchestra struck up a ragtime tune and the moment passed. Annie, however, saw that Clive's words had meant something to Jeanine, and she resolved to talk to her about it later.

After the luncheon was over, Annie went down into the third-class section of the ship, where she found Kathleen, as usual, struggling to keep the children occupied.

"Here, let me have that big boy of yours," she said. Snatching Michael up, Annie began to entertain him by joggling him on her knee. His head wobbled from side to side as he grinned tooth-lessly and chortled happily. "He's such a happy boy," she giggled.

"Just like his father," Kathleen answered quickly. Tears came to her eyes and she dashed them away. "I can't help it. I'm sorry, Miss Annie."

"That's all right. I understand."

"It was so hard to lose him. We had such a short time together."

"Why, he's not lost."

Kathleen looked up quickly. "Not lost? What do you mean, Miss Annie?"

"I mean when something's lost, you don't know where it is, but you know where your husband is. You told me he was a Christian."

"That he was."

"Then he's in heaven with the holy angels and all of God's people who have been gathered home. One day you'll go there and you'll meet him again. So he's not lost."

"But how can I be sure? I've not been a good girl, not really."

Kathleen's honesty touched something in Annie. She began to talk to her about Jesus and soon found out that the young woman only had a limited concept of God. She had no real concept of salvation. Annie, holding Michael, explained God's wonderful plan of salvation. She saw that Kathleen was listening carefully, her lips parted. It was a message she had never heard before.

"So I need to call upon God?"

"Yes, indeed. Ask Jesus to come into your heart, then you'll never be lonely."

And so Kathleen O'Fallon bowed her head and the two women prayed together. The children were quiet, which was a miracle, and soon Annie said, "Now, did you ask the Lord to forgive your sins?"

"Yes, I did, Miss Annie."

"And did you ask Him to save you?"

"Yes, I did. Am I saved now?"

"Indeed you are. You did exactly what I did when I was a little girl. Now you have to learn how to let God take over your life."

Annie stayed with Kathleen all afternoon. They read the Bible together, and it was a happy young woman who embraced Annie when she finally left, saying, "I feel different. I still will miss Sean, but I know I'll see him again. When I get to America, I won't know how to go on with God."

"I'll help you. You'll find a church, and there'll be people there

who will love you. That's the way it is. You're a part of the family
of God now."

★　★　★　★

The bridge was dark except for the glow of the instrument
lights. Captain Smith stood beside First Officer Murdoch, listening as he read off their progress. "Well, sir, we made 386 miles on
the twelfth, 519 miles on the thirteenth, and today, the fourteenth,
we've made 546 miles."

"Very good, First Officer."

Murdoch chewed his lower lip. "I'm worried about the ice,
sir."

"We're well out of the floes. There'll just be a few isolated
bergs. Put two good men up in the lookout with sharp eyes."

"Aye, sir. I'll attend to it." Murdoch waited until the captain
left and then appointed his two best men to serve as lookouts. "Be
sharp!" he said.

"Yes, sir!" they both said simultaneously, then ascended to
their perch.

As soon as they were seated, drawing their black wool coats
about them, they began to talk. They lit up cigarettes, and one tall
sailor named Jenkins said, "I'd rather be down below in my bunk
catching some shut-eye."

"Ah, it's a short watch," his companion replied. "Just think
about when we get to New York. What a time we'll have."

The two talked for some time. They rested as comfortably as
possible against the sharp wind. They had both been to New York
before and planned their good times as the *Titanic* moved relentlessly through the dark waters.

★　★　★　★

Radio man Jack Phillips held out a piece of paper to Lee Maddox. Etched lines of three upright creases appeared between his
eyes, and he said gruffly, "Well, there's another one, Lee."

Maddox took the piece of paper. "More ice?"

"Yes. That's six messages warning us about ice, and I don't
think the captain has seen any of them."

"Oh yes, he has. I took one of them up. I gave it to Officer
Murdoch. I saw him turn and give it to the captain."

"Well, if they've heard about it, they don't seem to be doing anything to act on it."

Maddox scratched his chin thoughtfully. He was a tall man of thirty with hazel eyes and a mustache of which he was unreasonably proud. He stroked it now and shrugged, "That's right. We're almost going full speed. I heard one of the officers say that we ought to be headed away from the ice fields."

"The way I hear it," Phillips said, "we're trying to set a record." He settled back and began to copy a message that was coming in over the radio. Maddox turned and left the radio room, going at once to the bridge. It was ten o'clock and First Officer Murdoch arrived at the bridge at the same time. He looked up at Maddox and snapped, "Well, what is it, Maddox?"

"Another ice warning, sir."

"I *can* read!" Murdoch barked, glaring at the radio man.

Maddox, who was unaccustomed to such sharpness, turned away and thought, *Murdoch is worried. He's nervous. I wonder if he knows something that I don't.*

The helmsman who stood with his hand gripped to the wheel had taken all this in. His name was Johnson, and he was an excellent helmsman and an excellent sailor. Ordinarily he would not think of questioning any action that his officers thought they should take, but now he said, "Sir, does the captain know about all this ice?"

Murdoch swiveled his head and glared at the sailor. "You just take care of the steering, Johnson! Let the captain take care of running the ship."

"Aye, sir."

Murdoch positioned himself, peering out over the green-gray waves that lapped at the side of the ship. The thought of an iceberg frightened him badly. He was not afraid of those he could see, but he had seen huge bergs with only a few inches showing, and he knew that such a berg could rip the bottom out of a ship. His brother had died at sea from such an encounter, and now Murdoch longed to reason with the captain to change course. He was a man of tradition, however, schooled in the etiquette of command on the high seas. It was not the first officer's place to bring his captain to any kind of judgment—especially a captain like Smith. Gritting his teeth, he thought, *I'll be glad when we get to New York. I'm beginning to hate this trip.*

★　★　★　★

Jeanine, Clive, and Annie entered the Café Parisien earlier that evening. The three had agreed to try it, and as soon as they stepped in, Clive said, "Why, you can imagine yourself at a sidewalk cafe on a Parisian boulevard."

"Yes, you can," Jeanine agreed. She seemed somewhat freer in spirit, and as the three sat down, she looked around, saying, "How many times have I sat down at a little place like this in Paris?"

There was a casual atmosphere about the place, and over in the corner of the room a string trio was playing softly. Ordinarily it was not a place where the wealthier passengers would eat, but rather a place to come between meals or after dinner. It was a favorite spot for the younger set in the first class, or those pretending to be young, such as a group of women that now laughed loudly over some joke three tables away from where the three sat watching them. Annie looked up at the ivy-covered trellises and then at the wicker chairs, which set the style for the place, and said, "I like this better than the Ritz."

"So do I," Clive said. He looked at a menu that a steward brought and said, "Look, they've got roasted squab on wilted cress."

"What's that?" Annie said.

"Squab? Didn't you notice it at lunch? It's simply a small game bird. Pretty common in Europe, and, of course, cress is watercress."

Clive ordered the squab and so did Annie, while Jeanine ordered calvados-glazed roast duckling with applesauce.

As they were eating, Annie said suddenly, "I'll be glad to get back to the States and get some plain roast beef. Or if I were back home at my parents', I could get the best steak you ever saw right off the cow that was walking around that morning."

The other two grinned at her. "I know what you mean," Clive grinned. "I get hungry for good, plain food, too. Seems like anything rich like this gets old quickly."

The three sat there leisurely eating French vanilla ice cream for dessert and spoke of unimportant things. Clive had been listening to Annie talk about her childhood, and he said abruptly, "Tell me about your conversion, Annie."

"My conversion?"

"Yes. How did you find God?"

Annie shot a glance at Jeanine, expecting her to make a light remark, but she saw that Jeanine was simply toying with her coffee, her eyes down. "I'm afraid I don't have a very dramatic testimony, Clive," she said.

"Tell me about it."

"Well, I've always envied those people who had dramatic testimonies."

Clive suddenly laughed aloud. "You mean like sixteen-car wrecks and an invitation?"

Annie could not help but smile. "Something like that. I always felt envious of people who had experienced that sort of thing."

"But you didn't?"

"No. It was very simple. I was only twelve. I'd been in church all my life and heard the Gospel, but for some reason one Sunday morning the pastor preached on the love of Jesus Christ. It was a simple sermon. I can't remember any of the details. He just talked about how Jesus loved people, how He went about healing those that were sick, comforting those that were in trouble, and suddenly I began to cry. And when the invitation was given, I knew I had to have that love in my life. So I went forward and the pastor prayed with me; he asked me to pray and I did." Suddenly tears came into Annie's eyes, and her voice was not steady as she said, "Ever since that morning, there hasn't been a day when Jesus hasn't been with me."

The sound of laughter came tinkling from other tables. There was a hum of voices, but the three of them sat there silently. Clive was examining Annie with a warm regard, and suddenly Jeanine said, "I think that's sweet, Annie. I wish my life had been like yours. You're the best woman I've ever known."

The unexpected compliment brought a flush to Annie's throat. "Why, that's too much, Jeanine."

"No, it's not," Jeanine insisted. She kept her eyes down and her face half turned away. "I've been suspicious of Christians for a long time. I hired you so that I could prove that you were a fraud and a hypocrite, and I've tried to make you lose whatever religion you claim to have." She looked up suddenly, and to the shock of both Clive and Annie, tears glistened in her lovely violet eyes. She started to speak but her voice broke, and without a word she got up and left the table, dabbing at her eyes with a handkerchief.

"I've never seen her like that, Clive."

"Neither have I."

The two sat there silent for a moment, and then Clive reached over and took Annie's hand. "I think this is Jeanine's time, Annie. God is speaking to her. I'm sure of it."

"Let's pray."

The three loud women across the room became aware of the two who clasped hands with their heads bowed. One of them began to laugh, but she broke it off sharply, then turned away. Others noticed the two also, including the steward. His name was Lee Watson. He was himself a fine Christian man. He longed to say a word of encouragement to the two and almost did, but then thought, *It is not my place. Anyway, they don't appear to need help.*

★ ★ ★ ★

At eleven o'clock Jack Phillips received an ice warning from the *Californian*. It was a message sent by Cyril Evans, and the tenor of the message was that the ice seemed to be more prominent.

Jack Phillips was sick of the reception he had gotten from his officers. It was not that he was upset with Evans, but he was upset with his own captain and with the first officer. He said roughly, "I don't want to hear about any more ice! You can shut up, Evans! I'm busy at important things. I'm working the wireless station at Cape Race."

On board the *Californian*, Cyril Evans grew angry. He ripped off his headphones, shut off his radio, and said angrily, "Well, if that's the way you feel about it, you can see how many more warnings you get from me!" He turned and left, then put the matter out of his mind. Back in the radio room of the *Californian*, the radio was silent, and Cyril Evans was quickly asleep in his bed.

★ ★ ★ ★

"So she said to me, 'You think you're a real man, do ya? Well, we'll see about that!'"

Mike Taylor drew his pea coat closer around him and grinned at his companion. "Harold, you're too young to have had all the experiences with women that you brag about."

Harold Simpkins, a native of Bristol, nudged Taylor in the ribs. "You think that, do you, boy? Well, when we get back you and me will go to Liverpool. I'll show you a time there. Why, I know a little blond bird just for you. . . ."

Simpkins continued to boast about his amorous exploits for the next ten minutes. He was interrupted suddenly when Mike Taylor came upright and stared out with disbelief at the gray waters ahead. It was dark, but he saw clearly the huge berg that loomed ahead. Grabbing the voice tube, he screamed, "Berg ahead! Berg dead ahead! Below there! Berg dead ahead!"

Simpkins began screaming also. "Iceberg right ahead!"

On the bridge, First Officer Murdoch stood stock-still, shock running over him, for he saw the huge mass of ice almost at once. Instantly he called out, "Ship's engine stop! Full speed astern!" At the same time, he watched as the berg seemed to loom ahead, and then he called for a hard turn to port. He stood there watching, willing the huge ship to turn, which it did not seem to do.

Finally First Officer Murdoch felt the *Titanic* answer the helm, but at the same time her forty-six thousand tons slammed into the wall of ice.

Murdoch breathed a sigh of relief. "We missed it! A little damage, but not bad." He spoke his words aloud and saw that Johnson, the helmsman, was wiping the perspiration from his face.

"It was a bad 'un, sir. But I think we're all right."

★ ★ ★ ★

Down below, Annie was in her cabin. She was still awake and had been praying for Jeanine. Suddenly she felt something odd. She could not define it, but the deck underneath her feet was trembling, and running to the porthole, she was shocked to see a wall of white ice.

"An iceberg!" she whispered hoarsely. The ship was bumping along and she heard metal creaking, and the thought came into her mind, *It's like a kiss of death.*

Annie did not know much about ships, but as she watched the ship scrape along the berg, she suddenly remembered Jeanine's words. "Not even God himself could sink this ship." The words touched her with a chill and she stood there, unable to think clearly. She could only pray, "God be with us."

CHAPTER TWELVE

"I'LL BE WITH HIM THIS DAY IN PARADISE...."

★ ★ ★ ★

Thomas Andrews, the managing director of the construction of the *Titanic*, had handsome, classic features and was a man of iron control, but when he traced the outline of the *Titanic* structure on a large blueprint, his hand was shaking. He took great pride in the ship, as he did all the ships he built, but this one he considered the crown achievement of his career thus far. Now he looked up with tortured eyes and said, "Captain Smith, the ship cannot survive. Too many of the watertight compartments have been ruptured." His voice broke slightly, and he cleared his throat, then added, "She is going down."

For a moment Captain Smith did not seem to understand the solemn words of Andrews. He stared at him with incomprehension and then, finally, as the truth broke upon him, whispered, "How long?"

"One hour. Perhaps two."

At that moment only Andrews, Captain Smith, and Johnson, the helmsman, knew the ship was doomed—except for those in the lower sections where the water was already flooding in.

Captain Smith seemingly could not function. Actually, he did nothing. He did not order the boats to be lowered until an hour after the collision. Perhaps the reason was that, as he stood there exchanging horrified glances with Thomas Andrews, both men knew there were not enough boats to carry all the passengers of the *Titanic*. The regulation required ships of more than ten thousand tons to carry sufficient boats for 962 persons.

The *Titanic*, originally designed for forty-eight lifeboats, was fitted with only twenty with a rated capacity of 1,178. Four of these, however, were collapsible and only of marginal use. Smith was a good mathematician, and as he counted the passengers and crew and measured those numbers against the boats, he knew that at least thirty-seven standard size boats filled to capacity would be necessary to save those on board. He was also aware that there had never been a lifeboat drill, nor were any of the crews assigned to any specific boat. The passengers would be of no help. Captain Smith realized that his career was at an end.

★   ★   ★   ★

Jeanine was lying down staring at the ceiling, her mind still troubled, when a rapid tapping on her door brought her sharply upright. She had undressed, and going to the door in her nightgown, she whispered, "Who is it?"

"It's me—Annie. Let me in, Jeanine!"

As Jeanine slipped the lock, Annie came rushing into her bedroom. "Quick, Jeanine, get dressed in your warmest clothes."

"What are you talking about?" Jeanine said, staring at her. "What's wrong?"

"It's the ship. We've hit an iceberg. She's going to sink."

"Let the sailors run the ship, Annie. It's not your place—"

At that moment Clive burst in without knocking. "The ship's going down!" he announced without preamble.

"Both of you are crazy!"

"Do you think so?" Clive asked grimly, his face pale. "Look at this." He took a coin out of his pocket, balanced it on end on a table, and said, "Watch." The coin rolled, picked up speed, and fell on the floor. It made a tinkling sound and lay there as the three stared at it. "The stern's going down and you've got to get on a lifeboat."

Jeanine still could not believe the news, but fear suddenly came over her as she saw the bleak expression in Clive Winters' eyes. "All right," she murmured.

"Put on all the warm clothes you have. That water is freezing out there. I'll get life jackets for us."

He moved outside the room swiftly, disappeared, and Jeanine looked around helplessly. "We'll have to take all of our papers with us."

"No," Annie said quietly. "We won't take any of those."

For the first time, Annie had refused to obey Jeanine's instructions. Now she realized that Jeanine was incapable of action. "Come along," she said quietly. "We'll put on the warmest underwear you have. I'll do the same. Then put on your black wool coat."

★　★　★　★

The alarm of the sinking progressed from the upper decks down to the lower decks slowly. There was no command to abandon ship, but the first-class passengers were awakened by the stewards. They were careful to inform them that there was no danger, but the ship had sustained damage. Down below in steerage there was no hint of such imminent danger. Kathleen O'Fallon was sound asleep with her children, Michael and Mary, not knowing that death was quickly approaching.

Jack Phillips looked up to see the captain come into the radio room. "Yes, sir," he saluted. He had already heard the rumors and now was not surprised at the dismayed look on Smith's face.

"Send distress signals at once, Phillips."

"Yes, sir. At once."

He began sending the distress signals almost immediately. The closest ship was the *Californian*, but the radio there had been shut off, and Cyril Evans, who might have been at his task even at this unusual hour, would have received the call. But the radio was dead and Evans was sound asleep.

★　★　★　★

Clive soon returned with three life jackets. "You have on your warmest clothing?"

"Yes."

Clive stared at Jeanine and saw that her face was pale. He could hardly hear her answer. "Are you all right, Jeanine?"

Jeanine could not answer him. She was petrified with fright. "We're all going to die, Clive," she whispered. Her eyes were pools of despair and seemed to be sunk far back into their sockets.

"No. There are lifeboats. Come along."

As the three of them reached the deck, it became obvious that something was happening. As he shoved his way forward, using his strength, one of the officers they did not know said, "Women and children only. No men, I'm afraid, sir."

Clive stared at the man, then said, "Very well. Take these two women."

The Strauses were there, and Isidor Straus was urging his wife to get on board.

Annie and Clive both turned as the woman said, "No, husband. We've been together too long. I will stay with you. Come now."

As the two turned away, Clive whispered, "That is some courage that woman has. Now, both of you, get into the boat."

Annie said, "No, I can't."

Both Jeanine and Clive stared at her. "You've got to get on the boat, Annie," Clive said quickly.

"No. Kathleen's downstairs with the children. Look around. You don't see any steerage passengers. I'm going to get her." She ignored Clive's call and heard Jeanine cry out, "Come back, Annie! Don't go down there!"

Already, walking was difficult because of the tilt of the ship. The decks were crowded as people fought to get at the lifeboats. She turned down the end of the corridor and began the descent. When she got down to one of the lower levels, she was shocked to see a steel grill across the opening. People were on the other side crying to be let out, but a steward stood there, his face pasty white, saying nothing.

"What are you doing?" Annie cried. "Open the door and let them out!"

"I can't. They're not permitted on the upper deck."

White-hot anger flooded through Annie. She slapped the steward's face and said, "You fool! Open that door! What's a rule or regulation? Give me the key!"

The steward's lips trembled and so did his hands as he reached into his pocket and extracted a key. "Your responsibility," he muttered, then turned and fled.

Annie unlocked the gate, and as it sprang back she was almost knocked to the deck by the stampede. Men and women, some holding children, some holding their suitcases, burst forth. She waited until the stampede was by and then hurried down as quickly as she could. She found Kathleen inside her room crying and holding her babies helplessly.

"It's all right, Kathleen," Annie said quickly. "Here, we've got to put the warmest clothes on you, and also on Michael and Mary."

The two women worked quickly. Kathleen was almost useless, but she grew better as Annie assured, "We won't worry about this. The Bible says that God will be with us. When we're in the valley, He's with us. There's also a verse that says something about the waters will not overflow us."

"But what will we do?"

"We'll get you in a lifeboat."

Snatching up Michael, Annie saw to it that Kathleen had Mary firmly in her arms and then said, "Let's go."

With their burdens in their arms, the two women made their way topside. The chaos they encountered was even worse than when Annie had left. She could not get close to the boats.

"Come on. There's another boat down this way that won't be so crowded." She looked out over the water and saw to her horror a boat leaving with only a dozen people in it. "The fools!" she whispered to herself. She did not know that the boat had been commandeered by Sir Cosmo and Lady Duff Gordon. They had simply climbed into the lifeboat along with Lady Duff's secretary and commanded the sailors to lower it. The boat designed for forty left the ship with twelve. They even refused to return to pick up more survivors after the ship went down.

Perhaps the most "dignified" response to the tragedy of the *Titanic* was that of Benjamin Guggenheim. When he realized there would be no escape from the cold waters of death, he went to his stateroom, put on his finest clothing, then went on deck to face his fate. He said to his steward, "I think there is grave doubt that the men will get off. I am willing to remain and play the man's game if there are not enough boats for more than the women and children. I won't die here like a beast. Tell my wife I played the game straight out and to the end. No woman shall be left aboard this ship because Ben Guggenheim is a coward."

Annie could not force her way through the crowd. She heard a voice behind her saying, "What's this, dearie? You can't get on the boat?"

She turned around to see Molly Brown, her florid face tense.

"It's not me. It's Kathleen and her two children."

"Two little ones, is it?" Molly Brown said. "All right. Let me handle this." She lifted her voice in a stentorian cry, "Get out of the way, you fools! There are two children here!"

Her cry rose above the babble of the voices, and miraculously a way opened up for them.

"Come along," Molly ordered. She whispered, "There won't be enough boats."

Annie looked around but could not see Jeanine. *Clive must have gotten her on another boat*, she thought with relief. She waited until Molly and Kathleen were in the boat, then stepped in and took her seat. As the boat lowered toward the water far below, she began to pray for all who would be lost that night.

★   ★   ★   ★

Clive had been waiting to put Jeanine into a boat, but it was filled to capacity. He said quickly, "Come along, there are other boats."

The two fought their way to the next boat, and by sheer strength Clive got Jeanine into a prominent position close to the rail. But then he glanced around and saw a woman with a small boy struggling to fight her way through the mob. "Wait right here, Jeanine," he said grimly. "I'll go help that woman with the child. Just step in the boat when the officer tells you to board."

Clive made his way through the crowd, and when he reached the woman, he saw that her eyes were glazed with fear. "Come along now," he said, "I'll see you to the boat."

Turning, he felt her pressing against him, and shoving men aside, he forged forward. He reached a point midway through the crowd when a hulking man in a dark suit loomed ahead. "Give way," Clive shouted. "There's a woman and child here!"

The big man was half-crazed with panic. He turned and struck Clive in the forehead with a massive fist. The force of the blow drove Clive to the deck, and his head was struck with such force that he lost consciousness.

The noise of shouts and screams came flowing back as Clive became aware that he was being trampled. Confused, he struggled to his feet, and then his mind cleared. His gaze swept the deck, and he could see that the ship was tilted at an extreme angle. He saw also that the lifeboat was in the water and was being rowed away from the ship. He could not see Jeanine but thought, *Thank God she made it!*

Clive knew he was doomed, but instinct drove him. He began to go toward the bow. The ship tilted more and more, and inside some of the staterooms they could hear tables rolling and dishes falling. Suddenly Clive started and cried out, "Jeanine! I thought you were on the boat!"

"I went back to my cabin to get my jewels."

Clive stared at her with shock but knew talk was useless. "Come along. We'll get you on one."

It was too late. The boats were all gone and the ship was now tilted at an acute angle.

"We've got life jackets," Jeanine said.

"They won't do any good," Clive murmured. "That water is freezing. Nobody could live more than a few minutes in that kind of water—half an hour at the most."

Jeanine seemed to be paralyzed. Her mind was chaotic, and her face was broken into lines that had not existed before. She reached out blindly, and Clive put his arms around her.

Clive's mind was working rapidly. He murmured, "We've got to find a way to keep you from freezing in the water, Jeanine."

"How can I do that without a boat?"

Clive suddenly straightened up and said, "Thank you, Lord!"

"What is it, Clive?" Jeanine cried.

"Just thought of something. Follow me!"

They had to go against the grain because everybody was moving toward the bow. The stern was already under, and the water was lapping over it. It was only a matter of minutes now. When they were halfway down the ship, almost to where the water was at their feet, Clive said, "Stay right here."

Jeanine shivered and tried not to look at the sea. All she could think of was death, and the idea of the cold depths paralyzed her with fear. Suddenly there was a clattering and the door opened. Clive was shoving a large barrel some feet high toward her.

He ripped off the top, saying, "Here, Jeanine, get in here."

"What are you talking about?"

"You've got to get in this barrel. It will float and you can stay dry in here." When he saw she didn't comprehend, he simply picked her up and put her inside. "Now," he said, "this was a beer barrel and it probably stinks like beer, but it will save your life, Jeanine. When the ship goes down, you sit down. Be sure you sit down or the barrel will tip over. I'm going to tie a canvas over the top so the waves won't wash over the top and sink the barrel.

You've got to stay dry until help comes. Do you understand that?"

Jeanine was in the barrel. She stared around wildly. "But what about you?"

"Don't worry about me." Actually this was the only barrel Clive could find. He had spent some time with one of the stewards who had shown him around the ship, and he had been amazed by the vast amount of alcoholic beverages. He had seen row after row of bottles of wine, champagne, and liquor of all kinds, but also barrels of beer. Many of them had been emptied already on the short voyage.

Now Clive looked at Jeanine and said, "I think God put this into my mind, Jeanine. He wants you to live. Now I'll go get some canvas and line."

Jeanine felt the tilt of the deck, and by the time Clive returned with his arms full of canvas, she knew he was giving his life for her. "I can't leave you! You'll die here!"

Clive was as calm as a man could be. He said, "I'm ready to meet the Lord, Jeanine. You're not. You must live, and you must take Christ as your Savior. You must do it now."

Jeanine listened as Clive began to speak of how to find God. She was weeping freely, and finally he put his arms around her and kissed her. "Remember, there was one man who loved you more than life itself. Find Jesus, Jeanine!"

Jeanine stared at him, and then his strong hands pushed her down. She sat down flat and put her arms around her knees as everything went dark. Clive wrapped the canvas around the top in three layers and bound it tightly. "I was always good at knots," he murmured, smiling grimly.

He began to work the barrel down until the cold water lapped around the base. Slowly he moved it until it was half-covered, and then the buoyancy took hold and it rose. "Good-bye, Jeanine—I love you!" he shouted, then maneuvered it over the side. The waves took it, washing it away from the sinking ship.

Clive Winters stood alone, watching the barrel bob on the choppy waters. He was calm and suddenly remembered what a minister had once said in a sermon long ago: *God will not give you dying grace this morning—for you don't need it, you're not dying. But when your hour comes to die, God will give you grace. Of that you may be certain.*

And it was true! Clive stood straight, his eyes on the barrel that was now almost invisible—and felt no fear. *I'll be with Him this day in Paradise,* he thought, and a faint smile came to his lips.

★ ★ ★ ★

Annie Rogers stood on board the *Carpathia.* She had been taken aboard at dawn, and her chief concern had been for Kathleen and the children. It took all of her strength to keep the younger woman from breaking down completely.

Now she said as she held Michael on her lap, "You see. You're all right, Kathleen. You'll be in America soon. We'll see that Michael and Mary have a good home."

"Oh, Annie, what would I have done if it hadn't been for you! I'd be dead with all the rest of them!"

Annie believed that Clive and Jeanine were dead. They had not been picked up by the crew of the *Carpathia,* and now Annie's heart was saddened and numb with grief at the loss of these two who had meant so much to her.

She finally went to her bunk and lay down, but sleep would not come. "Oh, Jeanine . . . Jeanine!" she moaned. "Why did you have to die?"

She didn't know how long she was there, but after a time, a knock came and a sailor stepped in. "Captain says come topside, miss."

She went up and found Captain Rostron. She had spoken to him before, telling him of her admiration. He had brought his ship through ice, dodging the bergs at full speed to rescue the survivors. After she had been on board, he had asked her gently, "Did you lose a husband?"

"No, but two dear friends."

"We're still searching," Captain Rostron had said. "But I can offer no hope."

Now as Annie came up on the deck, she saw Rostron standing by the side. He pulled her to the rail and pointed down. "Look!"

Annie looked over the side and to her astonishment saw Jeanine. The boat was almost even with the deck, and Jeanine cried out, "Annie—Annie!"

Soon the two women were in a cabin, and Jeanine was pouring out her story. Amidst tears, Annie listened, with her heart full for the man she had grown to admire.

Jeanine was shivering, although she was now in a warm cabin and bundled in blankets. She told the story of how Clive had saved her, then said, "He gave his life for me, Annie. He loved me that much." She talked for a long time about Clive, and then she looked at Annie and whispered, "When I was in that barrel with death all around me, I could hear the cries of those who were dying, and all I could think of was that Clive could have saved himself, but he didn't. He saved me."

"He was a loving man. He loved you greatly, Jeanine. You'll always have that."

Jeanine bowed her head and the tears flowed freely. She looked up and her lips trembled. "While I was tossed around by the waves, I was crying over Clive, and suddenly I began to think of Jesus. I thought of all the Scripture you had read me about how He died on the cross, and suddenly in the midst of death He seemed to be saying, 'I loved you enough to die for you.'"

"Oh, Jeanine, how wonderful!"

"I began to pray, Annie," Jeanine whispered. "And I told Jesus every wrong thing in my life, and I asked Him to fill that blank space that's been there for so long."

Jeanine looked at Annie, and there was a long silence, and then Jeanine drew a deep breath and said, "I've led the worst life any woman could lead, but I promised Jesus I'd give Him my life to use. I'm going to serve Him," she pledged, "as long as I live, any way He commands."

The two women joyfully embraced, and Annie knew a new life was about to begin for Jeanine Quintana.

PART THREE

AFRICA

★ ★ ★ ★

CHAPTER THIRTEEN

JEB FINDS A PLACE

★ ★ ★ ★

August had brought a searing heat to New York, and the summer of 1912 was one everyone would look back on with awe. On one of those hot Sunday mornings, Annie walked along Washington Street toward Kathleen O'Fallon's apartment, feeling the heat that seemed to melt her from the inside out. She was wearing a plain brown dress that clung to her, and drawing a damp handkerchief from her pocket, she mopped at her face. Overhead the sun was pasted in the sky like a huge yellow wafer, and even the horses passing her seemed to stagger from the force of the heat.

Passing by a group of children playing stickball despite the glaring sunshine, Annie smiled, thinking, *I guess kids would play in any kind of weather—even on the North Pole on top of the ice.* Turning down Thirty-second Avenue, a horrible memory of the *Titanic* going down leaped into her mind, and for a moment she closed her eyes, trying to blot out the scene. She had endured a recurrent series of frightening images of that terrible time, some that would wake her up in the middle of the night, and the few months that had passed since the tragedy had not mitigated the brilliant, flashing images.

The rattle of a riveter's gun startled her, and she twisted her head abruptly to look up at the towering skeleton of steel—a skyscraper that was rising out of the earth reaching for the sky. Annie shook her head, for she disliked skyscrapers intensely. She had grown up in a place where the eye could rest on distant vistas with nothing but land and trees and sky and clouds. To be buried now in the canyons of New York had grown more unpleasant the longer she stayed. The advent of the skyscraper built of steel frames meant that the windows in the new buildings could be larger, and at night sometimes the glare of the city lights depressed her even more for some reason. She had been reading some of the reformers who viewed the struggle between sunlight and gaslight as being symbolic of the struggle between vice and honesty. One of them, Maxim Gorky, in his visit to New York had said in a speech that Annie had heard: "At first it seems attractive, but in this city when one looks at light enclosed in transparent prisons of glass, one understands that here light, like everything else, is enslaved. It serves gold, it is for gold, and is inimically aloof from people."

As Annie moved rapidly down the street, the heat of the sidewalk almost like a griddle radiating heat, she thought of how she had spent her time since returning from England. It had been fortunate for her in a way that Kathleen had been in such great need. *It was like three babies instead of two*, Annie thought with a smile, for Kathleen had not a clue as to what to do with herself. Annie had thrown herself into finding a place to live and had spent her earnings on the project until Mark Winslow had heard about the situation from Jeb. Mark had insisted on paying the expenses for the young woman and her two babies and also on financing Kathleen's new venture—learning to use a typewriter.

Annie smiled again as she turned into the brownstone structure that had once been a mansion but had been converted to a rooming house when the neighborhood had gone downhill. Stepping inside, she mounted a sweeping stairway with carvings adorning the banister to the second floor. Turning to the right, she knocked on the door and it opened at once.

"Oh, I'm so glad you've come, Annie!" Kathleen smiled. "Guess what's happened?"

"I have no idea," Annie said, stepping into the room. "Well, what is it?"

"It's James Riley. He's offered me a job."

"James Riley? He's the young man from the newspaper, isn't he?"

"Yes!" Kathleen said, and excitement gleamed in her light blue eyes. "He came by yesterday and asked if I would like a job, and I told him yes." Two lines appeared between Kathleen's eyes, and a worried expression flickered across her face. "Do you think it's wrong, Annie? I mean, I don't know him all that well."

"Why, I don't see how it could be. He seems to be a fine man," Annie assured her.

"Oh, he is! He is! And he just loves Michael and Mary. He stayed over an hour playing with them yesterday before he left."

"Well, I think you need all the friends you can get, and Mr. Riley certainly seems like a nice man."

James Riley had appeared at the doorway of Kathleen's apartment seeking an interview. He was finding all the survivors of the *Titanic* with the intent of doing a series of stories for his paper, the *New York Times*. Annie had been favorably impressed with the man who was only in his mid-thirties, but his bright, cheerful face made him seem even younger. She smiled now to reassure Kathleen. "I think it will be fine."

Annie thought to herself, *I'm so glad Kathleen seems to have found a good job. But it would be wonderful if Kathleen could marry a good man who would be a husband to her and a father to the children. A woman needs help in this world.* Aloud, she said, "Well, it ought to be a good sermon this morning."

As always, Annie's approval was highly important to Kathleen. She had clung to her new friend constantly, and now she said, "Come on in and play with Michael. He's been crying for you for an hour."

"All right. I'll see to that young man. . . ."

★   ★   ★   ★

The sermon had been a very stirring one. The church had been so crowded that she and Jeb had been forced to be separated from Kathleen. She had whispered to Jeb that Kathleen had a job now. Jeb had whispered back, "At a newspaper, you say?"

"Yes. And with a good future. I just wish she could find a good husband now."

"Well, she's a beautiful young woman and has two beautiful children." He nudged Annie with his elbow and said solemnly, "Save a man a heap of trouble not having to fool around having his own children. A pair of them ready-made."

Annie gave Jeb a startled glance and saw the humor in his brown eyes. "You're just *awful!*" she whispered.

After the service the group separated, for Kathleen was never comfortable being away from her children. Mrs. Morgan, her landlady, had kept the children, but still, she said, "I want to get home." Kathleen smiled. "I'll see you both later."

"How does lunch strike you?" Jeb asked as they walked away.

"Strikes me fine. Where would you like to eat?"

"Some place cheap and good."

"How about Luigi's?"

"That's a good idea. Come along."

The two made their way to the small restaurant on Fifteenth Avenue where they had often gone. The proprietor, a burly man with flashing brown eyes and a head full of black curls, greeted them with a broad smile. "Ah, you've a come to have lunch with Luigi!"

"Bring us the best you've got in the house, Luigi," Jeb said grandly when he seated them at the table.

"I know. Spaghetti."

"That's right. Nobody makes it like you do."

"And no wine. Right?"

"That's right."

Luigi shook his head. "Spaghetti no taste good without wine. Why you no drinka wine?"

"Well, we don't drink any alcohol because we're Christians."

Luigi stared at them. "I'm a Christian, too! I go to mass every Sunday, but I drinka wine. Are you saying I can't be a Christian and drinka wine?"

"Oh no!" Annie broke in quickly. "He didn't mean that. It's just sort of a custom with our people."

"Funny sort of custom," Luigi mumbled. "You're missing a lot."

"Well, I suppose you're right," Jeb said. "But I guess we'll just have tea."

After Luigi left, Annie said, "It'd be hard to explain our feelings about alcohol to an Italian. I think they drink wine like water over there."

"I suppose that's true. When you get to Africa, you'll probably find the natives there drinking some kind of wine. Will you try to break them of that habit?"

"I don't think I'll be in a position for a long time to lay down any laws. If I can just tell them about Jesus and get them to see how He loved them, that's all I can hope for."

Jeb leaned back and studied the young woman. He was constantly surprised at how her face was a mirror that changed so often. Laughter danced in her eyes at times, and a healthy pride showed in her demeanor. She was a woman of integrity and determination. Despite her mildness, he knew she had a stubborn spirit set against the world's standards. Right now her face was in repose, and she had an expression that pleased him as he tried to find a name for it. "What are you thinking about?" he asked.

"Oh, nothing much." She suddenly leaned forward and put her hand on his—an unusual gesture for her. "I don't think you know how much you've done for Kathleen and how much I appreciate it."

The pressure of her hand on his was warm, and Jeb wanted to clasp it with his own but did not. "Why, I haven't done anything."

"Yes, you have. You went to Mark Winslow and he did something. If you hadn't told him, he would never have helped her."

"I wish I could do more."

Annie withdrew her hand and studied him carefully. He had a lean face and a prominent, dented nose. The large black horn-rimmed glasses he wore sometimes drew attention away from his eyes. They made him look bookish, but she knew he was very athletic and strong. In fact, he had won several prizes at running races, although he never spoke of it.

"I'm all through with my studies," Jeb said as soon as Luigi had brought the spaghetti and a salad.

Annie watched as he wound up long strands of it on his fork expertly, something she could never manage to do.

"I'll have to go to work soon."

"What will you do?"

"Don't know." He laughed at Annie as she tried to bite off a long strand of spaghetti. "Look. You do it like this. Put your fork in here, your spoon here. . . ."

Annie tried diligently but just did not have the knack for it. "I'll just have to gobble it down and bite it off the best way I can," she finally admitted ruefully. "It's so good, though. And I don't suppose anyone's watching except you."

Jeb ate for a while, listening as Annie told him about her activities, mostly going around looking for a sponsor from one of the mission boards.

"You haven't had any success at all?"

"No. Not a bit."

"Why don't you let Mark Winslow help you? I'm sure he'd be glad to."

It was not the first time Jeb had suggested this. He had told her often that Mark Winslow helped many budding young missionaries. His heart was in foreign missions, and it delighted him to be able to have a part in it.

"If you only knew, Jeb," Annie said slowly, "how tempting that is! It would be so easy, and I'm sure Mr. Winslow would do exactly as you say."

"Why not do it, then?"

"I just can't."

"Why not?"

Annie toyed with her spaghetti with her fork for a moment without speaking, then she shrugged her shoulders. "It's just that I feel that God has another way for me. I believe He wants to get me to Africa, but I just don't know what His plan is yet."

"Well, if you change your mind, I'm sure Mr. Winslow would be happy to help you." Jeb took a sip of tea, then asked, "What about Jeanine? Have you heard from her again?"

"Oh yes! She writes very regularly."

"How's she's doing?"

"Very well. I've been pleased."

"You told me she was baptized and had joined a church. What's she doing with herself?"

"Believe it or not, she's in Bible school."

"That'll be a shock for some of the Bible scholars there." Jeb grinned at the thought of Jeanine Quintana studying theology. "She's always so direct, but maybe she's changed her ways."

"I don't think she has, and I don't think she ever will."

"She'll be in trouble, then. When she was in the world, people didn't care much what she said. But now she'll be in churches and talking and moving in a different world altogether. She probably can't afford to be as outspoken."

"I'm not sure about that, Jeb." She sat there thinking of her friend, Jeanine, meditation turning her eyes mild and soft, and then finally said, "I think God uses the natural things that are in a person."

"How do you mean?"

"Well, I mean some people are slow and meditative, and God is going to take that mannerism and use it. Others, like Jeanine, are quick and impulsive. God can use that, too."

"You know, you may have something there. I always think of the apostle John as being sort of a dreamer, a slow chap to move. Although he did try to call fire down from heaven once."

"Yes!" Annie said with an edge in her tone. "I think about Peter. He was always impulsive."

"Always in trouble, too."

"Have to admit that. And Jeanine may have some problems with people who don't understand it, but she'll make it. I can tell from her letters she has a real love for Jesus."

"You two are certainly an odd couple. You're so quiet and gentle, and Jeanine comes on like a bull elephant. Or she did."

"We'll make it. God's going to do something with both of us, but I have no idea what. I know I'll be in Africa, and Jeanine will probably stay here, but God will use us both, even though we're so different. We're all God's people."

"Yes, we are. It'll be interesting," Jeb said slowly, "to see how God works all this out."

★　★　★　★

It was almost a month after this conversation concerning Jeanine that a loud knock sounded on Annie's door. It was just after dusk and she got up wondering, *Who can that be? I'm not expecting anyone.* Opening the door, she was surprised to see Jeb standing there, excitement glowing in his eyes. "Why, Jeb. What are you doing here?"

"I've got news. Can I come in?"

It was unusual for Jeb to ask to come in. Annie's landlady was very strict about gentleman callers. However, Jeb did not wait. He came in at once and turned around to face her. "A wonderful thing has happened, Annie! I've just heard about it, and I rushed right over to tell you."

"What is it, Jeb? Sit down. You're so excited you're about to pop."

"I can't sit down."

Coming over to her, he took her hands almost unconsciously. Annie was somewhat surprised, for Jeb had always been careful not to touch her. However, she saw that he had no thought except for what was in his mind, and she waited to hear what he was so excited about.

"I just heard today from one of the applications that I made, Annie. I've got an offer of a job."

"A job! How wonderful!"

"It's more wonderful than you think!" Jeb suddenly grinned and squeezed her hands. "Listen to this. It's a grant from a university to study the peoples of Africa."

"Africa! You don't mean it! You mean you're going to Africa?"

Jeb laughed and suddenly reached out and gave her a hug. "I'm sorry," he said as he stepped back. "I didn't mean to do that, but I'm so happy."

"It's all right, Jeb. Are you really going to Africa?"

"I really am. And they gave me a choice of the people I'll be working with. Guess which tribe I chose?"

"Why, I have no idea."

"You're not very sharp, then. What tribe have you been talking about for a couple of years?"

Suddenly Annie exclaimed, "The Masai! You're going to study the Masai people!"

"Got it the first time."

"Sit down and tell me all about it," Annie said.

The two talked for over an hour. Mrs. Mulligan, Annie's landlady, passed by the door once to inquire, and Annie said, "Come in and hear the good news, Mrs. Mulligan."

Mrs. Mulligan listened and said, "Oh, you're going all the way to Africa! Why, that's what Miss Annie's been trying to do, and here you're going off before her."

After Mrs. Mulligan left, Jeb turned quiet and rather meditative. Finally he rose and said, "Well, I wanted to tell you the good news."

Annie got up from the divan and walked over to the door with him. She turned to him and said, "I'm so glad for you, Jeb."

"You're not mad because I'm going and you're not?"

"No. I think it's God's plan for you. He hasn't opened the door for me yet."

Jeb had been so filled with excitement, and now that he had told Annie, something new came to him. She stood before him watching his face in that close and personal way that was a manner of hers. He saw her eyes light up and grow warm, and her face changed in a manner that he could not describe. She was everything he had ever longed for in a woman, and the loneliness that always lived in him somehow grew almost insupportable. She was a fragrance and a melody, and the walls that surrounded the two of them suddenly seemed to disappear. He reached out, put his long arms around her, and kissed her. When he drew back he saw her eyes lifted to him, narrow and watchful, but he saw something in them that he had not seen before.

Annie said, "Why did you do that, Jeb?"

"Why, Annie, I think you've known I've cared for you for a long time."

"I . . . I can't think of things like that, Jeb."

Suddenly, after the sweetness of her lips, a bitterness came to Jeb, and he spoke that which had been in his heart but which he had never said aloud. "I think if it were John Winslow, you'd care!"

Annie blinked and her head drew back. "You shouldn't say that. It's not true."

"I think it is," Jeb said. "I had better leave. Good night, Annie."

He left without another word and Annie Rogers stood for a long time looking at the door, her mind reeling at his comment. She turned and went to the window and watched him as he walked down the street, his back stiff, and she tried to convince herself. "No. It's not true! That was just a girlish infatuation." But she did not feel honest saying this, for there had been too many times when she had thought of John Winslow. Not as a young fifteen-year-old thinks of a man, but as a woman thinks of a man whom she might learn to love.

CHAPTER FOURTEEN

JEANINE TAKES CHARGE

★　★　★　★

Christmas was a good time for Annie Rogers. Annie had asked Kathleen to join her in Wyoming for Christmas. Kathleen had refused at first, but Annie had insisted that Michael and Mary would love the ranch.

They left New York and traveled west to Annie's home, and the interval was like a breath of fresh air to her. Her parents and brother were gathered there for the holiday, and she returned again to the joy she had known as a young girl growing up. It was a time of trimming the Christmas tree, exchanging presents, and singing the old Christmas hymns. During those days a sense of refreshment came back to Annie that had been lacking.

She got to spend a lot of time with both sets of her grandparents, Tom and Faith Winslow, and Dan and Hope Winslow, and with many of her cousins who were home for the holidays, too. Cassidy and Serena Winslow were there with their children. Peter and Jolie Winslow brought their three-year-old, Luke, and their one-year-old, Timothy. Annie especially loved little Kimberly Ballard, the four-year-old daughter of Jason and Priscilla Ballard.

She took long rides across the plains, savoring the cold and the snow. In New York City, the snow was dirty after a few hours, stained with the smoke from thousands of chimneys, and all the streets were defiled with the passing of horses still in prominent use in the big city. But out on the plains, as far as one could see, the glistening, crystalline whiteness after a snowfall hurt the eyes and at the same time delighted Annie.

From the moment they had arrived, Annie saw a different side of her brother. Bill was suddenly the perfect gentleman, especially when Kathleen was around. Michael and Mary loved all the extra attention Bill gave them, as well. Bill seemed to glow when Kathleen smiled at something he said or when the children begged him to tell a story or take them for a ride.

One night, when everyone had retired for the evening, Annie joined Kathleen in the guest room. "I hope you are enjoying your stay. I know my family has enjoyed having you here, especially my brother," Annie added with a smile.

Kathleen blushed a deep crimson. "Your brother is so nice to Michael and Mary."

"Just to Michael and Mary?" Annie queried with a grin. "I have never seen him act this nice for other children and certainly not for me. I think he has taken an interest in Michael and Mary's mother."

"You're just saying that," Kathleen protested, while trying unsuccessfully to hide her growing smile.

"Seriously, Kathleen, I think my brother is a wonderful man, and I hope something does happen between the two of you. He needs a good woman in his life, and you need a good man. And Michael and Mary could have a wonderful father." Annie then added, "Besides, we would really be sisters then, and I would have Michael and Mary as my nephew and niece."

"Thank you for being so kind," Kathleen replied sincerely. "I guess I can tell you that Bill has asked me to stay around here for a while to see how things go. I have been praying about it, and I think that God is leading in that direction. I was afraid to tell you, but you have eased my fears now."

Annie gave a small cry of delight and hugged her friend. "It is wonderful to see how God works everything for good for those who love Him and are called according to His purpose. God led me to you, and now He may be leading you to Bill. Let's pray that God will finish what He has started in our lives."

The two friends joined their hearts together in prayer to the One who was lovingly guiding their every footstep.

★   ★   ★   ★

Her family had begged her to stay longer, but after the holidays, it was time to return to New York. Annie's parents had again offered to pay her expenses to Africa, but times were hard for ranchers, and Annie knew there was no money to spare.

"God has a plan for me to get to Africa," she had told her father and mother at the station as they had hugged her. "Don't worry about me. When God has a plan, it will happen."

Annie then turned to her brother and said, "You take care of Kathleen now." She then turned to her friend, hugged her, and whispered, "God will answer our prayers." After giving Michael and Mary a hug, she boarded the train. As she looked back one last time at Bill and Kathleen, Annie knew in her heart that God had brought them together. The look on her brother's face when he looked at Kathleen was the last assurance Annie needed that all would be well.

Returning to New York, she had gone back to the old rounds of seeking an assignment from the missionary societies. She had insisted her health was not a factor, but her past history went against her. It seemed that in addition to this, the funds from all the societies were low.

"Finances are always a problem around Christmas," Reverend Harris Powell told her. He was the president of one of the smaller societies and had tremendous respect for Annie. "I'd send you in a minute if I could send anyone, Annie," he said regretfully. "But money is short right now, and with this recession going on, people seem to be reluctant to support missions."

The first of the year passed, and finally in the middle of January, Annie reached an all-time low. "I can't go on like this," she murmured to herself. "I can't just be a typist all my life. Maybe God intends for me to stay and help the missionary organizations to send others."

The thought saddened her, for she had truly believed all her life that God wanted her on the foreign field. Now she lay awake nights thinking of those who were going, including Jeb Winslow, who was already in Africa. She had heard from him, and his long letter thrilled her but at the same time filled her with a sense of unfulfillment.

The days passed slowly, and very rarely did she hear from Jeanine. Jeanine's letters had been regular at first, but then they had suddenly ceased. Annie had thought that perhaps she had fallen by the wayside. She had no one to talk with about her concern for Jeanine, but she wrote her mother, in whom she confided most things. *I'm afraid that maybe Jeanine found the Christian life too hard. It must be very difficult for those with great wealth, who have everything, to live as the Scripture commands. Perhaps I'm wrong—I hope I am.*

Annie was trudging homeward on a late afternoon in January after a trying day with the mission board, and despite her attempts to keep her spirits up, she was feeling quite depressed. The weather was dreary. Snow had fallen two days earlier but now was nothing but dirty slush in the streets. That which remained on the buildings was speckled with ashes and cinders. A gloom seemed to hang over the entire city as clouds glowered and the cold, wet wind bit to the bone.

Shivering and drawing her coat about her, Annie approached her doorway, dreading another weary night full of regret sitting in her room.

"Annie! There you are!"

Glancing up quickly, Annie saw Jeanine getting out of a taxi in front of her apartment house. She was wearing a dark blue and green plaid woolen cape with white fur around the shoulder collar with a matching fur hat and muff. Her eyes were flashing, and even in the dusk, there was an exuberance about her. Her violet eyes sparkled as she rushed forward and grabbed Annie, almost lifting her off her feet.

"Annie, I've missed you so much! Where have you been? I've been waiting over an hour!"

Annie was shocked at the sight of her former employer. She listened as Jeanine spoke rapidly, and then finally managed to say, "I was working at the mission board. I'm so glad to see you, Jeanine. I haven't heard from you in so long."

"I was wrong not to write you, but I had something going on that I didn't want to even talk about. I wanted to be sure that God was in it."

"Well, come inside. It's freezing out here."

The two women went inside, and as soon as they were in Annie's room, Jeanine said, "Tell me what you've been doing."

"Nothing much. The same as always," Annie said carefully. She was very familiar with Jeanine Quintana's moods, and she saw that the tall woman was almost quivering from the excitement she could hardly contain. "What is it, Jeanine? I can tell something's happened."

"I'll say something has happened!" Jeanine beamed. She

forced herself to quiet down with an effort, then came over and sat down on the divan beside Annie. "I have something to tell you that will probably shock you."

Annie could not help grinning. "You've shocked me enough already, Jeanine. Not again, I hope."

"No," Jeanine laughed. "Not in the old ways. Since I found the Lord, I've been sickened at times at what I did with my life. I've shed a lot of tears over the sinful life I led."

"You mustn't think about that, Jeanine. Put it all behind you. God has forgiven and cleansed you from all that."

"It's hard to do, but I'm trying. Now . . ." Jeanine's eyes gleamed as she reached out and took Annie's hand. "God has been speaking to me for the last month. At first I couldn't believe it. I just thought it was something that was in my mind. Maybe something I just wanted to do, but I've been fasting, and praying, and seeking God, and now I'm *certain* of what it is." She hesitated and then reached out impulsively and hugged Annie so hard that Annie almost lost her breath. Drawing back, she said, "God has called me to be a missionary—to Africa!"

For a moment Annie could not take in what Jeanine had said. It was so far from anything she had imagined that it seemed she had heard wrong. "To Africa?" she asked, staring at the other woman. "Are . . . are you sure?"

"I wasn't at first, but I am now."

"But, Jeanine, it's such a different sort of thing—I mean—"

"I know what you mean. I've been spoiled, and Africa's a difficult and dangerous place, and you're afraid I'll get there and won't be able to take it. Is that it?"

"Well—"

"Why of course that's what you'd think. I thought all that myself. But if God has called me, He'll give me the grace to see it through."

Annie stared unbelievingly. "It sounds so odd to hear you talk like this, Jeanine."

"It's not like me at all, is it? But it's me *now*. I can't tell you what life has been like. I've been studying the Bible day and night. Oh, Annie, I had some wonderful teachers at the Bible school." She laughed suddenly, saying, "They all cautioned me about one thing, and I'm sure you would agree with them."

"What's that, Jeanine?"

"They all said I shouldn't be too impulsive."

"Well, there may be something in that. New Christians do get impulsive sometimes."

Jeanine got up and began pacing the floor. She was utterly serious, and she seemed to be thinking it over, and then she turned and said, "Would you rather try to resurrect the dead or restrain a fanatic? I think it's easier to restrain a fanatic. Some of the faculty, even at the Bible school, seemed to have forgotten the excitement of what it's like to be saved, to be a new Christian, to be a child of God. It's all dull and academic! They get all of their theology out of books, but theology isn't in books, Annie. You know that better than I. It's walking around day by day with Jesus Christ inside. Isn't that right?"

Annie was very impressed with the dramatic change of spirit in Jeanine Quintana. Her violet eyes were glowing, and there was a gentleness and at the same time an insistence in her fine features. "That's right, Jeanine. I'm just saying that sometimes young Christians forget that there's a time to be cautious."

"Well, you can be cautious, and I'll be uncautious. Is there such a word?"

Annie could not help but laugh. "There is now. You just used it. Now sit down again and tell me all about it. Don't leave out anything."

The conversation lasted until suppertime, then the two went out and ate at Luigi's. Jeanine ate and talked with her mouth full at times, waving her fork around, and Annie sat quietly in shock and amazement at the difference. This was not the old Jeanine Quintana. One could never mistake the Spirit of the Lord that was in this woman!

"I'll tell you what we're going to do," Jeanine said. "You still haven't found anybody to sponsor you to the mission field, have you?"

"No. Not yet."

"Well, *I'm* going to sponsor you. You and I are going to Africa. I'm not even going to the mission boards to ask for support. God has given me plenty of money. He has given me a call, and I believe He's put the two of us together."

Instantly Annie seemed to hear from God in her spirit. *This is what you've been waiting for.* The words were not audible, but she knew God had spoken to her.

"Are you convinced that this is God's will for me to go with you, Jeanine?"

"Yes." Jeanine leaned forward, her expression intent. "I need somebody like you, Annie. You're right about my being too impulsive and too—well, *domineering* is the word many use. Straightforward and honest is what I call it. But anyway, I believe God would have us go together, and we're not going to be stopped by any mission board."

"Do me one favor, Jeanine."

"Of course. What is it?"

"Let's go to the mission boards first and see if they will sponsor us if you will pay the expenses. We don't need to go without a covering."

"A covering? What does that mean?" Jeanine asked.

"It means that we need to be responsible to someone."

"We're responsible to Jesus."

"I know, but there's more to it than that."

"I don't see that. Jesus has called us. He's our Lord, and all we need to do is go."

Annie felt that there was something wrong with Jeanine's idea of going off on their own. She had been at the mission boards long enough to discover that many who went out without coverings or responsibilities to others back in the States and on the field often came back having failed in their mission. She argued diligently, but Jeanine had her mind set.

"All right," she finally said, "we'll go see them. But you'll see, Annie. God intends for you and me to go free from anyone. That way we can do whatever we please without having to ask anyone!"

★ ★ ★ ★

The Reverend Josiah Crawford shifted uneasily in his chair and looked out over the heads of the two young women who had brought a great problem into his life. Reverend Crawford, a tall, powerfully built man with reddish hair and mild blue eyes, pulled his glasses off and began polishing them with a white handkerchief. It was a ruse he often used to gain time when he was not certain as to what to say. And the Reverend Crawford was not at all certain about the two young women who sat before him—well, that was not exactly true. He *was* certain of one thing. The African Mission Board would never sponsor these two unlikely candidates.

Finally he had used up as much time as possible on his glasses. So planting them firmly on his nose, he took a deep breath and said as gently as possible, "I am sorry, Miss Quintana and Miss Rogers, but the board was firm in their decision."

Jeanine Quintana said stridently, "I can't understand it. Did you make it plain to them, Reverend Crawford, that we would require no financial assistance?"

"Why, ah . . . yes, I did, Miss Quintana."

"So it must be something personal, I take it."

"Oh no!" Reverend Crawford said hastily. "Nothing personal at all. It's just that . . . well—"

"Don't tell me it's Annie's health. She's hasn't had a health problem in over a year now. Isn't that right, Annie?"

"That's right, Reverend Crawford. I'm healthier than I've ever been."

"Well, of course we all are hopeful that your physical well-being will continue, but—"

Jeanine interrupted. "If it isn't that, it must be me."

Actually, Reverend Crawford thought frantically, *it is you*. Several of the board members were women, and all of them were well aware of this woman's past. *I wish she had never come through that door*, Crawford thought desperately. He remembered the board meeting that had gone on for what seemed like hours with two of the women bringing up Jeanine Quintana's sordid past life. Crawford himself had acted as an advocate for Jeanine, but his pleas had gone unheeded.

"We cannot have a woman like that representing our organization!" Mrs. Asa Strother had said.

She was not only the wife of the chairman of the board, but she was on the board herself. She was an ex-missionary who had done good service but was old fashioned and out of step with the times, at least so Crawford thought. He did not say so, however, but had only added mildly, "But we must be careful about things like this. After all, if the woman has been converted—"

"Let her prove herself! She was on the *Titanic*. That was less than a year ago. God saved her life miraculously, but she's still a beginner. The Scripture says, 'Lay hands suddenly on no man.'"

"But this is a woman," Crawford had protested.

"Makes no difference. I am opposed and will remain so."

With the memory of that unpleasant meeting fresh on his mind, Reverend Crawford tried to soften the blow as much as possible. "I will tell you that I personally voted for your acceptance, both of you. But we have a board that makes these decisions, and in every case the majority rules."

"What were their objections?" Jeanine asked, and an impish light came into her eyes. "Was it because I was once a cigar-smoking, champagne-drinking, freewheeling modern woman?"

Suddenly Reverend Crawford could not help but smile. He liked this young woman's indomitable spirit. "I'm afraid it's something like that. It takes time to convince people, Miss Quintana."

"Time is what I don't have. Neither of us. Annie's been waiting for years to serve God in Africa. I know I'm young in the faith, but I strongly believe God's called me."

"I am not at all doubtful of that, and I think you have strength and courage and, above all—initiative. If the decision were mine alone to make, it would be very simple, but we have our rules, you understand."

Jeanine liked Reverend Crawford. He had a gentle spirit, and she saw the honesty in his mild blue eyes. "Well," she said as she rose, "I thank you for your time, Reverend."

"I wish it could have been different." Crawford rose and walked around his desk. "What will you do now?" he said.

"We'll do what I said we should have done at first," Jeanine said firmly. She glanced at Annie and smiled. "We've been to every mission board in New York City, I think, because Annie said we should be under someone's authority. I agreed to this. But now, since no one wants to sponsor us, I have a committee that will sponsor us."

Annie stared at Jeanine with astonishment. "You never told me about this! Who is this committee?"

Jeanine laughed heartily. "The Father, the Son, and the Holy Ghost! Not a bad committee, I would say."

Crawford laughed and put out his hand. "Not a bad committee at all. I will pray for you, Miss Quintana—and you, Miss Rogers. You both have wonderful spirits. You're going to shake Africa up, I'm afraid."

"You mean *I'm* going to shake Africa up," Jeanine said gaily. "Come along, Annie. We'll start our own mission. We'll be our own director and board, and we'll see what great things God will do."

Reverend Josiah Crawford went back to his desk depressed by the incident. "I don't understand the board," he said, speaking aloud to the painting of David Livingston that ornamented the wall. "Here are two volunteers with money, both obviously sincere and well-meaning. Miss Quintana is a little bit forward. She'll get her nose skinned, but she'll make it. She's got that kind of drive it takes to make it as a missionary. Well, God help them!"

★ ★ ★ ★

Jeanine Quintana knew but one way to get things done—and that was full speed ahead. She started the day after Josiah Crawford had rejected them, as she put it, and Annie thought she was caught up in the wake of some sort of tropical storm. Jeanine had her out early, and the two began making visits to all of the stores in New York that sold any goods that might be useful.

They barged into Lord & Taylor, on Broadway, and then, after sweeping through the store with Jeanine ordering everything that wasn't tied down, they moved across to Macy's. In 1902 Macy's had moved twenty blocks north from Sixth Avenue to Harold Square. It was the first store to be called a department store, and Jeanine took advantage of every salesman she saw. She asked to see Mr. Macy, and with Annie in tow, she informed him that the two of them were setting out for Africa and would appreciate a discount.

Mr. Macy stared at the beautiful young woman who totally outshone Annie. Jeanine had not changed except to become somewhat more modest. The moss green dress she wore was expensive and so was the jewelry. She had on a pair of emerald earrings that glistened in the sun. Her hair was done up with ringlets falling down in back and at the sides, and she wore a matching light green hat with a large dark green bow.

"Well, I must admit you're a funny sort of missionary, Miss Quintana," Mr. Macy grinned. "But I'll do my best. Everything you buy in the store will be fifty percent off."

"Could you make it seventy-five?" Jeanine wheedled.

Macy suddenly laughed. "I'll make it a hundred percent! Just don't drive me into bankruptcy."

By the end of January a mountain of supplies had been collected and piled high in several rooms in Jeanine's house.

"What are you going to do with your house after we leave?" Annie asked as she stood there amid the mountain of goods.

"I'm going to sell it." Jeanine was examining a .45 Colt. She had belted a black leather holster on her side and now was examining the weapon. She held it out, sighted it, and pulled the trigger. The click made Annie jump.

"You're not supposed to do that, Jeanine."

"It isn't loaded."

"Why do you want to take a gun?"

"We'll be traveling alone. I got one for you, too. Also, I got the finest hunting rifles that money could buy." Walking over, she pulled up a massive rifle and, holding it up, sighted along the barrel. "This one will stop an elephant."

"We're not going to Africa to shoot elephants, Jeanine," Annie said, staring at the powerful rifle.

"No, but they may decide to charge us. I'll have to give you shooting lessons."

"Jeanine, the ship leaves next Thursday, but I'm still confused about all this."

Jeanine put the rifle down and turned to stare at Annie. "What are you confused about? We've got our tickets, and I've already arranged to have all these goods shipped. We're on our way, Annie. It's what you've wanted for as long as I've known you."

"I know, but—"

"What's wrong with you? God's going to take care of us."

Annie did not know how to answer her friend. "Jeanine," she said, "there's such a thing as presumption. The devil tempted Jesus to throw himself off the temple and He said, 'Thou shall not tempt the Lord thy God.' "

A real surprise washed across Jeanine's face. "Why, I'm not tempting God. He's called us to go to Africa and we're going. Would you have us go without any preparation at all? Just get on a ship? That would be foolish, Annie."

Annie knew that Jeanine was right, but somehow she felt that something had been left out of their preparations. Actually she felt strange that they were going without any support, and she said quietly, "I wish we had a group behind us here."

"We'll get a group. Don't worry. When we come back on furlough, we'll go around making speeches, and maybe we'll wear our sun helmets and our revolvers. Lady missionaries back from wildest Africa." The excitement made Jeanine's eyes gleam, and she laughed and went over to put her arm around Annie. "Don't worry. Just trust me."

"I'm just a little apprehensive."

Jeanine shook her head. "Where's your faith, sister? We're going to show those folks how missionaries should act!"

CHAPTER FIFTEEN

TWO WITNESSES

★ ★ ★ ★

The *Carrie Bell* dipped down into the furrow of the gray waters of the Atlantic, then slowly rose again. She was not a passenger vessel but was designed for carrying heavy loads to different ports all over the world. Now she was heavy-laden, and as the winds turned the waters to freezing froth at times when she was struck broadside, she would wallow so much that officers and crew alike wondered if she would recover. The sea stretched out endlessly in all directions, and only a single sailor in the bow was occupied with tying down some gear. His name was Howie Satterfield, and it was only his third voyage on the *Carrie Bell*. He was a tall, lanky young man from Alabama who spoke with a soft southern drawl. His fair skin had been cooked by the sun, but now as the ship headed south, he looked eagerly forward, anxious for new adventures. Securing the gear, he made his way along the deck, proud of his sea legs. His parents were cotton farmers, and all Howie had ever seen of life was the backside of a mule as he worked the fields. He had waited until he was seventeen to announce he was leaving for an adventurous life at sea. And now he felt life could offer no more than to be a sailor aboard the *Carrie Bell*.

As the young sailor was making his way along the upper deck, Annie and Jeanine were struggling awkwardly to dress in the small cabin that had been assigned to them. There were only three cabins that could be used for passengers, and it was an interesting experience for Jeanine. After the opulent stateroom she and Annie had shared on the *Titanic*, the small cubicle aboard the *Carrie Bell* seemed almost like a prison cell. It consisted of a single room, ten feet square, with a single hard bed on each side and a chest bolted to the floor at the foot of each bed. A mahogany table with a chair that did not match completed the sparse furniture of the room. The mountain of luggage and equipment Jeanine had purchased was stored deep in the hold of the ship. The two had only what they could put into two suitcases, which they kept stored under their beds.

As Annie washed her face in the chipped enamel washbasin, the cold water gave her a shock. She was wearing a heavy woolen robe she had mercifully kept out, and she shivered inside, for there was no heat, of course, inside the small cabin.

Jeanine seemed totally indifferent to the cold. She slipped out of her nightgown and began to dress, talking all the time about the church service that was going to be held that morning. She pulled on a heavy white chemise of bleached flannel and then pulled up a pair of white flannel knickers. She wore a pair of tan jodhpurs, a scarlet blouse, and a pair of calf-high polished boots.

"I think it's going to be fun holding a service for the sailors, Annie. Don't you?" She sat down at the table, now that Annie had left to begin dressing, and began pulling at her hair that was so thick it tended to get snarls. She tugged at it, ignoring the pain.

"I think it's very nice of Captain Sheraton to allow us to have the service," Annie said. "The first officer told me that he doesn't usually do things like that."

"Well, he didn't want to at first," Jeanine smiled. She continued to brush at her lustrous black hair until it glowed and then began braiding it. "I had to turn on the charm. He's a pretty hard-nosed man, our Captain Giles Sheraton."

Annie slipped out of the robe, shivered, and began to dress. She put on a black wool skirt cinched at the waist with a black belt and a white high collar blouse with a black ribbon tied at the neck. Quickly she put on the plaid green coat she had bought at the last minute, thinking she might need it on the trip, although she certainly would not need such a heavy garment in Africa. She cast a doubtful look toward Jeanine and thought, *That's an outlandish outfit she's got on. I wish she wouldn't wear it.*

There had been some argument over Jeanine's choice of dress, but Jeanine had merely laughed. "The sailors will like it. I'll look like a woman in one of those Tarzan comic strips. I wish my sun helmet was unpacked. I'd wear that, too." Snatching up her Bible, she said, "Come on. Let's go."

As the two left the small cubicle and walked down the corridor, Jeanine asked abruptly, "Do you want to speak or do you want me to?"

"Oh, I think you should do it, Jeanine."

"Well, if you insist. Why don't you give your testimony first, and then I'll bring the sermon."

"That will be fine. I don't know what we'll do for music, though."

"Oh, you sing very well, Annie. We won't have a piano, of course, but surely some of these sailors will know a few hymns. Let's try it anyway."

When the two reached the mid-deck, the dining area had been turned into a temporary chapel. The tables had been moved to one side, and as Annie glanced around, she saw that about twenty men had come for the service. They all stood up as the two women entered and Captain Giles Sheraton came over to greet them.

"Good morning, ladies. Or should I say reverends?"

"Not reverend, if you please, Captain." Jeanine smiled at him fetchingly. It was ingrained in her to turn on the charm when a man was around, a habit from her former days. "I don't like the title reverend because I don't find it in the Scripture."

"What shall I call you then?"

"Oh, just our names will be fine."

"Very well, then, Miss Quintana. As you see, we have a fair congregation for you."

"Yes, we do. All of the crew wanted to come, but someone has to run the ship," said First Officer Charles Hodgson, a short, stocky man with a shock of black hair and piercing gray eyes. He smiled and cocked his head to one side, adding, "They're a pretty rough crew, ladies. They could do with a bit of religion."

"And how about you, Mr. Hodgson?" Jeanine said. "Are you saved?"

The question caught the first officer off guard. His face turned rather ruddy, and he stared at her as if she had asked something highly improper. "Why, I attend church when I can."

"That's not what I asked you," Jeanine said. She was totally aware that the captain and the rest of the congregation were listening, and she saw out of the corner of her eye that there were broad grins on the faces of the crew. *They like seeing the first officer called up short.* "The Bible says you must be born again. So let me ask it like that. Have you been born again?"

Hodgson grew even more crimson. "No. I'm not a believer."

"Well, I trust you will be. I'll remember you in my prayers."

Captain Sheraton had enjoyed the exchange between this flamboyant young woman and his first officer. He said, "I assume you'll start on me next. So to save you the trouble, I will tell you that I am a Christian, Miss Quintana. Not as good a one as I should be, but I am a believer."

"That's wonderful, Captain!" Jeanine turned her eyes on him, and her smile was warming. "We'll have to have some Bible studies together. What time would be suitable for you?"

A snicker went through the body of sailors who were listening, and the other passengers, two couples, found the exchange amusing also.

Sheraton was taken aback, but he took it in good spirits. "Why, we'll have to arrange a time. A captain is a busy person, you know."

"So is a missionary. I'll want to speak to every person on this ship before we reach Mombasa."

This announcement, Annie saw quickly, did not go down too well with the crew. She had been watching the sailors and the passengers and saw that all of them were fascinated by Jeanine Quintana. Her costume alone was enough to draw attention, and her aggressive mannerism was even more unusual. America still had many people, despite the women's suffrage movement, who felt that women should be quiet and modest. If the truth had been told, many would have said women should be seen and not heard in public. It disturbed Annie that Jeanine was so forward, especially forcing the issue in public, and she resolved to speak to her about it later.

The service began then when Jeanine said, "We are so glad that you've all come. We hope you will come every time we hold a service. I am Jeanine Quintana, and this is my fellow missionary Miss Annie Rogers. Either of us will be glad to talk with any of you at any time about your souls. Now we're going to have a song service. We don't have a piano or an organ, but we have Miss Rogers, who has a beautiful voice, to lead us. I have kept out some hymnbooks for your use."

Jeanine had planned for the evangelistic work on board the

ship. She had told Annie before leaving, "I read the biography of George Mueller. Every time he went on a ship, he spent his time talking to people about their souls. We're going to do the same thing. I'm going to persuade the captain to let us hold services, and we'll even have books. I thought about having a piano, but that might be too much."

Annie quickly passed out the books, smiling at those in the small congregation. When they were all ready, she turned to face them. She went to the front and said, "I'm really not as good a singer as Miss Quintana intimates, but I do love to sing the old songs of the church. I'm sure many of you will know them, and let me urge you to join in. You may not be the best singer in the world, but if you love the Lord, that's all He cares about. The first one was written by Charles Wesley, 'Oh for a Thousand Tongues.' We'll just sing the first verse several times, and that way those of you who don't know it can learn the tune."

> Oh for a thousand tongues to sing
> My great redeemer's praise,
> The glories of my God and King,
> The triumphs of his grace.

Annie did have a fine, clear soprano voice that carried well. Jeanine could not sing as well, but she made up in enthusiasm what she lacked in skill. Captain Sheraton joined in with a rumbling bass, and obviously some of the sailors had been brought up in a church. Many stood looking down at their feet, but by the time they had sung the first verse three times, Annie said, "That's just fine! Now one of my favorites that I'm sure you all know. This was written by a woman who was blinded when she was just a child. Her name is Fanny Crosby, and I love her hymns so well. You'll find it on page seven of your book. Join in with me as we give honor to the Lord Jesus."

> Blessed assurance, Jesus is mine
> Oh what a foretaste of glory divine!
> Heir of salvation, purchase of God,
> Born of his spirit, washed in his blood.
> This is my story, this is my song,
> Praising my savior all the day long.

The voices of the men rose up raggedly, but Annie was delighted to see that all of the men were trying. The visitors, one older couple and one middle-aged, shared a book and also joined in the singing.

Not wanting to stretch the service out, after fifteen minutes Annie said, "That was wonderful singing. Now if you'll be seated, I would like to tell you how I came to know the Lord Jesus." She began to speak quietly, and it was a moving testimony. She spoke of how she had found the Lord when she was only a girl, and then she related how God had spoken to her many times during her youth, telling her that she would be a witness for Him in Africa. She spoke of how the door had not opened for years, and added, "Sometimes God does not answer our prayers or show us His ways as quickly as we would like. But He is a loving God, and we must learn to wait on Him. It was only when Miss Quintana came into my life that all the pieces fell together. I will let her tell you her own story, but I will only say to you that the greatest thing in my life is loving God and serving Him. And I hope that each one of you will sense His love for you during this moment and during this voyage and for the rest of your life."

Annie sat down and Jeanine got up. Her face was glowing, and she began quite shockingly by saying, "I was saved in a beer barrel!"

She laughed aloud at the facial expressions she saw in the congregation. "That is not just shock tactics. It is literally true. Miss Rogers and I were on board the *Titanic*."

At this point everyone sat up and looked eagerly toward the flamboyant young woman. Her face was radiant as she added, "Up until the *Titanic* started sinking, I lived my life entirely for myself. . . ."

The crew, the officers, and the passengers listened, entranced, as Jeanine gave her testimony. It was a dramatic testimony, and she did not spare herself, speaking freely of the sinful life she had led. When she retold the story of how she had been saved from the *Titanic*, her voice grew husky. "I will never forget the unselfish love that Clive Winters showed for me. He could have gotten in that barrel and saved himself, but he died that I might have life. That was the first time I ever knew that love could be like that."

A silence had fallen over the room, and Annie thought, *She has a wonderful way of speaking. She can tell a story so well, and she's won their confidence.*

Jeanine continued by saying, "My sermon this morning will

be that you must be born again. I will read now from the third chapter of John's Gospel." She began to read, and then after she had read the story of Nicodemus coming to Jesus and being told by the Lord, "You must be born again," she began speaking from her heart.

"What is it to be born again? How can you be born again? And finally, what will happen if you are not born again?"

And it was a good sermon. She spoke of the first two points so well that she had her congregation in the palm of her hand. They listened carefully as she spoke of how Jesus Christ had to come inside the heart and used her own life as an example. It was apparent she had spent her time well at the Bible school, for she quoted Scripture easily, both from the Old and New Testament. The second part of her message, how to be born again, was abundantly clear. She quoted from the Book of Romans. "Whosoever shall call upon the name of the Lord shall be saved." She quoted from Luke, "Except ye repent ye will all likewise perish." She picked scriptures from the Gospels, from the letters of Paul, even from Revelation, and wove a net that caught the attention of her hearers.

But when she came to the third part of her sermon, what will happen if you are *not* born again, Annie's heart grew heavy. Jeanine began by saying, "You will go to hell. That's what will happen to you—and you will deserve it."

Her voice grew harsh and the ground she had gained was rapidly lost. Annie was praying, *Oh, Lord, don't let her do this!* But it was useless.

Jeanine reached the end saying, "Now, surely you must see the reason for this. You are sinners, and you must give up your sin so that God can come into your life. We're going to ask Miss Annie to sing, and as she sings I want you to come, you that are not saved, and I will pray with you. No one wants to go to hell. So I'm asking you to turn from your wicked ways this day."

It was a bad ending to what had been a good service. Her harsh words alienated the congregation. No one would meet her eyes, and after Annie had sung two verses, she said quietly, "We thank you for coming to the service. As Miss Quintana has said, if you want to speak to either of us, we will be available." She bowed her head and said, "Father, we thank you for your word, we thank you for the very life that you give us. Help us turn our thoughts to thee, for soon we must meet you face to face. And we ask in the name of Jesus that you will speak to every heart. Amen."

Annie saw with regret that most of the congregation was leaving quickly and that Jeanine was following them out. Her voice carried as she said to a middle-aged sailor, "I saw that you were nervous during the sermon. Are you saved?"

"No, ma'am, and I've got to be back at my station," the sailor said, pulling away from Jeanine's grasp.

Captain Sheraton came up to say quietly, "I enjoyed your testimony very much, Miss Rogers. It was a blessing to me—and also your singing."

"Why, thank you, Captain. And I want to thank you again for allowing us to have services."

Captain Sheraton shifted his feet rather uncomfortably. "Miss Quintana's quite . . . *direct*, isn't she?"

"She's a new Christian, Captain. Sometimes new Christians get overenthusiastic." She smiled, saying, "I heard one preacher say once that a new Christian thinks the world's on fire and that he's got the only bucket of water."

Captain Sheraton smiled. He liked this young woman very much, but he was troubled by Jeanine Quintana's method. "I wish you'd have a word with her. I realize that she's not a polished preacher yet, but she needs to learn. She did very well for most of the sermon, but then she grew, I thought, too demanding."

Annie could not say much, but she said, "I'm sure if we pray for her she will learn, Captain Sheraton."

After the service the two women walked around the deck. A feeble, pale sun shone through the clouds from time to time. As they braved the cold weather, finally Jeanine said impatiently, "Why did you end the service so soon? We could have talked to several of the men. I saw some of them were under conviction."

"Well, Jeanine, I felt like it was time." Hesitating for a moment, Annie knew now would be the best time to confront Jeanine. As tactfully as she could, she said, "Your testimony's so dramatic, and you did so well with most of your sermon."

"Most of my sermon!" Jeanine said. She turned to stare at Annie and demanded, "I take it you didn't enjoy all of it?"

"Doctrinally you were totally right. You had, I thought, the whole congregation right where we both wanted them to be. But the latter part of it was too harsh, Jeanine."

"Hell is harsh!" she said defensively.

"Well, of course it is, and people need to be told about the dangers of it. But you can't drive people, Jeanine."

"I won't water the Gospel down," Jeanine said firmly. She stared moodily out over the sea and said, "You're too soft, Annie. This is a tough world where people are dying and going to hell. I think it was Dwight L. Moody who said he was a brand snatched from the burning. That's what men and women are. They're like brands and already half on fire, and we've got to snatch them out and win them to Jesus."

Annie could not argue with this, but she knew deep in her heart that somewhere down the line Jeanine was going to have to learn to show more love and less aggressiveness.

★ ★ ★ ★

Annie arose early the next morning and, shivering in the cold, dressed. Jeanine kept covered up in a cocoon of blankets and blinked at her. "Where are you going?" she muttered.

"I can't sleep. I think I'll just take a walk around the deck." She left the cabin and began to pace the deck. She passed by the bridge up on a higher level and saw the first officer, whose eyes took her in. He did not smile, but nodded, and she waved at him cheerfully. *He didn't like what Jeanine said to him. I hope she gets a chance to show him a different side.*

She stood there thinking about the life that lay before her in Africa. She wondered how long it would be before she would get to see Jeb Winslow again. He was already working with the Masai people. She had gotten only one letter, a very brief one, but it was full of excitement, and he ended by saying, "I know I, perhaps, said too much about how I feel about you, but I could not help it, Annie. Please forgive me. But don't forget."

"Poor Jeb," Annie murmured as the wind whipped at her coat and blew her hair around her face. "I wish it were different, but I don't see how I can do what God's called me to do unless I'm free."

"Miss Annie, might I speak to you?"

Annie turned to see a tall, raw-boned young sailor standing there to her right. "Why, of course. I don't believe I know your name."

"Howie Satterfield, ma'am. Glad to meet you."

"Where are you from, Howie?"

"From Alabama, ma'am."

"I noticed you in the service yesterday."

"Yes, ma'am, I was there. And that's what I wanted to talk to you about."

Annie's heart suddenly warmed and she said, "Why, of course, Howie. Can we go inside or are you on duty?"

"Oh, I'm off duty, ma'am. We could go into the dining room. Nobody's there at this time of the morning. We might even get a cup of coffee from Cookie if you'd like."

"I'd like it very much, Mr. Satterfield."

"Oh no, ma'am. No mister. Just Howie is fine."

The two walked down the deck that tilted slowly with the roll of the *Carrie Bell* and entered the dining area. "I'll get you some coffee, miss," Howie said eagerly. "Would you care for an early breakfast?"

"No. Coffee will be fine."

"Sugar and cream?"

"Yes, please. Both."

Howie disappeared into the galley, and Annie sat down and prayed for guidance. He came back carrying two enormous white mugs, one with a spoon, which he handed to her. "That's got your sugar and cream, ma'am. I drink mine black."

Annie sipped the coffee and her eyes opened wide. "Oh, that's strong!"

"Yes, ma'am. Strong enough to float a horseshoe," Howie said somewhat proudly. "Takes a real man to drink coffee like this."

"Well, it's good all the same. Tell me a little about yourself, Howie."

Flattered by Annie's interest, the young man began speaking. He was not eloquent, but it was soon obvious that something was troubling him. Finally he said haltingly, "I've been . . . well . . . you know, thinking about the service yesterday."

Seeing the young man had come to some sort of a mental barrier and could not speak, Annie said with encouragement, "Was it something about the sermon?"

"Well, yes, ma'am, it was. About a man's got to be born again. I didn't rightly understand that."

Annie began speaking quietly and slowly, explaining the Gospel. Howie sat there forgetting his coffee and listened intently. When she had spoken for ten minutes, he shook his head and sadness came into his light blue eyes. "I don't reckon that's for me, ma'am."

"What's not for you, Howie?"

"Gettin' saved."

"Why, of course it is. It's for everybody. The Bible says, 'Whosoever will may come.' That includes you."

"Well, I'll tell you the truth, Miss Annie. I don't reckon the Lord would have nothin' to do with the likes of me. Not after what I've done."

Immediately Annie understood that something in Howie Satterfield's past was a tremendous barrier to him. She had encountered this before and now said gently, "It doesn't matter how bad a thing you've done. We haven't all sinned alike, but we've all alike sinned. The blood of Jesus washes us from all sin. There's a wonderful passage in Isaiah that says, 'Though your sins be as scarlet, they shall be as white as snow.' Isn't that a wonderful promise? And it's for you."

"Oh, you just don't know, ma'am, what I did."

Seeing the anguish on the young man's face, Annie said, "It's not necessary to tell me about it. I don't have to know what you've done."

Gratefully Howie said, "I think that's good, Miss Annie. Because I wouldn't want to say what I did to a lady, but it was bad." He hesitated and chewed his lower lip. "You really think God would forgive me no matter what I did?"

"I know He will, Howie. God wants one thing, a broken and a contrite heart for the wrong we've done."

"Well, that's me, I guess. I've been worried about it a long time, and while Miss Quintana was preaching yesterday, it just seemed like the Lord put a burden on me. But I didn't know what to do."

Annie talked with him some more and saw that there was an openness in his heart. "Howie, why don't we just pray, and you can be saved just like I was when I was a girl. It was a long time ago, but the Lord's been with me ever since. Would you do that?"

"Oh yes, ma'am. I would."

"Fine. I'll pray for you, and you tell God you've sinned against Him. He already knows about it, but He wants you to tell Him. Then you just ask for Him to come into your heart and give you a new life."

Annie bowed her head and began to pray. She had not prayed for long before she heard a muffled sound of sobbing, and she reached out and took Howie's hands and prayed fervently. When she had finished, she whispered, "Howie, will you ask Jesus into your heart?"

Right there in that galley, Howie Satterfield invited Jesus Christ to come in. As soon as he had done so, he looked at Annie and said, "I've done it, miss. Am I saved now?"

"Yes, you are, Howie. I truly believe you are."

"I don't feel too different," he said doubtfully. "Are you sure about it?"

"I'm sure that if you are honest with God, God will do exactly what He says. But it's important for you to do several things. First, you need to get a Bible. Do you have one?"

"Yes, ma'am, I do."

"Good. You begin to read it and I'll help you. And it's important that you talk to the Lord every day. More than once. And as soon as possible, you need to follow the Lord in baptism."

"I'll do all that, ma'am. You see if I don't." Howie Satterfield's eyes were bright as he dashed the tears away. "I thank you for talking to me, Miss Annie. I don't know what I'da done. I couldn't go on like I was."

"We've got several days. I've got a book or two that might be of some help to you, Howie, and we're going to have other services."

"I'll read anything you give me, Miss Annie," Howie said, then stood up and left.

Annie leaned back. She felt tired and drained but happy. Somehow this sort of work was exhausting. *It must be because,* she thought, *so much depends on it. I always get emotionally drained when talking to someone about their soul. It's so good to see a young man come to Jesus.*

Later that afternoon, Annie had another experience that pleased her greatly. Satterfield brought a friend of his to talk, Larry Dillon, a short, muscular man with fair hair and dark blue eyes. "I've been talking to my friend, Larry. He thinks he might like to know about Jesus, too. So I brought him for you to tell him."

"Why, I'm so happy that you're interested in your soul, Larry," Annie said quickly. The three of them went again to the dining area, for it was between meals, and in half an hour Larry Dillon had given his heart to the Lord. The two of them thanked Annie profusely, and as they left, Annie stared after them. "It's so easy when the Holy Spirit does it—and so hard when you try to do it yourself."

★ ★ ★ ★

The second service was not as well attended as the first, and although Annie did not speak it, she knew it was because some felt that Jeanine would be too harsh and would embarrass them in public. This time she had said, "Jeanine, let me speak this time. I feel the Lord's given me something."

"All right," Jeanine said, "but you'll have to do the singing, too. I just can't do that."

Annie had done the singing and then asked Jeanine to give a brief testimony. Jeanine seemed somewhat depressed. At least she did not enter enthusiastically into the service. The thought crossed Annie's mind, *Why, she's jealous!* But she pushed aside that thought immediately. *No. That can't be.*

Standing up, she said, "I'm no preacher and I don't need to tell you that. You will find it out immediately. But I have been studying my Bible lately, and there is a passage of Scripture that God has put into my heart. It's very simple. It's simply a phrase about Jesus. It says in the Scripture 'He must go up to Jerusalem.' That's not much of a text, but let me explain the lesson we can learn from that. Jesus was born of the Virgin Mary. He lived a perfect and sinless life for thirty-three years. He fulfilled every law that God ever gave without sinning one time, but there was one more thing for Jesus to do. *He had to go to Jerusalem.*"

She looked out over the congregation and saw that they were watching her curiously but silently. "Why did He have to go to Jerusalem?" she continued. "He had only one purpose—and that was to die. He had told His disciples this repeatedly, but for some reason they had deaf ears and did not believe it. Perhaps they didn't want to. We often don't want to believe the things we don't like. But it was true enough. You've all read the story, but I want to read again for you what happened in Jerusalem."

At this point Annie opened her Bible and read the story of the crucifixion of Jesus. She read it slowly, without great drama or flair, but simply. And even as she read it, tears came to her eyes as they frequently did when she read of the death and suffering of the Lord.

When she had finished reading, she said, "I'm going to talk to you about why Jesus died. Why he had to go to Jerusalem. . . ." For the next half hour Annie spoke without eloquence but out of a full heart. She spoke not only of the physical details of agony but how He had suffered in His heart when God's wrath was poured out upon Him. She explained why He had to hang there as the representative of sinful man. The room grew absolutely silent, and when she came to the end, she said, "Jesus had to go to Jerusalem. That is why He came to this earth. To die. I must go to Jerusalem, too—that is, in this life I must do whatever it is that God puts on my heart. And I think that each of us must somehow go to Jerusalem. Not the physical country, of course, where the Temple is, but to some point where God is leading us. I wonder this morning if some of you are not ready to begin your journey to Jerusalem. You may have done terrible things. You may have led a life that was not at all what God intended for you. But Jesus says, 'Come unto me all ye that labor and I will give you rest.' I'm going to ask you to stand. We're all going to bow our heads. And if during this time of prayer, any of you want to begin your journey to Jerusalem, it begins by taking Jesus Christ as your personal Savior."

Annie bowed her head with no more invitation than this and began to pray. Her eyes were closed, and she was praying when she suddenly sensed someone in front of her. Opening her eyes she saw the two young men, Howie Satterfield and Larry Dillon, standing there waiting. She finished her prayer and then waited for them to speak.

"We want to be baptized, ma'am. You said that that's what we ought to do now that we're saved."

For a moment Annie could not think of an answer, and then she said, "I'm so happy that you two have taken Jesus." She was aware of the crew and the officers watching closely. "But I can't baptize you."

"Why not, ma'am?" Larry demanded.

"Because I'm not authorized to do so. I'm not a minister, and I'm not a representative of a church. Baptism ought to be the first step toward serving God in a church." She had a happy thought then and said, "As soon as we get to Mombasa, it will be very simple. I have a relative there who's a missionary, and there's a large church. My relative, Barney Winslow, will be glad to baptize you. Will that be all right?"

"Oh yes, ma'am!" both men said instantly.

Annie dismissed the service and was pleased when one of the other sailors came by and said, "I'd like to talk to you if you've got time, Miss Annie. My name's Jerry Simms."

"Of course, Jerry. What about after lunch or whenever you're off duty?"

"Three o'clock will be fine, ma'am."

After Annie made the appointment, she turned to Captain Sheraton, saying, "Thank you again for letting us use your facilities for a service."

"No thanks necessary, Miss Rogers." He nodded and smiled. "Those are two fine young men. We've got some rough ones on board. I'd like to see them find the Lord, too."

"We'll pray that they will."

★   ★   ★   ★

Three days later the *Carrie Bell* docked at Mombasa. Both Annie and Jeanine were on deck watching eagerly as they prepared to disembark. "I'm so glad we're finally here," Annie said.

"So am I. I'm tired of this ship." There was something of displeasure in Jeanine's eyes. She turned and said, "I can't understand why I wasn't able to see any converts on this trip and you did."

"Oh, it doesn't matter who gets the credit," Annie said quickly. "We'll just thank God for those who have come to know His love. As a matter of fact, four sailors have been saved on the voyage, and even the first officer, Charles Hodgson, promised me to seek after God."

Annie could tell Jeanine was unhappy. She knew the older woman liked to be the center of attention, and she had seen this as a possible problem. She spoke for a while, saying, "It's sowing the seed that counts, Jeanine. The men heard the good sermons that you preached, and they'll carry them home. Why, there might be a dozen or more saved from the messages you gave."

"But I wanted to see it happen!"

"Well, of course we always want to see the fruit of our labor, but it doesn't work like that in farming. You go out and plant seed in the ground. You don't stand there looking at it. It takes a long time for it to come up."

"It didn't take long for you to see converts," Jeanine said pettily.

Annie did not know how to answer this, so she did not try. She looked down at the dock and said, "Look, they're putting the gangplank down, and I'll bet that's Barney Winslow right there. I've seen pictures of him, though I've never met him. I don't see my aunt and uncle. Come along."

They went down the gangplank, and sure enough, the first one to greet them was a tall man with black hair. "I'm Barney Winslow," he said. "I would guess you're a Winslow, too. Your aunt Ruth and uncle David send their love. They got called to a medical emergency, so they told me to tell you they will see you later. It sure has been a blessing having David Burns and your aunt Ruth join us as medical missionaries." He took Annie's hand and grinned. Barney Winslow was trim and fit, his face deeply tanned by the African sun. He shook hands freely with Annie, then turned to meet Jeanine Quintana. "We're glad to have you, Miss Quintana. We can use all the witnesses we can get here in this part of the world."

"I'm glad to meet you, Brother Winslow. Annie's told me so much about your life," Jeanine said. "I'm so glad we're here to help with the work."

"Well, I'll get your luggage. You can wait in the carriage. My wife's over there. She twisted her ankle, so she couldn't get out to greet you."

Annie suddenly laughed. "You don't know what you're saying, Brother Winslow—"

"Just Barney unless we're in formal circumstances."

"Well, Barney, then. We've got a mountain of luggage and equipment and gear on board. It'll take two or three wagons, I think, to cart it in."

Barney Winslow grinned. "Well, I've seen some prospective missionaries get off the boat without anything but the clothes on their back. But if what you say is true, I'm going to take you ladies over to meet my wife, and she'll take you in while I see to your luggage."

Taking them over to the carriage, Barney introduced the two women to Katie Sullivan Winslow, an attractive woman in her late thirties. And inside the back were their two children, Patrick and Erin. Katie said, "You come along, and we'll see that you get a place to freshen up."

"I'll take care of the baggage, but I think I'll have to hire someone to haul it, from what our new missionaries tell us. You go ahead. We're going to have a family get-together tonight. Your uncle David and aunt Ruth and niece, Eileen, Andrew and his family, us, and you."

"That'll be fine. It will be nice to meet Andrew. I've heard so much about him," Annie said.

When the carriage left, Barney went up the gangplank and asked for Captain Sheraton, whom he knew, for the *Carrie Bell* docked in Mombasa fairly often. The two greeted each other, and soon the process of digging the luggage out of the hold was under-way. As the work went on, Captain Sheraton said, "That Miss Rogers is a pearl, Reverend. She's a relation of yours, I understand."

"Yes, she is. Fine young woman, from all I can understand."

"Well, she's been a good influence on this ship. It's been a pleasure to have her."

Barney sensed something missing in Captain Sheraton's tone. "What about Miss Quintana?"

Sheraton did not answer at once. He was a slow-speaking man at times, thinking well before he gave his opinion. "That's a different story," he said finally.

"What's wrong with her, Sheraton?"

"Well, she thinks she's a man. Has to run everything. Very demanding."

"I hate to hear that."

"I'm sure you'll hate it worse. How will that sort of attitude go over with the natives?"

"Not well at all," Barney admitted. "But Africa has a way of taking some things out of a person."

"Well, she's got nerve. I'll say that," Sheraton grinned. "The next time I come I want a report on how they're doing. If they live, that is." He hesitated and then asked, "Do they know all about the fever that's killed half of you missionaries?"

Barney nodded, saying, "If they don't, they soon will. It's a different world they're coming to out here. They'll be two different women after a time."

"You keep your eye on Jeanine Quintana. She's apt to be a handful."

"I'll do that," Barney said. "But if she's as strongwilled as you say, she won't be paying much attention to me."

"Or anybody else, for that matter," Sheraton added.

CHAPTER SIXTEEN

THE GUIDE

★   ★   ★   ★

Reverend Andrew Winslow swept into the office with his hair almost on end. He had a habit of running his hands through it when he was excited, and now he was obviously extremely agitated. He was a dignified-looking man of forty, three years younger than his brother, Barney. Andrew was finer looking with chiseled features. His missionary work running the station at Mombasa and taking care of the needs of the surrounding area kept him from going to the interior, so he looked softer and much more "citified" than his older brother.

"Barney, do you know what that crazy woman's going to do?"

"Crazy woman! I don't think I know any crazy women, Andy." Barney looked up from the Bible he was reading and put his pencil down. He had been making notes for a sermon and now tilted back in his chair and examined his brother carefully. Barney did not like office work and preferred to be out in the villages, which suited Andrew fine because he preferred life in the city.

"I'm talking about Jeanine Quintana. You know very well who I'm talking about."

Barney grinned lazily. "What has she done now?" he said.

"She's planning to head out into the Masai country right away."

Barney's grin vanished. "That's not a good idea," he murmured. "She's not ready to go out to an outstation yet."

"Of course she isn't!"

"When did she tell you this?"

"Just this morning. She came breezing in and said, 'I'm going out to the Masai country' just like she would say, 'I'm going to the grocery store to buy some bananas.'" Andrew ran his hands through his hair, mussing it up even more, and shook his head in despair. "We can't let her do it, Barney."

"There might be a problem about that."

"About what?"

"About *letting* her do it." Barney stood up and went over to gaze out the window at the narrow street outside of the mission building. "She's not under our authority, you know. She's paying all of her own expenses."

"But I thought we had agreed," Andrew argued, "that she *would* be under our authority!"

Barney turned around and, moving over slightly, leaned against the wall. The flies were particularly bad this year, and picking up a swatter, he caught a group on the wall and eliminated them. "Pesky flies!" he muttered. "We've got to get these screens repaired."

"Never mind the screens. What about those two women? We can't let them go out to that country alone. They wouldn't last a week."

"I'm not so sure about that," Barney murmured.

"Oh, I know you. You always think everybody ought to head out as far as they can get away from Mombasa." It was an argument of long standing between the two. Andrew felt that it was important to maintain a strong base. It was his long-range plan to build a well-established church in the city and then slowly send out teams into the nearer stations.

Barney was just the opposite. He wanted to go as far as he could into the interior and often did, despite Andrew's protests. The two argued about it, but there was a genuine love between them, and now Barney knew that Andrew was partially right.

"I suppose we'll have to do something, but I don't know what."

"If only Jeanine were like Annie," Andrew sighed. He went over and plunked down into the bamboo chair with a red cushion and sighed heavily. "We get so many out here that aren't really called of God."

"Yes, we do," Barney said, "and there's nothing we can do about that. Those that are called will stick it out. Those that aren't won't." He grinned suddenly and said, "Remember what we used to say? 'Some got called and sent—some just up and *went*.' It'll always be that way. Some people think it's a romantic thing to go to Africa as a missionary."

"Yes, it is. I remember." Andrew grinned slightly. "I came with my head full of notions about how *romantic* it was."

"I suppose we were all the same, but there's no help for it. It takes a while for new missionaries to find out the truth. You remember what Livingston said about being a missionary?"

"Don't recall."

"Someone asked him when he went back to England what was the hardest part of being a missionary in Africa. They thought he would say something about the headhunters, or the cannibals, or the man-eating lions. And he sent them all into shock when he said, 'The pesky mosquitoes.'" He laughed then and said, "I don't know but what he said was right. We don't have much cannibalism left, but we've sure got plenty of mosquitoes."

Andrew shook his head impatiently. "That doesn't solve our problem. Barney, *you've* got to talk to Annie. She's a sensible young woman. She'll listen to what you say."

"I'll talk to her, but I can't make any guarantees."

"Well, you've got to do something! Jeanine Quintana is too impulsive and headstrong."

"Like me," Barney grinned.

Andrew suddenly laughed. "Yes. Like you. You talk to Annie, will you?"

"I'll talk to her, but she'll do whatever Jeanine says."

★   ★   ★   ★

At the same time these two were talking, Annie and Jeanine were walking the streets of Mombasa. During their brief weeks there, they had become very familiar with the city. It still held some bit of romance for them, especially the main street. It was lined with whitewashed buildings that gleamed in the sun, and the streets were crowded with donkeys, horses, mules, carriages, wagons, and a sprinkling of automobiles and trucks. As they walked down the street, they passed the meat market, and Annie wrinkled up her nose at the naked dressed carcasses that were hanging, most of them covered with flies.

"Smells terrible, doesn't it?" Jeanine said. "I could hardly eat anything for a week after we got here. You remember?"

"I have trouble now with the meat when I think about how the flies crawl all over it."

"Well, at the station Barney and Andrew take a little better care to keep the meat fresh."

The two walked on, and finally Jeanine said, "Let's go in for something cool to drink, if there is anything."

"All right," Annie agreed, then followed Jeanine off the street into what would have been called a restaurant, or a bar, in the States. It was a combination of both, as all establishments were in Africa. Strong drink was always available along with food. The two sat down and ordered lemonades, which the dark-skinned proprietor brought with a toothy grin. They sipped the cool liquid that had no ice but was kept in a hole, no doubt, to at least take the heat off of it. They talked about their experience, and it was Annie who said, "I got a note from Jeb. He's living with the Masai, you know. He wants to know when we'll be coming."

"Soon, if I have my way about it. But we may have to hog-tie Andrew and Barney if we're ever going to get on our way."

Annie sipped at her lemonade and frowned slightly. "I think we ought to listen to them, Jeanine. It's not like going out into Central Park in New York, you know. There are all kinds of dangers."

"We knew that before we came, and we've been over all that a thousand times. We'll be all right," Jeanine insisted.

"I think we should wait until we learn more of the language and perhaps more from the missionaries who have been here a long time. It might be better to spend a little time now than to go out and do something terrible."

Jeanine laughed. She was wearing jodhpurs, as usual, with a white blouse and a scarlet silk neckerchief knotted around her throat. She wore a sun helmet as well. It was her usual costume, and she tried to persuade Annie to adopt the same but without any success. Annie was wearing a simple pale blue dress that came down almost to her ankles and a pair of sensible brown walking shoes.

The argument went on for some time until finally Jeanine grew irritated. "Annie, don't you understand? Some of those Masai will die without Christ if we don't go preach to them."

"Well, of course that's true, but—"

They drank two glasses of lemonade in the relative coolness

of the cafe for half an hour. At the end of that time Annie knew that it was hopeless. She felt strongly that it was wrong that she and Jeanine were not accountable to anyone. In her scheme of things, Annie believed everyone should be accountable to someone. But Jeanine had no such inhibitions, and Annie knew there was no way in the world to stop her.

The two women left and went back to the mission station, where they had a quarrelsome meeting with Barney and Andrew. Andrew grew almost livid as he laid out his arguments against the two proceeding out alone. "Don't you see? It's not just a matter of your own safety, although that's important, of course."

"Well, what is it, then, Reverend Winslow?" Jeanine asked impatiently. She knew well what he would say but endured a lecture on how missionaries who do not know the customs of the natives could do great damage to the cause of Christ.

Finally he concluded, saying, "Just give it a few more months. That's all I ask."

"Months! We didn't come out here to sit in a mission station!" Jeanine exclaimed.

Annie said timidly, "Well, maybe just one month wouldn't hurt, Jeanine."

But this didn't satisfy Jeanine. Barney sat back and listened, for he had already seen that Jeanine Quintana had her mind made up. *She's a whole lot like I was when I first got out here*, he thought. *Some of the group wanted to stay in the city, but I wanted to go out right away and I did. Made a lot of mistakes. Maybe Jeanine's right. In any case, she's going.*

Finally, after Andrew gave up and left, a disgusted look on his face, Barney said, "Jeanine, I'm going to ask you to do one thing."

"What's that?" Jeanine asked suspiciously.

"I want to get you a good guide. Probably a native who speaks English well and who knows the Masai. I'd get another missionary if we had anyone to spare, but we don't. Will you wait for that?"

"How long?" Jeanine demanded.

"A week at the most."

Annie quickly said, "We can do that, can't we, Jeanine? It's only a week, and we'll need to organize."

"Yes, you will. It's going to take some doing to take all this gear with you," Barney offered. "In the meanwhile, the missionaries here are all enjoying your company. I'm sure your aunt Ruth is enjoying having you around, too, Annie."

Jeanine allowed herself to be persuaded, saying only, "One week, Barney, and then we're going, guide or no guide!"

★ ★ ★ ★

Three days passed after the conversation with Barney and Andrew, and Annie threw herself into the work of the mission station. She helped organize their supplies, but she stayed up late every night studying the Masai language. She had a good teacher, an old woman named Mali, who giggled at Annie's awkward attempts to speak the language. Mali herself spoke English in an interesting fashion, sometimes hard to fathom, but the two got along very well.

Annie also spent a great deal of time with her aunt Ruth and uncle David Burns. She discovered that her aunt had a great insight into the way of life in Africa. She told her, for example, "Annie, there are many Africas. They're all on this continent, but they're very diverse. Doctor Livingston's Africa, for example, was a pretty dark one. There are some brighter Africas that you'll encounter as time goes on, but one thing you'll never do is solve this mystery. It's wild, it's a sweltering inferno, it's a utopia, so some believe. It's whatever you wish." Ruth ended finally by saying, "But it's never dull."

The two had been walking along the streets of Mombasa as she spoke of this, and she finally said, "Do you know what black water fever is?"

"No. What is it?"

"About the worst thing you can have around here," Ruth said.

"Is it worse than malaria?"

"Oh yes! People that get malaria die. We don't know exactly what it is, but when the kidneys start producing what the natives call 'black water' it's all up with you."

"Is it very common?"

"More common than I'd like," Ruth said with a grimace. "We have a young man here who's got it and he's all alone. No friends. David and I stop by and see him as often as we can, but I wonder if you'd mind going by and visiting him."

"Of course, Aunt Ruth, if you think it would do any good."

"He always likes to talk to anyone, but it may be hard. It's pretty rough."

"I'll do whatever I can."

Ruth led her down one of the crooked, twisting streets that ran like a maze through the city to a door that she shoved open without knocking. Annie followed her, and inside she saw a man on a camp bed under a thick, sticky blanket.

"Davie, this is Miss Annie," Ruth said. "She's my niece and a new missionary. I thought you might like to talk to her."

Annie moved forward and was shocked at what she saw. What the Egyptians had done in fashioning mummies of dead bodies, the black water fever had done the same to this man. His face was a skull, the skin drawn over the bones, and he was all eyes, it seemed. They moved in their sockets independent of anything else. Annie's heart filled with compassion, and she moved over and sat down beside his bed.

"I've got some other patients to see. You two can visit for a while," Ruth said.

Annie nodded, then turned back toward Davie. The smell was awful! It was of death, and sickness, and of disease, but she tried not to notice. It was a struggle for her, for all her life she had been troubled to be with people who were extremely ill, even terminally so. She feared that more than she feared lions or hyenas in Africa, but she knew that death was a part of Africa, and this was her first encounter with it. She could not think of anything to say for the moment, and the man called Davie spoke first.

"Not very pleasant for you in here, Annie."

"Oh, it's all right. I'm sorry to see you feeling so poorly."

A silence hung in the room for a moment. The flies buzzed, as always, and Davie licked his parched lips and shrugged his emaciated shoulders. "I get lonely sometimes. Nothing to do but lie here and stare at the ceiling."

"Would you like for me to read to you?" Annie offered.

"No. Just talk. Tell me what you've been doing."

Annie discovered soon that Davie simply wanted to hear the sound of a human voice every day. When she paused during her rambling attempts at conversation, he whispered, "Lying here like this, you remember the strangest things. I remember people I hated once, but I don't hate them anymore."

Annie watched the sweat bead on his forehead and knew that he was feverish. "It's hard to be sick and alone. Do you have nobody here?"

"Doctor David and Miss Ruth come by every day when they're

not out in the field. I have an old woman who comes by and brings me something to eat—when she thinks of it."

Annie knew that Ruth and David had witnessed to the man, but she was determined never to miss an opportunity. "The Lord is all we have at times like this, isn't He?"

"Yes, He is. Doctor David led me to the Lord when I first got down. You know, this black water fever is about the worst thing you can have. I had malaria for years. Chills, fevers, nightmares, but when I saw the first black water from the kidneys, I knew I was dying. That I'd never leave this place."

"Don't say that. God's able to heal."

"Do you believe that?"

"Yes, I do."

"I don't understand it," Davie whispered. He was actually delirious now and said things that made no sense. He was all mixed up with when he was a young man, but he also said, "Doctor David did pray for me, but I didn't get well."

Annie hardly knew what to say. She was convinced the man was dying and did not want to offer any false hopes. She stayed with him for over an hour until Ruth returned. When she got up, she saw that Davie had drifted off into a fitful sleep. She followed her aunt outside and said, "Isn't there any hope?"

"I don't think so. He'll never get off that bed. It's sad, isn't it?"

"Why doesn't God heal him?" Annie asked passionately. And for one instant a violent mood shook her. "Why doesn't God heal him, Aunt Ruth? The Bible says if you pray, God will answer."

"I know. I've asked myself that same question a thousand times." She was wearing a plain white blouse with a brown skirt and half boots. Her red hair was pulled back and held firmly in place by pins. "I don't know. But I do know that God is love, and that if He doesn't choose to do something we want, it's because it's best for us. Who knows but what something terrible is waiting down the road for Davie, and God is going to take him out of it."

It was a thought Annie herself pondered many times. As a matter of fact, she found many of her thoughts much like those of this strong woman who walked beside her. Her eyes were warm and at the same time sad over the fate of her friend.

"Where's Jeanine?" Ruth asked.

"She went out shooting with some government official."

"She'd be better off spending time here learning how to minister to people. You'll have to watch her when you get on the field.

The Masai are proud people and very sensitive. Jeanine's going to have to be careful of her ways."

"Well, you know Jeanine," Annie replied.

"Yes, I do," Ruth said grimly. "She reminds me somewhat of how my cousin Priscilla used to be. But I still say you're going to have to watch her. I know it won't be easy, but I've seen many a missionary come to grief because they offended one of the Masai."

Annie did not answer, for she knew how hopeless it was to curb Jeanine Quintana's impulsiveness. As they continued on down the street, she said, "I'll come back to see Davie every chance I get."

"That's kind of you, Annie, and it's like you."

★ ★ ★ ★

The limit imposed by Jeanine came to an end on Thursday, and as Annie and the others expected, she rose, determined to leave that day. "I gave them a chance, didn't I, Annie? He hasn't been able to find anybody."

"Just give it another day or two. Barney said that he's sure he'll have a guide by then."

But Jeanine would not listen. The two were arguing about it, and Annie saw it was hopeless when a knock at the door interrupted them. When Annie opened it, Barney Winslow was standing there.

"Well, I see I came right on time."

"You mean you found a guide?" Annie said eagerly.

"Sure have, and you couldn't find a better one. You'll be a little bit surprised." He stepped aside and said, "Come on in, sir."

Barney turned to Annie then and said, "Here's your guide. I understand you two are old friends."

The sun was in Annie's eyes and she could not see the man, and then when he stepped into the shadows of the room, she could not speak for a moment.

"Hello, Annie. It's been a long time."

John Winslow stood before Annie smiling at her! He was just as she remembered him, tall, his auburn hair longer than before. He had the same wedge-shaped face and light blue eyes, and his skin was very tanned, of course, from the sun. He was thirty-one now, and there were fine lines around the edges of his eyes and at the corners of his mouth that had not been there when she had first met him years before on her trip west. She took the hand that he put out and found her hands enclosed tightly.

"Well, cousin, you've grown up to be a most attractive young woman. So I'll claim a cousin's privilege." He leaned forward and kissed her on the cheek, then grinned at her. "Kissing cousins!" He winked at Barney and said, "All we Winslows are handsome people, aren't we, Barney?"

Annie could not speak, her heart was beating so fast. The years seemed to fade away, and she was back again to the first time she looked upon John Winslow when he had saved her from the attack of a ruffian. Now the years had passed and she was not a fifteen-year-old girl any longer, but still in her heart something unique stirred at the sight of John Winslow. Something she had never felt before, and she whispered, "Hello, John. It's good to see you again. . . ."

CHAPTER SEVENTEEN

ON TO MASAI COUNTRY

★ ★ ★ ★

Annie Rogers had always considered herself a stable person not given to flights of fancy or excessive emotions. True enough, in her girlhood she had been caught up with reading fairy stories and romances of all sorts, including *The Knights of the Round Table*, in which she would fantasize seeing herself as Elaine rescued by the knight in shining armor, Sir Galahad. She had also delved deep into the romances of the day when any came into her possession—but never without a sense of shame and guilt. Somehow it seemed to her these romances were wrong, as mild as they were. Still it troubled her that she had this strain in her as she had passed from girlhood into adolescence and then finally to young womanhood. She had managed to at least partially subdue this strain of romanticism, and it had given her satisfaction to know that she had overcome such childish things.

One look at John Winslow, however, had brought her ideas concerning her own romanticism down like a house of cards. Just that brief encounter, and it was as if she were fifteen again! She had been almost speechless, managing merely to mutter a few words of greeting before excusing herself. She fled from her room at the first excuse and found herself aimlessly wandering the streets of Mombasa, struggling with the emotions that had erupted unexpectedly. She shook her head in confusion and turned down the land toward the market where vendors on both sides called out to her, begging her to stop and buy their wares.

She ignored them all until a small Arab wearing a dirty white turban and a disreputable robe darted forth and grabbed her by the arm, pulling her toward his small shop that consisted of an awning spread out over the sidewalk.

"See, English miss," he said, using the English language atrociously. "Fine pets for fine English lady! Look, a fine cat." He held up a rumpled ball of white fur and extolled the virtues of the kitten that looked half-starved.

"No. No cat," Annie said. She tried to pull away, but his fingers closed on her arm, and he pleaded excitedly, "Fine monkey. See!" Without loosing his grip he pulled her forward slightly and picked up a small gray monkey with large, soulful eyes. He clung to the Arab's shoulder and stared at Annie woefully.

He was the saddest-looking monkey Annie had ever seen, and she said, "No. I don't have any way to take care of a monkey."

"Oh, he would be delicious. Very good to eat," he said grinning.

Revolted by the words and by the thought of the fate of the melancholy beast, Annie pulled her arm loose and half ran down the street. She paid no heed to the cries that followed her from various vendors and finally made her way down to the coast. The harbor was dotted with small crafts, most of them with their sails furled. The beach was lined with fishermen who were cleaning their nets or repairing their boats. As she walked along, the air was filled with a multitude of voices that rose and fell, making a chorus to the waves that crashed upon the shore. The wind was brisk and Annie drew her thin coat closer around her. It was March and she thought about how at her home the spring would be pushing back winter's icy fingers from the frozen plains. As she walked along noting the starfish and sand crabs that scurried at her approach, thoughts of home suddenly made her feel a wave of nostalgia. She did not exactly think, *I wish I were home*, but the longing for home was there.

For over two hours she walked the beach, unconscious of her surroundings and not speaking to anyone. Finally she returned to her room, where she found Jeanine waiting for her impatiently.

"Where have you been?" she demanded. "I've looked everywhere for you."

"Oh, just walking around."

"Well, you picked a fine time to run off by yourself! We needed to talk about our plans and you weren't here."

"I'm sorry, Jeanine." Annie did not want to discuss plans with Jeanine, but it was obvious that she would have to. "What did you decide about leaving?"

Apparently Jeanine did not hear the question or at least she chose not to answer. She went over and sat down on a couch, pulled her legs up under her, and half smiled as she said, "Why didn't you tell me you had such a gorgeous cousin? He's a dream."

Annie stared at Jeanine. It was something she would have said before her conversion. She was well aware that Jeanine had known many men, and now it suddenly came to her that all of this experience still lay in her. She was still attracted by a handsome face or a lean, muscular form, and certainly John Winslow possessed both of these. "I never thought about it," she said. Instantly she felt like a hypocrite, for she knew that many times she had thought in exactly those terms. Disgusted with herself, she turned and went to the window and stared outside. She was aware that Jeanine was talking, and finally she was shocked when Jeanine suddenly appeared beside her.

"Wait a minute," she said, turning Annie around and staring into her face curiously. "I just remembered something—why, he's the cowboy that rocked your boat when you were just a girl, isn't he?" When Annie could not answer, Jeanine laughed with genuine amusement. "Why, you've told me all about that. How you went to Montana and he saved you from a fate worse than death, thrashed some bank robber or something and saved you and your friend Jeb. He's the one, isn't he?"

"Yes."

The brevity of Annie's reply did not escape Jeanine. Her eyes narrowed and knowledge flickered in her violet eyes. "I remember now. You told me you had a real case of infatuation. Well, I don't blame you. He's one of the most masculine fellows I've ever seen. But I'm surprised you're still stuck on him after all these years."

"I am not stuck on him!" Annie snapped angrily. "And I wish you wouldn't talk like that!"

Annie's voice was sharp, which was unusual for her, and in the silence that followed, Jeanine studied her friend's face. "Oh, it's like that, is it?" she murmured. "Well, I'm glad to see you're interested in some man. You sure haven't shown any sign of it since I've known you."

"Jeanine, I'm not interested in John Winslow in that way!"

"No? You could have fooled me."

"I wish you'd stop talking about this, Jeanine. It hurts me."

Shrugging her shoulders, Jeanine let a smile linger on her lips but said only, "Well, he's probably got a girl in every port—or I guess in every village, since he's not a sailor." She stroked her hair casually, then said almost inaudibly, "It'll be fun to have him along. We'll see what kind of a man he is."

★　★　★　★

Dorothy Hansen Winslow, Andrew's wife, and Katie had gone to great trouble to fix a special meal, since they were both aware that it might be the last they would be able to offer the two fledgling missionaries. It consisted of nothing very exotic. Eland steak and fried bananas were two of the more interesting items, but they had also prepared a large roast with new potatoes and a large pot of green peas, the common variety that grew in the area.

Annie liked both of the missionary wives. They were exactly the same age, thirty-eight, and very attractive women, although darkened by the sun more than would have been true in America. The kitchen and the dining area seemed full of children, although there were only five of them. Barney and Katie boasted of Patrick and Erin, while Dorothy did her best to sit on Amelia and Phillip, her own children. They were all between nine and eleven, which meant that they found it impossible to sit still and be quiet for more than five minutes at a time. David and Ruth's only child, Eileen, was a quiet five-year-old who never strayed too far from her mother.

"I suppose these children are a trial for you. You're not accustomed to them, Jeanine," Dorothy said after quieting her pair down for the tenth time.

"No. I'm not used to children, but I like to see lively ones." Jeanine's eyes sparkled and she nodded. "You certainly have lively ones here."

"I'll say amen to that," Andrew said. He had dressed for dinner more carefully than the other three men, wearing a gray suit with a white shirt and a blue silk tie. His reddish hair shone in the lamplight, and he was, without a doubt, the finest-looking man at the table. Across from him Barney showed the signs of a rough life. Some of the scars of his boxing career remained with him, including one ear that was slightly swollen and tiny scars around his eyes. He had also had his encounters in the African jungle, one with a lion that had left a claw mark down his left cheek. He looked rough and ready, whereas Andrew was far more sleek and sophisticated.

John Winslow had not dressed for dinner. He still wore the same faded khakis he had had on when he first arrived. He sat beside Annie, across the table from Jeanine, and had said very little during the meal. Annie learned from Barney and Andrew that he had not been in Africa long but had quickly become known as one of the best white hunters in the area. Barney had said, "He threw himself into it and picked up enough experience in a couple of years to put him on a par with most men who have been out here for ten. He really went native. Just lived off the country until he had covered it all."

Now as Annie avoided looking at him whenever possible, she was aware that Jeanine was watching her with an impish light in her eyes. She expected her to say something that would embarrass her, and surely enough she did.

"Annie's told us how you rescued her when she came to visit you, John. She made you out to be quite a knight in shining armor."

John's eyes flickered toward Jeanine, and he seemed to see something in her. He smiled and turned his head toward Annie. "She always made more out of that than it really was."

"What happened?" Ruth asked. "Tell us about it."

"Oh, when Annie and Jeb got off the train, I wasn't there to meet them as I should have been. One of the local fellows who went around trying to make himself look tough bothered them a little bit. I came along and discouraged him."

"It was more than that," Annie replied, her cheeks slightly flushed. "I think he would have become unbearable if you hadn't gotten there."

"Oh, he wasn't mean. He just smelled bad," John grinned. "I wasn't really a knight in shining armor. Just a dusty cowboy." He turned to Annie then, saying, "We had good times, didn't we, Annie? Long rides. I still remember them."

"So do I."

The conversation turned to something else, but just the comment from John that he still remembered their rides brought a warm glow of pleasure to Annie.

After the meal was over, Dorothy and Katie took the children and began the endless battle to get them ready for bed. David and Ruth left for their nearby home to put their little one to bed also. The others adjourned to the long room that served as a study for Andrew. It was lined with books, and a huge teak desk dominated the room. *Everything is neat and in order, which is like Andrew,* Annie thought. She took a chair over to the side of the room and determined to say nothing. She deliberately did not look at John Winslow but kept her eyes fixed on the others.

John had said practically nothing at supper, but as soon as they were alone, he walked over to the window, looked out for a moment, then turned and faced Jeanine. "Miss Quintana," he said. "I think you're making a serious mistake going off into the outland in such a hurry."

As always, whenever Jeanine Quintana was crossed, a rebelliousness stirred in her. She had not yet learned that this was part of her old life. To her it was simply the way she had always behaved, and now she acted exactly as Annie knew she would.

"Well, you can tell me your reasons for that, John."

"I expect you've heard them all." John shrugged, and reaching into his pocket, he pulled out a pipe. As he spoke, he filled it with tobacco from a worn, brown pouch, then struck a match on his thumbnail and lit it up. The blue fumes of smoke rose, and he spoke quietly but kept his eyes fixed on Jeanine as if he knew there would be trouble. In essence he repeated what Barney and Andrew had already said. He ended by commenting, "The Serengeti Plains isn't Central Park, Jeanine. There's not a policeman just down the street you can summon by a scream. It's a dangerous place. Death is lurking everywhere. It's part of that world."

"If I were afraid of a lion or any other beast, I wouldn't have come to Africa!" Jeanine snapped. "I'm sorry you should think we're just two helpless females and need a man along to take care of us, but I can't accept your judgment."

"I didn't think you would."

John Winslow's quiet words seemed to stir Jeanine's anger. She thought he was handsome enough, but she saw in him a rock-hard resolve and knew that the two of them would never get along—for she had exactly the same streak running through her. "You may be a great white hunter, John Winslow, but I want to tell you something. You don't know everything there is to know.

Why, you're not even a Christian, are you?" she spoke sharply and her face grew flush.

The stark form of the question made Annie flinch, and both Barney and Andrew glanced at each other uncomfortably. Only John himself was not stung by the harshness of the question.

"No, I'm not," he said without amplification.

"Well, if you were, you'd understand such things as this. God has told us to go and preach to the Masai and we're going. That's all there is to it."

"You have no idea what you're getting into," John spoke back adamantly, trying to lay out the difficulties of such a mission from a purely physical standpoint. The atmosphere became quite chilly.

Jeanine was obviously determined to go, and Annie gave a pleading look to John and said, "I know you feel this is wrong and foolish and even dangerous, but I wish you would go with us. I'd feel much better if you would."

John looked at Annie and found himself admiring her gentleness, which was such a contrast to Jeanine's aggressive and even arrogant behavior. He had made up his mind not to go, for he had told Barney, "I wouldn't put up with that Jeanine Quintana for a wilderness of monkeys." Now, however, Annie's face filled with concern caused him to change his mind. "Oh, I'll go," he said, "but under protest."

This should have been the end of it, but Jeanine's ire was up, and even after the meeting was over, she turned to Annie and said petulantly, "We'll get another guide. I don't think I can put up with John Winslow."

Alarmed, Annie said quickly, "Oh, we can't do that! It's taken a week for him to get here." She knew Jeanine very well and played upon the urgency. "If we're going to go, we'll have to take him with us. And after all, both Andrew and Barney say he knows the country and the natives better than anybody else."

Jeanine argued but finally allowed herself to be persuaded. "All right," she said grudgingly. "But it's his job to get us there safely and that's *all*. It's quite obvious he doesn't understand the things of the Spirit."

A sharp reply almost escaped Annie's lips. She came within an inch of saying, "And you don't understand the things of the Spirit either, Jeanine Quintana!" However, she had been long schooled in how to deal with Jeanine and merely said, "I'm sure it will be fine. You're anxious to go, and this is the quickest way to get there."

★ ★ ★ ★

"Why, you can't take all this gear!" John Winslow stood aghast at the sight of the storage room packed full of supplies of all sorts. He looked around with amazement and said, "You don't really think you can haul all this over land, do you?"

"We'll get trucks," Jeanine said. "I want it all to go." She saw this as the first skirmish in the war that she anticipated with John Winslow and was determined to win it. "If we need another truck, we'll get one."

"You don't know the Serengeti, Jeanine. You can put signs up that say there're roads leaving Mombasa, but they mean nothing. It starts out boldly enough, but after a few miles it dwindles into nothing but a trail running through a sea of red mud or black cotton soil. On a map it may look easy, but the trucks can only go so far. I think," he said with a smile, "whoever put up those signs outside of Mombasa pointing to different cities were incurable optimists."

"But surely we can make it through," Annie said.

"I don't think so, not all the way in a truck. We'll go as far as we can, probably halfway, then we'll have to hire bearers. So there's no point in hauling three truckloads of stuff. It would take fifty bearers to carry all these supplies, and it's going to be hard enough to get ten."

The argument lasted for nearly an hour, and finally John said shortly, "You can take ten trucks if you want to, lady, but I'm telling you that they will never get to where you're headed!"

He walked off, leaving Jeanine sputtering with anger. It was up to Annie again to calm her down. "Look, Jeanine. We'll go as far as we can with what we can carry this time. Then later on another truck can come with more. We may have to make several trips to get all this equipment there." She wanted to add that she had told Jeanine that carrying such an enormous amount of equipment was not wise, but she refrained from doing so.

Two hours later John Winslow came by and looked over the equipment Jeanine had put out. He made no comment on most of it, but he stopped dead still and pointed at an object. "What is *that*?" he demanded.

"My bathtub!"

John Winslow laughed out loud. "I don't think the Masai will know what it is. They'll probably think it's an idol that you worship. Anyway, you can't take it."

"I certainly *am* going to take it! I'm not going to be uncivilized and do without a bath just because I'm in Africa."

"Most of the people you'll preach to will never have had a bath except a ceremonial one," John observed. "Or when they fell in the river. But that thing is too heavy for bearers, unless you want to leave something behind—like Bibles, perhaps."

Jeanine flushed with anger, for she knew that the jibe revealed John Winslow's true feelings about their mission. "You can make fun of Bibles if you want to, but I'm taking the bathtub if I have to carry it myself!"

"That's fine," John said amiably. "It'll probably take two men to pick it up and put it on your shoulders, but that'll be an interesting sight. We'll get a picture of it. We can send it back home to your missionary board. 'Missionary carries bathtub to convert the Masai to bathing.'"

"You shut your mouth, John Winslow!" Jeanine cried out. Her eyes flashed and she stepped closer, as if she intended to slap him in the face. "Don't you make fun of our mission! It's for God."

"I'm not making fun of God or your mission. I'm making fun of you," John said. "It's stupid and ignorant and vain to carry that thing out there. But carry it on your back if you want to, Jeanine. That's the only way it'll get there."

Jeanine was furious, and it took Annie, Ruth, Katie, and Dorothy to calm her down. Finally, however, the truck was ready, and the three of them piled into the front seat. Jeanine wanted to drive and John merely grinned.

"All right. Don't ask me directions. I only drive. I don't give directions."

"You're trying to humiliate me in every way you can, aren't you?"

John shrugged and said, "I can't point out every chuckhole and quicksand pit between here and the village. If you're going to drive, you go ahead, but you'd better let me do it."

It was three in the afternoon and they could not get far before dark. "I think we might as well wait until morning," John said.

This was all Jeanine needed to insist on going now. "No! We're leaving right now. We'll go as fast as we can. I don't want to waste a minute."

Annie went by to embrace each of the women, Dorothy and Katie, and then shook hands with Barney and Andrew. She felt a momentary bit of sadness when she hugged her aunt Ruth and uncle David. She would especially miss her little niece, whom she had grown quite close to. They all wished her well, and Barney had them all stand in a circle and say a prayer. John Winslow did not join the circle but sat behind the wheel of the truck drumming on the steering wheel with his fingers. Finally the two women got in, and as they left the compound, Barney said thoughtfully, "Well, there they go. The Masai are in for some real surprises."

★ ★ ★ ★

As the truck rattled and shook and crashed into teeth-jarring holes, John gave Annie, who sat in the middle, a brief lecture on the country they were passing through. "There are really two distinct groups of people that speak Maa," he said. "The Masai proper and the Samburu. The Samburu are mostly farmers. The Masai don't approve of agricultural tribes. They say they don't follow the traditional Masai way."

"I can't get the geography in my mind," Annie said. "I've looked at a map, but I can't make much of it."

"Well, up to the north there is Kenya. Straight ahead is Mount Kilimanjaro. The Masai call it *Oldoinyo le Engai.*"

"What does that mean?" Annie inquired.

"The mountain of God. They see it as a gift from God, and the Masai worship in its shadow and pray for cattle and children. All this," he said, waving his free hand, "is a part of the Great Rift Valley. So over that way to the north is Kenya. Out to the south is Tanzania. The Tanzanian Masai have had less contact with the west, and that's where we're going. We'll circle around Kilimanjaro and stay in the area where the more traditional Masai live."

"Do you know many of them?" Annie asked.

"I lived with them for six months. They're a fine people. Very handsome and tremendously courageous." He shook his head ruefully. "If a Masai warrior was ever afraid of anything, nobody ever found out about it."

"What kind of religion do they practice?" Jeanine leaned forward to stare at John, and even as she asked the question, she could not help but admire the bronze planes of his face. Strength was in every line, and there was a steadiness that she admired in any person, man or woman.

"You'll have to ask them about that. They do a lot of worshiping, but I don't know what."

"Not the Christian God."

"I don't believe you'll think so. They live, of course, in harmony with nature, and this is very closely entwined with their reverence of God. As I understand it, they believe in one god called Engai. He dwells on earth and in heaven. He's the supreme god, and no one else can be called by that name."

"Why, that's what Paul found in Athens when he saw a statue to the unknown god. He said, 'Him whom you ignorantly worship I declare unto you.'"

"We'll have to get that nonsense out of their heads. I suppose they worship idols, too," Jeanine said.

John shook his head. "You'll have to find out for yourself, Jeanine. I do know this. There are two aspects of their gods. One is called *Engai narok*, the god who is black, and that's the good and benevolent god. The other is called *Engai na-nyokie*. He's the red or the avenging god, the god of anger."

"Do they have services of any kind?"

"Well, they pray as a community during the major ceremonies. Also you'll find out that they use many phrases that show they're aware of God's presence."

"Oh, I know!" Annie said. "They say *Engai tajapaki tooinaipuko mono*."

"Say, that's very good! Your accent isn't bad."

"What does it mean?" Jeanine demanded.

"It means, 'God shield me with your wings,'" John said. "You know any more, Annie?"

"Yes. *Engai ake naiyiolo*."

John laughed and leaned his shoulder against Annie. "I like that one! That may be my motto for life."

Again Jeanine was irritated. She had not spent any time studying the Masai language, and it aggravated her that she had to ask.

"It means, 'only God knows.'"

"Do you know this one, Annie? *Papala amoo etii ake Engai*."

"No. I've never heard it."

"It means, 'never mind because God is still present.' I use that one a lot myself when I get in a tight spot."

"You shouldn't be praying to some heathen idol!" Jeanine said.

John shrugged and said, "You might like this one, Jeanine. Some Masai prayers refer to God as male, but others as female. One song praises *Naamoni aiyai*. It means, 'The she to whom I pray.' Well, that's the extent of my Masai theology." He glanced at the sky, "It's getting dark. We're going to have to stop and make camp."

By the time they stopped close to a grove of oddly shaped trees called *baobab* and John had set up the tent for the women, darkness had fallen.

"Who's the cook?" John said.

"I'll do it," Annie said. "But there's not much cooking. We brought a ham and some fresh bread and vegetables. Aunt Ruth put them up for us."

John built a fire, and soon the three were sitting around it on blankets eating heartily.

Annie remembered her adventure in the market. "A vendor in the market tried to sell me a monkey," she said. "He said it was delicious."

"Oh, sure. Natives will eat anything. I guess that might be a problem," John said.

"Why is that?" Jeanine asked.

"Because if they offer you something and you don't eat it, it might insult them. Something to think about."

Annie laughed suddenly. "You know what I did? My teacher back in England told me that. So I brought a whole carton of hot sauce. I can put it on whatever I eat and kill the taste. I just won't ask."

"Not a bad idea," John smiled.

The three sat around the campfire, and soon John said, "You two had better get some sleep. It's going to be a long trip just to get as far as the truck will take us."

He was right about that, for it took two days to get as far as they could. By then the road had become impassable. They had passed through two villages, but nothing like a town, and all of the food Ruth Burns had packed they had consumed. They arrived at a small village on Thursday afternoon, and John said, "May take a while to hire porters."

"Why should that be?" Jeanine demanded.

"Well, it's a small village and there aren't many men available. I may have to scour the countryside to find some more."

"Pay them whatever they ask," Jeanine said waspishly. The truck ride had been hard on her. She was used to comfort, and the boiling sun and the dust that caked on her face and gritted on her lips had not put her in a good mood. "Money's no object," she said.

John did not answer but shrugged his shoulders. The next morning when he walked out of camp, leaving the two women alone, he was gone only a short time. When he came back he gave Jeanine an odd look. "It's going to take three days."

"Three days! That can't be! You didn't offer them enough money!" she insisted.

"It's not a matter of money. They're having one of their ceremonial periods. A religious thing."

"Well, I don't care!" Jeanine said. "We've got to have help. If you can't do the job, I'll do it myself!"

John grinned and pushed his hat back with his finger. He always wore an Australian type hat with the right side pinned up. "You fly right at it, Reverend," he said. "I'll be interested to see how it comes out."

Jeanine disappeared the next day, going to the village herself. She was gone all day long, and Annie grew worried about her. When darkness began to fall, John made a fire and began to cook a small antelope called a dik-dik. He was a good cook, but Annie was not hungry. Finally she said, "Are you worried about Jeanine? She should be back by now."

"She hates to get defeated, doesn't she?"

"Oh yes. She's very determined."

"Well, I think she's whipped this time. Money doesn't mean much to these people, Annie. Neither does time. They don't have watches or calendars. They take each day as it comes. They never get excited or hurried unless there's a war or a cattle raid."

"I think that's a good way to be, John."

He looked over at her. He was lying on his side on his elbow, and he studied her carefully. "I don't see how you two get along. You're an odd couple. You're so quiet and gentle, and Jeanine is— well—she's Jeanine."

"It took a while for me to get used to her ways, but you don't know where she's come from, John. You really don't." As the flames danced in the fire, Annie spent the next hour telling him the story of Jeanine's life.

When she had finished, John said, "Sounds like she's had a real adventurous life. Do you think she can make it out here as a missionary?"

"Oh yes. She just needs time and prayer."

"Well, there's plenty of time out here, but she's got to learn patience. These people won't be rushed." He sat up then, picked up a stick, and held it in the fire. It caught and he lifted it as if it were a candle. He watched it burn and then with a swift motion tossed it back on the bed of glowing coals. "I've never forgotten your visit to my family, Annie. I remember every bit of it."

"Oh, you couldn't!"

"I do, though. I remember you wore a brown dress that day we met, and you had little pearl earrings. You said your mother gave them to you."

Annie was rather shocked that he remembered such detail, but as he continued, he revealed that he remembered many details of the visit.

"I didn't think you were paying any attention."

"Why wouldn't I pay attention? It was a real break in my life. It was a good time for me."

"You were worried, though. I could tell that. And unhappy."

"Oh yes. I had the wanderlust. But it was good to have a visitor. Especially a pretty cousin like you. Do you still have that picture that Phil painted of you?"

"My mother does. She's very proud of it."

"Phil's done well by himself. He's famous now. Gets no telling how much money each time he paints a picture. I'm glad for him."

"I'd like to see him again. I liked him very much."

They were silent for a moment and then from the distance came a coughing roar. Annie blinked and sat up straighter. "Only a lion," John said carelessly. "No problem."

"They have such awful roars!"

"They do, don't they?"

"Do they ever purr like cats?"

"I don't think so. I believe a feline can either purr or roar, and it wouldn't help a lion much to purr when he's getting ready to fight."

John stared into the fire for a moment, then said, "Why haven't you married, Annie?"

"I . . . never found anyone—" She broke off and did not finish.

"I guess that's what describes me. I never found anyone, either."

"You never found a woman you loved?"

"Not really. I guess I never will now. I'm a confirmed old bachelor, it seems. Here I am at the ripe old age of thirty-one and still no wedding bells ringing for me."

"Could be hard on a woman being married to a white hunter."

"It'd be hard on a man being married to a lady missionary," John countered.

"I guess it would be," Annie smiled. "I'll be an old spinster and you'll be an old bachelor, and when I'm eighty years old, you can come and sit on my front porch and tell lies about how many lions you killed."

As they sat there Annie had a good feeling about it. It was the first time she had ever been really relaxed since they had left Mombasa, but it was broken when John suddenly sat up.

"There she comes," he murmured.

Annie had heard nothing, but she saw a shadowy figure and then Jeanine walked into camp. She was dirty and exhausted and angry.

"What's the matter, Jeanine?" Annie exclaimed. "Are you all right?"

"Those dirty thieves!" Jeanine said. She threw herself down before the fire and clenched her fists with anger. Looking up, she saw them both staring at her. "I found some men. I paid them in advance and told them where to meet me, but they didn't show up."

John Winslow knew instantly what had happened. "Probably some of the Kangori men. They're lazy and shiftless, not Masai, of course. They drift around this part of the world. Were they short and skinny and wore yellow headdresses?"

"That's them."

"Untrustworthy. Even if they had come, they couldn't have carried the loads. It'll take a Masai for that."

"What do we do now?" Annie said.

Jeanine stiffened her back. "All right. You can laugh now, John. You've got your own way. We'll have to wait until their ceremony is over."

"I'm not laughing," John said. "It's just a way of life for them. They're good men. You'll like them, Jeanine."

His words did not mollify Jeanine. She got up and went into the tent without saying another word.

"She spends a lot of time being angry, doesn't she?" John said quietly. "She had better learn to control that. Things go wrong in Africa. If she spends her time sulking in a tent every time something goes wrong out here in the Serengeti, she'll be in there a lot."

★ ★ ★ ★

The Masai porters arrived exactly as they had said and efficiently divided up the load. The head porter, whose name was something like Benji, stared at the washtub. "What is that?" he asked.

"It's what the tall woman uses to wash herself in."

Benji found this amusing. "Did you not tell her that we have rivers for that?"

"What is he saying?" Jeanine demanded.

"He wanted to know what the bathtub was, so I told him. He said there are rivers for that."

"Never mind what he says. Hire two more if you need, but I want that tub carried."

It required another trip to get more porters, but they set out with the copper bathtub in a cradle astride the shoulders of two tall Masai porters.

The trip was hard, for the women were not used to walking. Several times they had to stop and rest.

Annie was fascinated by the tall strong men. "They look so lean, but they're so strong."

"Kind of like a leopard, I guess," John said.

Finally, on the third day they reached the village and were met by a tall Masai and his elders. "This is Chief Mangu. Chief Mangu, these two have come to tell you about their God."

After hearing their names, Chief Mangu said, "You're welcome to our village."

"Thank you," Annie said quickly. "We are honored to be here." At that moment another voice spoke up, and Annie turned to see Jeb Winslow approaching. He was smiling.

"Hello, Annie. We meet again. It's good to see you again, Jeanine."

After the two women were ensconced in their tent, which Jeb and John set up, Jeanine said, "Every time we meet a man, there's something going on between you and him. First John and now Jeb. How many men do you want, Annie?" She was tired, but there was a teasing light in her eyes.

"Oh, Jeanine, don't talk foolishly!"

"Why, you can't keep your eyes off John. Anybody can see that."

Annie was even more fatigued than Jeanine. She did not possess the older woman's physical strength, and she had walked the last five miles on pure willpower. "Jeanine, I just wish you would keep your thoughts to yourself about John Winslow and me!"

Jeanine shrugged. "That might be best. Brother Jeb has feelings for you. I can see that. His eyes just lit up like a Christmas tree when he saw you."

"We're very good friends. That's all."

"John Winslow's not for you." Jeanine smiled slowly, her lips curving upward. She tapped her lower lip with a forefinger and nodded. "He's too wild for you, but I think I can calm him down a little bit. . . ."

CHAPTER EIGHTEEN

TERROR IN THE NIGHT

★　★　★　★

Annie could not understand what Jeanine had expected in a Masai village far away from the big cities. She herself had learned enough from missionaries who had served on the dark continent and from books she had pored over for years. It came as no surprise to her that the simple building of a mission station would be a gargantuan task. For Jeanine, however, the circumstances came as a complete and total shock. She took it for granted that things could be done immediately. It took her several days to understand that in this part of the world there were no carpenters, no labor unions, no employment offices. There was, in fact, nothing but the Masai themselves. It was a matter of pride with Jeanine that she could accomplish whatever she set out to do, but here in the wilds of Africa her expertise seemed to be of little use. She was a strong woman with a powerful strain of impatience running through her, but impatience would not serve her in this land.

"I can't understand why none of the men will agree to help me build a station. It seems a simple enough matter to me." Jeanine was walking around a plot of ground that Chief Mangu's sister occupied. "I don't see why Chief Mangu simply can't command the men to help."

John Winslow was sitting on a large rock. It was dull gray and worn smooth by countless rains and now was hot. Getting up, he stretched and observed, "That thing's too hot for me."

Jeanine stared at him. He seemed cool enough, although the

sun was beating down and she herself was completely soaked. "Did you hear what I said, John?"

"Sure I heard you, but it doesn't work like that in a Masai village." John grinned at a couple of Masai boys no more than eight or nine. They had small bows and were shooting at a piece of bark. "You're doing fine, men," he said in English, then tried to say it in their own language. He took their smiles and then held his hand up with his thumb and forefinger touching, making a circle. He spoke again and both boys suddenly raised their bows. One launched an arrow first and another immediately afterward, and both of them sailed right through the small circle made by John's fingers. He laughed and reached into his pocket and said, "All right. You win." He gave them a small piece of candy and then shook his head when they began to clamor for more. "No more. Later, but it was a good shot."

"Do they understand what you're saying?"

"No. Not unless I put it in their language, and I don't know enough of it."

"John, did you hear what I said about building a house?"

"Yes. I heard you."

"Well, what about it? Why can't I just pay Chief Mangu, and he can pay the men?"

"Men don't build houses among the Masai."

"What do you mean they don't build houses?"

"I mean the women build houses."

Jeanine stared at him. "I never heard of such a thing!" she exclaimed. "All the men do is sit around or go hunting and have fun, and the women have to do all the work."

"Doesn't seem to bother them." John was amazed at her irritation. "If you really want to see how a house is built, get Ayoho to show you. She's building one. Come on. You can have your first lesson."

The two moved across the flat, dusty earth, their boots raising small clouds. There was a smell of cattle and cooking fires, a rank odor that made Jeanine wrinkle her nose. She longed for a bath, but she knew it would do no good, for she would be hot and sweaty again immediately. As they made their way through a herd of cattle of all sizes and colors, some with enormous horns, John stepped closer to her and murmured, "Watch them. Some of these fellows can get pretty rambunctious."

Nervously Jeanine moved closer to John as they made their

way through the herd. When they emerged, John pointed. "There's Ayoho's place. Come on."

They approached the structure that looked very strange to Jeanine. She waited while John spoke to the woman who turned to face her. She was a beautiful woman with skin as black as ebony, and like all of the Masai women, she stood as erect as a soldier on parade. Her hair was woven into curls and fastened down, plastered tight against her skull, and she wore the traditional colored beadwork of the Masai women. Her garment was simply a piece of dark maroon cloth that covered her from the neck to just below the knees. She listened carefully as John spoke rather haltingly, then nodded an answer to him.

"What did she say?" Jeanine asked.

"She said she'll teach you how to build a house." John found this amusing. Yet his humor irritated Jeanine.

"You'll have to stay and interpret," she said.

"Glad to."

Ayoho showed Jeanine first how groups of houses were built on the inside wall of a tall fence made of saplings. The center of the *engang*, as it was called, was used to hold the numerous cattle.

A rough oblong shape was scratched into the dirt, then a trench was dug and saplings were buried sticking up. Smaller branches were woven into these, rounding off into the roof. Grass was packed all around, then plastered with cattle dung.

Ayoho led the pair into a finished house, and it seemed very small to Jeanine. She later made a sketch of it for use in a report or book she intended to write.

There was only one room and it was shared with the animals that formed the core of Masai life. There were no large windows, but light entered through openings in the side and roof. A hearth in the center of the dwelling served for cooking, warmth, and light.

As Ayoho began to speak, Annie came up and helped John do the interpreting. She had become fairly proficient unless the conversation got into areas she had no knowledge of yet. After she had finished the interpreting, she smiled at Ayoho and said something in Swahili, her own language. Ayoho smiled, her teeth white against her black skin, then she turned back to her building.

"Well, you're a certified housebuilder now. When are you going to start gathering your sticks?" John asked Jeanine.

"I'm not going to live in a mud house. We're going to have a

TYPICAL MASAI HOUSE

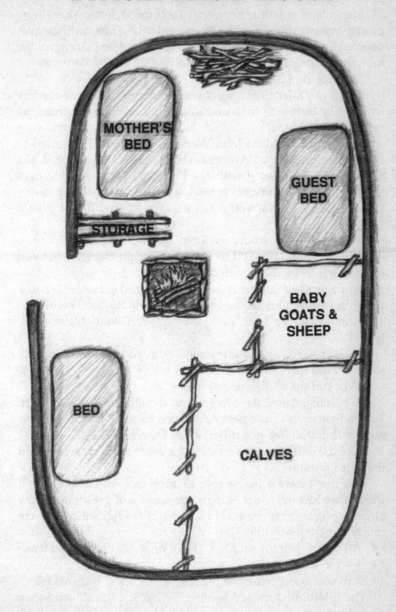

timber house. We'll have the wood cut and hauled in."

"That's one way," John said. "If you've got the money, it's a good way."

Annie was wearing her usual costume, a white dress now grown rather grubby with a day's hard work. Her red hair was covered by a sun helmet, and she said, "About our service in the morning. I don't see how we can do it without an interpreter."

"You can do it, Annie."

"No, I can't, Jeanine. I don't know enough of it yet. Someday I will." She turned to John and said, "John, would you interpret for us?"

The question caught John Winslow off guard. He turned to face her and shoved the Australian bush hat back on his head. His auburn hair was damp with the heat, and his light blue eyes seemed to glow against his tanned, wedge-shaped face. "I'm surprised," he said, "that you'd ask me. You know I'm not even a Christian."

"I know, but you know the language," Annie said.

"How do you know I'll be truthful? I might change what you say and tell them all to be Buddhists."

Annie grinned suddenly and her eyes crinkled up. She had a delightful smile. One seeing it could not help but smile with her, and she shook her head now, saying, "You wouldn't do that, John."

"Well, I have a good reputation with you. Better than with some I could mention."

"Will you do it?" Jeanine asked.

"If you like. You'll have to go slow, though, and I'm no expert. Too bad we didn't have Bert Feely here. He's the best interpreter around, but it's hard to get Bert away from Mombasa."

"Good. We'll have the service in the morning. How will we get the word around?"

"We don't have a newspaper to put it in," Annie laughed. "I think if we just tell Chief Mangu, the word will get around. He's already promised to come. How about if we have it over there under those baobab trees?"

"All right," Jeanine nodded. "We'll do it. Maybe we can teach them some simple songs."

"Are you going to do the preaching, Jeanine?" John asked.

The question surprised Jeanine. "Why, of course!" And then

she suddenly turned to Annie. "Unless you would rather do it, Annie."

"Oh no. I want you to preach. You do it so much better."

Something flickered in John Winslow's eyes, but he said nothing. "All right. I haven't been to church in a long time. I grew up in one, of course, but I've gotten away from my Christian raising."

Annie smiled, saying, "You'll get back to it, John. I know you will."

★ ★ ★ ★

Annie looked at all the people who had gathered for the meeting. Getting the crowd together was not difficult. Chief Mangu had done a good job promoting the service, and he himself sat with his large family directly in front of where Jeanine and Annie came to stand. Annie thought, *What an exotic place to preach the Gospel*. She looked over across the plains, and far beyond the herds of the Masai she saw the massive heights of Mount Kilimanjaro, the mountain of God, as the Masai called it. Sweeping her gaze around, she caught a glimpse of a small herd of zebras, almost too far off to see, raising a cloud over to the east. Overhead the ever present vultures were circling, waiting and searching for their next victim in the cycle of life and death that played itself out on the plains.

"I suppose we might as well start," Jeanine said. "Why don't you sing, Annie?"

Annie had prepared for this first service. She had translated one of the gospel songs into the Masai language with a little help from Chief Mangu. It was a simple song, "Jesus loves me, this I know, for the Bible tells me so. Little ones to Him belong. They are weak but He is strong. Yes, Jesus loves me. Yes, Jesus loves me. Yes, Jesus loves me. The Bible tells me so."

In a very faltering way, she asked them to listen to her sing and then try to sing it with her. She was quite intimidated by the ranks of tall Masai warriors. She could not help but think of how, in the past, they had been the fiercest of all African tribes. No one could stand before them. Now those days were mostly gone, except for cattle raids that no one could seem to get out of their system. Their skins glistened and they seemed totally unaware of the heat of the sun. She had seen one of the Masai step on a burning coal and not even notice it, so tough were the soles of his feet.

Now she began to sing, and when she had finished the song, she said, "Now you." This time when she began to sing, a few joined her, and by the time she had sung it four times, the sounds were echoing through the whole village. "Wonderful!" she said. "We'll just sing that one, but I'll teach you another one the next time."

Jeanine stepped forward then and stood under the shade of the single tree that seemed to be flattened out by the pressure of the heat. Her black hair was tied with a jeweled string behind her head, and she made a fetching figure as she began to speak. John Winslow, who stood to her right, kept his eyes on her and listened carefully. He felt awkward translating a sermon, but somehow not as awkward as if it had been Annie who had been doing the preaching. Actually, he thought it rather odd for Jeanine Quintana to do it. He had seen some streaks of stubbornness and willfulness in her that he did not like. *She's so different from Annie*, he thought, and his eyes went over to Annie, who was standing at a right angle to him, her eyes on the black faces that circled them. *She's just like she was when she was fifteen years old except she's a woman now. But Jeanine* . . . He looked back at Jeanine and refrained from shaking his head.

Jeanine, at Annie's insistence, kept the sermon short—no more than twenty minutes. She had been coached so that she would speak one phrase in English and wait until John had translated it into the language of the Masai. It was not an easy thing to do, for she longed to cry out and rush on ahead to tell them about the glories of God. She did not give her testimony, for a beer barrel would have meant nothing, nor would a ship. Her dramatic conversion would mean very little to any of the Masai. So she simply spoke of how people needed God in their lives.

When the service was over, the crowd remained still. Jeanine remarked with a startled expression, "What are they waiting for, John?"

"I think they want more singing and more preaching. Their ceremonies are very long. Some of them last two weeks. I believe," he grinned, "they think this was kind of a preliminary."

Annie and Jeanine exchanged frantic glances, but John said, "Annie, why don't you just sing some more? It doesn't matter whether they understand it. They like your singing and so do I."

Annie quickly agreed and soon her clear soprano voice was filling the village again. She was startled when the men suddenly began to leap upward during one song. She had seen this before.

It was a sport with the men. Standing flat-footed, they propelled themselves straight in the air. Some men, it was rumored, could leap as tall as their height. She never missed a beat, however, and glancing over at John, he winked at her and nodded encouragingly.

Afterward, Jeanine preached some more and John tried his best to interpret. Both women suggested that he was taking some liberties, but he only smiled back at them.

When the service was over, Jeanine and Annie went to the chief, and Jeanine put out her hand. It was a practice Chief Mangu was not familiar with, and he stared at her hand and looked at John, saying something. John responded and Chief Mangu's white teeth shone as he reached out and his big hand swallowed that of Jeanine Quintana. He then shook hands with Annie, then with John, and then went back to Jeanine. He repeated this several times until it became apparent that he was not going to stop.

John laughed and held up his hand. "It's all right, Chief. Usually half a dozen handshakes are enough." He listened as the chief replied, and then he turned and spoke to Annie. "He says that he'd like to hear more about this Jesus God."

"Wonderful!" Annie said. She looked at Jeanine and said, "See, it's going to be fine."

"Why don't we talk to them now about letting Christ come into their lives?"

Both John and Annie stared at her. "It's a little bit soon," Annie said. "These things take time."

Jeanine Quintana did not like things that took time, and her whole body revealed it. She stood stiffly and then threw her hands up. "All right! It'll take time."

As John watched her walk away, he said, "She's impatient, isn't she?"

"Yes. She's always had everything done for her. It aggravates her that she can't get her own way. But she's come a long way, John. You don't know how far."

"So have you, Annie."

Startled, Annie looked up at John Winslow. Her eyes were wide, and there was an air of vulnerability about her, as there always had been. John remembered this from when she was just a girl. It was still there, though she was now a woman pleasing to the eyes with a face that was expressive and at the same time quietly pretty. He liked her eyes especially, dark blue, almond-shaped with long, dark lashes. "I remember the first time I saw you," he said. "I think about it a lot."

The two turned and began to walk among the villagers, smiling and speaking to them. Annie was learning their names, and she kept a little notebook and wrote them down so she could practice saying them correctly. Ayoho had been helpful in teaching her new words. Now as she walked beside John, there was a peace in her, and she looked up at him. *Who would have believed I would be walking beside John Winslow here in the middle of Africa?*

Right then he turned and caught her eyes, and said, "I'm glad you're here, Annie."

"I'm very glad you're here too, John. We couldn't make it without you."

"Oh, I doubt that. You two are determined. You're going to make it all right."

★　★　★　★

Two days after the first service, John came in when the sun was just beginning to fall out of the afternoon sky. Thin tendrils of clouds trailed across the blue canopy that spread itself around Masai country. He greeted Annie, saying, "Had good luck. We can have roasted antelope. I'm not much of a cook, but even I can't mess that up." He looked around and asked, "Where's Jeanine?"

"Why, she went hunting."

Instantly John's face changed. His mouth drew into a tight line, and his voice was almost harsh as he said, "When did she go?"

"Oh, about an hour or two ago. I told her she'd better not stay out late."

John turned and ran at once to pick up his gun from the tent. He had leaned it against the tent support pole and began to rummage for ammunition. As he stuck it in his pockets and started out of the camp, Annie said, "What is it, John?"

"She's a fool! She doesn't have any business in a place like this. She thinks it's like her backyard at home."

Looking up, Annie thought the sky looked somewhat ominous. "You really think it's dangerous?"

"Dangerous? Of course it's dangerous!"

"You mean lions?"

"No. Not lions. It's the hyenas."

"Why, I thought they were cowards."

"They don't tackle a full-grown lion unless he's wounded, but they have the strongest jaws in Africa, and they find anything weak that's moving, especially after dark. They'll kill it." He pushed the bullets into the rifle, and there was a faint clicking sound as he put the safety on. He started to leave, then turned and said, "You can't go with me, but you'd better start praying for her. It just takes a few minutes to die here. A leopard could jump on her out of a tree and she'd never survive."

Annie nodded dumbly. "All right, John," she whispered. "Go find her and bring her back."

★   ★   ★   ★

Jeanine had enjoyed her jaunt. She had begun learning some of the names of the different flowers and plants and had recited them as she had gone stalking small game.

As she walked along the narrow trail, she began to think of how different things were. Time for Jeanine had always been a hard master. She had a sharp business sense and knew that time was money in her world back in the States. Everything ran according to the clock and to the calendar. One had to be at a certain place at a certain time. There were appointments that had to be fulfilled, and she had learned to live in that world so controlled by time.

The Masai, she had quickly discovered, had little sense of time. John Winslow had warned her of this, but she had learned it first-hand once when a warrior said he would come back soon. That could either mean ten minutes or a day or a week. It depended on what happened. She was only now beginning to understand why time had so little meaning. Their world was not complicated as hers had always been. They had no committees, they had no regular business hours, they lived by their cattle, and the young boys mostly took care of them. The women built their houses, but there was no hurry about that, either. Everything moved at a slow pace. It reminded her of a slow tide she had once seen coming in off the coast of New England, rolling slowly, never hurrying. So was life among the Masai people.

For Jeanine this was almost a tragedy. She wanted to get on with things. She had come to Africa burning with a desire to preach the Gospel. Time and again she had had dreams of natives coming and falling before God and letting Jesus into their lives.

Annie had warned her that it would not be like this, but secretly she had hoped that Annie would be wrong. Even now she wanted to build a building and had already ordered the timber to be brought, but she knew that the wood would be harvested by Africans and that the sawmill would be run by Africans, all with little sense of urgency. The trucks and bearers that brought the lumber back would not be in any hurry at all. So she was forced to bring her own busy life to, what seemed to her, a useless dead halt.

Jeanine stopped suddenly, for a slight movement caught her eye. Quickly she lifted her rifle and held absolutely still. A small antelope no bigger than a dog, called a dik-dik, lifted his head nervously and then stepped out into the clearing. Jeanine pulled the trigger and the shot took the small animal in the heart. He was dead before he struck the ground, and Jeanine felt a surge of satisfaction—the dik-dik would provide good food for her and Annie and some to share. She moved quickly to where the animal lay. When she tried to pick it up, she realized it was heavier than it looked. Nevertheless, she stubbornly put her rifle and her flashlight down and struggled to get the animal over her shoulders. It weighed no more than thirty pounds, but she had not gone far, only about a quarter mile, before her shoulders began aching. She looked up and was startled to see how dark the sky was. The afternoon had gotten away from her, so she hurried on, suddenly anxious for the security of the village.

Jeanine had always been healthy, but she underestimated the power of the African sun. She had not yet learned that it could drag the energy out of a person silently and without fanfare. She had noticed several times that she grew tired easily, but now, struggling along with the weight of the carcass, she began gasping for breath.

She halted and looked around wildly. She had left the camp walking east, but she had grown so interested in the flowers and the plants and in hunting itself that she had forgotten to check her position. Dropping the dik-dik to the ground, she grasped the rifle with both hands and turned in a full circle. This was even more confusing, and she said aloud, "Steady now, Jeanine. Just stop and think a minute."

But even as she stopped and thought and tried to figure out her position, it seemed that the sun was dropping lower and lower beneath the rim of the horizon. She started to remember stories she had heard from missionaries of helpless people torn to pieces by fierce leopards or attacks by lions. Even the thought of a wild African buffalo charging sent a shiver up her spine. Taking a deep breath, she made a decision. Knowing she could not carry the dik-dik, she left it where it lay, knowing that jackals and vultures would find it and finally ants and bugs and worms would finish off what they left. Nothing was wasted in Africa. She had learned that much.

She moved along a path, trying to convince herself that she was headed in the right direction, but after fifteen minutes, when it was almost too dark to see more than a few yards, she knew she was going the wrong way.

"I've got to go back," she said, and fear began to grow in her. It was an emotion she had not felt often, for she was a courageous woman, but this was not her world and she well knew it.

As she quickly backtracked over the ground she'd covered, she looked for the body of the dik-dik, but she had lost that, too. Now she was completely confused. The darkness grew thicker, and from far off she heard the coughing roar of a lion. Fear gripped her heart and she began to trot. She walked and half ran for over half an hour. The moon began to shed its silvery beams, but it was a cold and lifeless moon, unlike the jungle that was teeming with all kinds of life.

She did not know how long it was after that before something made her turn to her left. She caught a flicker of movement, and then it was gone at once. Instantly she lifted the rifle, ready to fire, but she saw nothing. Then suddenly to her right there was another movement. This time she did fire. The gunshot seemed to echo through the jungle much louder than when she had fired the rifle in the daytime. The echoes rolled through the forest and she thought, *Maybe someone will hear it and come and find me.*

She moved on quickly, straining her eyes to catch any movement. She knew, however, that her eyes were not as keen as those of her enemies that lived by tracking their prey.

The thought of leopards frightened her and she began to run again. But she had not gone far before she stepped in a hole and fell down with a cry. Her ankle twisted with a shooting pain, and the rifle went skittering across the grass. With a sob she threw herself forward, and just as she picked up the weapon, she saw other shadows. A baobab tree offered some shelter. With some thought of climbing, she started to make her way toward it. Her ankle would not bear the weight, however, and she had to crawl, dragging her rifle behind her. Finally she reached it but saw that the first limbs were too high for her to reach.

Real panic set in now at being alone in the African jungle filled with savage beasts. She put her back against the tree and held the rifle so tightly that her fingers began to cramp. Time passed slowly and she was sure that something was out there stalking her, but she could not see it.

Finally she sat down, for her ankle hurt so badly she could put no weight on it at all. Sitting there with her back against the tree, there was no question of sleep. She began to wonder what to do if something were to sneak up behind her. Awkwardly, she tried to move around, but she could not watch in all directions at once.

Right then a hideous scream rent the air, and Jeanine jumped at the sound of hyenas. They were back so far in the darkness that she could not make them out clearly, but then as they drew closer she saw the ugly underslung jaws and the high shoulders and the underdeveloped hindquarters. They began making their hunting noises then. She fired and they scattered in all directions, but then almost before the echo had ceased to reverberate throughout the darkness of the jungle, they began appearing again. Forcing herself to be calm, she reached to get her ammunition belt and to her horror discovered it wasn't there. She remembered then where it was. *I left it with my flashlight by the dik-dik.*

She checked her gun and saw that she only had two shots left.

The nightmare began then as the hyenas inched closer and closer. Ordinarily, they did not have prey like this. They were not bold as a rule, but there was something helpless in front of them, and they began moving in closer, chuckling with a ghostly sound rattling deep in their chests.

As they drew nearer, Jeanine began to pray aloud, "Oh, God, I've been so foolish. Get me out of this, please."

She continued to pray, and the sound of her voice kept the animals at bay for a time, but finally one came to stand no more than ten feet from her. He stared at her, and the coldness of his eyes sent a chill through Jeanine Quintana. She knew now that death was very close. She might shoot this one and one more. But when the bullets were gone, what would she do then? She shuddered at the thought of what their jaws could do.

During the next hour she kept them away but used up her two last cartridges. She knew the end was near, so she struggled to her feet by putting her weight on her sound ankle. When one of the hyenas crept close to her, she struck out with the butt of her rifle. He backed off, but there was a boldness in all the animals now, and she could see that she was ringed by them. They were moving closer, and she saw the huge leader getting ready to leap. She held the rifle in her hands by the butt, ready to strike with the barrel, but she knew they would tear her to shreds in minutes.

The muscles in the legs of the hyena bunched, and Jeanine saw him crouch. She heard the unearthly, evil laughter that rolled from his throat. Waves of fear and death washed over her. *I'm going to die*, she thought. Raising the rifle, she waited, and just as the animal was ready to leap, a shot rang out and the beast fell over, his legs kicking in the dust for a moment, then he lay still. More shots rang out. Two more hyenas went down and the rest vanished in the shadows.

Jeanine could not keep the tears from running down her face. When John stepped out of the darkness, she cried, "How did you find me?"

"I heard the shots. Let's get out of here."

"I can't walk." Jeanine found it suddenly hard to talk. Not only was her ankle very painful, but her legs were weak as well from the ordeal. She began to breathe very shallowly, and John Winslow reassessed the situation. "Tell you what. I can't carry you all the way to camp. We'll make a fire here, and in the morning someone will come looking for us."

Jeanine found herself gasping as if she had been underwater, and John said, "Here. Sit down. It was a close one, but you're all right now."

Jeanine Quintana sat with her back against the tree, her eyes closed. Her hands were trembling, and from time to time her lips would jerk in an involuntary fashion. Finally she opened her eyes and her breathing grew more regular. She watched as John found some dead wood and efficiently built a fire. Soon the very crackling of it and the smell of the smoke and the bright yellow and red flames seemed to bring her back to normal.

John sat down close beside her. "Not much to eat, but I got my canteen. It'll have to last until morning. Here, I have the remnants of two sandwiches. Half and half."

"I'm not hungry."

"Don't argue. Eat it."

Jeanine normally would have snapped back at John, but every

time she closed her eyes, she seemed to see the eyes of the hyenas as they surrounded her. Obediently she took the squashed sandwich and ate it, chewing slowly. When she was through, he said, "Drink a little water. Wish it were coffee."

The two sat there and John spoke quietly. He had seen fear shake people up like this before and understood that it had been a terrifying experience for Jeanine.

They were sitting rather close together when suddenly a hoarse cough from somewhere out in the jungle sounded, followed by a terrible roar. Jeanine could not help herself. Ordinarily she would not have done so, but now she grabbed at John. When he put his arm around her and held her close, she clung to him as if she were a child.

"It's all right. It's only a lion. He won't come into the fire."

Jeanine heard his words, but she found his arm around her comforting, and she held on to him. She could feel the strong muscles of his lean body as her arms encircled him. Since Clive Winters, she had not shown herself so vulnerable to any man, but neither had she ever been nearly torn to bits by wild hyenas before.

She looked up after a time and saw that he was watching her. The silver moonlight coated his face with its light, and he had an expression on his face she had never seen before. "What is it, John?" she whispered.

John Winslow had known women, but none seriously. He had been attracted from the first by Jeanine Quintana's beauty, as any man would be. And now as she lay in his arms, yielding and soft, he suddenly lowered his head and kissed her. She returned his kiss, but somehow he knew that her clinging to him was merely the result of her terrible fear. Still he held her, savoring her loveliness. She seemed to give him back as much as he gave her, and finally it was John who pulled away.

As John lifted his head, Jeanine Quintana realized she had been stirred by his kiss in a way that she did not understand. She knew men well, and she also realized she had held on to him and kissed him back more out of fear than of genuine affection. There was a weakness in her as a woman as well as a strength, and yet she did not want to admit this. She shoved him away and moved stiffly to put distance between them.

"Don't tell me you're insulted," John said.

"Don't ever touch me again!"

"I probably will, and you'll like it then just like you did this time."

Jeanine swung her arm, attempting to slap his face, but he was too quick. He pinioned her wrist, held it there, and shook his head. "You are what you are, Jeanine. Annie can be a missionary, but you will never make it."

"How can you say that? You don't know me!"

"Yes, I do! I'm no expert on women, but from what I've heard all my life about those who serve God, they have to have a streak of gentleness and generosity. I've never seen either in you."

His words seemed cold inside Jeanine's head, and she was hurt, for she knew there was truth in what he said. She would not admit it, however, and drew herself back. As the fire crackled in the darkness, making a tiny dot of brilliance in the blackness, she made up her mind. Although she did not speak out loud, she was thinking fiercely, *I will be a missionary! I will, and John Winslow will have to admit it!*

PART FOUR

MASAILAND

★ ★ ★ ★

CHAPTER NINETEEN

A MATTER OF TIME

★　★　★　★

The weeks seemed to drag for Jeanine Quintana, for in Africa time moves at a different pace—or appears to. She had been warned by Barney Winslow that she could not expect the Masai to keep her time.

He had grinned as he had said, "It's a matter of time, Jeanine. All of us who grow up in America are slaves to watches and calendars and clocks. The Masai's time is built in his spirit. He has no appointments to make or keep except those that concern his cattle or his rituals. You'll just have to realize this if you're going to be a successful missionary."

And Jeanine had sincerely tried to slow herself down. Being an impulsive woman of quick spirit, accustomed to a fast-paced life-style, it had been very difficult for her. Late one Saturday afternoon she was standing just outside the village watching a group of herdsmen. They were, she had to admit, a colorful group of men. She had long ago decided that the Masai were perhaps some of the most handsome human beings on the face of the earth. Both men and women had slender bones and narrow hips and shoulders, but with beautifully rounded muscles and limbs.

Now as the herdsmen plodded along with their cattle, she noticed that some of them still carried the leaf-bladed spears that had made them a terror to their enemies for decades.

She noticed one *morani*, or young warrior, who was painted with red ochre. As he passed by he grinned at her, and she nodded, giving him a greeting. His braids were greased and pulled up from the nape of his neck and jutted out over his forehead like the bill of a cap. There was something handsome and aristocratic about him, Jeanine had to admit, but still she was irritated.

"I don't see why they can't work a little more regularly," she muttered. Turning, she walked with a rapid stride back toward that section of the village where, for what seemed like months, she had been trying to get a church building erected. As she moved by the houses, rounded over and humped like huge strange beasts plastered with dung, she thought back over how difficult it had been just to do a simple thing like putting up a building.

First there had been the difficulty of getting the lumber cut. Then getting the lumber hauled over land to the village had been another gargantuan task. It had not come in all together in one large load but had dribbled in sporadically, hauled in oxcarts driven by somnambulant drovers.

Once the lumber was on the ground, Jeanine had drawn a deep sigh of relief but soon became disappointed by another delay. The lumber had come at a time when the men who would work on it had decided to go hunting. She had faced this problem before on the trail and had bitten her lips to cover her impatience.

Another problem had arisen when she had given instructions on how to build the building.

The warrior who had been in charge of the labor had explained things carefully to her. His name was Drago. He was like all the other warriors, tall, well formed, and with colorful beads dangling from his pierced ears. He spoke no English, which made things difficult, but Annie was able to translate his statement into something like, "It is a waste of time to build this building. We can make you one out of saplings and dung like our houses, only bigger." He had smiled then, believing the problem was solved. Jeanine had gritted her teeth, but stubbornly working through Annie, and through the use of pictures drawn on a tablet, she had shown Drago what she wanted.

Drago had muttered to his fellow workers, "The white-faced woman has no sense." A mutter of acknowledgment had gone around, and the workers had also become impatient with Jeanine.

Now as she walked up to where the base of the building was being assembled, she said, "Drago, you've got to get the men to work faster." Annie, who had been watching, came over and attempted to translate. "Tell him that the work is going too slow."

Annie hesitated. "Do you think that would be wise, Jeanine?"

"They're just lazy. Tell him!"

Annie did not translate Jeanine's words in the exact form in which she had received them. She said, in her faltering manner, "Drago, we would appreciate it if you could get the men to work a little faster."

Drago looked amazed. "Why?" he asked.

"What did he say?" Jeanine demanded.

"He wants to know why," Annie said.

"Wants to know why to work faster? To get the building built!"

A long and tedious argument took place then. Annie grew frustrated by her lack of ability with the language. It was like wading verbally through thick mud to put what Jeanine said into words that Drago could understand. Basically Drago was insisting that there was no hurry at all.

"Life is long," he said. "We have tomorrow and tomorrow."

Jeanine, on the other hand, was adamant and finally lost her temper and shouted, "You're just lazy! That's all that's wrong with you!" Then she turned and walked away, her back erect.

"The white God lady is not happy," Drago murmured.

"She's not used to your ways," Annie said gently. "Neither am I. You must be patient with us, Drago."

Drago turned to face Annie. The missionaries were an enigma to him, as they were to all his people. They had come to help, they said, but the language barrier had made it almost impossible for Drago and others to understand what form this help would take.

A smile touched Drago's lips and he nodded. "You are good God-woman, Mother Annie," he said, "but your friend has no respect."

Annie felt that Drago had put his finger right on the problem, but she had no way of explaining this. It was too subtle for her to explain in English, much less in their complex language. Carefully she tried to repair the damage as well as she could, but it was not easy. She watched as Drago ambled back to the structure and called the men back to work. As far as she could tell, they did not increase their speed at all after the scene Jeanine had made.

"I wish Jeanine wouldn't do that," she told herself, shaking her head almost in despair. But there was nothing she could do, so she just offered a prayer that a change would come into Jeanine Quintana.

★　★　★　★

Jeb Winslow had never been so happy. The food that he ate was repulsive to him at first, but he had adjusted to that. He had had malaria, which had dragged him down badly, but he had recovered. The sultry heat, the flies, the odorous smell that hung over every African village were all difficult, but he had adapted well and every day rose up thanking God that he had been allowed to come to Africa to study the Masai.

The sun was overhead as Jeb sat outside of the small hut he had built for himself. He was watching a group of children playing, for he had found the Masai family's life-style intriguing. He had begun by learning that the Masai adored children. It had touched him when he had first heard a devoted mother calling her child "My fragile bones" and another "The child of my beloved man." He had learned also that the Masai felt that a man with many children and few cattle was richer than one with many cattle and no children.

Leaning back and tilting his sun helmet over his eyes, he thought of how seriously the Masai took the rearing of their children. They sang beautiful songs that celebrated the birth of a child. One of them was called "Naomoni Aaayai." It was something like:

> "The one who is prayed for and I also pray
> God of the thunder and the rain,
> Thee I always pray.
> Morning star that rises,
> Thee I always pray.
> The indescribable color,
> Thee I always pray."

This is the song that every Masai mother would sing the day after a child was born. The next day a plump sheep would be slaughtered. Its fat would be melted down, and the mother would drink of it. The midwife was always given a choice portion of this animal.

Some families gave a first name when the baby was still very young. At this ceremony both baby and mother would have their heads shaved. He also learned that a child was often given a second name that was added to the first. The naming ceremonies were very colorful, for the mother would put on her best clothes made of soft lambskin. She would coat her face with heavy ochre and wear many beads and necklaces and earrings.

The mother cared for her baby, of course, but the baby also received much attention from sisters and from grandmothers. They would all tickle the baby, dance with it, and toss it in the air as the mother would sing,

> *"Grow up my child,*
> *grow up like a mountain.*
> *Equal Mount Meru,*
> *Equal Mount Kenya,*
> *Equal Kilimanjaro.*
> *Help your mother and father."*

All of this, and many other facts about the Masai people, Jeb Winslow recorded faithfully. He had remarked once to Annie, "I wish you had your typewriter here. My fingers ache from all this writing." Indeed, he had stacks of notebooks already, and now as he sat there in the warm sunlight, he was fascinated by the children playing before him. A boy of no more than three or four was holding a stick. This would be his fate, for all Masai boys became cattle herders and used sticks. This young lad was soon joined by a second. His stick had a sharp point, which Jeb saw was the forerunner of the spear that all warriors were privileged to carry. They started playing games, and one of the boys took a sharp cut, but he was not permitted to show pain or express anger during these games.

All around there were young children playing. The boys constructed miniature kraals out of the earth, just as English boys would make castles and American boys would make forts. Young girls played with dolls made from mud. They even had a game very much like jacks using stones or berries. Sometimes they played together, their favorite game being hide-and-seek, and like all children, they pretended to be grown-ups.

Getting to his feet, Jeb wandered through the village. He was greeted by many who spoke to him politely. The children were taught to call all elders "father" and all women "mother." He had learned that sometimes the children addressed adults by the name of their offspring, for example, Koto Meto would be the mother of Meto.

One of the warriors ambled up and said with a smile, "Good morning, Jeb."

Jeb returned his greeting. He was pleased that the man used his first name. "How are you, Talbi?"

Talbi indicated that all was well with him, and for some time the two men stood there talking. Jeb was especially gifted, it seemed, in languages, much more so than Annie, and did very well in the conversation. He also understood very quickly that Talbi had something on his mind. Jeb had fallen into the rhythm of life adopted by the Masai. If he had been at home in America, he probably would have said, "What's on your mind, Talbi?" But such a direct question was not asked here. There were certain rituals to be observed, and it was easy to insult the Masai by rushing into things.

Jeb simply stood there speaking idly, his eyes running over the village, waiting until Talbi finally felt that it was the time to bring up whatever was on his mind.

"We are glad you are in our village, Jeb."

"Thank you, Talbi. It's good of you to have me here as a guest."

"Mother Annie, she is a good woman."

"Why, yes. She certainly is."

A silence then seemed to fall upon the conversation, but Jeb knew that Talbi had not said what he intended to say. He seemed to be having difficulty saying it, and finally he seemed to postpone it by saying, "It is time for me to eat."

Jeb grinned, for he knew that Talbi was making sport of him. "I'll join you," he said.

Talbi did not laugh openly, but his dark eyes showed a flash of humor.

"Come," he said.

As Jeb strolled alongside Talbi, he thought about how vital cattle were to the life of these people. Their herds supplied milk, the staple of the Masai diet, and the people had learned to make a sour form of yogurt from it. Babies were given *ghee*, which was their name for butter. It had been strange to Jeb, but he discovered that animals usually were not slaughtered for their meat, except on special occasions, such as when a woman gave birth or when warriors went on retreats to gain strength. Most food was shared in the Masai community, and whenever one killed a cow, everyone who wanted to eat meat that day joined in. However, he had also had to learn that milk and meat must not be eaten at the same time, since the people there were convinced that tapeworms were the results. He asked, "Talbi, why will your people never eat meat and drink milk on the same day?"

"Because it would betray the animal to feed on it while alive by drinking its milk, and then also after it is dead to eat its meat. So we must decide which we will do that day."

They reached the herd and Jeb stood by as Talbi, with the help of one of the other warriors, selected and held a cow firmly by the head. Talbi borrowed an arrow and wrapped a thong just behind its tip. Carefully he knelt and drew the arrow back only a few inches. When he released it, it pierced the jugular vein of the heifer, which gave a start but was firmly held. A calabash, a hollow gourd, was placed beneath the cut and the blood was drained into it.

Quickly Talbi staunched the flow of blood, then drew off some fresh milk into the calabash. He sloshed it around, then the Masai warriors gathered around, their eyes gleaming with fun.

"Here, you first, Jeb."

This had happened before, and Jeb knew that very few white men had been able to join the Masai in their favorite food. He had steeled himself to it, however, and had come to the conclusion, "Well, we eat livers and hearts and gizzards of animals. What's the difference?"

Lifting the calabash he took several swallows, wiped his lips with his shirt sleeves, then patted his stomach. "Good," he said. "Thank you, Talbi."

A murmur of approval went around. Talbi drained the rest of the mixture of milk and blood from the calabash and said, "You are the only white man who knows what is good to eat."

"If you were in my country, you would have to learn to eat some strange things."

Talbi and the others wanted to know about this, and Jeb found himself explaining popcorn and candy and ice cream.

Finally Talbi led Jeb away and they stopped under the shade of a baobab tree. Evidently the sharing of the meal had opened Talbi's mind, but he still did not come right to the point. Instead, he said, "You know. Our people use every part of our cattle."

"Is that true?" Jeb said, although he knew it was.

"Oh yes. We drink the milk and the blood, we eat its meat, we use its urine for medicinal purposes but also to wash calabashes. We use its dung to cover our houses, we make containers of its horns, . . ." He continued on explaining that the hoofs were used for ornaments, the hide for clothing and shoes, for house and bed coverings, and rope. He ended by saying, "All of our ceremonies must include part of our cattle in one way or another. It is through our cattle we have attained our life. We consider little else to be of any value."

Indeed, Jeb had understood that almost from the beginning.

The two stood there talking, and finally Talbi said abruptly, "The people do not like the missionary lady, the tall one." He would not even use her name.

"She's got a good heart," Jeb said quickly.

"She is too forward and too brash. She is not like Mother Annie."

Talbi apparently had finished what he had come to say. He turned and walked off, and Jeb stood looking after him. Finally he strolled through the village to the tent Annie and Jeanine shared while a hut was being built for them. They had insisted on getting the church built first and then building their own accommodations.

He found Annie preparing a meal and she greeted him warmly.

"Come in, Jeb. Chief Mangu killed an antelope and brought us a quarter. It's almost done."

"It sounds good," Jeb said. He sat down on a stool, one of the two he had made for Annie and Jeanine. They could not sit on the ground comfortably, he knew, so he had constructed it of a top and three peg legs he had whittled himself. He watched her and thought of how well she had adapted. Like himself, she had fallen into the rhythm of the village. She loved to do small things and would watch the people for hours when she was not busy with her own work. Now she brushed the smoke away from the fire, where she was roasting several chunks of meat. Looking up, she smiled and said cheerfully, "No salad today."

"It's all right. It reminds me of the meals we had back at Luigi's. Remember?"

Annie had removed the chunks and was putting them onto wooden platters also carved by Jeb.

"I think of them often. Why, I'd like to have a big plate of his lasagna right now."

"Yes, or spaghetti." Jeb took out his knife and began to carve the meat. "Ouch! It's hot!" he said.

The two sat there chewing on the meat, which was rather tough but quite tasty. Jeb did not know how to bring up the subject but finally said, "You know, Annie, I think Jeanine is trying too hard."

Annie shot a glance at him. His face was serious and she happened to think, *I wish he weren't so serious all the time*. She knew he had had a hard life as a child and wondered how much of that still remained with him. "I know, Jeb," she admitted. A thought came to her and she asked, "Has someone complained?"

"Well, the people here think Jeanine is too brash."

Annie chewed a small morsel of meat for a time, then swallowed it. "I don't know how to tell her, Jeb."

"She's not the kind of person you can tell things to, is she?"

"No, she isn't, but she's got to adapt. She won't survive otherwise. I pray for her every day, and I hope that you do, too."

"Of course. It's a new life for her. So different, isn't it?"

"It's hard to believe that she's here. She's had everything she's ever wanted out of life. She used to gratify her every whim, and now she doesn't have those things. You and I had some discipline growing up, but Jeanine didn't have any. I think it's going to be very difficult for her. It already is."

"Well, whom the Lord loves He chastens, so she may have to be chastened a little." He smiled and got to his feet. "We'll pray for her. Now, come along. I want to show you something."

Annie laughed and got to her feet. "You always want to show me something."

"It's so fascinating, isn't it, Annie? I'm so glad to be here. I'm not a missionary like you, of course, but I've learned to love these people."

Annie suddenly stood stock-still. "You know, Jeb, sometimes I think that's all a missionary is. Someone who loves people and wants to help them."

Jeb flushed. He appreciated any compliment from Annie, and he said, "Thank you, Annie. That was a kind thing for you to say. Now, come on," he said eagerly. "You've got to see this."

★ ★ ★ ★

Annie looked up and felt a rush of pleasure to see John Winslow striding quickly toward her. He was wearing, as usual, faded jodhpurs and black boots that came up to cover his calves. The strong muscles of his chest and his shoulders were revealed through the thin white shirt. The Australian bush hat was pushed back on his head, and his eyes lit up as he saw her.

"Hello, John. I didn't expect to see you."

Pulling his hat off, John stood before her, a rueful expression on his face. "I didn't expect to be here," he admitted.

"You sound like you're sorry of it."

"It's not that," Winslow said quickly. "But I've got a client camped just outside of camp. I mentioned you and Jeanine to him, and he insists that you come out and have dinner with him tonight."

"Well, I think that's nice. We don't get many dinner invitations," Annie smiled. "As a matter of fact, we haven't had any where they didn't offer us blood and milk."

"They tried that on you, did they? It's one of the hardest things I ever had to do," John said. "When they offered me that awful mess, I drank it down and smiled. Later I went out and vomited."

"You did better than I," Annie laughed. "I just said no and so did Jeanine. But you sound like you don't want us to accept the invitation."

"It's not that at all. I just don't think you'll like him very much."

"Who is it, John?"

"He's a German named Fritz Rutger. Got more money than he needs, so he comes out once a year and spends a fortune on a safari."

"You shouldn't mind that. He pays well, doesn't he?"

"He's not my kind of man."

The statement intrigued Annie. "What's wrong with him?"

"I just don't like him. He shoots everything that moves and he's a terrible shot. He nearly shot me yesterday." He laughed suddenly and looked much younger. His white teeth seemed to flash against his golden tan, and the breeze, which was stirring slightly, blew his auburn hair down over his forehead. He brushed it back as he answered. "I have to practically put him in a position where the muzzle of his gun is touching the game. A fellow could get hurt like that." He looked up and nodded toward Jeb, who was approaching. "Hello, Jeb. Got an invitation for you."

"What kind of invitation? Not that any won't be welcome." He listened carefully as John Winslow described Rutger and then said, "I'd eat with Judas himself if he had some good grub."

"He's got that all right." A wry expression swept across John Winslow's face. "He brings his own chef along."

"Oh, that's not true!" Annie protested. "You're teasing us."

"I'm not. He does bring his own chef along, a Frenchman. And not only that, he brings his own champagne and caviar."

"That's the only invitation I need," Jeb said. "I'm getting so tired of my own cooking, I'd eat anybody's food. I'll even put up with your Mr. Rutger. Are we all going?"

"I haven't asked Jeanine yet, but you can bet she'll come," John grinned. "Don't you think so, Annie?"

"I'm sure she will. She may even drag out an evening dress, although I didn't bring anything like that."

"When does this big feast take place, John?" Jeb asked.

"He sent me in to get you." Looking up at the sky, he estimated, "It must be about four. Why don't you just come along now?"

"I'll go get Jeanine and we'll get ready."

"Well, that may take a couple of hours," John winked at Jeb, "knowing how slow women are."

"Not me. I'm hungry for some caviar. I had some on the *Titanic* and didn't like it, but I think I'd like anything out here after a steady diet of antelope."

The two men sat down on a log to wait, and Jeb listened as John described his client. "It's clear you don't like him," he said. "But I suppose you have to take whoever comes."

"Takes a lot of money to go on a safari. So you're right. I have to take what I can get. How are things here, Jeb?"

"Every day is about the same."

"But you like it, don't you?"

"I really do."

"You're a strange fellow. I didn't think you'd make it out here. You were all white and soft, but you've toughened up a lot." He glanced over in the direction of the tents where the two could hear the excited voices of the women. "I didn't think they'd make it, either."

"They're going to make it. They'll do fine."

"Even Jeanine?"

"Well, she's going to have a hard time of it along the way. But you know, she's got some quality I can't quite put my finger on."

"Hard-nosed arrogance."

"Oh, that's on the outside. Deep down inside I think there's something else. You know, she talks a lot about that fellow who died for her. The one who got her off the *Titanic* alive. She's never really gotten over that."

"She never says anything to me about it."

"I think you two are a little bit too much alike."

"Hey, I resent that," Winslow said. "She's rich and I'm poor."

"You know what I mean, John. Both of you are pretty stubborn. Lock you two up in a room together," Jeb grinned, "you'd probably kill each other."

"Heaven forbid! Well, here they come." Getting up, John Winslow watched the two women as they approached. "Rutger will be pretty surprised at Jeanine. I wonder why she dragged that outfit along. Nowhere to wear it out here in Africa."

Jeanine was wearing an unusual outfit, at least for Masailand. She was wearing a deep red skirt made of fine silk. It came down to her ankles and showed off her black heeled shoes. Her blouse was white, high necked with delicate lace surrounding the neckline, and ran down into a V along the bodice, where it was tucked into the high-waisted skirt. The blouse had short, puffy sleeves that came to just above her elbows and were tied with white ribbon neatly in a bow.

"Well, you look beautiful, Jeanine," Jeb said.

"Thank you, Jeb." Jeanine turned and smiled at John, which was rather rare. "So you're going to take us out to dine tonight."

"I'm just an errand boy. You'll have to thank Rutger for the food. Come along, and remember, you have to be nice to him. He's rich and they're used to it."

"I'm rich, too," Jeanine said. "He'll have to be nice to me."

John Winslow studied her as they moved along. "That's true, isn't it? How much money have you got?"

Jeanine was not often shocked, but this did silence her for a moment. "People don't usually ask that."

"I'm just curious." John smiled and added, "I like to say things that set you back. Just like you like to set people back."

Jeanine suddenly laughed and turned to look at him. "You're a brute," she said, "and you're probably right about that. Both of us like to show off a little bit, don't we?"

"Sure. But those two back there, they're good people. You and I, we're bad."

Jeanine enjoyed his teasing. He was a handsome man, and she found his appearance pleasing. "Tell me more about Fritz Rutger."

As they walked along, Winslow told her all he knew about the man, but when they reached the camp, even Jeanine was shocked. "Some setup, isn't it?" Winslow said.

"How many people does it take to carry that tent?" The tent Jeanine spoke of had a high peak and looked like it belonged in an Arabian desert. It was made of some sort of buff material, and it moved slightly in the breeze. It was a huge circle at least thirty feet in diameter, and rose high in the air.

Fritz Rutger was sitting in a canvas chair outside of the tent. He rose at once and came to greet them. "Ah, you've brought our guests, John. Please introduce me."

Rutger was a tall, muscular man in his late forties. His hair was clipped short in the Prussian manner and was a premature gray. He had very pale blue eyes, thin lips, and a broad face with a scar that ran down his left cheek. He wore a pair of spotless white trousers with a light green shirt, and a pair of soft house slippers adorned his feet. When he heard the names, he said, "Glad to meet you, ladies, and you, too, sir. Suppose we have our meal first and then we can talk."

The meal was scrumptious. It included exotic canned meats such as tuna and caviar, and there were at least four different kinds of fresh meats. Rutger drank often out of the wine, and John Winslow joined him, although he drank of it sparingly. Fritz laughed at the others. "I forgot that you are missionaries, and tee-totalers, no doubt."

They were sitting around a table that was covered with a spotless white tablecloth and crystal glasses. It was like a table in an elegant New York restaurant, and even Jeanine was impressed.

"I haven't had a meal like this since I left New York, Mr. Rutger. Everything is excellent."

Rutger beamed at her. His face was beginning to glow from the many glasses of wine, and it was obvious he was impressed by Jeanine. "Ah, my dear Miss Quintana, I have read about you and your adventure on the *Titanic*. Most extraordinary. I would like to hear your version of it."

Jeanine glanced around and Annie nodded encouragement. She began to speak of their experience on the *Titanic*, and when she got to the point where she was saved from death, she smiled and said, "So I was saved by the grace of God, you see, Mr. Rutger."

"Please call me Fritz." The German leaned forward and studied her. "I myself have been very close to death more than once. Has it changed your life?"

"I gave my life to God in that barrel, and I've been trying to follow His will ever since."

"Admirable! Very admirable indeed!"

The meal went on for a long time, with Fritz Rutger drinking far too much, and finally John said quickly, "I'd better get the ladies back to the village. I wouldn't want them to go alone."

Rutger protested, "I'll say when the meal is over!"

"I'm afraid not, Fritz," John said firmly.

Rutger's face flushed. He was accustomed to having his way, and it was obvious that he felt John had challenged his authority.

"I'm the one that pays the bills, and I will say when the meal is over!"

"Fritz, you can say all you want to. I'm taking the ladies back."

"You're fired!"

"Fine! You can send the check to my address in Mombasa."

On the way back to camp, Annie said anxiously, "John, you're going to lose your client."

"No, I'm not. He won't even remember it. He's half-drunk now, and he'll drink himself into a stupor. In the morning he will have forgotten all about it."

"Not a very pleasant man to work for," Jeb observed.

"No. He's not."

Later on when Annie and Jeanine were alone in the tent getting undressed for bed, Jeanine observed, "I rather admire John. I've had my clashes with him, but he's a strong man." She had slipped on a nightgown, and now she pulled the sheet back and got onto her cot. She leaned over with her hand under her cheek, which was her customary way of sleeping, and said, "You still think about him a lot?"

Annie knew that Jeanine was very interested in her feelings, but she refused to answer. "Not much," she said. "We've got too much to do."

★ ★ ★ ★

The next day was Sunday. As usual, the three white inhabitants of the village met for a service. They were surprised to see John Winslow walk in just before they began.

"My client's got a terrible hangover. I thought I'd come to church."

"Will you interpret for us again, John?" Annie asked.

"If that's what you want. Jeb could probably do as well, though."

Jeb shook his head. "Not quite. I'm still learning."

The service went very well. Annie was the speaker and Jeanine had little to say. It lasted a long time, for they had learned that the Masai loved long services. John seemed to enjoy the interpreting, although more than once he had to say, "I don't know how to say that, Annie." The statement was having to do with being born again, and John shook his head. "They know about being born once, but this being born again. I don't even know how to put it into their language."

Annie smiled. "Maybe you can think on it and talk with some of the Masai, then the next time one of us uses it, you'll have a word for it."

Afterward the two went around the village. John knew many of the warriors, and he had a real respect for the chief. The feeling was mutual, and they spent some time speaking of unimportant things.

John went back to his camp after the service, but he returned later that night. He found Annie sitting in front of her tent. "Where's Jeanine?" he asked.

"Jeb's explaining some of his work to her."

"Mind if I sit down?"

"Oh no. Please sit down, John."

Winslow took his seat and leaned back. He had removed his hat. Now he ran his hands through his hair. "What are you doing?"

"You'd laugh if I told you."

"That's all right. You shouldn't mind a laugh every now and then. As I recall, some of the Wesleys got more than laughed at when they started their ministry. They got hit with rocks."

"Yes, but they were serving the Lord. This isn't anything like that." She hesitated, then laughed quietly. "I'm keeping a journal."

John Winslow grinned. "All young ladies should keep journals. Why don't you let me take it back to camp and read it? I'm sure I'll find it fascinating."

"No—no!" Annie said quickly. "I couldn't do that!"

"Aha! Deep dark secrets, eh?"

"Nothing like that. Just very private."

The two sat there talking and finally Annie stood up. She put her journal inside a special wooden box that Drago had made for her. "Is it too dark to walk?"

"Pretty much. Leopards sometimes come in to see what they can pick up. Even inside the kraals. They make no noise at all when they're hunting. But we can walk a little."

As they strolled along the perimeter of the camp, silver moonlight flooded the kraal. Annie was feeling rather strange. John Winslow had always had a peculiar influence over her, and now as he walked alongside her, she was stirred. He turned to look at her.

"You look very nice, Annie," he said unexpectedly. "I think Africa agrees with you."

Annie was flustered and did not know what to say. "Just the moonlight," she said.

"Yes. Romantic, isn't it?"

Annie did not answer for a moment. "I don't know. I don't know much about romance."

John Winslow was surprised at her remark. He stopped, and reaching out, he turned her toward him. "You need some romance in your life. You can't work all the time. Of course, there's nobody here to romance, is there? Except me. Just a beat-up, old white hunter."

"You're not beat-up and you're not old."

"I'm a white hunter, though. I'll never get married, I don't suppose. No woman would put up with the kind of life I lead."

Annie did not know how to answer that and she stood quietly. Finally she said, "I'd better go in."

"All right, Annie. I'll walk you back to your tent."

After John had left she sat writing in her journal, but she could not write much. It amounted to only a few sentences. "Do I really care for John? Ever since I was a girl, I thought I did. I've never had thoughts of any other man in a romantic light, and now he's here. And we were in the moonlight together. I feel so strange and so confused. I think, God, you'll have to sort it all out for me."

With a sigh she closed the journal, put it back in the box, and then went to bed.

CHAPTER TWENTY

A BITTER ENDING

★ ★ ★ ★

July had come to the great Rift Valley, but for Jeanine and Annie there was nothing to remind them of the summers they had known. Africa has only two seasons that last roughly six months each: the rainy season called *alari* and the dry season called *alamei*. In November the rainy season starts with short rains that continue until May. From then until October the weather is dry. The cold months in Masailand are July and August.

It was on a Sunday morning that Annie awoke realizing she was cold. The hut Jeanine had hired the natives to build was an improvement over the tent in some respects. It had a wood floor, and since it was raised off the ground on poles, there was little danger of snakes or other unwelcome guests creeping in during the night. The large windows covered with screen let in the breezes during the hot season but also let in the cold air during the cooler times.

Lying in her bunk, dreading getting out into the cold, Annie suddenly was amused. "I came to Africa knowing I'd suffer hardship, and now I'm afraid of a little cold weather. Lord, help me to get over this crazy desire for the things I left behind."

The patterns of the Masai had become part of her own internal clock. As soon as a blanket of green grass replaced a dry one, she would watch a new cycle of life begin. The tribe would move their herds to the open country. They worked harder to care for their cattle, for the herd was their life, as she was often reminded by the Masai themselves.

Lying flat on her back soaking up the warmth from the stiff gray blanket, a picture came before her eyes. It was a portrait, almost, of the land where the Masai lived. She saw the thorny acacia trees that rose up out of the grassy savannah. She thought of the broad lakes and the meandering rivers she had seen in her short travels, which contrasted so dramatically with the flat, seasonal, and parched lowlands that rose toward the softly rolling hills. And then she thought of Kilimanjaro, Kenya, Maru, great, tremendous, and distant mountains that stood like watchtowers over the plains. They put a ring almost like castle walls around the land where she now lived.

The air was always fragrant, it seemed, with leleshwa leaves, and she took pleasure in the Serengeti that teemed with herds of grazing zebras, antelope, and wildebeests. At times she heard the scrubby forest echo with the crash of elephants on the move.

She heard a soft voice calling her name and was startled. She had not heard footsteps, but she rose up on one elbow and answered. "Is that you, Drago?"

"Yes, Mother Annie."

"I'll be right there."

Annie slipped out of the cot, thinking with amusement at the name they had given her. There was something touching about the Masai habit of calling every woman "Mother," but it made Annie feel odd. Quickly she slipped into her warmest clothes. She still refused to wear the jodhpurs that Jeanine took such pride in, but she put on heavy stockings, a thick petticoat, a woolen vest, and brown half boots with laces running up to the ankles. She slipped into a warm, light blue dress, then quickly pulled her hair back and knotted it. Grabbing her helmet, she moved toward the door.

"Where are you going?" Jeanine's sleepy voice spoke up.

"I'm going out on a honey gathering trip with Drago. You go ahead and sleep." Annie left knowing that Jeanine would sleep at least another two hours. Stepping outside, she found Drago waiting for her. He stood on one leg, the other leg bent so that the heel rested on the knee. It was the stork position the Masai men used when they were waiting or simply watching their herds. He wore a simple dark red toga, and blue beaded earrings of a circular pattern dangled from his ears.

"I'm ready, Drago."

"We go." Drago led the way from the village. It was still dark, and overhead a splash of stars seemed to be frozen in an ebony sky. Annie did not speak to Drago, and they covered ground at a tremendous rate. Leaving the village, they took a circuitous route around the herds of cattle that were watched by alert guardsmen who spoke to them as the sky in the east began to turn a golden gray color. By the time they had traveled for over an hour, the sun was part of a blazing crimson disk clearing the mountains in the east.

Finally Drago stopped and said, "We are here." He spoke very slowly and chose simple words, for he was proud of Annie's advances in his language. He stood waiting for her and smiled suddenly. He was a handsome man, tall and well formed, with the lower two middle teeth missing, as was true of all the Masai. The baby teeth were removed and later the permanent ones. Annie had asked about this and discovered that at least one of the reasons was that if anyone got tetanus they could be fed through a straw until it passed away.

"What do we do now, Drago?"

Drago said, "Now we get the honey." He seemed to enjoy lecturing to Annie about the habits of his people. "We must have honey, Mother Annie. It is used to make the beer that is drunk by the elders and the guests at all ceremonies."

Annie listened as he spoke slowly and then said, "All right. What can I do to help?"

Drago seemed to be finding some sort of amusement in the situation. "Usually," he said, "I would bring a boy to help me. But since you insisted today, you will be the boy." The thought of her trying to get honey tickled him and he laughed aloud. "You are a boy, Mother Annie!"

"All right. What does the boy do?"

"Come with me."

He led her to a steep cliff and pointed downward. "There are our bees. It is a difficult spot to get at."

He had brought a bag over his shoulder, and now putting it on the ground, he removed a long hide rope. Without explanation he tied it around Annie, knotting it just under her arms.

"You will go down and put the honey in this bag."

Annie was startled. "But won't they sting me?"

"Not if you are quick. It is cold and they are asleep. If you are not quick," he warned, "they will certainly sting you."

Annie swallowed hard. She had not bargained on this. But she had learned that the Masai valued courage in man or woman more than almost any other virtue. To back down now would be to lose face, so she said, "All right. You tell me what to do." She listened as Drago explained that it simply involved reaching in, scooping out the honey, and getting away as quickly as possible. "I will pull you up as soon as you cry out. Are you ready?"

"I'm ready."

Annie found herself being lowered over the edge of the cliff. It was not a sheer drop-off, so she found places for her feet to rest on. When she passed by the hole in the wall, she saw that the nest was right on the edge. She did not see any bees, but, nevertheless, she was rather frightened. She heard Drago say, "Just scoop the honey into the bag. Get what you can and then crawl out."

She had found a place to stand on a six-inch ledge, and drawing a deep breath and praying a quick prayer, she opened the leather bag and reached in. Quickly she scooped handfuls of raw honey mixed in with comb, expecting any minute for the bees to swarm out. She had scooped out some eight or ten handfuls when a low humming began and a bee suddenly flew right past her eyes.

"Now, Drago!" she cried out, and instantly she was swayed up into the air. Drago was tremendously strong, and he pulled her up hand over hand, seemingly as if she were stuffed with feathers. When she reached the top, he grabbed her and set her down and took the bag from her. Looking inside he chuckled. "You are a good boy, Mother Annie. We have posho honey. Come, we go home now."

The two made their way home, and when they reached the village, Drago taught her how to separate the comb from the honey. Then he mixed it with water and some roots that he had ground small. He poured it then into a large, round calabash, a specially made hide container. This would be placed near the fire. With constant tending the mass would ferment within two weeks. And on the third week, as Drago explained, it would be filtered and divided into as many gourds as would be needed for the number of guests.

"You will have your own gourd when we have our ceremony."

Annie wanted to say that she did not drink strong drink, but somehow she did not say it. *I can at least make a show of joining in,* she thought. *Liquor is not the problem for the Masai as it is for other peoples of the world, apparently.* She had not heard of a drunken man or woman since coming to live with the Masai. It was one of those decisions she found necessary to make constantly. When she was on the *Titanic*, she had not touched even one sip of wine, even though Jeanine and others had urged it upon her. There it had been a test. Here with the Masai she was in a different world. The mild beer they made was part of their ceremony. If she were invited to join, that would be an honor, and she would have to pray much about how to handle this particular situation.

★ ★ ★ ★

"Well, you just getting up?"

Jeanine looked up to see John Winslow standing in the door of the hut. There was no front door, merely an opening they covered with a net to keep the mosquitoes out.

I'm glad I was dressed, she thought, but she only said, "Hello, John."

"Have you had breakfast yet?"

"No. I was just thinking of getting some."

She went to the door and stepped outside. "Do you have another drunken German on safari with you?"

"Not this time. I'm doing some work for a geographic society."

"Really? What kind of work?"

"Join me for breakfast and I'll tell you about it."

He had pitched his tent just outside the kraal, and one of his assistants, a short, muscular native named Bolo, had prepared a delicious breakfast of eggs and fried eland steak.

"Where's Annie?" John asked as they sat back drinking coffee.

Jeanine was enjoying her breakfast tremendously. She sipped on the coffee and stretched luxuriously. "Oh, she went out early looking for honey with Drago."

John Winslow laughed. "I hope she doesn't come back like I did the first time I went looking for honey. Couldn't see out of my eyes for three days."

"Really?" Jeanine was worried. "I hope she doesn't get into anything like that."

"Drago's a good man. He wouldn't risk her. He might tease her a little bit, though."

"Tease her? You think he'd do that?"

"Why, sure. The Masai have a tremendous sense of humor. It's a little bit sophisticated. They've got a dry wit, but odd things amuse them, and to them we're pretty odd. Do you know what they call us?"

"What do you mean call us?"

Sipping his coffee, John said, "They call us *L'ojuju*."

"What does that mean?"

"It means 'the hairy one.' I guess they've seen a lot of beards. The Masai don't have heavy beards."

The two sat there enjoying the sunrise, and John said, "I'm going to take a look at some elephants. I'll be bringing a client through next week, and some of the herds have moved in close. Have you ever seen elephants up close?"

"No. I've seen a few at a distance."

"Would you like to come along?"

"Yes. I'd like it very much. Are you going to shoot one?"

"No. Not this time."

It took only a short time for Jeanine to get ready. The earth was warming up now, but she still brought a heavy coat along. She left the village striding along with John, the two of them moving across the plains until after a two-hour hike they came to where the landscape changed.

"You see how most of the tall trees are knocked down? Only scrub things here?" he asked, gesturing with his hand.

"Yes. Why is that, John?"

"Elephants do it." He was carrying a .470 Rigby elephant rifle, and his eyes constantly moved from point to point. "Elephants probably destroy more vegetation than anything on the continent."

"Really? How is that?"

"Well, when they go crashing through, they destroy everything in their path. They seem to love to butt against big trees and rub against them. So the herds are destroying many of the taller trees. Of course, when they knock the trees down and the trees die, sometimes there are fires that burn for months, and those fires waste the dry grass. So here in the Serengeti, fire and elephants together have converted hundreds of miles of acacia woods to grassland."

"That's bad, isn't it?"

"Well, the range of the plains' game has increased, but it's robbed other species of their habitat." He continued to give her a short lecture on elephants as they moved along into thicker woods. "You know, Jeanine, an elephant can eat as much as six hundred pounds of grass and boughs in a single day, and as I say, it's a destructive feeder. Tears up trees and uproots shrubs."

"What will happen?"

"Why, nothing much, I suppose. Elephants have been destroying woodlands for thousands of years. Maybe it's just a part of the natural cycle of this part of the world. My dad would say that it's the way God made it."

"Do you think so? That God does things like this?" Jeanine glanced at John Winslow's face. "Do you believe God is that interested in everything we do?"

"It's the only answer I have. I had it from the time I could remember." He said nothing for a while, then added, "I wish you could meet my parents, Jeanine. They're the best Christians I've ever known."

"That must have been a wonderful childhood."

John laughed. "I didn't think so. I was a little bit of a rebel. Annie could tell you something about that."

"Do you think you'll ever come to have your parents' faith?"

Suddenly John turned and faced her. His face was utterly serious, and he did not answer for a moment. The question had touched something deep within him, and he studied her countenance for what seemed like a long extended moment. "I hope so, Jeanine. There's got to be more to life than the few years we've got here. I can't deny the Bible is true. It's the only anchor I know of. I went through a time when I thought I would be an atheist, but all during those times, all I could think of was my parents and their faith. I thought of Barney Winslow and other Christians I had met who had been faithful almost unto death. Did you know Barney got clawed by a lion out here and killed it with his bare hands?" He shook his head in marvel. "He must have been tremendously strong. He got astride the lion and choked him. Some tribes here still call him Lion Killer."

"He's a wonderful man," Jeanine admitted.

Turning, John said little more. He was deep in thought, and Jeanine knew his mind was on the question she had asked him about God and his faith. She had an impulse to try to pressure him to make a profession of faith. It was her nature to be aggressive. She wanted whatever was at hand to be done at once. Drago had called her the "now woman" because everything she wanted had to be done now for Jeanine. Still, some bit of wisdom came to her, and she thought, *Not now. You've got to learn to wait. You've made a start. Now God's working in his heart and will do whatever is needed to bring him to faith.*

They had not gone too far before John turned and said with a glint of humor in his eyes, "Aren't you going to try and convert me, Jeanine?"

Suddenly Jeanine began to laugh. "You know me too well," she said. Her eyes were sparkling then, and the strange purple hue gave them a most enticing character. She had wide, mobile lips that expressed her moods more than she wished sometimes, and now as she looked at John, she shook her head with chagrin. "That's exactly what I wanted to do."

"I thought so. As a matter of fact, I was expecting it. You can't do that, Jeanine. It might work once in a while, but with the Masai especially, they won't be driven."

"I know you're right, but it's just my nature."

The two were standing beneath a baobab tree, and from far off came a strange sound. It sounded like "*Chough—chough!*"

"What's that?" Jeanine exclaimed.

"Rhino. No danger from them." John Winslow's mind had not left the question, however, and he stood for a moment, lowering the butt of the heavy rifle to the ground. "You can't push people. You'll never catch a husband like that, Jeanine," he said.

Winslow's words startled her. "What brought that on? You think I'm after a husband?"

"Isn't every woman?"

His bold comment irritated Jeanine. "That's what all you men think, that every woman is out to snare them. I think it's egotistical."

"I think it's experience."

"Oh! Have you been besieged by women panting with desire to marry you?"

"Well, not exactly, but after all, it's a natural thing, Jeanine. There's nothing wrong with it. God made us that way." He smiled again. "That's what Dad would say."

"Well, I've had enough chances to get married. I could have been married when I was sixteen years old. You wouldn't believe how many men wanted to marry me—for my money."

The words had a bitterness that rang loud and sharp and clear. Examining her face, John said quietly, "That's been a problem for you, hasn't it? I suppose it would be for a wealthy woman. You'd never know if a man loved you or what you had."

The insight of the tall man beside her made Jeanine blink her eyes. "Yes," she said quietly, "that's exactly the way it is. I probably never will marry."

"Seems a waste."

His words surprised her and she looked up, saying, "What does that mean?"

"It means you were made to be loved by a man—and to give love to a man."

"Well—" Jeanine was taken aback. She had had so many harsh clashes with John that she could not put his words into perspective. "Where did all that come from?"

"From observation. You're a pretty tough cookie on the outside, but Jeb told me once that despite all that diamond hardness on the outside, there's a gentleness you're afraid to show."

"Jeb's getting to be quite a psychologist, isn't he?" Jeanine was surprised and at the same time strangely pleased. She had not been called gentle since she could remember, and now she looked down to her feet for a moment, savoring the compliment. Looking up, she asked, "What do you think? Is it there?"

"Yes. It's there. But I don't know if you'll ever let it get out. What I think, Jeanine, is that we build walls around ourselves. Some people build them of different material. Inside we're one thing, but we build a wall of money or pride or ambition, and that real part of us that's inside can't break through that hardness. So usually it shrivels up and dies."

Once again Jeanine was amazed. She had not thought she'd discover this kind of insight in the tough white hunter who stood beside her. "How do you break down the walls, John?" she asked quietly.

"I think God has to do it."

Jeanine was very quiet. She thought of Annie and the gentleness that not only was on the inside of the woman but expressed itself in every aspect of her life. Finally she said, "I think you're right."

Then John Winslow broke the spell. It was as if he had revealed too much of himself and said, "Well, come on. I'll show you some elephants."

The discussion left Jeanine thoughtful, but soon she was forced to put it aside when they reached a point when Winslow spoke.

"All right. You're going to see elephants like you've never seen before."

The air was quiet, but as they advanced, she was aware of a mass moving in front of her. She had been told that elephants travel in matriarchal groups led by a succession of mothers and daughters. John had slyly said, "You'd like to be an elephant. Then you could lead the parade."

Now as they crouched behind some acacia trees, John whispered, "There's the leader. She's the oldest cow, probably. That one may be fifty years old and past breeding age, but she's got a good memory."

"I've always heard that elephants never forget."

"I think that's true—about water holes and dangers, at least. They have an instinct about the seasons and always know what to do."

Jeanine watched as the elephant mass moved like gray lava, leaving behind ruined trees, twisted and broken off at the trunk. Finally John whispered, "Look."

Putting her gaze in the direction he gestured, Jeanine saw six enormous elephants emerge from the trees. They were lashing the air with their trunks, and their ears were stuck out at right angles like huge fans. She watched as they forded a deep gully and then appeared again not a hundred yards away. There was a terrible crackling of trees as they shoved their heads against the acacia trees and seemed to take pleasure in destroying them.

The rest of the herd flowed by in perpetual motion with a strange grace, and she noticed that their ears were like great delicate petals.

"They make a lot of noise, don't they, John?" Jeanine whispered.

"Sometimes they do, but we could turn around right now and find one right behind us. They can sneak up that close without a sound."

Involuntarily and with a start of fear Jeanine whirled but saw nothing. When she turned to face John he was grinning. "It wasn't there that time, but it's not a bad idea to look behind you every once in a while. Look at that fellow there."

Jeanine looked to her left and there, about fifty feet away, stood a huge, mighty bull elephant. He had come through the scrub and the dead wood as quietly as a shadow, and she could see the flies that gathered on his trunk.

"Can he see us?" she whispered.

"No, but he can smell us."

Jeanine noticed that John was holding his rifle in a half-ready position, and she looked up at the mighty animal that stood facing them. Suddenly he lifted his trunk and expanded his ears like dark wings. He seemed to fill the air, and the air was split wide open by a scream that shook her down to her marrow. She had never heard anything like it, and she could not even move as the beast moved toward them. She saw John lift his rifle but he did not fire. The beast was only forty feet away when he stopped. He seemed to be peering at them through his little eyes, but then suddenly he lowered his trunk, flattened his ears, and walked calmly away.

"He was pretty close," John observed.

"Yes."

"I thought for a moment there I might have to shoot him." Winslow turned and said quietly, "That was a little bit *too* close, Jeanine. Were you very frightened?"

"Yes."

"So was I. It takes a well-placed bullet to stop one that close. I shouldn't have brought you out here. It's too dangerous. Let's get back."

The two made their way back to the village, and when they told Annie about the elephant, she shivered. "I probably would have fainted."

"I nearly fainted myself," John grinned.

"Were you really afraid, John?" Jeanine asked.

"Of course! A beast like that forty feet away? I've seen what they can do. A man would be crazy not to be afraid. You don't think I'm one of those fearless white hunters, do you? Never afraid of anything?"

"I thought you were," Jeanine smiled. "It's good to know you've got a weakness."

"I've got a suitcase full of them. Come over to my camp for supper tonight and I'll take them out one at a time."

After John left, Jeanine was very quiet. Annie finally questioned her, "What's wrong, Jeanine? Was the elephant hunt that frightening?"

"It wasn't that," Jeanine said slowly. She hesitated, then said, "I had a little talk with John, and I nearly made a terrible mistake."

"What mistake?"

"He talked about his parents and their faith in God. I nearly tried to force him into becoming a Christian."

"I think he's had an experience with Christ in his life already."

The words surprised Jeanine. "Why, what makes you say that?"

"Hasn't he told you about the time when he was a boy when an evangelist came through and he prayed at an altar?"

"No. He didn't tell me that. He just said that he was a rebel."

"So was the prodigal son, but he was still a son. I think that's who John Winslow is. He's been running from God all these years. I think I can see the Spirit of God in him. Barney told me the same thing. He has a lot of confidence. We've been praying together that John would come back to God. I'm glad you didn't force him to become a Christian. It might have been hurtful."

Jeanine was shaken by what Annie had told her. She had not yet learned that discernment was an essential part of a Christian's life.

★ ★ ★ ★

December had come and Jeanine had almost ceased to think about her conversation with John on their way to watch the elephants. For a time it had had left an impression on her, and she had modified her aggressive behavior, but as the months had passed and she seemed to see no result from their labors, impatience began to have its way with her once again. And now she was determined again to make things move faster. She had said to Annie, "We haven't seen a single convert since we've arrived. Something's wrong."

Annie had shook her head. "Nothing's wrong. We're planting seeds. When you plant a seed, you don't dig it up every day to see how it's doing. You water it and let the sun shine on it, you pray over it, and God will grow it. Don't you remember the parable about the seed? The good seeds are going to come, Jeanine. You have to be patient."

Jeanine had ignored this good advice. She had her jaw out and her mind made up to talk to Manto, who was the spiritual leader of the tribe. *If I could win him to Jesus*, she thought, *the whole village would listen. They have such confidence in him*.

Manto, a tall, gray-haired man with deep-set brown eyes, listened as Jeanine pressured him to throw out his old gods and come to the God that she proclaimed to be the Truth. He tried to explain some of his beliefs to her, but she was impatient. Finally her anger flared, and she said, "You are a pitiful example of a leader! We've come to bring you the truth and you won't listen! Well, your sins be on your own head!" She turned and stormed out, and Manto sat staring after her.

The same day, after Jeanine's explosion, the two women had a visitor. It was the chief himself who had come, and there was a sternness in his eyes that neither woman had seen before. He said without preamble, "You must leave our village. You bring trouble."

Jeanine whirled and saw that his eyes were fastened on her. She reacted, not with humility and confessing her faults as something deep within said she should do, but the old Jeanine, the aggressive woman unable to take rebuke, suddenly rose up within her and she lashed out. "Very well! I'll leave your village! There's nothing here anyway but a bunch of ignorant savages!" she shouted, then whirled and left to go to the hut.

Annie said, "Chief, she's a good woman. She just makes mistakes."

"Let her make her mistakes somewhere else." Chief Mangu put his eyes on Annie and said, "Mother Annie, you are welcome. We know you love our people. Our ways are different, but we are listening to you. But your friend cannot stay. She divides the peace." He nodded and said, "Aia," the good-bye of the Masai.

Annie went to find Jeb. The two had become even closer during their time in Africa, and when she told the story, he got up at once, concern in his eyes. "We've got to talk to her. She'll have to apologize."

"She'll never do that, Jeb."

"She *has* to. It's the only way. These people are proud, as you know, Annie. It's a good and quiet pride. But Jeanine's pride is the bad kind. She simply wants her own way."

"Come along. Maybe we can convince her together."

But Jeanine was beyond convincing. She listened stonily as both Jeb and Annie begged with her to ask the chief's pardon and also to ask Manto's forgiveness.

"I haven't done anything wrong," she said stiffly. "We came here to preach the Gospel."

"But that's not what you did. You demanded that Manto obey your commands," Jeb said quietly. "I'm no missionary, but I know enough about the Bible to know that the Gospel works when God draws people, not when we herd them like they were cattle."

"Jeb, this is none of your business!" Jeanine snapped.

"I think it is," Jeb said. "I live with these people. They don't see many white people here. They're looking at us to see how we act and what we do. To see if we have honor, if we have love and dignity, and when we don't have it, do you think they don't see that?"

"Well, I know your opinion of me! You won't have to worry about that," Jeanine said bitterly. "I'm leaving!"

"Please, Jeanine," Annie implored. "Don't leave! God's not through with you here."

"Well, God may need me, but I haven't seen it. It just hasn't worked. I'm going home. I suppose you'll stay here, Annie, but I can't take it anymore. I've had enough."

The argument went on for some time, but the next day Jeanine hired four bearers to take her personal possessions back to Mombasa. "I'm going to take a ship from there," she said, "and never see Africa again."

Annie had tears in her eyes. "Please don't do this, Jeanine. Please don't!"

Jeanine knew within her heart that Annie was right, that Jeb was right, and that she was wrong. But her pride was too strong, and she went over and kissed Annie on the cheek. "You're a good woman, Annie. Better than I am. I'm just not strong enough, or good enough, or whatever it is that God wants me to be. Goodbye."

Annie stood beside Jeb, tears running down her cheeks. He put his arms around her, and suddenly she fell against him. "It hurts, doesn't it?" he whispered.

"She's come so far, Jeb, and now she's throwing it all away."

"We'll have to pray that that doesn't happen." Jeb held her while she wept, and then finally she drew back. He wiped the tears from her face with a handkerchief, then shook his head. "Jeanine's going to find out what it means to run from God. Somehow He will help her!"

CHAPTER TWENTY-ONE

A MATTER OF COURAGE

★ ★ ★ ★

"You can talk all you want to, Barney, but I'm not going back. I'm leaving Africa and I'm going back to America."

Barney Winslow was filled with consternation. Jeanine Quintana had arrived in Mombasa the previous afternoon and had come storming into his office announcing that she was leaving. Barney had tried to reason with her, but she had turned on her heel and walked out without another word.

It was not the first time a missionary had failed in Africa, and Barney had been acquainted with many of them. He had gone at once to his brother, Andrew, and Andrew had shaken his head sadly, saying, "I was afraid it would happen, Barney. She may not be missionary material."

Barney had disagreed. Perhaps because he had seen some of his own aggressiveness in Jeanine. He had slept poorly that night, tossing and turning so much that he disturbed Katie, and finally had risen well before dawn and gone out to walk and pray. He had waited until ten o'clock, then had gone to the hotel where he had asked for Jeanine. She had come down, and there was a stony expression on her face that would brook no argument.

"Could we have a cup of tea?" Barney said. "There's a nice restaurant down the street."

"We can have tea, but it'll do you no good. I've made up my mind."

Barney was stubborn enough himself to realize that arguing

with someone like Jeanine Quintana was useless. Instead he asked about Annie and about Jeb, and after three cups of tea, he was pleased to see that some of the anger had left her eyes. She was not wearing her customary "missionary" outfit but had donned a pale green dress and wore European black patent shoes. Her skin had been tanned by the African sun, but now she wore a garden hat, and her hair had been washed and now fell freely down her back.

"I'd like to hear what happened to bring this change of heart in you, Jeanine," Barney said almost casually.

Jeanine took a deep breath and shook her head. "Oh, it was my fault. I am sure of that. I had a conflict with Manto, the chief elder, and he asked me to leave the village."

Must have been some conflict, Barney thought. Aloud, he said, "Manto's a pretty easygoing fellow and a good man, I think. I've known him a long time."

Jeanine shrugged her shoulders and stared down into her teacup. She swirled the pale amber contents and watched it as if it had some great meaning, then looked up and met Barney's eyes. "Probably my fault. I'm what I am, Barney, and I can't change."

Barney allowed a smile to turn the corners of his lips upward. "I think I said about the same thing once, Jeanine, but I think all life is a matter of change. The only people that don't change are dead people. Those of us who are alive change. Sometimes for the better, sometimes for the worse. I've gone through both changes."

"No. Not this, you haven't. I've heard the story of your life, Barney, and you've been a wonderful missionary." Suddenly tears came into Jeanine's eyes. She could not help it. She had fought them back all night and now she dashed them away. "Well, I've become a weeping woman, but I'm just not constituted to be a missionary. Annie is, though, isn't she?"

"Annie's what she is. She's what God made her. And so are you, Jeanine. There are going to be times," Barney said carefully, "when that which is in Annie is what's necessary. But there are going to be other times when her personality and her ways won't do. It will take a strong individual to press through. I think your only trouble is that you've been aggressive at the wrong times."

"How am I supposed to know the right times?"

"Comes with time and breaking. God has to do some breaking in all of us, Jeanine. You know my story. I had to wind up in Sing Sing Penitentiary before God got my attention."

Jeanine had heard Barney's story, how he had been a prize-fighter and had fallen into evil ways and finally wound up in the penitentiary. He had been converted there and come out to blaze brightly for God, first in a waterfront mission station and then across the face of Africa. She admired him tremendously and said so. "I guess I just don't have what it takes, Barney," she said. "I'm going home."

There was such finality in her words that Barney could only say quietly, "I think you're making a mistake, Jeanine, and I'm going to pray that you will see things differently."

★　★　★　★

The knock on the door startled Jeanine. She had been lying on her bed trying to nap. The three days she had spent in Mombasa waiting for a ship had been hard. If there had been a ship leaving, even if it had been going around the world before arriving in New York, she would have taken it. But there was nothing due to make port for at least another week. She had kept to her room, avoiding Barney and all the other missionaries, and had had to force herself to eat. Bitterness rose in her and she could not seem to fight it down. She tried to read the Bible, but the words would blur or they would seem to have no application to her. When she tried to pray, it was almost impossible. She could say the words, but they seemed to go nowhere. She was reminded of the line from Shakespeare's play, "My words fly up, my thoughts remain below, words without thoughts never to heaven go." She had spent anguished hours on her knees, sometimes leaving in the late hours to go walking on the seashore. The whispering of the waves did not soothe her but reminded her of her own restlessness.

"Who is it?" she said, coming off her bed and brushing her hair back with her hand.

"It's me—John."

For a moment Jeanine thought of telling him to go away, but with a shrug she went and opened the door. "Hello, John," she said. "You want to come in?"

"Yes."

John Winslow was wearing a faded khaki shirt and a pair of worn dark blue trousers. As usual he wore black leather half boots and carried his bush hat in his hand. He stood before her, and she could not read the expression on his face.

"Do you want to sit down?"

"Yes. I want to talk."

"I suppose Annie sent you. Or was it Barney?"

"It was Annie. She and Jeb are worried about you." He sat down in one of the two chairs in the hotel room and seemed restless. "I'm worried about you, too."

"Well, you can stop worrying. It's all over. Nothing to worry about." There was a bitterness in Jeanine's voice. She walked to the window and stared out with her back to him, adding, "It was a good idea that didn't work. I'm just not cut out to do this sort of thing."

"I wouldn't be so quick to say that."

Turning to face him, Jeanine crossed her arms and stared at him. "I've given you enough evidence, John. You're a pretty sharp fellow. You've told me often enough that I'm too rough, too aggressive, too brash. Weren't those the words you used?"

"Maybe I did, but those words apply to me, too."

"You weren't trying to be a missionary."

Winslow leaned forward and put his hat on the floor. He hesitated, then stood up and walked over to her. "I said some harsh things to you, Jeanine, but I meant them for your good."

"Oh yes. I'm sure of that. Annie means good, and you mean good, Barney and Jeb mean good. Everyone means good."

Winslow stood there quietly considering the woman before him. He thought of all he had heard about her, how she had denied herself nothing. He thought, *If I had her advantages, I'd be just like her. We're the same inside.* Aloud he said, "You're feeling pretty sorry for yourself, aren't you?"

"Is that what you've come here to say? To tell me I'm feeling sorry for myself?"

"You think you're the only one who has problems, Jeanine?"

"Of course not."

"Yeah, I think you do. At least you don't think of other people's problems. Annie has problems, too, or maybe you haven't noticed. Maybe you don't know Barney's problems. He's got a child that may have a life-threatening disease."

This startled Jeanine. "He never told me that!"

"Did you ever ask? Have you talked with him about his children, about his life, how he's getting along?"

"Well, no—"

"Well, why haven't you?" He waited for an answer and saw

that she was struggling. "You've been too concerned with your own problems, Jeanine. I don't deny that you've got them. All I'm saying is that there's more to life than what goes on in our own living room."

"I know that, John."

"I don't think you do. Look, Jeanine, I know you're hurting. I can see it in your eyes. Well, I'm hurting, too."

Startled by his words, Jeanine parted her lips with surprise. She saw for the first time that his face was filled with strain. There were lines she had not noticed before, not just of fatigue but marks of some inner strain. He was a strong man, able to handle problems as well as anyone she had ever met, but now she noticed a stoop to his shoulders and that his eyes were cloudy with something she could not define.

"What's the matter, John?"

"Are you sure you can take time from feeling sorry for yourself?" John said sharply. Then he shook his head. "I'm sorry. I didn't mean to say that. Yes, I've got problems."

"What is it? Can you tell me?"

Winslow hesitated. He had been struggling inside his own spirit for days now. He had spoken to no one, but now in the quietness of this room, the anguish that roiled in him suddenly leaped out. "What's my life, Jeanine? I lead rich drunks around who kill all the animals they can, and most of them stay dead drunk. That's a real meaningful life, isn't it?"

Jeanine blinked her eyes with astonishment. She had not seen this side of John Winslow. "It's not like that, John."

"Isn't it? What good do I do?"

"Why ... you give pleasure to people. That's worth something, isn't it? What about the work you do for the Geographical Society?"

"Make a virtue of everything you can in me, Jeanine, but for the last few days I've been ready to hang it all up, except there's no place to run to." His shoulders seemed to stoop even more, and his voice grew almost inaudible. "Ever since I was a kid, I ran away from reality. Soon as I could, I left my home looking for adventure. Well, I found adventure. And what's in it? Nothing!"

Involuntarily, almost, Jeanine reached out and put her hands on John's shoulders just beside his neck. "I hate to see you like this," she whispered.

The touch of her hands brought a surprise to John Winslow.

She was standing very close to him, and he saw something that shocked him. He had been told by Jeb Winslow that there was a tenderness and a softness in this woman. He had never seen it before, but he saw it now. It stirred something in him, and he said quietly, "I've made a wreck of my life, Jeanine."

"So have I."

The simple admission was more than John had expected. He saw her lips tremble, and that she was a beautiful, desirable woman. All the old longings that were in him suddenly arose. He reached out and pulled her close. She did not resist, and he whispered, "I don't know what to do. I guess I feel like you did when you were on the *Titanic* and thought you were going to drown."

Jeanine was intensely aware of his strong arms as they enclosed her. With all of her misery she was crying out inside for some assurance. She sensed the same thing in him as she reached up and pulled his head down. "You're going to be all right, John." She pulled his head forward and kissed him, holding to him tightly. She felt his arms tighten around her with a strength she needed. She had always thought she was a strong woman, but the months of failure had drained her of that confidence. His lips were firm on hers and yet not demanding. It was as if they were exchanging some sort of courage, and she held him tightly.

It was a strange experience for John. She was a beautiful woman, desirable, but always before there had been an iron will in her. Now her soft form pressed against him, and he felt the brokenness he had never felt before. Her lips were soft and gentle and seemed to exert a force of their own. There was but one brief moment and then he lifted his head. "I don't know what's happening to me. I think I'm so mixed up I don't know what to do."

Jeanine was still in the half circle of his arms, and she felt more vulnerable than ever. The softness and gentleness that all of her life she had kept buried deep within seemed to be rising to the surface. "I feel the same way," she whispered. "I don't know what it will take to put my life back together."

"You've got to try, Jeanine."

"No. It's too late for some things. But it's not too late for you."

"Promise me this," he said. He could smell the faint perfume that she wore, and an urgency arose in him. "Promise me you'll stay for a few weeks. There's always time for God to do something."

"I'm surprised to hear you say that."

"It's what my dad and my mother always said. There's always time for God to do something. I heard it a thousand times. It's really a matter of courage, Jeanine. I always thought I had plenty of that. I can climb on a wild horse or face a charging buffalo, but to face myself and my life and what it is, I feel weak and washed out."

Jeanine leaned against him and put her face against his chest. She was aware of his heart beating strongly, and she heard herself whispering, "I'll wait a few weeks, John. Maybe there is time for God to do something—for both of us."

★　★　★　★

Annie sat on a fallen log close beside Jeb, so close that their shoulders touched. Both of them were watching the dancers who seemed to be packed together in a phalanx. They had come to witness one of the many ceremonial dances of the Masai. This time the reason was so obscure that neither of them really understood it, but, as always, the ceremony had a dignity and a magnificence that both of them loved to watch.

The dance had begun, and the warriors, spears upright, began hopping, one by one, as they circled. They followed the long, leaping Masai trot that in times of cattle raids and even in wars carried herdsmen three hundred miles or more over the plain. John had once said to Jeb, "There's no point trying to outrun a Masai. They have legs that can run forever."

As the two watched, the dancers began to tremble and shake, and two or three stepping out from the main body began to leap straight up and down, their spears glinting in the sun. They shot their chins out as they rose and stamped with their right foot as they touched the ground. The upright spears and the clubs were twirled all around. Some of the dancers were shattering the air as they clapped their hands in rhythm, shouting, "N-ga-ay!" One of the men in the circle began to chant in a guttural voice, and it became a litany. Another began to orate in the background as the young women and the old men who were watching became excited. A fat infant with a necklace of dik-dik bone was bouncing next to Annie on its mother's bare shoulders.

Some of the elders sat in the hot shadows of the hut as the dancers began to cry out, "UM-Bay-AY-uh!" They said this over again as the dance picked up into a litany. The greased red faces of the dancers glowed with sweat as the men moved in perfect circles. Always there was the glint of the spears as the sun caught them, turning them into diamond brightness. The metal arm coils of the dancers glittered in the sun, and the chant and whooping became at times exultant, at times mournful, but always harmonious.

The dance went on for some time, and finally Annie and Jeb saw with regret that it was over.

"That's some dance, isn't it, Annie?"

"Yes. I've never seen anything like it. They're so full of joy and sorrow at the same time. Our people can't express themselves like that in dance, can they?"

"No. I guess we do it in other ways, but the Masai have a genius for it."

The two walked around for some time after the dance, and finally they found Chief Mangu standing under the shade of an acacia tree watching the herds as they slowly lowered their heads to eat. "Come," he said, "and talk with me."

The two went over. Both of them had learned to admire the chief. His son, Rentai, stood listening carefully to his father. The relationship between the two was close, Annie had noticed, even for a Masai warrior and his son. She saw that the boy's eyes were fixed earnestly on the tall figure of his father, and from time to time Chief Mangu would look at him with approval.

It was one of those times when Annie realized how fragile her relationship was with the Masai. In anguish she had cried out, "Oh, God, I am so different. How can I make them understand who you are?"

Now they wandered for a time over a small hill called a *kopje*, which overlooked the plain. Her eyes searched the ground for adders, cobras, and mambas, all of which were to be found in this area. As they moved along, a small antelope appeared, climbing to the crest of a red termite mound. He watched them carefully, then went bounding off in impossible leaps.

They passed several agate-eyed agama lizards that seemed to materialize from nothing. They were a brilliant blue and orange, and their heads were swollen and seemed to be an off shade of pink. As the four passed by, they began to hiss audibly.

Chief Mangu laughed. "They think we are here to get their territory and we might. They're very good to eat."

Finally they came to a stop and watched as a Thompson gazelle suddenly appeared. He moved along, dipping his head toward the stiff blades of grass.

"What's he doing?" Annie whispered.

"He's got a little gland right by that black spot under his eye," Jeb said. "He pierces it with the sharp tips of the grass and leaves a waxy black deposit on it. Do you see?"

"Why does he do that?" Annie asked.

"Because he wants to mark his home," replied Chief Mangu. "It is good for everything that lives to have its place. The animals need to know and so do the Masai." He turned to the two and said, "What is your place, Mother Annie?"

Annie smiled. "The world is God's home. He is everywhere. So everywhere I am, my Father is there."

The statement seemed to excite the interest of Chief Mangu. "That is good," he said. "We Masai know we have only one place, however. You are a stranger here. You are not of our people."

"We are all of one people," Annie said gently.

Mangu considered this and finally said slowly, "Sometimes the black god brings rain, but the red god does not want it. The black god lives in the good rain, and the red god brings the drought, but sometimes I think the black god and the red god are the same god who brings both good and evil."

"There is but one God, Chief Mangu. The evil that comes is the result of our wrongdoing, but God is a Father who wants the best for His children. He loved the world so much that He sent His only Son, Jesus, to die."

"Tell me about this Jesus again."

Annie was shocked. She had felt what seemed to be the indifference of the Masai, even of Chief Mangu, but now out of the blue suddenly he said, "Tell me about Jesus." She breathed a quick prayer and began speaking evenly but with warmth and obvious love.

Jeb Winslow said nothing. He was praying that Annie would find the right words that would touch the heart of the tall Masai warrior. He heard her tell how the world went bad and was doomed, and how God the Father sent His only Son to die on the cross as a substitute. She spoke for some time, and then Mangu looked at his son.

"I think I could not give my son for anyone."

"Most of us could not," Annie said. "But God loves us that much."

"I would hear more about this Jesus."

There was a moment's silence, and Mangu seemed to realize that he had somehow startled the two. He smiled and said, "I have a word for you, Mother Annie."

"Why, I would appreciate your wisdom, Chief."

"The white hunter. He is not for you."

Annie had been shocked earlier, but now she was speechless. She exchanged quick glances with Jeb, who seemed to be equally startled. "What do you mean, Chief?"

"You have eyes for him as a lover, but he is a wanderer. He is not like you. I counsel you to put him out of your heart."

Annie felt her face flush and put her hand on her neck as if to conceal it. She could not think of one single word to say and finally whispered, "I thank you for your words of counsel, Chief."

After they got back to the village and separated from the chief and his son, Jeb was strangely quiet. "I think the chief gave you good advice, Annie. I know you've been in love with John all your life, but he's not for you."

Annie turned to face Jeb. "That's not all you have to say, is it, Jeb?"

"I've said it all. I don't want your heart to be broken. John's a fine man, and I think God's going to do something with him, but you two don't belong together." He suddenly smiled and said, "I've told you how I love you, Annie. I won't burden you with it again, but give heed to what the chief says. I think he saw something in you, and I know that I'll never change."

Annie watched as Jeb Winslow turned and left. A warmth came to her then, for she realized that he did love her. Such a love as this cannot leave a woman unchanged. It gave her a sudden gush of pleasure as she realized that at least one man in her life loved her for herself. She thought of the years she had enthroned John Winslow as the ideal of manhood, but now looking at Jeb, she thought, *He's stronger than John in many ways.*

CHAPTER TWENTY-TWO

SIMBA!

★ ★ ★ ★

"A beautiful day, Annie," Jeb said. He stopped on top of the hill and waited until Annie came to stand beside him. From where they stood, they could see a band of green that lined the bases of some steeply rising cliffs. Far off, the Mountain of God, Mount Kenya, was clearly outlined against the sky. It was a magnificent cone, crystal white and perfect as few volcanos are.

The two stood there looking toward the mountains and the hills beyond that seemed cloaked in the blue haze of Africa, and everywhere there were birds. Annie was proud of herself, for she had learned to name them. "That's a stone chat," she announced and pointed to it. "There's a flycatcher."

Jeb joined in the game. "I never saw so many different kinds of birds. Look, there's a kingfisher. Not like the ones we had back at home, but he is beautiful, isn't he?"

"It's odd. Kingfishers live in the dry woods in Africa. At home they're always around water."

"And the owls grab the fish, and the eagles eat the insects," Jeb added.

The two began walking again, descending into a more wooded area. The world seemed to stand still, and high above, a hawk rose on the thermals. They heard the crashing of trees from a small herd of elephants knocking them down. They crossed over a brook and then a small pond, where bush buck and water buck lifted their beautifully carved horns to watch their coming. Their tails switched and they watched cautiously, but they did not run.

For a long time they wandered, always looking for the Mountain of God as a landmark. "I'd like to go down into that crater someday," Jeb murmured.

"Can you do that?"

"I think so, but it's sacred to the Masai. I doubt if any of them would go there any more than we would go rushing into the Holy of Holies."

Clouds began to settle, and the wind blew across the waste of coarse tussock that stirred like a living thing across the wide plains. Far off they could hear the chough-chough-chough of the rhinos. "Kifaru mkubwa," Annie whispered.

"Yes. Big rhino. I'd hate to get caught by one of them. Have you seen one of them at a dead run? They'd outrun a man easily."

They passed by a group of wild banana fronds, and from far off, smoke-plumed villages filled the landscape. The clouds overhead seemed to be almost light lavender, and as they moved rapidly across the slate gray sky above, the two made their way into a shaded area. Goldenback weavers occupied the trees overhead, and long stalks of purple amaranth dangled from the boughs. It was a lush, wet area, and a frog chorus suddenly began to sound in the afternoon air while a bush shrike chestnut wing came rushing in as if to defend his territory.

"Are you tired, Annie?"

"I think so. I don't really know." But Annie listened with pleasure as Jeb started to sing. He liked the old songs, "The Old Rugged Cross," "Amazing Grace," and although he sang effortlessly, his voice seemed to fill the clearing as they made their way back toward the village.

As Annie listened it suddenly occurred to her, *I'm thinking more about Jeb than I am about John.* The thought came into her mind unobtrusively. It was as if someone else had put it there rather than being something she herself had thought of. She considered it as they made their way through the meadows that surrounded the village. A band of ravens, startled at their appearance, rose with a rush of wing, making black periods against the sky. From time to time she would look over at Jeb. His face was now tanned almost as dark as that of John Winslow, and the spare diet and heat and exercise had planed the features of his face down. He was not gaunt, but there was a strong, masculine attractiveness to the slant of his jawbone and the firmness of his mouth. His arms were bare up to the biceps, and they were tanned also and swelled with muscle that had not been there when he had left the States. She found pleasure observing him without his knowledge, and then he turned and caught her looking.

"Why are you looking at me?"

"Because you're so beautiful." Annie made a face at him.

"I am, aren't I? I look better than that baboon we passed back there."

"Oh, much better than that! You're at least as attractive as a warthog."

Jeb laughed. "You know how to make a fellow feel a hundred feet high, Annie."

The two walked on until they finally arrived back at the village. Turning to Jeb, Annie asked, "Can we work on the translation later today, Jeb?"

"Yes." The two had started a free translation of the Bible so that it would be very simple. The King James was fine for those who grew up with it, but there were expressions in there that even gave Annie and Jeb problems. It was not that they wanted to rewrite the Bible but to simplify it. They had worked on it for long hours and had come to find a real pleasure in it.

They did work on the translation all afternoon, and just as the sun was going down over the mountains, they heard John Winslow's voice. They were seated outside of Annie's hut, and looking up, they saw the white hunter come striding in. "Hello, John," Annie smiled. "I'm glad to see you."

"Have you been to Mombasa?" Jeb asked.

John nodded. "Yes. I went to talk to Jeanine."

"Has she left yet?" Annie asked almost fearfully.

"No. I persuaded her to wait a few weeks." Taking off his hat, he wiped the sweat from his brow and shook his head. "She's in bad shape spiritually." He looked down at the hat that was in his right hand and murmured, "Well, who isn't?"

Something about the question touched the hearts of both Jeb and Annie. They gave each other a quick glance, and Jeb said, "Come along. We'll fix something to eat."

"Yes," Annie said. "*Karibu chai.*"

Winslow smiled faintly. "Welcome to tea," he translated. "All right. I could eat a little."

"Come along. I'm trying a new menu. One that the chief's sister gave to me."

The two men followed her to the fire in back of the house. As the two men sat down on stools, Annie began to stir maize meal into boiling water. This made a white paste called *ugali*. It was the chief staple all over East Africa. When it was boiling, she chopped up meat and vegetables, and even added a little gravy that was left over from a previous meal.

She stirred it until it thickened and then said, "Supper's ready."

The three pulled their stools closer to a stump that had been left for a dining room table, and Annie set the bowl out in front of them. She closed her eyes and said, "Father, we thank you for this food. In Jesus' name."

"Amen," Jeb grinned. He reached over and picked up some of the ugali in his hand and rolled it up into a ball. Then he took a bite of it and nodded. "Not bad."

The three ate out of the common bowl, and Annie murmured once, "Not very fancy, is it? Can you imagine what people at home would think of this?"

John said little during the brief meal. Finally he said, "I've been invited to join in on a lion hunt tomorrow."

"You mean you're taking a client out?" Jeb inquired.

"Oh no. The chief invited me to go." He leaned back and pulled his pipe out. He packed it, lit it up, and when the purple clouds of smoke began to rise, he nodded. "It's his boy's first hunt. That's important to a young man, you know."

"It is, isn't it? I don't quite understand it. I guess it's sort of an initiation into manhood."

"More or less," Winslow nodded. "It follows a set procedure." He leaned back and listened to the sounds that came across the village, a mixture of voices and far off a cry of a distant hunting bird. The sounds had become natural to all of them now, but he was always watchful and listened more than a man would back in the States. "The day before the hunt some of the warriors tell the others where to meet. In the morning at dawn a warrior with a metal bell attached to his thigh will circle all the nearby kraals to remind the warriors of the hunt."

"What's the bell for? A wake-up call?" Jeb asked.

"Yes. When the warriors hear the bell, they rush out fully armed and go to the meeting place."

"Could we come and watch?" Annie asked.

"I'm afraid not. It's strictly for warriors."

"Then it's sort of an honor to invite you along, isn't it?"

"I guess so."

"What do they do then?"

"Well, they start out in a long, loose line. It's a sight to behold the way those fellows can cover ground." He laughed, saying, "They'll probably leave me two or three miles behind. They always put the best runners in front, and those with the heavy shields will follow behind. When they sight a lion they call 'eele,' and you hear this all down the line. Eele—eele—eele! The warriors in the front chase the lion and try to tire him out."

"It's very dangerous, isn't it?" Annie asked.

"It can be. Lions have different temperaments. Some are cowards. They run for their lives at the first sight of danger. Some of them will just run a few hundred yards, then they'll turn around and run right at you. Sometimes they are too full of meat from a meal to run. They always try to stop and vomit to get lighter. This gives the warriors a pretty good shot at them."

"Tell us about how they actually kill a lion with a spear. It seems impossible."

"It would be for me. It's hard enough with a gun."

"Will you take your gun tomorrow?"

"No. That wouldn't be permitted. I'm just going as a guest." He puffed on his pipe and watched the smoke spiral and then continued speaking slowly. "The warriors in front always wait for those in the rear to catch up. They try to circle the lion first at a good distance, and then they sing songs."

"Why do they do that?"

"Oh, I suppose they're trying to hypnotize the lion. They close in slowly until they're at a spear-throwing distance. The lions seem to know which warrior will attack them first. He'll go for him every time, it seems. Sooner or later a courageous warrior will run in and throw his spear. After he hits the lion he runs out of the circle and waits with his sword in hand. The other warriors throw themselves into sort of a barricade throwing spears. Sometimes they succeed and sometimes they don't."

"They sometimes get to the warriors, of course," Jeb said.

"Yes, they do, and that's pretty serious. It's a matter of honor with them. The warrior who spears the lion first proclaims the name of his family very loudly. Sometimes he calls out the name of his lover." He grinned and winked at Annie. "You don't have to worry about me doing that. I'll be standing there without even a knife, so if the lion makes for me, I might break a speed record."

"What happens after they kill the lion?"

"Well, the warrior who first spears the lion takes its mane and its tail. The second takes a paw. They stick their trophies onto the end of their spears, and they come back singing and perform a dance around the lion's carcass. Then they head on to celebrate, but they won't celebrate if any of them have been wounded. You'll probably see that tomorrow. It's something to see. The Masai warriors will put on their ceremonial gear, those ostrich plumes on their heads and then lion's manes or eagle feathers. They'll perform a procession, and when they come home, they'll send someone to inform the village. Then they make a triumphant entrance. 'Warriors have killed a lion! Warriors have killed a lion!' everybody will cry. They fall into a kind of frenzy. The Masai call it *emboshona*. They'll all cry out, 'Such are the Masai warriors!' All the girls will decorate themselves, because the two most attractive girls will dance with the first two warriors who spear the lion."

Annie and Jeb listened with fascination, and finally John looked at them and shook his shoulders together. "I'm talking like an old woman," he said. "Getting old."

"No. I'd give anything to see it," Annie said quietly. "You ought to write it down. People at home would love to read something like this."

"I'm no writer."

"How do you know until you've tried? Promise me you'll write it down," Annie said.

"Yes," Jeb said. "I need material for the book I'm writing. I might even put you in a footnote," he grinned.

"Deliver me." John rose to his feet and said, "I'm going to bed. It'll be early in the morning. We'll leave about three, so I won't see you until we get back with our trophies."

"Can we pray for you before you leave, John?" Annie asked.

John Winslow stopped. He stood there silently, and then said softly, "I don't think anybody's done that since Mom and Dad did when I left home. If you like, go ahead."

Jeb and Annie went to stand beside John. She took his hand and held it firmly, and Jeb put his arm around the broad shoulders of the white hunter. Annie prayed a brief prayer, and her voice was full of concern, then Jeb prayed also. He ended by saying, "God, this is your man. Protect him and protect all of the warriors. In Jesus' name."

John stood there a moment feeling the warmth of Jeb Winslow's arm and feeling the firmness of Annie's hand. "Thanks," he said huskily, then turned and disappeared into the gathering darkness.

★ ★ ★ ★

"Simba is near," Chief Mangu whispered. He waved his spear toward the east, then looked at his son. "Can you smell him, Rentai?"

"Not yet, Father."

"Clear your nose out then. A Masai must smell as well as see."

John Winslow stood a few feet behind the chief and his son. They had left well before dawn, and he had found it difficult to keep up with the warriors. They, of course, ran in their full, free swinging gait and never seemed to tire. Although Winslow was in good condition compared to most men his age, still he was gasping for breath more than once. He never quit, though, and had seen the look of approval in Chief Mangu's eyes.

"Now, Winslow, the men will move in and the circle will tighten."

John Winslow nodded. It was a sight to behold. The sun was just beginning to rise high in the sky, and they had arrived at a spot where the hard plains were bare with only a whisper of grass. The animals kept to the ridges where the grass was shortest. They had passed wildebeests that seemed to run in that tilted whirl of slopes. Their black tail tassels hung on the wind behind. Winslow knew they were a favorite food of the lion. Wherever there were wildebeests, there would be lions not far off.

The dawn seemed to hold something ominous about it, and it seemed that a tinge of gloom had come to him directly from the surroundings. He had experienced such feelings before and never paid much attention to them, but now for some reason there was a tenseness in the back of his neck that he could not shake off. A great stillness that seemed to hover over the landscape made him restless, and far overhead a peregrine falcon sailed across the sky and on down across the valley. It was a beautiful day, but John was tense and had to remind himself to relax his muscles.

For some time it seemed that nothing would happen. Winslow followed as Chief Mangu and Rentai moved ahead. Rentai did not even have a spear, for he was not old enough, nor had he passed through the rite of manhood. And no uncircumcised male could take part in a lion hunt. Still, he could observe, and what he saw he would one day put into action.

As the circle drew smaller and smaller, Winslow suddenly saw a movement ahead. Even as he saw it Mangu whispered, "Simba!" He watched silently for a moment, and then as the beast came into view, he turned and said, "A fine lion. Mkubwa simba."

Winslow's eyes were at least as good as those of the chief, even if his legs were not. "Fine animal," he said quietly. He felt defenseless standing there without a gun, and the restlessness that had come with the dawn seemed to rise in him. He tightened his jaw, for he was aware the chief was watching him carefully.

The chief gave the order and slowly the circle tightened. The lion, a magnificent black-maned male, suddenly coughed, then split the air with a tremendous roar. He made a dash in one direction and saw his way blocked, reversed his course, and then ran straight in the opposite direction. He had not gone far, however, when one man stepped forward. It was Drago. The man's arm drew back, and the polished head of the spear flashed in the light.

"A bad throw," the chief muttered. "Drago will be clawed."

But the lion did not run for Drago. He changed directions and for some reason headed straight toward where the chief stood.

"Back, Rentai!" the chief said, ordering his son out of danger. He advanced quickly, leaving Winslow and Rentai standing watching the scene.

The lion headed straight toward the chief, who assumed the classic stance of the spear thrower. He waited until the lion was only a few yards away before releasing his spear. The lion, however, for some reason changed directions and the spear flew over his head. John thought, *The chief's a dead man!* But the lion did not attack the chief, who by then had snatched his sword out. Instead he ran right by, passing within ten feet, and now was on a dead run for Winslow and Rentai.

A lion running at full speed can cover the ground in no time. John saw that he was headed straight toward Rentai. He called out the boy's name, "Rentai, run!" but he knew it was hopeless. Without giving thought to the consequences, he threw himself forward, waving his arms. He saw the lion's yellow eyes fasten on him and the mouth open as a fierce roar emanated.

He had no time to think anything else, for suddenly the lion was upon him. He felt the steely muscles and smelled the fetid breath, and he suddenly felt an excruciating pain in his left arm. Desperately he kicked at the lion's belly, but it was hopeless. He felt the claws again tearing at his side, and he thought, *This is it. This is death.* But suddenly the lion gave a coughing sound, and Winslow sensed that his attention had been distracted. He rolled over and saw that his entire arm was covered in blood that was flowing in a rich stream. His side was torn also and matted with crimson blood. When he saw that an artery had been cut in his arm, he had the presence of mind to whip off his belt with his right hand and twist it around his upper arm. At the same time he saw the warriors had closed in, and the lion now lay with three spears in him, coughing out his defiance . . . and then lay still.

The chief ran back at once. "Are you all right, my friend?"

"How is the boy?" John asked.

Chief Mangu reached out and pulled the boy to him. "He was not hurt. You threw yourself into the lion's jaws."

"Couldn't let Rentai get hurt. He's too good a man for that," John Winslow said, then he gasped and said, "Would you mind holding on to this? I don't think I can—"

Chief Mangu quickly reached forward and held the belt that was keeping John alive. He saw Winslow's eyes flicker and then the body went limp. He began calling out orders, shouting at the top of his lungs.

★　★　★　★

Annie was sewing a rip in one of her dresses when Jeb suddenly appeared. "Annie, it's John. He's been hurt." Dropping the cloth and needle, Annie leaped forward. She ran out the door following Jeb. They saw the procession coming and instantly noted that four of the warriors were carrying a litter made of hides.

Rushing forward she looked and saw John white as paste, his eyes closed. His entire side was covered in blood, and the chief was holding on to a tourniquet.

"John," Annie cried. She looked up at the chief and said, "Is he dead?"

The chief looked at her with compassion. "No, but he may die. He is badly torn."

"We've got to get Doctor Burns," Jeb cried. "I'll go to Mombasa."

"No," the chief said, "you are too slow. We will send our fastest runner."

He barked out commands, and a rather short, wiry Masai named Polesi listened carefully and then sprang into action. He disappeared from the village at a dead run, and the chief looked down at the pale face of John Winslow. "I think it is his time to die. He is a brave man." Grief and sorrow were in his voice, and he looked at Annie, saying, "He saved my son's life. It is like your Jesus who died for another, is it not?"

Annie could not answer. Fear came up into her throat and she looked at Jeb. "He can't die, Jeb," she whispered.

"No, God won't let him do that. Come. Let's move him into your hut. That's the best place. We'll do what we can until your uncle comes."

CHAPTER TWENTY-THREE

THE DARK VALLEY

★　★　★　★

"How is he?"

Annie looked up from where she was sitting on a hand-built chair beside the cot where John lay. Jeb had come in so silently she had not heard him. "Not any better."

Jeb chewed on his lower lip and thrust his hands behind his back. "Why doesn't Doctor Burns hurry up?" he grated through clenched teeth.

Annie could not answer. It had been two days since the runner had left. Chief Mangu had assured them that the runner would arrive within fifteen hours, but getting the doctor back was another thing.

"He may be out on his visits to the outlying villages," Annie said wearily. Her eyes were gritty with sleep, her lips were dry, and a sour taste lay in her mouth. She got up and stretched her back and looked down at John Winslow. "His fever is going up again."

"If we only had something to give him!"

"Well, we don't have anything, so we'll have to keep him bathed with water-soaked cloths."

"All right. I'll be sure there's plenty of water as cool as we can get it."

Jeb left and Annie sat down beside the bed. Her mind cried out for sleep, for she had slept only in snatches since John had been brought in. She and Jeb took turns, but even when she was lying on her cot, she was in an agony of prayer. Somehow through all of this she had learned that her love for him was for one Christian to another. Still she thought of his parents at home and his brother and knew that they would be devastated if this wandering one died in a hut in Africa.

She put her hand on John's forehead and his eyes fluttered. He licked his lips and stared at her. His eyes were sunken back in his head, and he tried to sit up and involuntarily grunted with pain. He looked down at his arm that was bound up, and it was as if the arm belonged to someone else.

"Be still, John. You must drink some water."

Quickly she poured water into a cup and held his head up. His flesh was burning like fire. He gasped at the water thirstily, and then she lay his head back. "Uncle David's on his way. He'll be here soon."

John looked at her. His eyes were yellowish, and his lips were cracked and parched. It was as if the fever burned any fluids that he drank instantly. Looking at his arm, he closed his eyes. "Don't let them take off my arm, Annie."

Annie wet a cloth and put it on his forehead. "John, they may have to. The arm was terribly torn."

"Don't let them take off the arm. I'd rather die."

Annie did not argue, but she purposed in her heart that if she had anything to do with the decision, she would rather save John's life. A man with one arm can do fine things that a dead man cannot.

Jeb came back soon with a calabash full of cool water. The two stripped off the sheet and began applying the cool, damp cloths to the fevered body. This went on for over an hour, and finally he said wearily, "I think he's all right now. The fever's going down. I'll sit by him a while. You go get some sleep."

Annie shook her head. "I can't sleep. I'll just sit out on the porch."

She left and went out and stood under the moonlight. When she looked up she saw the moon was clear and sharp and perfectly round. She could see the pebbled and pimpled surfaces roughly spotted by the clash of meteorites eons ago she had heard Jeb mention one time on a walk.

For a long time she sat there letting her mind drift, but always it returned to two people, John Winslow and Jeanine Quintana. Winslow appeared to be the most grievously wounded, for his physical condition was bad. But Annie prayed no less for Jeanine. She knew that spiritual problems are worse than physical problems. And John and Jeanine needed spiritual touches in their lives.

She felt the tread of a step as Jeb came to sit down beside her. He heaved a sigh and shook his head.

"I'm afraid for him, Annie. He's very sick."

"I know. How do we have more faith?"

"I don't know, but I know you can't work up faith," Jeb answered. He thought for a while, then said, "I read a cynic once who said faith is believing what you know ain't so."

"Well, I think that's the truth," Annie said. She leaned over against Jeb and held on to his arm. She was so weary that she felt like she might fall over. "Faith is always believing something that's not so. God calls those things that are not as though they are. You remember what he said to Abraham?"

"I remember."

"He said you'll have a son. He was in his nineties when that promise came, and his wife had been barren. So Abraham had to believe what couldn't be true."

The two sat there for a time, and the moon crept slowly up into the sky. They watched as small clouds drifted across, hiding the face of the silver disk temporarily. They sat in the half light of the moon, and finally when the cloud disappeared, Jeb said, "I love you, Annie. I have for a long time."

Annie Rogers knew that something was happening. She could not put a date on it nor a time, but she knew that at some point in the recent past she had begun to realize that Jeb Winslow was more than just a good friend. It was all entwined with the idea of her girlhood infatuation for John Winslow. Slowly she had come to realize that what a girl of fifteen might feel had little in common with what a woman in her twenties could feel for a man. She now knew that Jeb was a fine man. For years he had been faithful and endured her infatuation for a man who he knew was not right for her. She felt his warmth as she leaned against him and said, "Do you really love me, Jeb?"

"Yes."

"You'll have to be patient with me, Jeb. I've been confused for a long time."

Jeb suddenly freed his arm and put it around her. With his free hand he turned her face toward his. "You're the dearest thing in my life except for God himself, Annie. I don't know if you could ever learn to love me half as much as I love you, but I'll be faithful to you, and I want to marry you."

Annie saw the honesty in his fine eyes. Her lips trembled and suddenly he bent and kissed her. His lips remained on hers, and unlike other caresses, she felt this was a holy confirmation. He was strong and masculine, and the embrace was something she had yearned for, and now it had come. She clung to him and salty tears fell down her cheeks. When he lifted his head they touched her lips. She removed a handkerchief, wiped her face, then whispered, "I think I love you, Jeb. Can you wait until I'm sure?"

Exultation ran along Jeb Winslow's nerves. It was something he had never expected to hear. He pulled her up against his side and held her hand. "I can wait," he said gently.

★ ★ ★ ★

The runner reached Mombasa, but he had difficulty at first finding the mission station. It took him almost half a day, and finally when he stood before Barney Winslow, he poured out his story. "Mother Annie says tell doctor that white hunter is badly hurt."

"How was he hurt?" Barney Winslow demanded.

"By a lion. She says send help."

Instantly Barney sprang into action. He informed Andrew of what had happened and set out immediately to find David Burns. Unfortunately it was David and Ruth's day at a distant village, but that did not stop Barney Winslow. He told his wife, Katie, "I'm going to find David, and I'm going to take him to the village myself if I have to."

"Tie him hand and foot if you have to. We must do all we can for John."

"I'm leaving you to pray while I go," Barney said. The two embraced, and when he stepped back, he said, "I've got to tell Jeanine."

He went at once to Jeanine's hotel. When he knocked at the door she opened it. "Bad news, Jeanine," he said.

"What is it? Is it Annie?"

"No. It's John. He's been clawed by a lion. I'm not sure he'll live."

To Jeanine it was like being struck by some powerful fist in the stomach. She had never once thought of anything happening to

John Winslow. She stood there, the blood draining from her face, and suddenly her knees felt weak.

"Here," Barney said quickly. "Sit down, Jeanine. I know it's a blow for you."

Jeanine allowed him to help her sit down on the bed, then she whispered, "Tell me." She listened as Barney told what little he knew, then said, "I've got to leave right away. David is at a village that's located pretty far out. I'll have to find him and then get him there as quick as I can."

"I'm going with you, Barney."

"You can't do a thing. You just stay here and wait."

"No. I'm going."

"You'll slow me down," Barney said.

"If I slow you down, run off and leave me. Give me ten minutes."

Barney was going to argue, but one look at the tense face of the woman before him stopped him. He said, "He means a lot to you, then."

Jeanine did not know how to answer. "I think he does," she said finally. "But I didn't know it. Wait down in the lobby. I'll be down in ten minutes."

★ ★ ★ ★

When they reached the village, Jeanine was exhausted. Barney and David Burns were accustomed to hard treks. When Barney and Jeanine had found him, David had agreed at once to come to the village to treat John. He had left Ruth to care for the ill in the village in which they had been working. They had made long, hard marches each day, and each night Jeanine had fallen to sleep in utter exhaustion. She had been awakened each morning by Barney, who said, "Can you go on, Jeanine?" She had blindly crawled out of her blankets, washed her face, and endured the hardship. More than once Barney had urged her to wait behind or at least to allow him to let the bearers carry her. Stubbornly she had said, "No. Don't lose a minute."

Now they were in sight of the village and Jeanine felt her heart beating hard. *Would he be dead?* was the question that had come to her many times and came to her now.

The smoke in the village slowly spiraled upward, and as they entered, the first person they met was Jeb Winslow. Instantly Barney spoke. "Is he alive?"

"Yes."

"Take me to him," David said.

As David and Jeb turned and hurried toward the house, Barney turned to see Jeanine, who was standing there as if she had no strength. She had lost weight and there were circles under her eyes. "Come along, Jeanine. Let the doctor look at John. You sit over here. I'll get you some fresh water and something to eat."

"No. I can't eat anything."

"I'm the doctor, you're the patient. I'll make you some tea."

By the time Barney had made tea over a quick fire that one of the Masai women had built and Jeanine had drunk it, her color had come back. "I'm afraid of what David will say."

"Jeanine, never take counsel of your fears," Barney said quietly. "I know it looks bad, but nothing is too difficult for God." He sat quietly beside her, then reached over and took her hand. "Don't be afraid," he whispered. "I've had a feeling about John Winslow for some time. Since I've first known him, I felt that God had a work to do in him. I don't think He's going to let him die until it's done."

The two sat there until finally David Burns and Jeb came outside closely followed by Annie. As the three walked over, Jeanine tried to read the expression on Burns' face. Annie came over and slipped her arm around her.

"I'm glad you've come back," she whispered.

"How is he?"

David looked at Jeanine and spoke to her. "He's alive, Jeanine."

"Will he live?" Jeanine blurted out.

"That's in God's hands," David said. "I've done about all I can do. I can sit beside him, but you can do that as well."

"Will you stay, David?" Jeanine asked, and there was a plea in her voice.

"I'll stay as long as you need me," Burns said gently. "Now, why don't you go in and see your friend."

As Jeanine left, David turned with a question in his eyes. "I don't get those two, Barney. What are they? From what I've heard about Jeanine Quintana, she doesn't get too upset about other people's problems."

Barney shook his head. "I think this time she has. You know one man died for her saving her from the *Titanic*."

"I've heard about that. Must give her a funny feeling. But this one isn't dying for her."

"I don't think it matters," Annie said. "I think she loves him, and he did save her life once from hyenas. Did you know that, Uncle David?"

"No I didn't. It would be rough having two men that saved you die, wouldn't it?"

"I don't think she could stand it," Annie said. She put her arm through Jeb's and said, "Come on. Let's go pray for them. That's all we can do now."

★ ★ ★ ★

The lives of the people with white skins within the Masai village were completely taken up with the welfare of John Winslow. David Burns stayed for two days and then finally said, "Miss Quintana, I would stay, but there are others who need me rather desperately. I need to get back and help Ruth. But I won't leave unless you say so."

Jeanine Quintana had changed indeed! Her lips trembled and fear came to her, but then she said in as strong a voice as she could muster, "You have to care for others. You've done well to stay with us this long, and we're all grateful to you."

David said haltingly, "I've seen men hurt worse recover. If he endures the infection and the high fevers don't kill him, he'll be all right."

"What about . . . his arm?" Jeanine asked, her voice quavering.

"It may be stiff, but I patched it together as well as I could. He won't lose it, though. The main thing now is to keep the fever down. Try to get him to eat. Good nursing saves more people than good doctoring, I think sometimes."

"Good-bye, David. I hope to see you again soon. And we're very grateful."

As David packed his kit and got ready to leave, he was joined by Barney. "Are you going back with me, Barney?"

"No. I'll stay here and see how things come along. Thanks, David."

"I wish I could be more encouraging, but it could go either way. I've seen it so many times."

"He's a strong man, if that means anything."

"It means a lot. Has he turned to the Lord yet?"

Barney hesitated. "I think he has. He's gotten away from the Lord, but I've seen something in him recently that's given me hope for his return."

"Well, Ruth and I will keep praying." David shook hands with Barney, turned, and spoke to his guide.

The two left at a quick pace and Barney wandered through the village. There was nothing really to do, but he felt inclined to stay and see after Jeanine. He went by the house of the chief and saw his wife standing there. "God be with you," he said in the Maa language.

"And God be with you." The chief's wife smiled slightly and said soberly, "How is the white hunter?"

"He is still very sick, but we hope that God will make him well."

"You believe that God can do that?"

As always, Barney never missed a chance to spread the Gospel. He stood there talking easily in very simple terms about the goodness of God. He quoted several verses but, of course, the woman didn't know the Bible was the Word of God. Still she examined him with vigilant eyes.

Finally she said, "Do you think it was God who saved my son or the white hunter?"

"Both."

"How can that be?"

"I think God loves your son and wanted him to live. So I think He used John, the white hunter, as a means of saving him."

"He is a brave man. Not even some Masai warriors would leap into the jaw of a lion without even a knife." Admiration shaded her tone and she shook her head. "My husband thinks he is brave enough to be a Masai."

Barney smiled. "That's a high compliment indeed."

The chief and his son came up at that moment and the chief asked how John Winslow was doing. When Barney had told him, the chief asked, "He is your blood?"

"Yes. He's of my tribe and my clan. We have the same name."

"If you are as good a man as he, you are a good man indeed."

"I do not think I could have done what he did."

Chief Mangu stared at him. "We have heard the tale of the time when you killed a lion with your bare hands."

Barney shifted uncomfortably. He felt not in the least heroic and said finally, "That was a long time ago. I hardly even remember it."

"How could a man kill a lion without even a knife? I would hear the story." He drew his boy closer. "My son needs to hear it also. You understand we are in debt to the white hunter."

"What he did was much braver than what I did." Barney went on to minimize his own deed that had taken place many years ago and was now faint in his memory. He knew he was still revered in this part of the world among the tribes there, but he always discouraged it, for he did not want to take the glory from God.

"God helped me once when I needed it, just as He helped you through the white hunter."

"Mother Annie says that God is the Father who gave His son for all men."

Eagerly Barney nodded. "That is the truth. There is one God, and He is the God of love."

"Is He a God of strength as well?"

"Yes He is. The cattle on a thousand hills are His. He owns everything. He made everything, and when the time came to help me and you, He died that we might know what life really was."

For some time he stood there talking to the chief, then after leaving, he thought, *Thank God the chief is listening. I saw the interest in his eyes. I think it's a real breakthrough. If John Winslow never does anything else, he's done something this time.*

★　★　★　★

At first it was just simply a blackness that was warm at times and cold at other times. At times he did not know the difference between the freezing cold and the burning heat that came and went. He felt hands on him, and sometimes the burning would be assuaged by coolness he felt on his face and body. From time to time a light would break through, and he would see a face, almost always the same one. He would try to talk, but his lips were cracked and parched.

He lay there with no sense of the passing of time. Confusion came and went like a wave as he would awaken, and then he would be plunged back into the darkness. Finally, however, he opened his eyes and found that he was not suffering from the bone-cracking fever. He licked his lips and found them dry and cracked, and slowly he turned his head. A woman sat in a chair slumped over, and at first he could not recognize her. As his mind cleared, he thought, *It must be Annie.* But then she lifted her face, and he whispered, "Jeanine."

Jeanine came awake in one swift moment. She had spent the

long vigil beside John's bed, and now she had no strength left of her own. But when she heard her name whispered she came awake at once.

"John," she whispered tenderly. She rose and came over and put her hand on his forehead and her other hand on his chest. "Your fever is gone," she whispered.

"How . . . how long have I been here?"

"A long time."

His mind was fuzzy and vague, but her features were sharp and clear. He studied her for a moment, then finally said, "You look tired. How long have you been here?"

Jeanine did not answer. The tears that filled her eyes now came running down her cheeks, and there was a thickness in her throat. "You're going to be all right, John," she whispered. "You're going to be all right."

He lifted his arm, although it felt like it had a fifty-pound weight on it. He touched her cheek and felt the tears that coursed down them. "I remember. You've always been here every time I woke up."

"Yes."

"Why did you come, Jeanine?"

She did not answer, for her chest was heaving and she could not stop the tears. She leaned forward and lay across him, holding his head with her hands. His body was still warm, and she knew that all his strength had been drained by the fever. His hand came up and stroked her hair, and she choked, "John, I thought you were going to die."

John Winslow held the weeping woman. His mind was becoming clearer now, and he realized that he had almost died. "Thank you, God, for bringing me out of it," he whispered. And then when Jeanine straightened up, he reached up and touched the tears on her face. "I never thought I'd see that. I've never seen you cry."

"John, how do you feel?"

"Terrible."

She smiled then. "You'll feel better soon."

"That's good," he said. He licked his lips and added, "I'd hate to think I'd feel this bad the rest of my life." He lifted his arm again and tried to flex it. "It hurts something fierce," he said.

"It's going to be all right. A little stiff maybe, but you have it. God has done a work in you."

309

"Could I have some water?"

Quickly Jeanine turned and filled a glass.

"Help me sit up."

He sat up in bed and blinked his eyes. "The room is going around," he complained.

She spilled some of the water down on his bare chest, and he asked for more. He drank three glasses and finally Jeanine said, "No more for now."

"I feel like I could drink the ocean dry." He sat there watching her as she put the glass back. When she came to stand beside the bed, he said, "Sit down, Jeanine."

She sat down and he reached out and she took his free hand. "Tell me how you got here." He lay there listening as she related the news. When she had finished, he asked, "Why did you come, Jeanine?"

"I thought a lot about it, John," she said. "One man gave up his life for me . . . and now you saved my life, too. And I couldn't stand the thought of it happening again. I'm not worth either one of you, John."

John Winslow lay there for a long time without speaking. He held her hand and she felt the warm pressure of it. He saw the weariness of her face, but there was something in her eyes that spoke of more than grief and sorrow. "I can't believe that you cared enough to come and nurse me."

Jeanine Quintana could say only, "I did care, John. I do care."

John lay there thinking about his past, and after a long time, he said, "I've been thinking about the time when I gave my heart to the Lord. I was only a boy, but I meant it then, Jeanine."

"I'm sure you did. Annie did the same thing. Oh, how I wish I had found Jesus when I was just a girl."

"I didn't follow the Lord for all these many years, and it's hard to believe He still loves me and cares for me. But I have to believe it because the Bible says so."

"He does love you. Why, He even loves me."

"I need God in my life," John said. "Only you and Annie can help me. I want to come back to God and serve Him the rest of my life."

Jeanine began to weep. "I can't stop crying," she said. "I'm just a weepy woman, but I know God loves you, John." She almost added, "And I love you, too," but she knew she must not say that. He was weak and helpless, and when he was well, there would be other things for him. Now, however, she began to pray that God would make His presence known in John's life.

As John lay there listening to Jeanine's voice, he began to pray with her, and soon he felt the peace of God come into his heart. Looking up, he whispered, "This is it, Jeanine. I've come home again. I haven't known the presence of God since I was a boy, but I know it now."

Jeanine felt a joy rush into her spirit. "Thank God, John. I thank God that you've come home."

CHAPTER TWENTY-FOUR

WHAT WILL GOD DO NOW?

★ ★ ★ ★

The small stream that began high in the mountains enlarged itself several times. By the time it reached within a mile of the village it had become, even during the dry season, a substantial current. Naturally, in a land jealous of water, animals came and went constantly. The herds of zebras would foul it from time to time, but it soon cleansed itself.

At one point in a bend, a rather large pond had been formed, and it was here that a large crowd had gathered for the baptism of John Winslow.

Jeanine's heart was filled with joy as she stood beside the pool. She had spoken earlier in the day to Chief Mangu as well as Manto. The words did not come easy for Jeanine to apologize for her offensive words and behavior toward these village leaders. From the encounter came a deeper understanding among the three of them.

The line of black, glistening bodies that surrounded the pool looked like an ornament. The Masai had been informed by their chief that the ceremony would be attended by all of the elders and as many others that would choose to come. Now it seemed a sea of black spread outward over the grass. Their colorful beads added a splash of color to the scene, and many of them had painted their faces with red ochre. The warriors had brought their buffalo shields that were highly decorated. They formed what seemed to be a wall surrounding the pool.

Not ten feet away from where Jeanine stood, a green monitor lizard four feet long scrambled out of the pool into the confines of the stream and disappeared. Speckled butterflies flickered through the shade, and far overhead a dog baboon had his breakfast, a bunch of red berries he had picked on the ground level. At one end of the pool a white-browed water-bottle bird with his neck feathers raised and his whole body shivering made a strange cry that startled Jeanine for a moment.

John stood beside his kinsman, Barney, but his eyes found those of Jeanine Quintana. The two seemed to be alone for that one moment, and when Jeanine smiled, John's smile quickly grew on his own lips.

"Are you ready, John?"

"I'm ready, Barney."

The two men waded out. Both were dressed in white pants and white shirts. They had both removed their shoes, and as they waded out waist deep Barney felt a thrill. "I've never seen anything more beautiful than this, John," he said. As he turned John to face at right angles, he said, "Look at that. The whole Masai tribe has come to your baptism. I wish we could get pictures of it."

"Don't worry. Annie's taking care of that."

Barney turned his head and saw Annie fiddling with a camera she had set up to photograph the whole thing.

The water was cool and John let his eyes run over the beautiful black faces, interrupted only at intervals by the few white people that had come from the mission at Mombasa.

"I wish my parents were here to see this, Barney."

"They'll be very proud of you. They already are." Lifting his voice, he said, "My dear friends. We have come here to celebrate the new birth of our brother, John Winslow. He is come to be obedient to his God. This is not what makes him a good man. The Father of love has made him that in his heart. What we are doing is celebrating the change that has come into his life as he follows Jesus Christ. . . ."

Barney preached a miniature sermon ten minutes long, but no one grew tired or weary or bored. Chief Mangu and his family stood foremost in the circle, and his eyes never left those of the two men clothed in white. He felt his son pressing close against him and whispered, "See, a brave man and a good man. That is what a Masai should be."

And then Barney Winslow said, "And now in obedience to the commands of our Lord and Savior Jesus Christ, and upon your profession of faith in Him, I baptize you, my brother, in the name of the Father, in the name of the Son, and in the name of the Holy Spirit."

Barney put his hand behind John's back and lowered him into the water. When he came up with the waters of the stream running down his face, he turned a brilliant smile on Jeanine and said, "Amen, and God be blessed forever."

"Glory be to God and the Lamb forever," Jeanine echoed. She hurried forward with a towel, and as she handed it to John, she said, "It was lovely, John. It made me want to be baptized all over again."

And then the crowd came, all wishing John well. All wanted to shake his hand, and finally he stood in front of Chief Mangu, who did not offer his hand. Instead he bowed deeply and said, "When you have time I will hear more of Jesus."

"I will be honored to tell you of my Savior, Chief. Will tomorrow be suitable?"

And then finally the Masai turned back to their village, and Jeanine stood beside John.

John said quietly, "Well, you did a good job of nursing me, Jeanine." He held up his arm, and the scars that would be there for the rest of his life appeared livid. He flexed it and said, "I've got the feeling I won't be a white hunter anymore."

"What will you do?"

"I think I'll just stay in Africa and see what God's going to do with the Masai."

"I think God's put you in that place. You saw how the chief greeted you. I think you can win him to Jesus."

"You're the missionary. Not me."

Jeanine dropped her head. "I quit when the going got hard. I'm ashamed of myself, John."

Quickly he reached out with his right hand and took hers. "We all do things that we shouldn't. You can't leave, Jeanine. God wants you here. You, and Annie, and Barney, and all the missionaries, and even a beat-up, old white hunter, or ex-white hunter."

"I'll stay if you want me to, John."

"That's my girl. Come now. Let's walk along this stream, and I can tell you what I've been thinking about. It's about ways to make a living. You see, the Geographical Society . . ."

★ ★ ★ ★

Barney looked up to see Annie and Jeb enter his office. Their faces were beaming, and when he opened his mouth to greet them, he was interrupted by Jeb.

"I want to marry your relative, Reverend Winslow."

Barney's jaw dropped open. He closed it with a click and began to smile. "Why are you asking me?"

"Well, you're basically our pastor. I've already talked to Mr. and Mrs. Burns and gotten their permission to marry their niece." Jeb's eyes were glowing, and he turned and hugged Annie. "I love this woman and she's agreed to marry me. Will you do the honors, assuming you give your permission?"

Barney Winslow laughed. He came over and hugged Annie and then shook Jeb's hand vigorously. "Of course you have my permission. It's a match made in heaven."

"Well, it took God a long time to put it together. I did everything I could to prevent it," Annie said. "But I've been overwhelmed." She put her arm around Jeb and was shocked at the feeling that ran through her. Once she had opened her heart to his love, her own heart had overflowed. It was like nothing she had ever experienced before, and her joy showed in her eyes.

"You two will work together, and we'll see the kingdom of God grow."

"Well, I'm no missionary, but I'm in Africa for the long haul," Jeb said. "You can be my song leader. You have the most beautiful voice in Africa. You do the singing and I'll do the preaching."

There was much light talk, but Barney finally said in a more sober tone, "I'm happy for both of you, and your families will be, too. We need people like you in Africa, both of you."

Jeb was completely happy, but suddenly he frowned. "What do you think about Jeanine, Barney? Will she stay?"

A slight smile touched Barney Winslow's lips. "I think she will."

"Do you know something we don't?" Annie asked suspiciously.

"Well, I'm no prophet. Neither am I the son of the prophet," Barney Winslow said. "But somehow I feel that God is up to something."

★ ★ ★ ★

"What in the world is that?"

"That?" John said, looking in the direction of Jeanine's gesture. "That's a pangolin." The animal that he pointed at looked something like an armadillo. It had overlapping armor on its back and on its legs and tail. "Ugly rascal, isn't he? He looks like the armadillos they have down in Texas."

"I suppose he might look nice enough to a female pangolin."

John reached out and took her hand. They were walking along a well-worn trail overshadowed by towering trees. Overhead a troop of monkeys went chattering through the canopy of trees, shouting and screaming at one another, and then their voices faded in the distance. John stopped and said, "You know what the Masai warriors do with pangolins?"

"No. Eat them?"

"Probably, but they do something else." He took her other hand and they stood facing each other. "They make ornaments out of their plates."

"Why do they do that?"

"The Masai think that pangolin plates make a man lucky in love. So if a warrior wears one, he gains the favor of his sweetheart."

"Do the women think the same?"

"Oh yes. I've seen many a maiden loaded down with pangolin plates."

Suddenly there was a lightness in Jeanine Quintana's spirit. She had felt ridiculously joyful since John's recovery, and the two had grown steadily closer together. At his baptism it had been all she could do to restrain herself from crying out with joy, and now she wished she had. A sly look came into her eyes and she squeezed his hand. "Why don't you go take a plate off that fellow and tie it around your neck."

John laughed and said, "Do you think it would help my case, Jeanine?"

Jeanine grew more serious. "I don't think you need any help. I'm always saying the wrong thing, but I'll have to tell you this. I love you, John."

John felt her hands tighten on his and saw something like fear in her eyes. He knew then that she was afraid of his reaction, and he said, "I'm glad of that."

"Why?"

"Because you're the only woman I could ever be happy with."

Jeanine dropped her head and did not answer for a long time. "What's the matter?" he asked.

"You . . . wouldn't want a woman with my past."

"I've got a past, too, Jeanine. But the past is washed away. We start where we are from this day. I would have asked you to marry me before, but—"

Quickly Jeanine looked up, her lips parted. "Why? Why haven't you? What's wrong?"

"You've got a calling as a missionary, and I don't have that calling."

"I can't help that, John," Jeanine said. "I don't have any shame left. I love you whether you love me or not. I have to say it."

John pulled her close and kissed her. Her lips were soft and gentle and he kissed her cheek, then he stroked her hair. "Maybe God is giving me another calling. To be a husband of a missionary."

"I'd like that very much," she said.

"Do you know what, Jeanine? I think that you and I could spare two people a lot of misery."

She looked up. "What do you mean by that, John? What two people?"

"The two other people we might marry if we don't marry each other." He held her tightly then said, "We're both strong-willed. So perhaps we ought to marry just to save those other two people a lot of misery."

"John Winslow, what a thing to say!"

"Just a thought." Then Winslow grew more serious. "I'm going to stay in Africa. I love this place. I could never be happy in any other setting."

"I'm so glad."

"You were leaving, Jeanine. I take it that's out now."

"Don't remind me. I was harsh and so wrong."

"Well, let's not put ourselves down. We've both been wrong." He held her tightly and then said, "You're stubborn and I'm stubborn, but do you know what I think about that?"

"What?"

"Think what stubborn kids we'll have."

"Oh, John, don't say that!"

He laughed, then kissed her, saying, "Come along, Jeanine.

I've got things to talk to you about. We've got a life to plan here. I've got ideas about working for the Geographical Society. That way I can stand behind you and Annie at the mission station, and we'll just see what God's going to do."